THE BREAK

THE UNBROKEN SERIES: RAINE FALLING

SHAYLA BLACK
JENNA JACOB

DREAM WORDS LLC

THE BREAK

A DARK ROMANCE SAGA

THE UNBROKEN SERIES: RAINE FALLING TWO

NEW YORK TIMES BESTSELLING AUTHOR

SHAYLA BLACK

USA TODAY BESTSELLING AUTHOR

JENNA JACOB

THE BREAK
The Unbroken Series: Raine Falling (Book 2)
Written by Shayla Black and Jenna Jacob

ISBN: 978-1-956445-00-8

This book is an original publication by Shayla Black and Jenna Jacob

Cover Design by: Rachel Connolly
Edited by: Chloe Vale and Shayla Black

Excerpt from *The Brink* © 2021 by Shelley Bradley LLC and Dream Words LLC

Previously published as *The Young and The Submissive*

AUTHORS' NOTE

The Unbroken Series: Raine Falling is a serialized succession of novels meant to be read in order:
The Broken
The Betrayal
The Break
The Brink
The Bond

We hope you enjoy reading these stories as much as we did writing them. Happy Reading!

Shayla Black and Jenna Jacob

ABOUT *THE BREAK*

One woman. Two Rivals. Countless secrets...

Raine Kendall has everything a woman could want—almost. Sexy, tender Liam O'Neill is her knight in shining armor, but is he too good to be true or could their growing connection actually last a lifetime? To complicate matters, she can't shake her feelings for her commanding boss, Macen Hammerman, especially after the mind-blowing night he stopped fighting their attraction, took her to bed, and ravished every inch of her.

Now there might be consequences.

While Hammer can't stop coveting Raine and counting the days of her cycle with glee, Liam resolves to keep her for his own. But she stubbornly refuses to open the corners of her scarred heart. Determined to win her for good, Liam risks everything. Though once he puts his plan in motion, she proves as elusive as smoke. It's a bitter pill when he needs Hammer's help to bring her home. And Liam can't help but wonder...will Raine ever be his again or will he lose her to his ex-best friend for good?

Chapter
One

Macen "Hammer" Hammerman stifled the mundane conversation with his assistant, Raine Kendall, and stood, bracing his hands on the desk between them. Though his office door stood open—he wasn't "allowed" to talk to her otherwise—they were as alone as they'd been in weeks. It was now or never. He had an important question to ask.

"Tell me something, Raine. Your period is what, five days late?"

Blood leached from her face. "Wha—I... How would you even know that?"

Because it was his business. After six years of being her mentor, caretaker, and employer, he'd recently given in to his gnawing hunger and fucked her in every way known to man. And recklessly, he'd done it without a condom. Since admitting how much he wanted her, he couldn't seem to stop. But the elaborate collar that now dangled from her neck strangled him with one indisputable fact: She was owned. Taken. Completely off limits. Property of another.

That son of a bitch, Liam O'Neill. His former best friend.

"Kind of blows your theory that I've always looked through you, doesn't it?" He smirked. "Since you came to Shadows, I've kept tabs on your cycle every single month. You promised you'd let me know if you were so much as a minute late. I've been waiting."

She pretended to scan through the pages of her notepad. "I promised to tell you if I was pregnant. Right now, I don't know anything. We need to finish discussing the Thanksgiving menu. I hope you bought cranberry sauce."

"Cranberry sauce? Really?" He cocked his head, his tone a warning.

"Don't do this, Hammer."

He leaned closer. "In case you've forgotten, it was *my* cock riding *your* pussy, precious. So I'm not shutting up until I have an answer."

A rosy flush suddenly stained her cheeks. Hammer smiled. She hadn't forgotten the passion they'd shared any more than he had. It had haunted him, day after day, night after night…

Raine scrambled to her feet, clutching her notepad and pen. "I have enough for the menu. We're done here."

"We're not," he barked. "Sit down."

She tossed her things on his desk and crossed her arms, glaring up at him. The swells of her pillowy breasts spilled from her V-neck tank. She looked sexy when she was mad. "So you can harass me again?"

Yes, Raine would see it that way. Christ, he needed to dial back on the confrontation, figure out how to drag information from her without distressing her even more.

"So we can finish talking. It's not my intention to upset you," he murmured.

She gave him a skeptical stare.

"Sit. Please." He waited until she complied, then he sat across from her. "You know I'd normally rather fucking swallow glass than say I'm sorry, but I owe it to you to shove this apology past my pride. That night, my need to mark you as mine overwhelmed my better judgment. It was selfish and reckless. I'm sorry."

Raine sighed, some of the starch leaving her. "You were drunk."

"That's even worse. I was pissed off, too. And hurt. To me, Liam's claim on you didn't mean shit. He messed with your mind and played you, just like he played me."

"You don't get to decide if my relationship with him is meaningless. I was afraid, and Liam took care of me. He still does."

A fact Hammer hated. "Why do you think he took such a sudden interest in you?"

"Why do you care? You and I were a mistake. Move on. I have."

No way. "I made *love* to you that night, Raine."

She squirmed and looked away. "And your 'love' was so meaningful, you couldn't wait the next morning to tell me that I wasn't woman enough for you."

Hammer reached across the desk and grabbed her chin, forcing her gaze to his. "Sixteen days, ten hours, and thirty-seven minutes ago, I heard your screams of ecstasy as I drove into your sweet little pussy. And you were so much woman that it changed me."

Raine shivered in his grasp. She tried to act like he didn't affect her, but he knew her way too well to believe that.

"So you don't want a slave you chain to your bed every night anymore?"

"I'll always want that." In fact, he could picture her as his, collared, naked, wet, kneeling… He swallowed down a surge of arousal. Raine wasn't built for that kind of submission, and he couldn't expect her to change for him. "But I've always wanted you, too." He reluctantly released her. "And every time you submit to Liam, I can hear that son of a bitch all over you through the thin walls. It hurts like hell, but I still listen and remember the taste of you on my tongue."

"Stop." The pulse picked up at Raine's throat. She pushed out of her chair and whirled for the door, leaving her pad and pen behind.

Hammer rushed around the side of his desk and grabbed her elbow. He'd tried not to crave her. Impossible. Raven hair, rosy lips, porcelain skin. Striking. Sensual. Soft-hearted. For weeks, he'd struggled to overcome his addiction to Raine, but every time he looked at her, he suspected he'd relapse really fucking soon.

"Let go." Her breathing sounded rushed, shallow. Aroused. "Please."

"Give me one more minute." As he pulled her closer, she trembled. "For six years, I wasn't honest with you about how I felt. I'm sorry for that, too." He spun her around and delved into her blue eyes. "But I won't apologize for touching you. That would be a lie."

He'd said as much as he could without confessing that he loved her and always would.

"Seriously, Hammer. You can't say things like that."

"Too honest?"

She hesitated. "Inappropriate."

"We passed inappropriate when Liam…" *Sank balls deep into your virgin ass, and I had to watch you thoroughly enjoy it.* Hammer cleared his throat. "Claimed you."

Her black lashes fell softly to her cheeks as she closed her eyes. "Macen…"

"It's done. You seem to have everything you've ever wanted. If Liam makes you happy, I'm glad."

Or he was trying to be. But standing this close to Raine and knowing he couldn't slide her beneath him again was eviscerating his restraint.

She scoffed. "You've never tolerated anyone blowing smoke up your ass. Neither will I."

Hammer pressed closer, barely resisting the urge to rub his hard cock against her. "What do you want to hear? That it's not smoke I want to fill your ass with, precious?"

She tensed. "I think you've said enough."

Because she belonged to Liam. *Right.*

Hammer sighed. He'd been the center of her life for years. Now Liam had stolen her away and taken his place. Hammer's only consolation was that he suspected she shared even less of herself with the Irish prick. Her stubborn, sometimes secretive behavior was a far cry from the loving deference a Master sought from his collared submissive. Which meant she probably wouldn't tell Liam about this conversation. She should, but...that was Raine. He loved her independence, even if it sometimes made his palm itch.

The vixen needed firm guidance. She might seem fragile on the surface, but her will could be iron. Idly, Hammer wondered if Liam would figure out that overindulging Raine wouldn't give her the boundaries she required before she crashed and burned.

"You're right." He smiled wryly. "But I'm being honest."

"If you don't have anything else, let me go. I'll have Thanksgiving dinner ready on Thursday at three."

"One more question. Has your period ever been late? I can't remember a single instance."

She closed her eyes. "Leave it alone."

"Like hell. I didn't take responsibility for you like I should have that night, but by god, I will now. If your period hasn't started by Black Friday, you won't be shopping. I'll be taking you to the doctor."

Raine jerked from his grip. "I'm perfectly capable of visiting a doctor myself."

"But I know you won't go without a push. Consider me your personal bulldozer."

"I'm not your responsibility anymore. I'm Liam's."

And wasn't that a kick in the balls?

"I want to be very clear, Raine. If you get a positive result from that test, everything changes. Every. Fucking. Thing. I will take care of you—in every way."

"I have to go." Her voice cracked.

In a flurry of dark hair, lace, and ruffles, Raine dashed toward the door. Hammer surged from his chair, caging her between the wall and his body, breathing on the back of her neck. God, she smelled good.

Fear, desire, dread—he felt them all pinging off of her as she shivered. "Hammer…"

Pulling together his restraint, he eased back, trying not to torture himself with what he couldn't have. Nearly three weeks without a woman—without her—was killing his self-control.

"I'll let you run away for now since it's what you do best, but I'm not letting this go. Be ready by eight a.m. Friday morning."

Liam O'Neill clutched the little box in his hand and rehearsed the speech in his head again. He prayed this package contained the key to his future with Raine. Maybe they could finally find some bloody happiness—and he could convince her that he intended to stay. Would she stop hoarding chunks of herself then? Of course, she'd push back at first, but she needed this. One day, she would agree.

As if his thoughts had conjured her up, his little hellcat tore out of Hammer's office and barreled down the hall, fists clenched. She nearly charged straight into him.

He pocketed the box. "Raine?"

She stopped short, trembling, blue eyes wide with panic. His fury—always simmering these days—began boiling.

Hammer, that fuckwit, had rattled her.

The need to protect rode Liam hard as he gripped her shoulders. "Tell me what happened."

Instantly, Raine's walls went up, and she shut down. *Here we go again...* Every day the same shit—him struggling to reach her, her hiding behind her defenses. So far, no amount of gentle cajoling or patience had convinced her to believe in him. After a couple of weeks as her Master, he'd seen only the merest glimpse into her soul.

Most men would have given up on her, but Liam's divorce had proven that if he wanted a relationship to last, he had to try harder. He'd never bothered to work his way into his ex-wife's soul or bared his own to Gwyneth. He couldn't make that mistake with Raine. She'd seized his heart, gripping it more tightly every day until he wondered if he could even breathe without her. He had no bloody idea if she would ever love him in return, but he'd do whatever it took to earn her trust.

Liam pinned her to the wall. "I've asked you what happened. Answer me."

She tried to wriggle free. "Nothing."

An evasion and a lie. Bloody hell.

Maybe things would be different if he could persuade her to leave Shadows, Hammer, and all the distractions. Maybe then he could win her over. But Raine refused to budge. This was the only place she'd ever known safety, and she felt obligated to Hammer for taking her in as a teenage runaway. But that wasn't her only reason. How fucking long would she pine for a man who refused to give her any part of himself that wasn't temporarily engorged?

"Give me the truth," he demanded.

Worry furrowed her dark brows, strained her delicate face. "Just hold me. Please don't let me go."

Her begging reached into his chest and tugged. "It'll be my pleasure, love, as soon as you tell me what Hammer did."

"Let's not talk about him. Or anything."

She clutched his lapels and brushed her lips over his. Then she did it again. Her next kiss turned urgent. He drowned in her sweet mouth for a lingering moment, knowing he should pull away.

Too often, Raine tempted him to carry her off to their bed, bare her pussy, and sink deep inside her when she sought to divert his attention. More than once, he'd lost himself in the pleasure that eclipsed everything but the explosive desire between them. When he succumbed, they never discussed what troubled her—which suited her fine and dandy. For Raine, talking through her problems was akin to peeling the flesh from her very bones.

But she hadn't smiled in a week. Giving into her manipulation wasn't going to help that.

Liam forced himself to set her away. "Wait for me in our room. I'll be along in a few minutes."

"Just forget it. Please." Raine plied him with another desperate kiss. "I'd rather be with you."

He sent her a stern scowl. "What part of 'wait for me' did you not understand?"

"It's not important."

"I'll decide that." He pointed down the hall. "Go."

With a sigh, she plodded down the hall, a sad slump pulling at her shoulders. Liam gritted his teeth against the stab of guilt. Sorting out this mess would do a lot more to help her than sex.

Dragging in a steadying breath, he watched her disappear into their room, then charged toward Hammer's office. Steeling himself, Liam shoved his way inside and slammed the door.

The bastard looked up from his paperwork and frowned.

"What the fuck just happened?" Liam demanded. "I let Raine spend a few minutes with you, and she left distraught."

"Don't come into my office looking for a fight, O'Neill. You won't like how it ends, and neither will Raine. For some reason, she likes your face the way it is."

"What did you do to *my* sub?" he snarled.

Hammer stood with such force, his chair rolled and hit the metal filing cabinet behind his desk. "Worried that I grabbed her tits? Copped a feel of her pussy? Fucked her? All with the door wide open?"

"You want her. So whether the door was open or closed wouldn't matter if you thought you could get away with it. Of that, I'm sure."

"What did Raine say? Or haven't you figured out yet how to make her communicate with you?" He crossed his arms over his chest with a sneer.

"I want your side of things."

Hammer snorted. "So she didn't tell you shit. Let me clue you in on a little secret: You'll need a crowbar to open her up when she walls herself off, like she's doing right now."

"That's no secret. *I'll* deal with that. Did you touch her, yes or no?"

"I didn't break the Code of Conduct." He tugged stiffly on his suit coat.

"Let's not pretend that honoring the Code would mean a damn thing to you if not for your fellow Doms' disapproval. Respect Raine enough not to make this situation any more difficult and tell me what happened."

"I'm not making it more difficult; I'm ensuring that she runs back to me when you figure out she's more than you can manage. *I* know how to handle her."

The silky threat in Hammer's voice crawled up Liam's back. He swallowed an answering insult. He needed answers more than he needed a fight—no matter how badly he wanted one. Hammer blamed him for losing Raine, obviously so enraged that he could barely see straight. And Liam couldn't forget—or forgive—that Hammer had done his bloody best to plant a seed in her womb the moment Liam took her for his own.

He rubbed at the knot at the back of his neck, staring at Macen. "If you care about her at all, put her needs first for once. Tell me what has her rattled."

"I didn't take any liberties, so stop busting my balls."

"I don't care about your balls. I'm here to protect Raine."

"Yeah?" Hammer gave him a hard glare. "You don't seem too worried. Do you know how many days late her period is? I sure as hell do."

There was the proverbial punch in the gut. Raine's monthly *was* late… just as he'd suspected. Liam closed his eyes, damn near crippled where he stood.

Hammer knew the answer to the question Liam had asked Raine many times. No matter how Liam had tried to wrest it from her, she'd danced around the truth, as though possibly being pregnant by another man was none of his goddamned business.

What else was she keeping from him? Time to pry Raine open and find out.

Liam turned away and opened the door.

"Wait," Hammer called him back. "I want you to know that night with Raine was the only time I haven't gloved up since Juliet. I'm clean. She really is just scared and lashing out. It's how she copes. Don't take my mistake out on her."

Liam didn't turn back, just curled his hands into fists. "Fuck you."

C HAPTER
T W O

R aine paced, wringing her hands, her head a tangle of a thousand thoughts. Damn it, she always let Hammer push her buttons. Why hadn't she gotten him out of her system? She bit her lip. In three days, he was going to force the truth on her, and it terrified her.

What if she was pregnant? God, did she even know how to feel about that? On the one hand, blessed. She loved kids. She loved Hammer. She loved the idea that her six years of unrequited love for him might bear fruit. On the other hand, if she was carrying the child of Liam's former friend, she didn't expect the man to stay. Despite his assurances, why would he?

As she fingered her collar, Raine felt her expression crumble. Crying wouldn't change the fact that she loved two very different men for very different reasons. If Liam left her... Well, she had no one to blame for her stupidity but herself.

Suddenly, the door opened, and she spun to face him, bracing herself for the confrontation she'd desperately tried to avoid. He looked somewhere between somber and furious. Her heart sank. She had no doubt what he and Hammer had discussed. Today she'd gotten the message loud and clear that Macen wanted to separate her from Liam. One topic could do that very quickly.

Raine ran to him and threw her arms around his neck, all too aware that if things turned out as she feared, this might be one of the last times she held him. She clung and inhaled his musky scent. He was all man. Her rock. Her greatest comfort. Her most tender lover. And he was slipping through her fingers because she was an eternal fuckup.

"Liam..." She pressed her lips to his, willing him to kiss her back, lower her to the bed, and forget about everything else.

He cupped her face and studied her. The dark eyes that usually caressed her with such caring now dissected her with a razor-sharp stare. "We need to talk."

Panic seized her heart as Liam led her toward their bed. Though Raine knew she owed it to him to discuss her problems, that only made them more real.

As she sank to the mattress beside him, she looked into his beloved face. His stormy eyes wrenched her heart. She'd done this to him, taken this strong, gorgeous man and turned him inside out. Guilt crushed her.

"Can't we talk later?" She caressed a hand down his chest, letting it drift lower and lower... "I've missed you." Her eyes teared up. "I'm begging."

"There's nothing I'd enjoy more than to bury myself between your thighs, love, but you can't distract me from this. Stop trying."

If they had this conversation now, it would only end in disaster. "There's nothing to talk about. Hammer and I got into an argument. We were discussing the menu for Thanksgiving and—"

"Thanksgiving?" He scowled. "Did you make plans of your own, then?"

She blinked in confusion. "Not plans of my own. I just assumed... I always cook for Hammer." Immediately, she saw that Liam had taken her words the wrong way. "What I mean is, I always cook so that he can host a Thanksgiving dinner for the 'orphans' of Shadows. You know, the people with no other family and nowhere else to go. They'll spend it alone if I don't fix this dinner, and it's too late to hire a caterer now."

Liam cursed. "And when were you thinking of telling me? Am I even invited?"

"Of course!" Dismay spread through her. He looked angry. But worse, he looked hurt. "I assumed you knew about the group dinner. We have it every year, but..." *Oh no.* A fresh wave of worry overcame her. "But you haven't been here long enough to know. I'm so sorry."

His expression didn't soften one bit.

Raine swallowed. "Really. I've been so..." *Preoccupied.* "Busy. I didn't realize that I'd never mentioned it."

"I had a special surprise planned just for the two of us."

Shit, she just kept digging herself a deeper hole with him. "I didn't even think that you might want to do something else. Next year..."

Raine couldn't finish that sentence. Next year, if nature had taken its course, she'd have an infant, and Liam would be long gone. Even the thought filled her with terror. Still, what else could she do? Hammer and the others were counting on her. Serving this meal every Thanksgiving was one of her greatest pleasures.

"If we can do whatever you had planned on Thursday night, I'd be thrilled and honored to go with you," she ventured.

And maybe, if she was lucky, Liam would have her somewhere else on Friday so she could avoid Hammer and the doctor appointment he'd threatened. Yes, she was putting off the inevitable, but she just couldn't face the future now.

He glared at her, his face forbidding.

Raine rushed to reassure him. "Thursday night, I'll be done with my responsibilities here and I'll be all yours again."

"You're not all mine now, sub?" He rose to his full height. "Am I only your Sir when it's convenient for you?"

Oh, shit… "That's not what I meant. Of course I'm yours." Liam usually wasn't much for protocol and honorifics, but she couldn't mistake his demeanor. Raine resisted the urge to shrink back against the headboard. "Sir."

The title had almost no impact on him. He still glared at her with dark eyes full of disapproval. "Don't forget it."

"No, Sir." God, she hated feeling unworthy, like she never did anything right.

"The private Thanksgiving I had planned for us? I'll flush that down the fucking toilet."

Her dread soared. "I feel terrible about disappointing you, especially on Thanksgiving. I want to enjoy what you planned, but I can't let twenty-five others down. How can I make it up to you?"

"By telling me how late your period is."

She felt the blood drain from her face. "I told you last week that I wasn't late."

A dark brow jetted up. "And this week?"

"Liam…"

"What did you call me?" He glowered, tangling his hand in her hair, pulling just enough for her to feel the sting.

"Sir."

"Better. Now answer me. Hammer apparently knows exactly how late your period is, while I have no bloody clue."

Damn Hammer for not keeping his mouth shut. "I didn't say anything. He's been counting days. I've tried not to upset you—or anyone—until I knew something for sure."

"You must have some idea whether you're pregnant, Raine."

"How should I? I've never worried about this."

Liam whirled away and stormed into the adjoining bathroom. After the rustle of plastic, he returned a moment later, carrying a box. He slammed it on her nightstand.

A pregnancy test.

Her heart stopped.

"I bought this for you last night. Let's end the worrying." Liam crossed his arms over his chest. "Take it."

She backed away. "Don't make me. Please…"

Her pleading did absolutely nothing but make his expression colder.

"I've been patient."

He had been, just like he always was. She had no right to expect more. But she needed it so badly.

Raine shook her head. "I can't. I'm too scared to pee on that stick and find out for sure. I'm afraid the truth will drive you away."

That was as honest as her courage allowed.

His mouth turned down in a disapproving scowl. "Is that why you and Hammer fought?"

She nodded. "He threatened to take me to the doctor on Friday if I still haven't started."

"And you wanted to avoid that so badly, you were going to 'let me' take you away Thursday night, after dinner at Shadows?"

"No, I really do want to be with you," she choked. "I'm sorry. About the test, Thanksgiving…" She tried, but nothing would stop her tears. "About everything."

"I don't want you to be sorry. I want you to be honest," he shouted. "Open up and tell me what's bothering you. Your fears. Your insecurities. What the fuck you want for dinner. Whether or not you're pregnant. I'm sick to death of being in the dark. I won't be treated like the bloody wanker you find ways to dodge."

"You're not, I swear. Liam…I'm scared."

"I know you are, but if you won't face the truth or trust me to help you…" He gritted his teeth. "Then my hands are tied."

Shame engulfed Raine. She knew she didn't share things with Liam the way she should. He'd stripped her soul so naked once before, and she'd cowered behind her walls since. They couldn't have a genuine exchange if she continued this way, but anxiety drove her to shut him out.

"I'm trying." She couldn't make the tears and the sorrow stop. "You may not believe me—"

"I'd believe you if you'd take the damn test."

Raine crossed her arms over her chest, every muscle in her body shriveling. "I'm not ready. I can't face it. Not yet."

"How long do you need? How many days is enough? Or will you still be burying your head in the sand when you're giving birth?"

"How long should it take me to accept that my whole life could be changing and I could lose everyone who means anything to me?" she shouted back, tears streaming. "I know you've been patient. I know I'm being illogical. I know you're pissed off. I'm *trying*."

"No, you tried when I had you alone at my lodge. You opened up that night. The minute I brought you back here to 'help' Hammer because he so desperately needed you…" Liam rolled his eyes. "You stopped. You've fed me nothing but shit since. Clearly, I overestimated your desire to submit to me."

"You didn't. Not at all."

"Then what the hell is your problem? I've told you time and again that I'll stand by you, no matter what. But I might as well be talking to a brick wall." He tossed his hands in the air.

"Because no man has ever lied to a woman?"

"When have *I* ever lied to *you*, Raine?" Mouth flattening into a grim white line, he released her hair. "I've nothing else to say now."

Liam turned his back on her.

Shock blanched her system, followed by an icy drench of guilt. He hadn't lied to her—ever. Her father had. Hammer had. And she'd accused Liam of their sins.

Raine stood, looking at the tense set of his broad shoulders, his muscled back, his clenched fists. She forced herself to approach him. "That was unfair. I'm sorry. Liam… You're right. You've always been wonderful. I don't know how I could possibly deserve you."

No apology or verbal bridge-mending was going to reach him now. Raine wanted to tell Liam how much she loved him, but saying it now would seem disingenuous. And making herself that vulnerable to him petrified her.

God, she was like a yo-yo, swinging between revealing the vulnerability he coaxed from her and shrouding herself behind her barricades like a coward. Raine knew she couldn't keep holding out like this, but years of fears and insecurities didn't melt away overnight.

And that test on the nightstand—the elephant in the room—only magnified everything.

"I don't know what to say," she admitted. "I always manage to screw up everything good that happens to me. And you're the best."

She worked up the courage to reach for his shoulder, but he jerked away. His rejection hurt like a physical blow.

"Please don't shut me out." Raine sniffled, dying inside. "I want to open up and share everything with you... I'm trying to trust and believe you. But I've never done that with anyone. Honestly, I'm lost. I'm not trying to be a bitch."

He whirled around with narrowed eyes. "Did you just swear at me?"

Raine winced. "It slipped. Sorry."

She just kept fucking up the words. He was too angry to hear them now anyway. Time to show Liam how much he meant to her. She only knew one way to do that.

With shaking fingers, Raine peeled off her lacy tank, shimmied out of her short skirt, unclasped her bra, then removed the last of her barriers, her thong. With shaking hands, she folded everything at his feet and sank to her knees, bowing her head. "Punish me, Sir. I've earned it."

"You've more than earned it."

As the weight of his words settled over her, Raine felt his stare rake her, scorch her. She couldn't stop trembling.

"Love?" A hint of coaxing warmed his voice as he hooked a finger under her chin and lifted it. She had no choice but to meet his gaze. "Are you afraid of me?"

Despite his size and strength, Liam was gentle at heart. Of course, he'd punished her before, but always in a way designed to make her think more than hurt. Right now, he was all big bad Dom. Though she'd never seen this side of him, he didn't frighten her. In fact, as anxious as she was, his power was like a beacon. She was deeply drawn to it.

"No, Sir. Never."

"Then present."

Her tummy knotted as she leaned forward and skimmed her palms along the rug until they stretched above her head. Ass lifting from her heels, she arched up in offering to him and rested her forehead on the carpet. Then Liam knelt beside her.

"Look at me." His too-controlled tone sent a chill down her spine. She forced herself to comply, bracing for the worst. The heat of his body surrounded her. His warm breath fluttered over her ear. "I know you're scared and worried about the 'what ifs.' But I've told you over and over that I expect you to share everything with me. You're not doing that."

Her heart wanted to. Her head hadn't yet gotten the memo.

"Five days." Her voice shook. "I'm late by five days."

Liam sucked in a breath like she'd punched him with her words. Raine closed her eyes.

"I told you to look at me."

She swallowed hard and did as he'd commanded, wishing he wouldn't force her to see his disappointment.

"Are your cycles often irregular?"

"Not since I lived with my dad. I think stress caused it. I'm under a lot of pressure now."

"Finally, some bloody honesty. Was it really so hard for you to tell me that?"

She bit her lip. "I didn't know how to start the conversation. 'Hi, honey. I'm worried I might be pregnant by your best friend.'"

"Take the test."

"I'm scared the results will disappoint you. I hate that." Tears flowed again. "So much."

The silence dragged on. Pain and frustration filled his face. God, she just kept hurting him. Maybe it would be better if she left. She hated to stay where she only made matters worse, and the urge to escape now pressed down on her chest until she couldn't breathe. But he and Hammer were both right; she always ran. She couldn't honestly say that she'd done her part to hold the relationship together if she left now.

"Say something. Please..."

Liam sat back on the bed, his face closed. "Put yourself across my lap and spread your thighs for me. Show me your cunt. I want to see what's mine."

Raine rose from her knees and stepped closer, knowing any display of uncertainty would only make the punishment more painful—not physically. She wasn't concerned about that. But mentally? Emotionally?

She tried to snare his gaze, but he looked right through her. Disquiet filled her all over again. Still, she dredged up the courage to sprawl across Liam's lap.

"Tell me your safe word."

"Paris," she breathed.

Liam gave her a sharp nod. "Count until I stop."

Raine drew in a rough breath, knowing he'd light into her ass at any moment. Instead, he made her wait. She twitched, wondering when he'd get on with it. The seconds dragged into minutes, which seemed like days. Still, he did nothing for a long, silent while but stare at her vulnerable bare backside. She resisted the urge to fidget.

Finally, he smacked her ass, his hand branding her with the feel of his palm and each finger. It burned into her like fiery, oozing lava. And it was oddly soothing.

"One." She sobbed.

He kept going.

Today, he didn't warm her up and he didn't hold back. Each slap stung like a bitch. Pain sizzled over her skin, burned down into her flesh. He scorched her through and through. She focused on the sensations he gave her and welcomed them.

Slowly, with each rhythmic smack, the cacophony of thoughts all yelling through her brain quieted. Suddenly, there was a blessed peace, broken only by the *whoosh* of his hand, the slap and its echo reverberating through the room, the high-pitched sounds of her crying out the count, his heavy breathing...before the cycle started again. Somewhere along the way, she lost count and lost herself, fading out to a lovely place where she began to float away from all her problems. From everything but Liam, her anchor. Her love.

Raine didn't know how much time had passed when the spanking abruptly stopped. Her muscles felt like melted chocolate, her thoughts like oozing honey. She breathed him in as he grazed his big palm over her hot flesh.

Long moments passed as she curled her arms around his leg, holding tight. "Thank you, Sir. I feel calmer."

As he sat her up on his lap, Liam ran a soothing hand down her spine and cradled her to his chest. Her head lolled back, and she stared up at him, feeling her heart in her eyes. That didn't scare the hell out of her as much as it used to.

"How do you do that?" Raine whispered. "How do you always know what I need?"

"I wish I did. I don't pretend to have all the answers, but I'm here and I can bear the burden. Do you not realize how much I need to do that for you?"

"I promise, I'll try harder."

He sighed. "Stop telling me what you think I want to hear. Show me."

Raine wanted to please him. "How?"

Liam didn't answer her, just lifted her up and laid her out on the bed, bound her wrists in the cuffs attached to the frame, then grabbed her ankles and spread her legs wide. Despite all her angst, arousal bloomed. She ached for his attention, but stilled her writhing to please him. Raine knew she didn't deserve to be rewarded, but she needed him desperately.

He tore free of his clothes, dropping them where he stood. She watched hungrily. The sight—strong jaw, broad chest, corrugated abdomen, muscled thighs, and a hard cock in between—made her yearn for him. His rigid flesh jerked in need as he crawled between her splayed thighs.

With a feral gleam in his eyes, he hovered over her and stroked his long, thick shaft. A mewl of impatience slipped from her lips.

"Is this what you want, Raine?" With his free hand, he dragged his finger through the folds of her moistening slit and teased her clit. "What you need?"

"Yes. Please, Liam."

Instead of giving her more, he lifted his finger away. His expression blanked.

"Sir. Sorry. Yes, please, Sir."

He didn't give her what she wanted. "Do you like it when I share myself with you? Does it make you feel close to me?"

She nodded. "It does."

"Treasured?"

"Yes, Sir."

"You like watching me stroke myself, don't you, Raine? Does it make your cunt juicy with desire? Do you want my dominance? Ache for me to fuck you?"

She nodded feverishly. "Always."

"Ah, love," he murmured. "How do you want me? In your ass? Down your throat? Filling that tight pussy until you're mindless with wanting to spill over me as you come?"

He circled her straining clit. She moaned in utter supplication, her stare riveted to his every move, silently begging for more.

"Any of it. All of it," she cried.

"I can tell you want me." His silky rasp reverberated in her ear. "I smell your arousal."

"Liam..." she cried breathlessly.

Then his voice hardened to steel. "But I don't think you understand, Raine. You *will* tell me what hurts you, keeps you awake, frightens or upsets you, makes you laugh and cheer and every fucking thing in between because you are *mine*. Until now, you've given me nothing except what I yank out of you under duress. Even then, you dance pretty around the periphery, clinging to me with your soft body and batting your lashes to distract me from your problems. I've given you a lot of slack in your rope. All you've managed to do is hang yourself."

His words sliced her to the bone with guilt. From the time he'd approached her about becoming the best submissive she could be until this moment, he'd tried everything to reach her. Still, she remained half-frozen—in love with him but torn. Yearning to surrender everything but terrified.

"I know I need to do better."

"You need to decide what you want."

"You, Liam. Always you. Your touch. Your approval. Your under-standing."

"Then you have to do your part. I won't tolerate just some of your effort or half of your soul anymore."

He meant it. Raine saw the gravity on his stern face, in the hard glint of his eyes. If she wanted to keep him, she had to find the courage to surrender. She had to figure out how to give him the power to hurt her and trust that he wouldn't.

"I know." Raine teared up. "You're so capable of making a woman feel special and showering her with devotion." She didn't see what she could possibly give him in return, and didn't that sound pathetic? "I feel like I'm bringing you nothing but problems. Wouldn't you rather just have my body?"

"I already have your body, sub, splayed out and wet just the way *I* want it." Again he teased her cunt, sliding his thumb upward to rub her clit while inserting first one, then two fingers through her cream and deep inside her. "Making you beg and scream has been a heady pleasure from the start."

Raine cried out and arched up for more, trying to drown the dread snaking through her with the euphoria of his touch.

He bent to her ear, his voice brutally gentle. "We don't have a problem communicating when I'm fucking you into oblivion." Then he withdrew his fingers, leaving her cold. "It's here." Liam tapped her forehead, right between the eyes. "This is where I lose you, where all our troubles lie."

"You're right. I know. I said I'd try harder."

"But what you meant is that you'll find more creative ways to hide from me. Close your mouth. Don't deny it. If you lie, I'll truly punish you and I'll make sure you don't like it."

Foreboding mixed with her arousal to create something so confusing, Raine had no idea what to say. "I understand, Sir."

"Then prove to me that I'm important enough for you to knock down your walls and learn to trust. Show me I'm not wasting my breath."

"I'll do my best. But it's not that simple. You don't understand."

His brows slashed down in a thunderous frown. "Really? Your father hurt you and Hammer pretended he didn't want you for years, so now you think you're not good enough for any man, and if I see the real you, I'll run screaming in the other direction like some bloody nancy? Is that what you *think* I don't understand?"

God, it was as if he'd shoved her in front of a mirror, then sliced her to the bone so he could force her to watch herself bleed. Though she'd done her best to hide, he still saw right through her. It felt like being naked in the middle of a crowd. Panic threatened. She tugged at her bonds, struggling, though she knew it was pointless.

"Stop," Liam growled. "Damn it, Raine, how do you expect to learn to surrender when you spend so much of your energy fighting me and yourself?"

She had nowhere to escape his penetrating stare. Her heart chugged. The moment felt so intimate. So petrifying.

Raine closed her eyes and turned her head away.

He grabbed her cheeks and forced her to look back at him. She didn't have the guts to open her eyes and see what was on his face. Disappointment? Anger? Scorn?

"The only way you'll be escaping me now is by using your safe word. Say it or look at me."

Using her safe word when he wasn't physically hurting her would be the coward's way out. He was trying to help her learn to give more of herself. She *needed* this lesson. But he'd already seen so deeply inside her, more than maybe anyone ever…

On that fateful morning he'd offered to train her, he'd told her that he intended to split her open like a ripe peach. She'd been almost smug in the belief that she'd never give him that power. Damn, she'd been a fool.

Hitching in a sob, she forced herself to open her eyes, though she couldn't see him through her thick tears.

A voice in her head told her that sharing all of herself wouldn't be as scary as facing an executioner. It would probably be beautiful. Raine still didn't know if she could do it.

"I know the fact that I'm not giving myself over to you is damaging. I just keep trying to solve my problems so I don't have to bother you."

"It doesn't work that way, and you know it."

In her head, Raine did. A plea for his reassurance sat on the tip of her tongue, but she silenced it. She had to give him control.

"Raine…" He wiped her tears away, his fingers terribly gentle.

Her heart wept. Liam was so kind, so tender… She blinked up at him, resisting her every instinct to crawl back inside herself and hide.

"Good. Stay with me now."

He eased down her body, his lips dragging over her skin, sucking slowly at each nipple before he lowered his mouth to her pussy and took a long, slow lick. She shuddered with the sensations of her soul splitting open and oozing need, her body wired and alive.

He groaned. "The taste of you, love… So perfect on my tongue."

"Liam," she sobbed and writhed. "Help me. Tell me… What do you want?"

"You, Raine. All of you. From the sweet to the tart and everything in between." He sucked her clit between his lips, pulling and scraping the bud with his teeth. She arched her hips, desperate for more of his mouth on her. Liam only pulled back and slapped her clit. "You're not in control here. Give it to me."

She choked back a cry, her pain melding to pleasure as he slid two fingers in deep, grazing the sensitive bundle of nerves.

"We could be so good together, if you'd just trust me."

"It's not you," she swore.

"I know. But I want to be the man you finally let in."

His incessant fingers drove into her pussy, his thumb swirling over her clit. Panting and whimpering, she arched, waiting and hoping for his command to come.

"You burn so sweetly for me. And you're so close to orgasm you can almost taste it, can't you?"

"Yes!"

He pulled away from her quivering pussy, then straddled her body. His engorged cock hovered inches from her mouth, the weeping crest glistening. Mouth watering, she opened to take him deep between her lips.

Instead, he leaned over her and unfastened the cuffs, setting her free. Then he rolled to her side, no longer touching her. "All right, then. Stroke your pussy for me, Raine. Make yourself come. Show me how much you want me."

Raine would far rather have Liam touch her, but he'd given her a direct order. He was allowing her pleasure. She didn't dare question him or ask for more.

With a jagged sigh, she slid her fingers to her swollen clit. In seconds, she was panting, falling over the edge as a hard, fast climax tore through her. Even as her thighs tensed and her body shook, the orgasm was hollow, a parody of pleasure. It left her wanting.

And she knew exactly what was missing… Liam.

Reaching for him, Raine murmured his name.

He grasped her wrists. "Did you enjoy that?"

Physically, she had. But emotionally, knowing that he hadn't allowed her to give him pleasure in return left her feeling wretched, empty, and wracked with guilt. "Not without you. I feel like...you gave and I took, but it was one-sided."

"Exactly." He backed away from her and off the bed. "Now you know what I feel every damn time you try to satisfy me with scraps of yourself. I can't dominate what you won't submit. I've tried to do it all for us, but I can't, no matter how much I want you."

His words were a silken slide down a razor blade, delivered so softly. But it cut her heart wide open.

He picked up his clothes and silently began to dress. Raine sat up and watched, pressing her lips together in mute horror and trying to hold onto her tears. There was no sense arguing with him when he was right.

Once he'd zipped his pants, Liam looked down at her with such profound sadness. "Hear me well. Half of you is no longer an option, Raine. I'll have all or nothing. I won't make you take the test before Thanksgiving. That gives you almost three days to prepare yourself for the result. But if you haven't started by Friday, you will be going to the doctor. *I'll* be taking you."

CHAPTER
THREE

Liam resisted the urge to slam the door between him and Raine. As he eased out, he released a ragged breath. Thankfully, he didn't see Hammer. But Liam had few doubts that his old mate had been listening to his entire exchange with Raine through the wall. The fuckwit probably itched to insist again that she was more challenge than he could master.

Unfortunately, Liam's problems didn't end there. His cock stood as hard as a ship's stern and twice as swollen. His balls ached so badly he couldn't walk straight, let alone think. As he adjusted himself, he considered finding an empty room and some privacy. Of course, he'd ten times rather have drowned in Raine, helpless and tethered to his bed. The ferocious need to own her all the way to her pretty toes twisted him inside. But no matter which way he took her or how often, Raine never truly surrendered.

Maybe he'd finally reached her today. At least she'd been more honest. But did that mean anything? Raine was like a damn jigsaw puzzle. The tactic that revealed a part of her today wouldn't work tomorrow. Just after he'd collared her, he'd whisked her up to his lodge and chipped away at her defenses until she'd exposed her soft side. Now that he'd breached her again, he feared she would only hide once more.

Liam resisted the urge to punch the wall. Where the hell did he go from here? He couldn't give up. If he ever solved her, the heart he uncovered would be big and beautiful. And *his*.

If that day never came… Hell, he didn't want to think about that.

In his pocket, his phone buzzed. Liam grabbed it and scanned the screen, smiling at the name of his friend and fellow Dominant back home.

"Hello, Seth." Liam ducked into an empty room down the hall. "Enjoying the snow in New York?"

The other man scoffed. "You'll be enjoying it soon yourself, so don't gloat too much."

"I'm not coming."

"You won't be home for Thanksgiving?" No mistaking the surprise in Seth's voice.

"Afraid not. I made other plans, but they fell through. Now it's too late to get a flight, so…"

"You mean I'll have to fist this turkey all alone?"

Liam rolled his eyes. "You're a sick bastard, you know that?"

"And proud of it. So why are you staying in L.A. for the holiday?"

"Well, for one, I don't want to freeze my balls off," Liam teased.

"It might be cold as fuck here, but at least I don't have to worry about the state falling into the ocean."

"True." Liam leaned against the wall and rubbed a thumb and forefinger at his gritty eyes. "Look, I know I said I'd come back for the week, but circumstances have changed. There's this woman…"

"Tell me more."

"She's a beauty and a spitfire, Seth. You'll like her, assuming I can ever figure out how to persuade her to come home with me."

"It's that serious? You haven't spent more than fifteen minutes of 'quality time' with anyone since Gwyneth, but it sounds like you have more than a hard-on for this girl. What'd she do, put you under some kind of spell with her voodoo pussy?"

Liam laughed for the first time all day. "Something like that."

"Aww, don't worry. You're always cool, collected, and smart. You'll figure out how to sweep her off her feet. If not, you know some awesome knots. Just tie her up and carry her away." Seth chuckled. "What about Hammer? When we talked last month, you said he wasn't himself. Did you figure out what's up with him?"

"Well, funny that. His problem is the same as mine. Raine. She's the girl I told you Hammer took in years ago, remember? He's in love with her. The fucked up part is that she's in love with him, too." Liam sighed. "And now, she's wearing my collar, but there's a good chance she's knocked up with Hammer's bairn."

"Whoa! What the... It sounds like a fucking soap opera."

Liam grunted. "It feels like a fucking soap opera."

"How the hell did all that happen?"

"For years, Hammer refused to admit how he felt about her. But he wouldn't allow any other man near her. I tried to help them both, but—"

"Help? Meaning that you gave her attention to see if Hammer would claim her in a jealous fit?"

Seth knew him well. "Raine needed a bloody guiding hand and some damn affection. What woman doesn't deserve that? Hammer sure as fuck wasn't giving it to her."

"I guess he finally did or she wouldn't be knocked up."

"Oh, he did. As soon as I took her for my own. So now he hates my fucking guts. I'm not too fond of him, either."

"Holy shit." Seth whistled.

Liam sighed. "Jesus bloody wept, it really does sound as fucked up as it feels."

"So which one of you is Raine actually with now?"

"It's supposed to be me, but I don't rightly know."

"What shit are you guys smoking out there?" Seth huffed.

"I almost wish I had some. Half the time, I don't know whether to laugh, scream, or jump off a bloody bridge."

"You know the easy answer. Share her, like you did Juliet."

It sounded so simple. Nothing could be more impossible.

"No chance in hell," Liam said.

"Why not? You'd both get the girl. She'd feel more secure, get more guidance…"

"Hammer may have shared his wife with me, but Raine? I think he'd rather castrate himself. I don't want that daft prick touching her, either. Besides, he seems convinced that sharing Juliet caused her death. I'm not sure why exactly, but he won't risk it again."

"Do you think he's right?"

Liam closed his eyes and didn't say anything for a long moment. "I've asked myself that a thousand times. Hammer and I have never talked about the end. He was so shut down, and I wasn't there. I never wanted to pry. I just know that Juliet wasn't communicating with either one of us. Neither is Raine."

"Shit. Do you think she's unstable enough to pull a Juliet?"

"I doubt it. She's emotional but bloody obstinate."

"You should tread carefully until you're sure."

Liam sighed. "I know, but…I'm in deep, man. I love this woman."

"Love?" he asked incredulously. "Oh dude, but if her heart belongs to Hammer—"

"She cares for me, too. At least, I think she does. But Raine is confused, Seth. And so damn vulnerable."

"I suppose that suggesting you pack a bag and take a red-eye home is out of the question?"

"Fuck that. I don't hear a fat lady singing yet. It's not over."

"Are you sure you're not wearing earplugs?"

"Sometimes I'd like to, but Raine's crumbling. I can't leave her now. Everyone else in her life has."

Seth blew out a stunned breath. "Do you have a game plan?"

"I'm working on it. First, I need to find out if Raine is pregnant. Then…we'll see."

"If she is, what the fuck are you going to do?"

Liam shook his head as the image of Raine swelling with Hammer's spawn made him grit his teeth. "Not much I can do except be there for her. But fuck…"

The silence hung between them, the gravity of the conversation weighing them both down.

"I'm sorry for the hell you're going through." And Seth's voice said that he meant it. "Either way, you need to reach Raine before she falls apart. I know you'll hate this idea, but can Hammer do it? Does she trust him?"

Did she? Liam had always assumed she did. But Hammer had figured out how late her period was; Raine hadn't volunteered the information. So maybe not. "As much as she trusts anyone, I suspect, but it's not a lot."

"Just a suggestion, but maybe you and Hammer need to stop trying to claim your territory by planting your um…flag, and—"

Liam growled.

"And work your shit out," Seth continued. "It might take both of you to reach her."

"He wouldn't lift a fucking finger to help me now." Not that he wanted Hammer's help.

That saddened Liam, too. Over a decade of friendship gone in a flash, ripped apart by their unyielding determination to possess and claim the same woman.

What a bloody fucking debacle.

"One of you has to swallow your pride. Working together might help you and Hammer kiss and make up. You've been friends too long to fight like this," Seth pointed out. "Remember, Raine has to come first."

"She does. But she has to *want* to do the work. So far, she's dodged every attempt I've made to help her."

"She's not trying at all? That changes a lot, then."

They talked about Raine's behavior and pounded out a rough idea designed to help him reach her.

"You hate it." Seth didn't even ask; he knew.

"Every bit," Liam admitted. "But I see the wisdom. I'll have to think on it."

"It's not a move to make lightly, for sure," Seth advised. "But you won't be happy unless you've earned her whole heart and total surrender."

The following morning, Raine chopped some nuts for a loaf of banana bread, pausing to flip on the light in the oven to check her red velvet cake. Fresh baked chocolate chip cookies cooled on her left. Their scent wafted to her nose and should have tantalized her. But it didn't. Hammer's favorite, apple spice muffins, sat on the table behind her. Their smell should have perked her up too, but no. The yeasty bread rising under the dish towel nearby looked ready for the oven. She'd already baked a plate of cinnamon rolls and set them nearby.

And she wasn't any calmer than when she'd walked into the kitchen at three a.m.

Liam hadn't come to bed last night—at least not the bed they shared. Raine tried desperately not to believe that he'd found someone else's. Never before had he disappeared without a word. But she knew exactly what he meant to convey: he was more than frustrated with her refusal to take the pregnancy test, Thanksgiving… everything.

If something didn't change, she wouldn't be able to keep him much longer. At the thought, panic gripped her throat.

She'd texted him this morning to tell him that she missed him, but he hadn't replied. Her only consolation was that his clothes still hung in the closet. She hoped that meant he was coming back, but she was also aware that he could send for them from New York.

What if she'd driven him away for good? She pressed her hand to her lips to hold in a sob.

In the doorway behind her, she felt a presence. Just by the way the air stirred, she knew Hammer stood, watching her. He'd see all the baked goods—and he'd know exactly what they meant.

She dragged in a steadying breath, then dumped the nuts from the chopper into the batter, avoiding his gaze. "Good morning. I'm just baking. Help yourself."

Hammer crossed the room and stepped into her personal space, telling her without a word that she wasn't going to escape whatever he had to say. His thick fingers gripped the counter near her waist, and she felt his body heat along her back. Why the hell hadn't she worn more than her panties and a tank top? Under his stare, she felt naked.

"Everything looks delicious, precious. Tell me, is it that bad?"

She forced herself to shrug. "I couldn't sleep. I was bored, so I baked."

A humorless chuckle rolled from the back of his throat. "This is me you're talking to. You only bake enough for an army when you're deeply troubled. Tell me, did the bed feel a little empty last night?"

Why the hell was he taunting her?

She slammed her spoon on the counter. "It's none of your goddamn business."

"Turn around." He waited until she complied with a sigh. "We're going to talk."

"Is this official club business?"

"Liam may let you negotiate. You know I won't. Sit down. Now."

She braced her hands on his chest, pushing him away. "What the fuck do you want from me? To hear that I screwed up? Yep. You're right. I royally muffed everything. Happy now?"

"Liam is sleeping off a bottle in a spare bedroom down the hall." He paused, his voice softening. "Alone."

God, he could have said most anything else to her and she would have held it together. A fight? Bring it on. She'd love one of those now. Instead, he'd disarmed her with compassion. Damn him.

She and Hammer might have had a bumpy personal relationship, and he might have blown arctic and heat wave on her in the past, but he was still the person she trusted most on this planet. She knew without a doubt that he always wanted what was best for her—even if they had different ideas about what that was. So Raine had a hard time resisting the urge to throw herself against him and cry out her concerns, wrapped in his familiar arms. She couldn't. He would take on her burdens without hesitation, but that wasn't fair to either him or to Liam.

She had to keep it to herself. And that made her feel so damn alone.

"Thank you. Please don't make this tougher for me. If you're here to remind me that this is day six without a period, believe me, I know."

With a grim expression, he pulled out a chair and extended his hand. "I don't want to talk about your period. Friday will come soon enough." He poured a cup of coffee, then plucked a muffin from the plate and took a bite. And he moaned. "You spoil me with these. They're the best I've ever tasted. Now put your ass in the chair."

Raine hesitated. There would be no avoiding him. *Tenacious bastard.*

With a sigh, she eased her butt, still sore from Liam's paddling, onto the hard wooden chair, trying not to wince.

"A little tender, are you, precious?" he drawled. "Yeah, I heard."

And wasn't that completely embarrassing? "You didn't have to listen."

"I told you I like hearing you moan, even if it's not for me."

She scowled at him. Then when a little ache tightened behind her clit, guilt pricked her. She looked away. "Hammer..."

"I said I was going to be honest from now on, remember?" He sat at the head of the table and leaned toward her.

"Then I'll be honest, too. I don't want to discuss Liam with you."

"That's too bad because we're going to chat. Look at me, Raine." She raised her gaze and wished her heart didn't stutter in her chest every time he stared at her. "What did Liam punish you for yesterday?"

"Do you really have to guess? You couldn't wait to tell him how late I was. I'd been holding him off with vague answers, trying not to worry him until there was something to worry about. But you basically goaded him into demanding I take a pregnancy test. When I refused, we stumbled onto the topic of Thanksgiving...and now everything is a fucking mess. Don't be surprised if he packs up and leaves." At the thought of never being with Liam again, tears spilled like acid from her tired eyes. "And then I'll be to blame for both coming between you and your best friend, *and* driving away one of the kindest men I've ever met."

Raine stood, her chair scraping the tile floor. She tried to dart past Hammer. Since he sat between her and the door, he merely leaned back and grabbed her wrist. He stood, his heavy brows slashing down with…what? Anger? Concern?

"If you're unhappy with me, take a number." She swiped at the hot tears on her cheeks. "I should have left, you know. That night we fought. If I had just walked out, you and Liam would still be pals. You'd both be happier. And I wouldn't be around to fuck everything up."

"Sit down, Raine, and stop beating yourself up." Hammer exhaled, his stare heavy. He waited until she complied, then sat again. "Now talk to me."

God, she didn't want to spill her guts. Just the thought of this conversation made her stomach roll. And Liam would be furious if she opened up to another man, especially Hammer.

Shaking her head, Raine blinked back more tears. "I can't."

"Okay, then listen. You didn't come between Liam and me. I don't want you carrying that weight on your narrow shoulders, girl. This isn't the first time we've butted heads, and I can pretty much guarantee it won't be the last. We may not have fought this seriously before, and I might be pissed as hell at him now, but I still love him like a brother."

He tried to smile, but she could see it was strained at best. Another avalanche of guilt pressed down on her.

"Why did Liam punish you?" he asked again. "If it's because you haven't started your period yet, I'll kill him."

She shook her head. "That's not why, and you can't. What happened yesterday between Liam and me is our business. But you're smart. You can read between the lines. Put yourself in his shoes and imagine why you'd be deeply disappointed. You won't be far off the mark."

"Yes, I can read between the lines, but I want you to explain it to me. Let me hear *your* interpretation."

"Why do you do this to me? Stop trying to pry me apart. It's over. It's done. The lesson for me is that I suck at relationships."

Hammer slammed his fist on the table, rattling the plate of muffins and her nerves. "Tell me."

"Apparently, he didn't like the way I tried to spare him the pregnancy scare. I hate dumping my crap on him. Or on you. I'm capable of taking care of myself."

"Answer the fucking question."

"I did!" she insisted. "God, you're like a damn dog with a bone. Let it go."

Hammer leaned back in his chair, crossed his arms over his wide chest, and flattened his mouth into a tight line. His pissed-off Dom face.

This wasn't good…

"Let me rephrase," he growled. "Tell me what submissive rule you broke."

"Probably all of them. Why do you give a shit?"

Without a word, Hammer stood and walked to the counter. He grabbed a clean wooden spoon and returned to the table, hovering over her and clutching it in a white-knuckled grip. "What lesson was Liam teaching you? You either tell me now or I'm going to bend you over the table and beat your ass with this."

Raine hunkered down in her seat and rolled her eyes. "You would."

Damn, she hated sounding like a pouty teenager. She needed to get her shit together.

"In a fucking heartbeat," Hammer tossed back.

"Do I need to remind you again that I'm not yours to punish?"

"I care about your needs more than I care about Liam throwing a hissy. And frankly, I think if he'd seen the way you behaved this morning, he'd agree with me. Now talk or I'm going to enjoy every fucking whack."

Ugh, talk! She *hated* that word. But at least being angry with Hammer was better than being the guest of honor at her own pity party. "Communication, all right? I wasn't totally honest, I guess. And he thinks I don't trust him. God, do you have to badger me?"

"Obviously I do." He set the spoon down gently and sat again. "And I suggest you stop provoking me to change the direction of the conversation."

Yeah, she'd kind of figured he was onto her.

"You're afraid Liam is going to leave you? Well, if you behave with him the way you just did with me, I guarantee he'll walk out that door and not look back. A Dom thrives on total surrender. You're not letting go. You'll have to, Raine, in order to receive."

"I know that!" Sadness, anger, and disappointment in herself all formed a lump in her throat that threatened to choke her. "I'm not stupid."

"You're not. But you're too fucking stubborn for your own good. Do you like being this miserable? You must. You're not doing a thing to change it, and you're the only one who can."

Raine bit her lip, despair rolling over her. How did she change herself? "I know."

Hammer's expression softened. "I can see how badly you're falling apart. Don't think for one second that Liam can't, too."

"Rooting for your rival?" She swiped at her leaking eyes. "Things were easier when you thought of me as your sister."

"I may be a twisted fuck, but I'd never masturbate to thoughts of my sister, precious."

She felt a flush crawl up her cheeks as heat burst through her body. It might be wrong, but on some level it gratified her to know that Hammer wasn't any more immune to her than she was to him.

"I know I'm walking a thin line even talking to you like this since you wear Liam's collar. So instead, consider this some friendly advice. Stop being so damn afraid to share yourself. If you won't be honest with Liam, then for fuck's sake, take his collar off and stop wasting his time."

This tumultuous crap plaguing her, mostly of her own doing, completely exhausted Raine. But she didn't know how to get off the merry-go-round. She didn't know how to stop hurting. "I need him."

Pain flashed in Hammer's eyes. "Then you have a decision to make."

"That's what Liam said." Morosely, she snagged a muffin from the plate and picked at it. "Are you pushing me so hard toward him because you still think you're bad for me?"

He hesitated. "I've seen a change in you. As much as I hate to admit it, that's Liam's doing. He reached you in a way I hadn't. Obviously not deep enough yet."

She laughed bitterly. "We both know he'll give up before then, if he hasn't already. I'm kidding myself if I think that ripping my soul open for him is going to make much difference."

"If you go through life scared that the other shoe is going to drop, you're going to miss out on a hell of a lot of good things."

"Probably," she whispered. But trusting that someone would be there tomorrow? Nothing was more difficult—or terrifying—for her.

"Raine..." He swallowed tightly and leaned toward her, cupping her chin with his broad hand. "Am I bad for you? Probably. You're not wired for what I want, and I couldn't live with myself if I crushed your spirit. But I'm happy you're in my life. Will I always want more? Yes. Is that your fault? No." He bent, his hazel eyes delving deep. "I want you to be happy. Promise me you'll do whatever it takes to make that happen."

He was willing to sacrifice his heart for hers. It was kind and noble— two things that didn't come easily for Hammer.

Raine had never felt more unworthy in her life. "I don't know how."

"Then learn. It will be uncomfortable, maybe even painful, but you can. Now do it."

Chapter Four

The tantalizing aromas of Thanksgiving dinner made Hammer's mouth water as he entered the dungeon, now transformed into a makeshift dining area, complete with buffet tables, draped in turkey-themed cloths. He cast a nod to the club members seated at the long table as several submissives carried in platters of food, adding them to the already bountiful spread.

Raine set a heaping bowl of mashed potatoes down and headed back to the kitchen. Hammer's focus naturally slid to her ass as she scurried away. Had she taken his advice yesterday morning and opened up to Liam?

The Irish prick sidled up to him. "Stop staring at Raine or I might change my bloody mind about you living another day."

Hammer turned to scowl at him. "What the fuck are you talking about?"

"Raine started her period this morning."

Liam's declaration slapped Hammer. He froze, rolled the words around in his head. Finally, the meaning of those words dawned on him. They seized his guts, sucked his veins dry, stabbed his heart. His faint but stupid hope of sharing a life with her died.

Goddamn it, he'd wanted Raine to be pregnant.

Without a word, he stormed away from Liam toward the privacy of the liquor storage room. Slamming the door behind him, Hammer took refuge in the small, shadowy space. He leaned against the steel-framed racks of booze, dragged in a jagged breath, and closed his eyes.

What if Raine had been pregnant? Would he have hauled her to a Justice of the Peace for an unfulfilling five-minute ceremony? Then what? Watch her pine for Liam? Worry that she'd come to regard their marriage as a mistake? Hammer roughed a hand down his face. Would he have shoved his inner beast deep into the recesses of his soul and ignored the clawing hunger to make her his slave until it drove him insane?

"Fuck."

Maybe. But that didn't stop his slew of regrets. Visions of a precious little girl with raven hair and big blue eyes, just like her mommy's, raced through his brain. She'd be inquisitive, headstrong, and need his protection. He could almost hear her sweet giggles as he slung her on his back for pony rides or see her yawn as he tucked her into her frilly pink bed and kissed her little button nose good-night.

Or would they have had a boy? Hammer blinked against the sting burning his eyes as he pictured a little imp with Raine's eyes and a mischievous smile. He and his son would have played ball in a lush green yard and rolled around in autumn leaves. The boy would have sneaked frogs and worms into the house to scare his beautiful mother with a grin.

Daddy, Daddy, Daddy! Hammer heard the little voices calling in his head.

None of that would happen now.

Grief sat on his chest like an elephant.

Hammer pounded his fist against the wall. Until this moment, he hadn't let himself acknowledge how much he yearned to be a father, a role model, a defender. And how much he wanted all that with Raine.

With a few words, Liam had managed to dash all those hopes.

Hammer believed things happened for a reason. And he knew what that was: Raine deserved better than him. He'd had years to claim her, but he hadn't tackled his fears and seized the opportunity. Now he could only man up and stop dreaming about what would never be.

With a curse, he jerked three bottles of wine off their rack, turned on his heel, and braced himself to see relief in Raine's eyes.

As he entered the dungeon again, she carried the turkey, all sliced and steaming, to the table. Her black dress showed a hint of cleavage and bared thighs he remembered locking around him as they rocked together in pursuit of pleasure. God, would he ever look at her and not crave the chance to make her his own?

Hammer looked Raine's way. Her red-rimmed eyes stood out in her pale face. She'd been crying. Not in the last ten minutes or her nose would be red, too. But recently. Their stares locked for a moment. Her chin trembled. Those blue eyes looked so tormented with...what?

Before he could decide, she jerked away with a frown and set the turkey on the table. Then she pasted on an overly bright smile. "Come on, everyone. Time to eat."

As everyone took their seats, Hammer pulled out Raine's usual chair, directly to his right, for her. With her sitting close, they might be able to talk discreetly. Instead, Liam led her to the opposite end of the table and helped her into a chair, widening the divide between them more.

Hammer's stomach took a nosedive. A volatile mix of anger and pain skewered him.

He should be thankful for a thriving business, food aplenty, as well as the good friends he had and the good times they shared. Right now, he could only focus on what he didn't have: Raine, the chance to have a family with her, or even any of her goddamn warmth in his life.

To his left, his friend and Shadows' resident sadist, Beck, nudged him. "Everyone is staring at you, man. Stop looking at Raine like she's dessert, make a quick speech, and let everyone dig in."

Quickly, Hammer raised his glass, thanking his extended family for coming to share this day with him because he treasured each and every one of them, blah, blah, blah. He was running on autopilot, probably reciting the same speech, more or less, that he had for th⌐ past eight years. In the back of his head, he kept wondering why he hadn't changed his ways and snapped Raine up when he'd had the chance. If he would have put the past behind him, he could have had a new life with her. *Woulda, coulda, shoulda.*

As the guests all raised their glasses to him, he watched Liam cup Raine's cheek. She sent his old pal a shaky smile, then downed most of her wine in two swallows. Hammer didn't like how pale she looked. And he would kill to know what she was thinking.

"Dude, you *really* have to stop staring at Raine," Beck warned in a low voice. "Liam is going to take your head off if he catches you. What the hell is your problem?"

"Raine's not pregnant," Hammer hissed.

"You should be happy, then."

"Do I look happy?" He flashed a seething look Beck's way, then stared down the length of the table at her again.

Had she been crying in relief that she'd started her period? Or disappointment that his child wouldn't grow there? Hammer wasn't sure when—or if—he'd ever find out.

Without looking away, Hammer filled his fork with food and slid the contents in his mouth. He had no doubt everything was delicious as always, but he couldn't taste a thing.

One of the newer Dommes, Mistress Hillary, complimented Raine's cooking. The girl smiled stiffly and murmured her thanks. When the exchange was over, Raine's brows drew together. She rubbed at a spot between her eyes. Hammer studied her pained expression. Damn it, of course she was hurting. He knew the symptoms. He'd seen them dozens of times. And from the blithe look on Liam's face, he didn't have a clue. Raine obviously wasn't letting her Dom in on her problem.

Clenching his jaw, he tossed his napkin on the table and stormed over to her, leaning down to whisper in her ear. "Let me get your medicine. You need to take it and lie down."

Raine shook her head in refusal. "Later."

Stubborn little brat.

Gritting his teeth, Hammer marched down the hall. Her stare raked his back. Once in his quarters, he rummaged through his bathroom cabinet and picked through his toiletries until he found Raine's medication.

Frustrated with her and wishing like hell that she was his to punish, he stalked back to the feast and slammed the bottle of pain killers on the table in front of her.

Liam raised his head, scowling as he picked up the bottle and read the label. "What the hell are these pills for?"

Hammer ignored Liam and stared down at Raine with a raised brow. "Do you want to tell him or shall I, precious?"

Anger flashed in Liam's eyes as he studied Raine. "Tell me what?"

She lowered her guilty gaze. "Hammer, I planned to take one and explain everything to Liam after dinner," she said in a low whisper. "Please sit down. I'll handle it. Everyone is staring."

They were, and Hammer didn't give a shit. He resisted the urge to shake her. Did Liam have any idea how badly she deserved to be taken over a knee and thoroughly spanked? He stomped back to his chair, then eased down and glared at her. She raised her chin and still didn't take a fucking pill. In fact, she whispered furiously to Liam and ignored the bottle, pushing food around on her plate. More color seeped from her face as the pain obviously grew worse.

Why was the stubborn minx refusing to help herself?

Jaw tight, Liam set the bottle aside and pinned Raine with an expression that promised confrontation after dinner. Hammer approved. If she wasn't going to take care of herself, and he couldn't, someone had to.

After the awkward meal, Raine served dessert and coffee. She was moving slowly, but thankfully the other subs helped. After a blessedly brief chat, most everyone agreed to follow Beck to his place for beer and football. The rest of the members headed home, leaving him alone with Liam and Raine.

The second the door shut behind the last of the dinner guests, Liam turned on her, grinding his jaw and gritting his teeth. "Are you in pain?"

"It's not that bad," Raine tried to assure him. "I'll—"

"Are you in pain, yes or no?" All hint of nice had disappeared.

She dropped her gaze. "Yes."

"Then take the damn pill."

"I will." She sent him an imploring stare. "Liam, don't be angry. It's just a headache. I'll be fine."

"Just a headache?" Hammer scoffed. "Yeah, and I'm Godzilla."

He stared at her in disbelief. He hadn't seen her this shut down in years. Before this week, she'd been making strides with Liam. Little ones, but…progress. What the hell was going on inside her head now?

"Yes, that's all." Then she turned a pleading stare on Liam. "As soon as I do the dishes, I promise to be a good girl, pop a pill, and go to bed."

"No," Liam snarled. "You'll take the fucking pill now, sub. I'm waiting."

Hammer had never heard Liam speak to her so harshly. But she needed it.

Raine looked like she wanted to argue, but a jolt of pain hit her again. She winced, then silently opened the bottle and swallowed down a pill.

"Good." Liam nodded. "Now I'll clean up the mess. You go to bed. We'll talk about this later. And Raine, there *will* be consequences."

What little color had been in her face drained away.

As raw as it chaffed Hammer to see her under another's care, the time had come to share a bit of insight with his ex-friend. Someone needed to clue Liam in, and if she was too bottled up or independent to do it, he would. After all, Raine's welfare wasn't a point of contention. Which one of them got to fuck her was. But the girl's health was by far more important than this pissing match.

"It's not 'just a headache,'" he told Liam. "She's suffering from a migraine. I've taken her to several specialists over the years. Each said these episodes are hormone related. Every month, she gets a migraine early in her cycle. When they start, you'll need to make her stop what she's doing and give her a pill, then put her to bed. The medication she should have taken when I brought the bottle will knock her out. She needs that *and* about ten hours of sleep in a dark, quiet room to recover."

Raine sighed wearily. "Macen, you didn't even give me a chance to explain." She turned to Liam, her gaze pleading. "Can we talk about this privately?"

That expression tore at Hammer because he remembered when she used to look at him for forgiveness and approval.

"No. I'll talk in front of him, Raine. He knows more about you than I suspect you'll ever allow me, so there's not much point in doing this in private, is there?"

"Just…hear me out. I was feeling all right until right before I served the food, so I thought I could make it through dinner and finish playing hostess before the pain hit. But it got bad really quickly. I didn't want to announce my problem to everyone or hold up the meal." She sent Hammer a quick glare. "So don't make it sound like I intentionally withheld information from Liam." She reached for the other man. "I'm sorry if it seemed like I was keeping you in the dark. I wasn't, I swear."

Liam raised a skeptical brow. "That's a lovely speech, but I'm not convinced you would have explained if Hammer hadn't forced your hand. I doubt you'll ever let me know the real you."

His voice iced over with a cold rage Hammer had never heard.

Raine gaped at him, the fear and heartbreak naked on her face. "That's not true."

Liam sighed. "I wake up each day wondering when I'll step into the next pile of shit because you've either forgotten, decided I didn't need to know, or simply hadn't bothered to forewarn me. How do you expect me to care for you, love—and I do love you—if you won't share?"

Hammer's knees nearly went out from under him. For the last month, he'd been imagining that Liam would knock on his door someday, Raine in tow, and wash his hands of the girl because of her stubborn, wary ways. But hearing Liam talk so openly about the love he felt for her, and knowing that Raine thought she needed him...Hammer feared that day wouldn't be coming anytime soon.

"You say you care about me and want my dominance," Liam went on. "Yet you don't trust me enough to communicate something as basic as your health. That's sub 101, and you know it. I'm deeply disappointed, Raine." Liam turned away as her eyes spilled over with tears. "Hammer, thank you for informing me about my sub's problems. I'll take it from here and ask you to mind your own fucking business from now on."

Hammer bristled. Liam wanted him to mind his own business? Never going to happen where Raine was concerned, especially now that he knew she had walled herself off nearly to the point of suffocation. He had to get more involved, not less.

Suddenly, Raine blinked rapidly, swallowing hard, swaying on her feet. Hammer inhaled a sharp breath. Fuck, he knew the signs…

Surveying the disheveled dinner table, he lunged to retrieve an empty bowl that had previously held green beans. As he raced back to her, Raine slapped one hand on her stomach, then doubled over with a cry and fell to her knees.

"Liam," Hammer shouted, trying to shove the bowl under her face. "She's going to be sick."

Raine pushed the bowl away, squinting against the light streaming through the open windows. Pain wracked her face. "I'll be fine."

"Bullshit," Hammer growled, then addressed Liam. "She waited too long. It's about to get bad."

Worry stamped Liam's face as he lifted Raine into his arms and strode from the room with her. After Hammer snagged her pills off the table, he pushed past Liam and jogged backward to keep the bowl under Raine's face, just in case.

"Take her to the bathroom," he called out as Liam kicked open the door to their room.

Raine winced and turned her face from him. "Get that bowl away. I smell green beans."

Hammer didn't budge.

Once inside the bathroom, Liam eased Raine to her feet. She shoved the man out, then slammed the door, locking it between them.

Hammer gaped, itching to shake Liam and demand that he knock Raine's door—and her fucking walls—completely down. Another part of him felt sorry for the poor bastard. Liam had done everything right as a Dom to reach her. Now, he just looked stunned. No, flattened.

The man didn't know how to help Raine. And fucking aliens would invade before the proud girl ever asked for what she needed.

As anger soared, Hammer pounded at the portal. "Open the goddamn door, Raine!"

Seth was right; this *was* just like a fucking soap opera. Nothing that had happened during these last few hellish days made a lick of sense. The only good thing had been Raine starting to bleed. But his relief hadn't lasted long before her silent tears had cut him to the quick.

Liam shut his eyes. The bloody Thanksgiving feast had been a special hell all its own. He'd been unable to be thankful for a fucking thing. Just when he'd assumed the rage festering inside him couldn't get any worse, Hammer had proven again that he knew Raine intimately, in every sense of the word. It was a blow far more effective than any punch Hammer could have thrown. Liam was all too aware that, though he learned something new about her every day, it was never enough.

Did Raine need him at all? Would she ever?

Furious and wrung dry, he stared at the bathroom door. Never had the temptation to walk away from someone equaled his determination to stay and see it through to the bitter end.

The time had come to force this intolerable situation to a head. His conversation with Seth circled through his brain again. And Hammer pounding on the bathroom door, demanding Raine let him in so he could care for her... Liam shook his head. Hammer didn't want him here, either. It was the final bloody straw.

"Go away," Raine protested weakly from behind the door.

"In your dreams. Open the door," Hammer yelled.

She didn't budge.

"Open the fucking door, Raine, or I'm busting it down!" Hammer pounded on the wooden slab again.

Liam shoved Hammer aside. "I'll take care of her. She's my responsibility. Bugger off."

Hammer flipped him an incredulous stare. "Do you know how to take care of her when she's sick like this? Do you know what she needs?"

"Stop screaming." Her frail voice cracked with pain. "You're making it hurt worse."

Then Raine's retching came, a terrible choking hurl. The sounds of her suffering breached the door. Once, twice, she emptied her stomach. Liam closed his eyes. He felt so bloody helpless.

Hammer growled, then shoved his left shoulder into the portal.

The wood creaked, but held tight—until Liam pushed him aside and kicked at the handle with all his might. The lock gave way and the door opened, flooding the dark room with light.

Raine knelt on the floor totally naked, one hand braced on the porcelain commode. The other held back her raven mane. Her dress was a puddle on the floor. As Liam rushed in, she turned and winced, squeezing her eyes shut.

"Love?"

She turned to sag limply against the nearby wall, her knees curling to her chest. Even in the dim light, she squinted, looking spent and pale and defeated. "The light. Hurts."

The sight of her cut him to the bone. He ran to the blinds and yanked on the cord, muting the afternoon beams filtering through the window. But he had no fucking idea what to do next.

Hammer skidded to his knees at her side, stroking her hair. "Precious, are you feeling better?"

She nodded weakly. "Bed."

"Of course." Hammer's tone sounded almost like he spoke to a beloved child.

Ignoring her nakedness, he flushed the toilet, grabbed a glass of water and a cold cloth, then set them on the basin before he helped her to her feet.

Liam stared. How could he protest? Raine needed care, and he didn't know how to give it to her. All he could do was watch and absorb the never-ending nightmare.

Hammer wiped her face gently and instructed her to rinse her mouth. She did it slowly, her eyes half closed. Carefully, Hammer gathered Raine's long hair in a gentle grip, searched around for a band, then secured it inexpertly away from her face.

Why hadn't he bloody thought of that?

Then Raine's strength seemed to give out. As she melted against him, Hammer scooped her up and took *his* woman to the bed they shared. Liam raged at the sheer injustice of the moment. Though Hammer was helping her, it chafed.

It would be easy to turn and walk through the door, leave the two of them to sort everything out and catch that red-eye to New York Seth had suggested. Had that been just yesterday? But the Dominant inside Liam roared, as did his heart. *Mine!*

"That's enough, Hammer. She can thank you for your care and consideration once she's well. I've no doubt she will. But I'll see to her from here. Anything I don't know, I'll figure out. Once she's settled, I'll meet you in the kitchen."

He didn't raise his voice, but the hard tone brooked no argument as he tore off his shirt and toed off his shoes.

Hammer gave an angry jerk of his head. "Fine. Raine needs another pill since she threw up the one she took earlier." He fished out the bottle, set one tablet on the nightstand, and pocketed the rest.

Liam glared. "What if she needs more?"

"Then come find me. I'll start cleaning the dishes." Hammer walked out before Liam could object.

Unfuckingbelievable.

After retrieving another glass of water, Liam climbed on the bed and drew the blankets over her naked body. Curling up beside her, he drew her into the circle of his arms. Holding her close now felt so bittersweet.

"Take another pill, lass." He lifted the glass of water to her white lips and held her head up so she could swallow.

Pain had carved itself into her features. Raine could be so strong that he'd never imagined seeing her this weak.

Bloody hell...

"There, love," he crooned. "Can I get anything else for you?"

"No." Her voice was barely above a whisper. "Thank you. Will you hold me?"

"Of course. Rest now."

Raine seemed to use the last of her energy to blink up at him. "I'm sorry...about everything."

Yes, he was, too.

CHAPTER FIVE

ammer stepped up to the table and began clearing plates. "I'll be cleaning this mess up all fucking night."

He worked on autopilot, stacking the dishes next to the sink while his brain whirled. Liam might be fed up with Raine now, but the minute the man eased up, she would revert to giving only the tiniest morsels of herself so she didn't have to truly bare her soul. When would she realize that refusing to share the real her with everyone who cared wouldn't lead her to the fulfillment she craved?

Cursing, he carried another stack of plates into the kitchen. The entire room looked like an atomic bomb had detonated.

"And she was going to clean this mess up with a goddamn migraine? Right…"

At the sound of angry footsteps, Hammer turned to see Liam striding into the room, barreling down like a train. The prick didn't say a word, just launched a solid right hook into his jaw. Dazed, Hammer stumbled back, colliding with a stack of dishes that teetered on the edge of the counter, a breath away from crashing to the floor.

"Back the fuck away from Raine. She's not your 'precious.' She's mine."

He narrowed his eyes, massaging his chin, and stared at Liam. "Do you feel better now?"

"Not really. I'd rather smash your teeth down your throat, you selfish wanker. You could have had Raine any bloody time in all the years she's been here, but ever since I collared her, you can't seem to stay away."

"What the hell? She got sick. I tried to help her, asshole."

"By undermining me. And I still haven't forgiven you for dragging her to your bed the second I claimed her. Why won't you go the fuck away?"

"Because it's my club, thank you very much. We both know that last-minute training collar was a convenient way for you to get her into bed. Pot, meet kettle."

"Piss off, fuckwit." Liam rubbed at his knuckles.

"What's really got your dick in a twist? That she loves me? That she wants me? Or that she feels safe with me and doesn't want to leave Shadows?" Hammer expected to feel his friend's right hook again any second. Instead, hurt flared in Liam's eyes.

"We're bloody stuck here because a BDSM club is the closest thing Raine's ever had to a real home. And she can't break her connection with you because you won't leave her alone long enough to let her."

Guilty. He should have given Raine a proper home outside the club. He should have backed the hell off when she'd accepted Liam as her Dominant. But if he had, he would have lost Raine, probably for good. His guts clenched at the thought of her no longer in his life.

"You break her heart and fucking make her cry," Liam railed on. "And me? Hell, you can't stop laying on the accusations, taking every cheap shot you can."

And didn't that make him feel like a thousand kinds of an asshole? For years, Hammer had clung to Raine like a safety line. He never drew her to his shore, just gripped the goddamn rope tighter and tighter, afraid of losing her and the contentment she gave him, equally terrified that if he embraced her, he'd destroy her. If being with Liam made her happy, he should drop the rope and let her go.

His lungs burned as he tried to suck in a breath. Panic set in. His conscience screamed in the back of his brain that he should do the right thing...for once. But even if he kicked himself in the ass for not giving her what she needed, he was still a selfish bastard. In the end, he couldn't give her up.

"Liam—"

"Shut the fuck up. Sometimes I wonder why I'm bothering when neither one of you seems to want me here. I'm sick to death of fighting you both."

Liam sounded damn close to giving up on Raine. Somehow, that wasn't nearly as satisfying as Hammer had imagined. In fact, he'd never seen the man so near the end of his rope, not even when Gwyneth had betrayed him.

Guilt oozed through his pores. Hammer would rather cut off his nuts with a rusty blade than examine this shitstorm, but no avoiding it now. He'd been blinded by his goddamn jealousy. He'd been too busy backbiting and lashing out to see that he was not only neglecting to consider Raine's needs, but destroying a brotherhood.

Hell, he *had* been a fuckwit. He should say something, offer an olive branch of some sort. This feud wasn't helping Liam, himself, or Raine.

"Listen—"

"Not another bloody word." Liam gave Hammer a mighty shove, sending him stumbling back. "Raine needed guidance for six fucking years, and you did little but isolate and ignore her. You would have contorted yourself to help any other sub grow. If another Dom had treated her the way you have, you'd have killed him. What happened to you?"

Juliet.

"I used to look up to you," Liam went on. "I don't know who the fuck you are anymore."

The man's temper and accusation sparked his own. "You're not perfect yourself. You didn't have my permission to touch Raine, but you took her anyway. You knew I was in love with her. Some friend you are, forcing me to watch you fuck the only woman I've cared about since Juliet. You don't know who I am? Fuck you. That street runs both ways."

"Oh, quit your bellyaching about how I stole Raine from you when you were too daft to make her yours in the first place." Liam's face tightened, his fists clenching. "I won't apologize for falling in love with her. At least I've tried to put her first. For years, Raine begged you for attention, but you were too busy dancing the mattress tango with every other sub. Think what you want of me, but the way you've treated the so-called 'first woman I've cared about since Juliet' is despicable. If you truly care for Raine, you'll let her go. If not, you're going to destroy her. And there'll be no mending this rift between us."

"I share a decade with you—a roof, a bed, my goddamn wife—and you're ready to toss our friendship out for a woman you've been fucking for three weeks?"

"Are you a relationship guru now who knows exactly how long it takes to fall for someone? I love Raine. That eats you up. Admit it."

"Damn straight it does, just like the fact that I love her too crawls up your ass and festers. You know the difference? I shared. I opened my fucking marriage to you because I thought Juliet needed you. Raine needs me. And you tell me that I can only talk to her about work with the door open? Nice reciprocation, asshole."

"I invited you back to New York after I married Gwyneth."

"What was I supposed to do in the middle of your newly wedded bliss besides be your third wheel?"

"I asked you to live with us so we could share her. I didn't think I had to spell out the obvious."

"I wanted no part of that bitch. Liam, she didn't give a shit about anyone but herself."

"It has nothing to do with her. You were too bloody busy with your club and your endless parade of fuck bunnies."

"Every one of those subs kept me from returning to New York so you didn't have to go through the hell with Gwyneth that I did with Juliet."

Liam gaped at him. "You dipping your wick in every hole was somehow for *my* benefit? I've got to hear this."

"I didn't share Gwyneth with you because I worried it would ultimately drive her to something reckless."

"Like Juliet? That's ridiculous. Your wife was quiet and meek— nothing like Gwyneth. Juliet was a bit screwed up, too. Lousy excuse, Hammer."

"Yeah?" Hammer whirled around, panting between clenched teeth as he searched for something to throw, to hit, to fucking break. "When you called to tell me that you were filing for divorce, what was the first question I asked you?"

"You asked why." Liam shrugged. "So? What are you blathering on about? You know why Gwyneth and I split up. She liked my money. Oh, and she liked fucking her personal trainer and his boyfriend. What does any of that have to do with Juliet?"

"I asked you why you left Gwyneth because I gave a shit. Because I cared about *you*."

Hammer kicked the wall, then grabbed a plate from the counter and hurled it across the room. Hearing the crash and seeing the white china shatter wasn't nearly as satisfying as he'd hoped.

"Why the devil are you breaking the dishes?" Liam stared at him as if he'd lost his mind.

"You never asked *me* why," Hammer whirled back on Liam, his chest heaving. "Didn't you care why Juliet swallowed a whole fucking bottle of pills in the middle of a Sunday afternoon? You called. You said all the right things." He choked. "But you never asked why. You weren't fucking there when I needed you most."

Rage poured out from him like hot bacon grease, sizzling his skin, burning away all his self-control. He wanted to hurt something, destroy it, preferably Liam. The dumb prick stood gawking at him like he was still trying to figure out the puzzle. Goddamn if that didn't infuriate him, too.

Hammer reached for the next plate on the stack and zinged it across the room, the splintering of the delicate china firing up the beast inside him.

Liam stared, blinking, barely breathing. "Hammer, I didn't... Can you stop destroying the place long enough for me to say something? Christ, man. You'll wake the fucking dead! Or worse, Raine."

Liam grabbed the next plate away, and Hammer felt a fresh wave of fury crash through his head as he lurched to snatch it back. "Give that to me!"

"No. You obviously want to talk about Juliet and what I didn't do right. How was I to know? Before I could even come home, you had her cremated and buried, like you'd filed her away in a dusty cabinet. I didn't even get to say good-bye. I thought you just wanted to forget her and move on."

Hammer clenched his jaw. He'd been keeping the lid closed on this can of worms for years. *Keep pushing, and I'll open it right up.* "You assumed, but you didn't care enough to ask."

"I didn't pry," Liam insisted, putting the plates out of Hammer's reach, then crossing his arms over his chest.

He scoffed, his temper rising. "You didn't want to know why my wife and your lover killed her goddamn self without expressing an ounce of unhappiness to either one of us?"

"Of course I did." Liam stepped closer, his voice dropping. Goddamn it if he didn't look somewhere between concerned and compassionate. "I offered to drop my project at work and come home. *You* said not to bother, so I tried to talk to you over the phone. But you were aloof, so I backed off..." He shook his head sadly. "I wasn't disinterested, Macen. Jesus, I'm sorry. I didn't realize you felt like this. When you kept pushing me away, I thought you needed time to process. When you moved out here, I assumed you needed space, a fresh start..." He hung his head. "I worried that I was a reminder of a time you wanted to forget."

"I wish to fuck I could," Hammer said miserably. "I changed coasts, changed careers, and changed lives. Nothing made me want to really live again until Raine."

"Shit. I didn't start with her to hurt you. I know I'm a bit late, but..." Liam swallowed. "Why? Why did Juliet end herself, then? Do you know?"

"Yeah, and you don't want to."

"I do or I wouldn't have asked."

The backs of Hammer's eyes ached. His throat closed up. "She left me a note. She wanted more attention."

Liam rubbed at the back of his neck. "Frankly, mate, I'm not sure either of us could ever have given her enough attention. She was a bit starved, no matter what we did. I suppose it didn't help that work kept me away for the last six weeks or so, but I called her. She knew I was coming back."

"She was tired of being our 'fuck doll.'"

"Juliet said that?" he asked incredulously.

"Yeah, and neither of us realized she felt that way."

"You're right." Liam blew out a breath. "The last time I saw her, she kissed me and told me to hurry home. Why didn't she tell us that? She always struggled with communication, but—"

"She was pregnant." Hammer dragged a hand through his hair and let loose a jagged breath as he slid down the wall and sat surrounded by broken crockery, miserable and defeated. "Eight weeks."

Liam gaped. "Did you know?"

"Not until I read it in her note. I should have paid more attention."

He swallowed, looking visibly pale. "Whose baby was it?"

"She wasn't sure and she couldn't handle the shame of not knowing whose name to list on the birth certificate. She knew we'd never let her go if she was pregnant, and she didn't want to raise a child in our 'den of depravity.' Instead of communicating, she chose sleeping pills over life with us."

"Fuck me dazed." Liam slid down beside him, staring at the wall on the far side of the kitchen. "Didn't you think the truth was important enough to share? Or did you imagine that I wouldn't care?"

"I tried not to dump this on you. I tried to be a *friend* and save you this shit. Look how you repay me."

Liam's rage went from zero to zoom. He turned red, betrayal in his eyes. "You son of a bitch! You tell me all this *now* and pass it off as a favor? I would have been by your side in a heartbeat if you had bothered to fucking tell me."

"Well, as a friend, you should have *asked* why. And now you've taken Raine from me. What sort of friend does that? All I've got left is Shadows. You want that, too?" He jumped to his feet and fished the keys out of his pocket. "Here you go. Don't come back to me for anything else. I don't have a goddamn thing left to give you."

Liam's eyes widened as he staggered upright. His mouth hung open as if Hammer had just punched him. "I don't want those." He shoved the keys out of Hammer's hand. They skittered across the floor. "Now what the fuck are you saying? That Juliet was *my* fault?"

"Damn straight," Hammer roared, shoulders back, chest heaving.

"How do you figure that?" he railed in return. "I didn't shove the pills down her throat."

"Besides not being there for her, you still hit the clubs, still fucked all the subs. She knew that, and it crushed her."

"She said that in her suicide note?"

"It was obvious. And she knew that you were hardly a monk while you were in Miami on business. I know exactly what you were doing the night of her birthday. Or who you were doing. How do you think that made her feel?"

Liam scowled. "We spent hours negotiating everything before we started sharing her. Exclusivity wasn't part of the deal. She'd seen me with other women and never seemed to mind."

"Of course she minded," Hammer shouted. "Do you think she liked feeling as if she wasn't enough for you?"

Liam sent him a sharp glare. "And Juliet told you she felt this way? Or is this how *you* feel?"

"That's great. Pin it on me." Hammer threw his hands in the air. "You've taken two women from me, but you won't take an ounce of guilt. Perfect."

With fists clenched around the chair, Liam ground his teeth. "Fine. You want it to be all my fault? Okay, it is. It's all my fucking fault. Juliet would have been beyond happy if I hadn't agreed to *your* invitation, invaded your marriage, and fucked up your lives, so I'll take every ounce of blame. Now you can sleep at night. Feel better?"

No, he didn't, not one fucking bit. His whole body clenched in knots.

"Yeah," he lied. "Your turn to carry this load around, asshole. And if you fuck up Raine too, I'll rip your head off and shit down your throat."

"Trust me, I'll take care of Raine. All day, all night, in every way she needs."

Hammer surged closer. "You barely know her. I might not have watched over her perfectly before you barged in, but she wouldn't even tell you the date she should have gotten her period. *I* can damn well make her talk. She needs a strong Dom. She needs *me*. And if I get a chance to be with Raine again, you can bet your ass I'll take it."

"It's not enough that you hoard this secret, then lay it on my shoulders eight years too late. But you also spew out that you'll fuck *my* Raine again, given the chance. I ought to shove your fucking balls up your ass and make sure the only way you can find them is with a toothpick."

Hammer opened his mouth to rage back, but the door pushed open suddenly. Raine stepped in, squinting against the light. She surveyed the damage with a frown, her hair pulled haphazardly away from her pale face. The ancient T-shirt she wore looked at least four sizes too big and swallowed her up.

With a pained frown, she stared at them both as if they'd lost their minds. "What's going on? Why are you shouting?"

Liam glared at him, then scooped Raine up in his arms. "It's nothing, love. Let's get you back to bed. I'll come with you."

Hammer could only watch the other man take the woman he loved away, maybe this time for good.

Two hours later, Hammer sat on the edge of his bed, swirling a tumbler of Scotch, his thoughts circling like the amber liquid. He'd lost the grip of his icy control in the kitchen with Liam. Why the hell had he suddenly unloaded years of anger and dumped it on the man? Had he expected Liam to magically wash away the layers of blame and make everything better? Hammer scoffed. By finally vomiting out the truth, he'd managed to purge a lot of resentment. Why didn't he feel any better? He should have confronted Liam and his own guilt years ago. He just hadn't had the balls to wade through the shit. He really didn't want to now.

"Mind if I join you?"

Hammer zipped his stare to the doorway to find Beck leaning against the frame, his arms folded across his chest, eyeing the decanter of Scotch on the nightstand.

"Help yourself." Hammer nodded, raising his glass in the air, toasting his own stupidity. "What are you doing here? I thought you'd taken everyone back to your place for beer and football."

"We caught the last half of the game, then they all bailed. I came back to see if the club was still standing. What the fuck, man? I don't think I've ever sat through a more uncomfortable Thanksgiving. What do you have planned for next year, pissing in the gravy?"

Hammer issued a humorless chuckle. "You missed the fun part."

"Yeah, I kind of figured. When I couldn't find anyone, I peeked in the kitchen." Beck gave a low whistle. "It looks like World War Wedgwood hit that place. So who won?" Beck asked, cocking a brow as he pulled up a chair across from Hammer and took a seat.

"No one." Hammer sighed in disgust. "I royally fucked up, man."

Beck swallowed down a healthy gulp of Scotch and hissed. "What did you do this time?"

Hammer filled the sadist in on all the ugly details as he refilled their glasses.

When he was done, Hammer closed his eyes. He could still see Juliet's pale, naked body lying on their bed. Her blonde tresses spilled out over the gray silk sheets; white foam congealed around her blue lips. Her eyes were open, lifeless, staring past him as if he wasn't there. And he hadn't been when she'd taken her own life. When the world had crumbled beneath Juliet's feet, she'd given up, welcoming the end without him.

"I should have told Liam how much guilt I was drowning in a long time ago. But I didn't." Hammer rubbed at his forehead. "He was so young, and I thought I was protecting him because he wouldn't be able to handle the truth. Besides, she was *my* wife. Liam had signed up for sex and good times, not...all that. I didn't know how to cope, so I shut down. I shouldered all the responsibility for her death. When he moved on to a normal life and got married, I resented the fuck out of him. I just kept getting more and more pissed off. I ended up blaming him for pretty much everything."

"You're a dumbass." Beck shook his head.

"Yep." Hammer groused, then downed the contents of his glass and filled it once more. "I accused him of helping to push Juliet over the edge because he frequently fucked other subs."

"Is that true?"

"I don't know. Maybe." Hammer sighed. "She never told me how she felt. About anything."

"You're an even bigger idiot than I thought. You blame Liam for maybe upsetting Juliet because he couldn't keep his pants zipped. But you *know* your manwhoredom crushed Raine and you didn't take responsibility for that one whit. Really, dude?"

"I know. I was just pissed as hell and looking for a way to unload my guilt." Shaking his head, he swirled the liquid in his glass and watched it turn. "What Juliet did completely shell-shocked me. I didn't have a fucking clue how to deal with it. I sure as hell couldn't bring myself to examine my own role too closely. Blaming him was easier."

"Are you examining it now?"

"I'm trying not to. Hence the Scotch," Hammer replied, then tossed back a healthy swig.

"Yeah, that'll really do the trick," Beck drawled.

"No, it won't. Trust me. I've tried for years." But that didn't stop him from pouring another. He tipped back the glass in a futile attempt to wipe away the memory. Sure, it numbed his guilt, but never eradicated the stain from his soul.

"So maybe you should stop trying to drown your crap. Dissect it and then let it go. Hell, who knows, you just might end up a happier son of a bitch."

"What makes you think I'm not happy?"

"Gee, I have no clue." Beck shook his head. "You've got to come clean with Liam."

"Why would I do that after he stole Raine?"

"Stole? Let's cut the shit, shall we?" Beck leaned in and narrowed his eyes. "You owe Liam an apology. And then you need to pull your balls out of your purse, cupcake, and tell Raine how you feel about her. See what happens."

"Don't you have a home to go back to?" He glared, nursing his drink.

"Aww, but digging in your head is a lot more fun." He slapped Hammer on the shoulder. "Besides, you need a friend who's not afraid to put a stop to your big ol' boo-hoo pity party."

Hammer winced. "Don't hold back, Beck. Tell me how you really feel."

"I'm trying. Pull your head out of your ass, unless you enjoy the smell. If you didn't tell Liam anything about Juliet's death, how could you expect him to take half the blame?"

"She killed herself, and he never asked why. What the hell?"

"What would you have done in Liam's shoes? The woman you're sharing in an open relationship offs herself, and her husband won't talk to you."

Hammer drained his glass, wishing he could strangle Beck for such an ugly goddamn question. "I guess…" He sighed. "Fuck, if I'd been Liam, that would have been my sign to keep out. He said he didn't want to pry, but I think he blamed me."

"But he didn't tell you that?"

"No."

"So you're assuming?"

"Shut up, Freud." He poured more Scotch. "You're a vascular surgeon, not a shrink."

Beck shrugged. "I did my nine weeks' psych rotation. I'm almost qualified."

"Then why don't you examine your own life? There's plenty of shit there."

"Nah. I'm screwed up, but not nearly as much as you." Beck chuckled.

"Fuck off."

"Seriously. Stop drowning in your booze and go apologize to Liam."

"He won't listen to a damn thing I have to say, especially after I told him I'd fuck Raine again when I got the chance."

"And you decided to pour gasoline on the fire, why? Weren't the flames hot enough for you?" Beck shook his head. "You've got way too much pride, Macen, and it's biting you in the ass."

"It's not the first time."

"And probably not the last." Beck paused. "What drew you both to Juliet? What was she like?"

Hammer sloshed back another stiff swig. "Quiet. Refined. Proper. She was a lady. The downside was, she didn't like conflict or confrontation."

"I just can't see you with a quiet girl. You need the challenge of a spit-fire sub." He cocked his head. "Like Raine."

Hammer winced. "I know. Her sassy attitude makes me want to smack her ass and fuck her breathless. I can't get her out of my blood. I've tried."

"Too bad you haven't tried being honest with everyone."

"There's the door, fucker." Hammer pointed. "I didn't invite you in to unravel me. I'm not one of your pain sluts."

"So you're going to shove me out, like Liam. Newsflash for you: I don't have a dog in this hunt. I don't care what you do, except that I'd like to see my friend smile once a decade. We don't have to talk about a damn thing. We can get staggering drunk, then you can deal with your own mess tomorrow. And while you're at it, stop badgering Raine for not communicating because you're no better."

Yeah, Beck just kept digging in his head and figuring all his shit out. Wasn't this fun? Hammer downed the last of the liquid in his glass. Beck snatched it away.

"I hate you." Hammer scowled.

The other man laughed. "Good, then I'm doing my job. We drinking or talking?"

"Talking," he conceded, shaking his head.

"Happy to hear it. Now tell me how Juliet went from good girl to sex slave for you two?"

"I got off on pushing her past her comfort zone. It was like pure power pumping through my veins, and it fed the fuck out of the beast inside me. So I kept pushing and pushing..."

"You're supposed to do that as a Dom."

"Yeah, but she almost never pushed back. Once, I brought in a Domme. Juliet did safe word out of that. So I took her to a dungeon to see what tripped her trigger. The only thing that seemed to catch her eye was Liam sceneing. When I approached him about Juliet, he was all over it. Hell, he was twenty-one, but he had a firm understanding of the power exchange."

"So he joined you?"

"For a night, at first. But I loved it. I thought she did, too. Knowing I could make a proper wife fuck another man did it for me. I thought she liked connecting with her inner bad girl, and they seemed to click, so I asked him to stay for good. By the time I found out it made her feel like a whore, it was too late. I mistook her silence for submission."

"You didn't ask a ton of questions before you changed the relationship?"

Hammer hung his head. "Not enough. I was drunk on power and not a shining example of a Master."

"Wow. That's not the man I know. I seriously can't see you not forcing Juliet to communicate. You nearly talk subs to death."

"Oh, I tried to talk to Juliet, believe me. Every time I sat her down and told her I needed to know how she felt, she'd give me a placid smile, tell me she loved me, shower me with kisses, then usually give me a blow job. I bought into her acquiescence, thinking she was the perfect submissive. I should have dug harder, but she never gave me any reason to. But she taught me a valuable lesson. That's why I harp on subs now about communication."

"Hammer, she didn't give you anything to work with. You did the best you could with what you knew. After all, there were two people in that marriage. She made her choices."

He shrugged, but he couldn't unload the boulder of guilt from his back. Instead, he took his glass from Beck and poured another shot. "But it was my job to take care of her, physically, emotionally, and mentally. I failed her in every way."

"What happened next?"

"After her death, I shut down. I was alone and miserable. I couldn't stay in New York. Too many memories. Too much hurt. I didn't know where to direct my rage, except toward Liam. I couldn't pin it on Juliet. She was a victim of my desires and my ego."

"Wait a minute. She wasn't a victim. She didn't tell you how she felt and she didn't give you a choice. She took the power. Weren't you pissed at her for taking her own life?"

"Livid. I know that's part of the death process, but I wondered if I'd ever really known her. I thought I loved her, but how could I love a stranger?"

"I'm not speaking ill of her, but it sounds like she was repressed, depressed, and just fucked up."

Hammer flubbed through a laugh. "Maybe. A little."

"Haven't you beat yourself up enough yet? Are you sure you don't have a little bit of a masochist in you?"

"You wish." With a shrug, Hammer stared down into the alcohol. "Good strategy. Wait until I'm drunk so I'll talk."

"Hey, it worked."

"Prick."

"That's Sir Prick." He snickered. "So neither you nor Liam had any hint that Juliet was unhappy or contemplating suicide? Or that she was pregnant?"

"Nope. That mistake cost me dearly."

"That explains why you dole out Raine's medication. And why you've always kept track of her cycles. I had no idea it was that bad, man. I'm sorry."

Beck's words were slathered in sympathy. Hammer didn't need it. He just wanted the regret and shame eating him up inside to go away.

"I can't believe you've been carrying this crap around all these years." Beck looked as blown out of the water as Liam had earlier.

"Yep, until tonight when I puked up every ugly bit of it, right onto Liam." The memory of utter shock on his old friend's face slid through Hammer's veins like black, oily sludge.

Beck's eyes grew wide as if suddenly struck with understanding. "Well, now I know why you won't tell Raine you're in love with her. All these years you've wanted to claim her, but..."

"I'm no good for her," Hammer interrupted. "She deserves a better man and Master."

"Yeah? And everyone can see you're doing so great without her," Beck mocked.

"I never said that."

"So all the submissives you take to bed are what? Substitutes for Raine?"

Hammer leveled a look of warning toward Beck. "You're stepping over a line. Watch yourself."

"No. I'm not going to candy-coat it for you, and deep down you don't want me to."

True. "They're not substitutes. They're able to handle what I need. When I'm rough and strict, it silences the guilt screaming in my head."

"What about the night you spent with Raine. Guilt then?"

Hammer's hand tightened around his glass. "She silenced it all. There was nothing but peace."

"So why don't—"

"I don't deserve to have it silenced. Don't you understand? I failed Juliet. I'll be damned if I fail Raine."

"You think Raine might check out like Juliet someday?" he asked Hammer.

"No. Never."

"At least you've gotten that much through your thick skull. Raine may not be the greatest communicator, but she's a fighter, Macen. You know that."

Yeah, he did. All the years he'd spent with Juliet he'd never truly seen his wife's soul. No matter how he'd tried, it had been like looking through smoke. He could see Raine's bright beacon as clear as day. She wasn't a quitter. The girl could be so damn self-sufficient. She'd left that prick of a father as a kid, and without fear of how she'd survive, drew from her inner strength to forge a better life for herself. Hammer knew what Raine would do if she were unhappy, and it sure as hell wasn't swallow a bottle of pills.

"I might have to hunt her down," Hammer said. "But I'll never have to bury her. If I'd thought for two seconds that I might, the possibility of her being pregnant would have sent me into a panic."

"Then stop projecting your guilt over her and Liam, and start being honest with them both. Hasn't Juliet taken enough from you? Maybe your child, nearly a decade, your happiness? Do something, idiot! Otherwise, you'll just keep wasting away your life."

"Thanks for holding back."

Beck snorted, but he was right. Hammer had wasted so much time. How much longer was he willing to throw away over shit he couldn't change?

C H A P T E R
S I X

Unleashing his frustration on the punching bag had done nothing to alleviate Liam's rage. Every morning in the week following Thanksgiving, he'd slipped away to the gym to escape Shadows and the pressure cooker of problems there, if only for a while. After nearly an hour of the repetitive rhythm, sweat dripped in his eyes and his muscles screamed…but he still couldn't fatigue himself enough to silence the chaos crowding his head.

Finally, he stripped away his gloves and headed to the shower. As he sagged against the tile wall and let the hot spray cascade over him, he tried to decide what the fuck to do next. His options were limited. Stay or go? Fish or cut bait?

Liam sighed. Hammer was a secretive asshole and his rival for Raine. But he also made a hell of a sounding board, and ironically Liam missed him now.

Once dressed, he headed out of the gym and fought the morning rush. As soon as he pulled into the car park of the first beach he encountered, Liam took out his cell and rang Seth.

When his friend answered, he heard the sound of a woman's soft voice in the background.

"Hey, it's me."

"This had better be good, Liam. The things I'm willing to forego for a friend has its limits."

He could hear the laughter in Seth's voice and smiled faintly. "I wouldn't call any of this good, but I could use an ear."

Seth sobered. "You got it. What happened?"

Liam leaned his seat back a bit and stretched out. "How much did you know about Juliet's death?"

"Just that she committed suicide."

"You didn't know why?"

"No," Seth answered. "I figured you'd know far more about that than me."

"I would have thought so, too." Liam sighed. Exhaustion and frustration tugged at him. He swiped at gritty eyes. "Macen finally told me."

He related the conversation to Seth. Afterward, his friend said nothing for a long moment. "Holy shit."

"That sums up how I feel. Hammer held all that in for eight fucking years."

"He never hinted why Juliet had done herself in?"

"Not once. Not during any of our phone calls, not when I stood beside him at Juliet's grave on the anniversaries of her death and we talked about old times. Not in the two months since I moved out here. Never...until last week."

Seth whistled. "You must feel run over by a truck."

"I was in shock at first. Now, I just keep thinking what the fuck? Hammer blindsided me. Then he blamed it all on me. Fuckwit."

"You feel betrayed." Seth didn't ask.

"I do. And how am I supposed to feel about the fact that Juliet might have killed herself because of my baby?" Somewhere between incredulous and wretched, for sure. "Even though I didn't know and I can't do anything about it now, guilt is eating me."

Juliet's suicide was ancient history, but Liam's wound felt fresh.

"She chose to end it without talking to either one of you," Seth pointed out. "Don't beat yourself up. So are you and Hammer talking now?"

"We haven't since that night. I can't decide if I should beat the fuck out of him or apologize for missing the boat completely."

Liam couldn't bury his anger toward Hammer...but he could only imagine what the man had assumed all these years. That he didn't care. That Juliet hadn't mattered. That the grief of losing his wife meant nothing. Strictly looking at Hammer's version of events, Liam supposed he came off like an insensitive prick. He cursed himself for not following his instincts and rushing home from Miami.

Had Hammer's resentment spurred him to take Raine to bed the night Liam had first claimed her? It wouldn't surprise him if Macen had purposely tried to get her pregnant, too.

Bloody rat bastard.

And no matter how fucking angry he was, Liam couldn't rail to anyone at Shadows. Who would listen? Hammer? Liam rolled his eyes. Raine? Well, if Hammer had never told the man sharing Juliet's bed about his wife's tragic suicide, Liam doubted his old pal would have whispered a word of it to Raine. Not that Liam wanted to spill their dark past to the bruised, half-broken girl. He wanted to earn her trust, and telling her that story wouldn't help the cause.

"It's a tough break, man," Seth commiserated. "But how the fuck were you supposed to know what happened if no one told you?"

True. But that didn't eradicate his guilt or halt the need to unleash his wrath.

"To add insult to injury..." Liam gripped the steering wheel until his knuckles turned white. "Hammer made it clear, that he'll take what-ever opportunity presents itself to drag her back to his bed again."

Seth paused. "Clearly, he's being a douche, but what's more important to you? Is it preventing Hammer from taking Raine to bed again or serving the needs of your sub? We already talked about this. If she needs you both—"

"So the last sub you cared about, you wanted your friends fucking her?" Liam countered.

"Don't try to make this about me. Focus on Raine. What are you really afraid of? Is it just that she'll spread her legs for Hammer again? Or that she'll ultimately choose him over you?"

The question made Liam's heart seize. Hell, Seth saw right through him. "Hammer is too screwed up for her."

"Maybe confessing to you means he's finally letting go of the past. I understand you're pissed off at him, but what does *she* need?" Seth sounded infinitely patient.

That made Liam want to grit his teeth. "I'll give her what she needs, damn it!"

"All I'm hearing is your jealousy. You've got to put Raine before Hammer and your anger. So far, you've done everything right for her. Don't stop now."

Why did Seth have to be so damn right?

Liam sighed in defeat. "Asshole."

"It's asking a lot of you, I know, especially when you're not sure where you stand with her."

"She's shouted her love for Hammer to the rafters. But me? I don't know."

"I get that you're afraid that Raine will run back to Hammer, maybe for good. But you can't control the choices either of them make. You can only focus on your own."

"The plan we discussed last week…" Liam swallowed tightly. "I don't know if I've ever done anything more difficult."

"You told me then that she's crumbling. If she doesn't get what she needs, what then?"

Liam raked a hand through his hair. "I know, you bastard. Shut up."

"You came to me for help—twice. We came up with this plan together."

"I told you then it was fucking terrible. It could all blow up in my face."

"It could. But if you do nothing, it will. Unless you're not sure Raine is worth the effort and sacrifice?"

Liam didn't hesitate. "She is."

"Then do what you know you've got to. I'm here if you need anything, but you have to keep it together and focus on the needs of your submissive."

"You're bloody good at nagging," he groused.

Seth chuckled. "Do you want me to come out there and help you keep your head screwed on straight?"

It would be damn nice to have someone in his corner. "If you can, I'd be grateful."

"I'm on my way, Faultline U.S.A."

Liam let out half a laugh. "Thanks, Seth."

"You're welcome. Now fuck off and leave a man in peace. I'll let you know when I land in L.A."

After a somber trip back to Shadows, Liam sat at the foot of his bed, watching Raine sleep as he gathered his fortitude. She looked so damn beautiful—peaceful—in his bed.

The serenity on her face wasn't real.

The lass would never be whole if he didn't follow through with his plan. And he would never be whole without her. Dread nearly crushed him. But Seth was right; he had to put his fears aside and help her. The worst part was knowing that it wouldn't matter how gently he proceeded, the impact could be vicious.

Fuck.

His heart twisting, Liam reached out for Raine, stroking the luscious leg she'd thrust out from the covers, reveling in her soft skin. It was his…at least for the moment—just like she was.

How had the girl branded his soul so quickly? Raine was everything he'd never known he sought. Parts vulnerable, funny, tart, giving. Mysterious. Clever. She oozed sex. The Dom in him wanted to own her. The man in him wanted to conquer her. Liam shook his head. Hell, he sounded like a knuckle-dragging ape.

What he should be pondering was the ways in which he could imprint himself on Raine in return. He'd told her he loved her a hundred times. She'd never returned the sentiment. Liam felt sure it was, at least in part, because she didn't believe him. How could he make her understand his devotion before their conversation? How could he make her *believe* his love?

"Raine, wake up." He caressed his way up her body, then scooted closer, bending to smooth the dark locks back from her sleep-soft face, willing himself not to get lost in her.

God, he wanted to make love to her again. It had been eleven days, but it felt like forever.

Her dark lashes fluttered open to reveal her sleepy blue eyes, her expression welcoming as her lips curled up in a little smile. "Morning, Liam..."

She sat up and snuggled into his arms. He embraced her, savoring her closeness while he could, breathing her in, tangling his fingers in her silky hair, nuzzling her smooth cheek.

"Raine," he whispered finally. "I need to talk to you."

"Hmm." She purred into his neck, her breasts soft against his chest. "It's so early. Come cuddle with me again. You're so warm, and I'm happy when you're next to me."

In typical Raine fashion, she stalled any discussion that might result in him peeling away her layers and exposing her vulnerabilities. She kissed her way up his neck, across his jaw, angling toward his mouth, enticing him. Liam gritted his teeth.

"Not now. I'll give you ten minutes to use the bathroom and ready yourself. Then I want you back here, flat on the sheet, hands above your head, with your thighs spread wide and that gorgeous pussy open. And I want your full attention. Understood?"

Her eyes opened wider at his low demand. "Yes, Sir."

Sparks ignited down his spine. "Best get a wriggle on, then. The clock starts now."

Raine sent him a kittenish smile as she rose and disappeared into the bathroom. When he heard the soft snick of the door closing, Liam prepared the space with everything he might need, methodically setting items in their place. He slid into that heady Domspace he always enjoyed with Raine. Not since their time at the lodge had he felt so in control of himself and their scene. He'd allowed too many distractions to derail him since then, but now, thanks to his conversations with Seth, he felt focused, steady.

He just hoped like hell that Raine understood the message his actions meant to convey.

Moments later, she emerged from behind the closed door, hair and teeth brushed, face scrubbed and glowing, collar on. She wore nothing else, and that was precisely the way he liked her. His cock stood tall.

As she surveyed the room and saw everything he'd set out, a smile of anticipation lifted her lips. That, he expected. But the hope in her blue eyes surprised him.

"I've missed you. The last few weeks have been so..." She stopped herself, just when she might have said something important, and caressed his face with a soft, clinging stare. "I'm glad you're here and that you want me."

Her voice said that she'd been worried by the possibility that he hadn't after their Thanksgiving row, but she didn't verbalize it. That frustrated Liam. "No matter what you think, I've always wanted you, Raine. From the very first minute I laid eyes on you."

She smiled, and he swore he could see her heart in her eyes. Something far deeper than desire lay there. Why wouldn't she just bloody tell him?

Liam caressed the silky hair at her crown, then cupped her cheek. "I've tried to voice how I feel about you. I'm still not sure you actually understand how strong my feelings have become, but now isn't the time for talking. Open yourself to me and let me show you."

"I'm not very good at telling you my feelings." She brushed a kiss across his lips. "But I'll do my best to show you, too."

Then she lowered herself to the bed, legs parted, arms over her head, just as he'd requested. It was a sight to behold. Her rosy nipples cresting plump breasts, the long, lean line of her torso leading down to sleek thighs, and the strip of dark hair above her otherwise bare folds made him ache and sweat.

As Liam hovered above her, he couldn't look away. Sexually, everything between them had always been as hot as a live wire, urgent, connected. This was one place her submission shined. Raine gave him everything in bed. But sharing her whole body was a thousand times easier for her than sharing even a part of the woman beneath.

Unbuttoning his shirt and shrugging it off, he toed off his shoes, and sat on the chair opposite to strip off his socks. He still couldn't take his eyes off her, all gracefully arranged and spread out before him. He growled in satisfaction as she spread her thighs even wider, displaying *his* cunt and his ass, both reserved for his pleasure alone. Sorrow and pride blended, beautiful and bittersweet.

He pushed the melancholy aside. By god, regardless of today's outcome, she would feel him so deeply inside her—mind, body, and soul—that she'd forever hold a piece of him close.

He unfastened his belt and unzipped carefully over his straining erection. His cock already wept for her, throbbing to be enveloped in her silken heat. He forced himself to be patient.

Walking to the bed, he reached for the cuffs, securing her wrists and ankles. He heard the soft quiver of her indrawn breath, then watched her test his restraints.

"You'll not be going anywhere until I say so. While you're with and under me, I'm going to talk to you with my mouth, my hands, my body. I want you to listen and tell me what I'm saying to you. Be specific, Raine. I want to hear about the sensations, your level of intensity." He leaned over her, knee pressed to the mattress between her legs, and delved into her eyes. "More important, find the words to tell me how my actions make you feel. Do that for me."

"I'll do my best to communicate."

He leaned into her face, pinning her to the bed with a firm stare. "Your *very* best, Raine. Nothing less."

Sudden apprehension rolled across her expression. She grasped his displeasure, lingering since Thanksgiving. She felt it. But she didn't broach the subject. In fact, they hadn't spoken at all about that day. He'd tried. The first time she'd lured him to silence with a blow job, and he cursed himself for letting her lead him astray. The second time, she'd suddenly remembered a task she'd neglected to finish to ready the dungeon for play that night. Liam had followed her, still talking... only to be stopped short when he spied Hammer and Beck already in the room. He hadn't bothered trying to talk to Raine again.

Now he'd get her attention.

"I expect you'll let me know how you're feeling with the colors of the traffic lights. Do you remember?"

"Of course."

"And tell me your safe word."

"Paris."

"Excellent." He released a little slack in the chains attached to the cuffs at her ankles and bent her knees to make a cradle for him.

Wretchedly eager to feel her, Liam covered her body with his own— and forced himself to do nothing more than rub his cock along the wet, engorged lips of her sex. Raine whimpered and tried to wriggle her hips to align the head with her opening. Sliding inside her was so tempting. It would be so easy to simply let the pleasure take over. But so unfulfilling in the end.

Liam pulled back. "I told you to communicate what you want, not wiggle. Do I have to punish you before we start?"

"No." She swallowed, hesitated. "I, um...like it when you touch me. I miss having you inside me. I want to feel you now."

At her words, he barely managed not to snort. Raine had a bad habit of topping from the bottom that made his inner Dom roar to subdue her. "Eventually."

He nipped at her ear, laving the lobe with wet kisses. As she moaned in appreciation, he reared back enough to cup the hot, silky weight of her breast in his hand, kneading it firmly all the way to the tip. Rolling and pinching her tight nipple, it swelled and lengthened between his fingers. He rolled beside her and nipped at the base of her throat, then suckled her nipple, even as he reached for a clamp.

She hissed as he slid the little alligator-toothed implement into place. She gasped sharply with the shock of pain and pleasure. He waited for her to speak. She didn't.

Running his hand over her warm skin and reaching for her other breast, he pinched and laved its tip, then applied the twin clamp, reveling in the way she tensed, then exhaled out all her tension with a low moan.

"Raine?" he prompted.

"Green."

"And? Use your words."

"All the sensations in my body are centered around my nipples."

"Do you like it?"

She gave him a shaky nod, inky strands of her hair brushing the tops of her pale breasts, flirting with the clamps. The sight of her flushed and aroused beneath him played hell with his self-control. He forced himself to rein in the urge to fuck her.

"I love it. The pain is just enough to excite me. It sounds odd, but I feel so female and submissive when you bind me this way."

"Not odd at all. It's designed to."

Liam tugged on the little chain between the clamps, loving her shaky little gasp. "How does it make you feel, knowing I'm giving you these sensations?"

Her lashes fluttered before she focused on him. "Desired."

"Good. You are, love."

On hands and knees, he settled himself over her, then brushed the hair from her eyes, waiting until she met his stare. "So beautiful. You're not like any woman I've met."

A wry smile played at her lush mouth. "You mean I'm more challenge than submissive."

"You're both. You've always intrigued me. How did I make you feel when we first met?" He cradled her breast, thumb caressing the inner curve.

"Intimidated," she admitted. "You were polite to a fault. With a smile, you tried to set me at ease. But I realized you were assessing me and drawing conclusions."

"I was studying the woman who had Hammer tied up in knots. How did the way we spoke make you feel?"

"Scrutinized."

Liam shook his head, pointing to her chest. "In here."

She took in a shaky breath. "Nervous. Dizzy. Watched. A little excited."

"That's good. You filled my head that day. Your face, your scent, your voice. You were like a tingling in my spine, surprising but not unwelcome."

She lifted her face toward him, and Liam didn't resist the need to kiss her. Rather than diving into her mouth and taking all he wanted, he teased her with a brush of lips, then lifted away. He did it again, lingering a little longer before he pulled back. But fuck, she lured and addicted him. He parted her lips and dove in for a long, exhilarating moment, moaning when she arched beneath him. Before he lost himself in Raine, he eased back, peppering her cheeks and neck with his kisses.

"Stop pulling away!"

Liam heard the frustration in her tone. It ramped up his need. "Do you give the orders, sub?"

"No," she whispered, suitably chastened. "I'm sorry, Sir."

"What made you demand more?"

"I want more."

"I want a billion dollars, but you don't see me robbing banks for it."

She sighed. "That's different."

"Tell me how."

"You're right in front of me, looking at me like I mean…something to you."

"Everything," he corrected. "You mean everything to me."

Raine lowered her gaze. She was still afraid to believe him, damn it to hell.

"Keep going," he demanded.

"When you look at me like that, I…it makes me feel good inside," she spoke, but she'd gone quiet. "Worthy. Your touch says you value me."

He cupped her cheek, then caressed his way down to cup her chin, lifting it to make sure she had nowhere to look but at him. "Do you feel treasured when I touch you this way?"

A little flush splashed across her cheeks. "Yes."

"You feel that I care for you, love?"

She hesitated. "Y-yes."

Liam felt her body tighten, saw her expression start to retreat. He was approaching her comfort zone. She didn't have a hard time loving, he realized. She had a hard time believing that anyone loved her. If he could change that, she would feel secure revealing her devotion in return. His chest twisted up. Raine might be closed off, but she had such a big heart to give. He wanted it for his own.

"I do, Raine," he reassured her. "I've told you many times."

He bent to press his mouth fully onto hers, sinking in for a slow melding of lips, an unhurried stroke of her tongue, and a shared breath. Liam anchored himself in the moment, never rushing, always simply letting her feel how much he wanted and adored her.

Her response began cautiously, as if she wasn't sure whether to believe all the affection in the kiss. With every sweep, he met her, giving her a bit more, always there to guide her, catch her, encourage her.

The hesitation left her gradually, an inch of starch at a time softening, until she opened completely and whimpered, giving him all her passion in that one kiss. Desperation poured from her. And need. With every moan and glide of her tongue, she told him that he mattered to her. She loved him. Liam felt waves of it from her. This was part of what addicted him to her, not just her beauty or sexuality, but the way he could *feel* her vulnerability, need, and caring when he held her.

With one fist in her hair to keep her close and the other clamped onto her hip, he broke away. "Where are you?"

"Very green," she breathed.

"What did that kiss make you feel?"

Raine shrank back a bit. A little furrow appeared between her brows. He tried not to grit his teeth in frustration.

"There's no right or wrong answer, love. I only ask because I care."

She relaxed. "Languid. Connected to you."

"I'd hoped you would say that." For starters, anyway. He ran a hand up her soft, smooth torso to her breast, brushing his knuckles across the swell. "What did that kiss tell you about my feelings?"

"That you were there for me." She had a harder time getting the next words out. Liam watched her struggle and urged her to fight. "That you care."

That shouldn't be news to her. "Of course I do. But I always want you to feel it."

She nodded. She didn't speak, but her stare never wavered. Hope and need and a silent pleading for his affection all lay there. She wanted more and wanted to share herself.

Anticipation charged his blood. "Something you want to say, love?"

Raine blinked, bit her lip, then shook her head and lowered her gaze. She was so bloody bottled up. Liam forced down more disappointment. He refused to give up.

Lowering himself to his elbows, he settled his face closer, brushing his lips over hers. "You can tell me anything."

"I know."

No, she didn't. He sighed.

Shimmying down her body, he knelt to kiss the insteps of her little feet and nip at her toes. The ticklish girl giggled, then watched him with wide eyes, her expression somewhere between awestruck and afraid. Bloody hell, there was a wealth of information on her face. She'd been fucked—by the bastard who had taken her virginity, by Hammer, even by him—but no one had truly taken the time to show her his caring through touch. It made him doubly determined to reveal his heart without words now.

He kissed his way up her smooth legs, lingered at the soft caps of her knees, laving his way up her thighs, until he breathed over her pussy. The lass was wetter than he'd ever seen her. The closer his lips came, the more ragged and uneven her breath turned. She thrust her hips at him. He pinned her gently to the mattress.

"No, love. Where are you?"

"Green." She couldn't get the word out fast enough.

He smiled, then blew a hot breath on her slick folds and rubbed the pad of his thumb right above the plump flesh. "What does my touch make you feel now? Tell me."

"More than wanted. Like…no one else matters more to you. It sounds crazy, but—"

"No. You're exactly right. I'm proud of you."

With both thumbs, he opened her cunt to his gaze, his tongue. Liam lifted her hips high, his hands banded about her thighs, as he buried his face in her folds, eating her slick flesh like a man starved. He kissed the most feminine part of her with his whole body, giving her all the thoroughness he'd bestowed on her mouth. Even though his cock wept, hard as steel and pounding with need to be inside her, he lingered, aroused, encouraged, brought her higher.

Intoxicated by her slippery musk sliding across his tongue, he hummed his approval against her softness. "Does that make you feel cared for?"

"My head is swimming," she panted. "My blood is rushing. My pussy aches."

Easy responses to confess, and probably ones that had stroked his masculine pride in the past. Now he wanted more. "Good. What about your heart?"

"I…can't imagine you giving that intensity, in that way, unless it meant something to you."

A better response, but still not what he sought. "Yes. But what do you feel in your heart when I do this?"

He bent to give her another loving, longing lick deep in her furrow, delighting when she tensed under him and softly moaned, writhing.

"It makes me feel like...you want me to know that you care."

"I do." She danced around the words he really wanted to hear. Her insecurities and needs all glimmered in those blue eyes. She'd nearly drowned him at first glance; nothing had changed, especially the fact that she was too afraid to tell him how she felt.

But he still had more ways in order to help her try.

Crawling up her body, he rested his weight on one elbow, his face level with her breasts. After a quick tug on the chain, he released one nipple, sucking it directly into his mouth, soothing it even as he drew more blood to the tip.

"Raine?"

"I tingle. I ache. I...need. Liam..."

"What does my touch say to you?"

"That you know how to play my body so well."

"Look at me." He waited until she complied. "Why would I have paid so much attention to you, love?"

"I matter." She whispered the words, and he almost didn't hear. Almost as if she was afraid to voice the guess or jinx herself.

Liam grabbed her shoulders, his stare penetrating her, reaching for her soul. "You always have."

He rewarded her by removing the other clamp and treating the nipple to a thorough coaxing with his tongue. He filtered his fingers through her hair, loving the little groans and whimpers that slipped from her throat.

Liam couldn't stand it anymore. He had to be closer to her.

Covering her body with his own, he sank into her mouth and simply lost himself. No woman he'd ever fucked in a club, taken in a casual hook-up, shared with another, or even married had ever awakened this fever in his heart. Just Raine. He stopped trying to give her messages and simply let everything he felt pour all over her.

As he did, Liam pressed himself against her, his cock burrowing ceaselessly back and forth at her cunt, bumping her clit and avoiding the tantalizing well that coated his cock with her cream, promising nirvana if he'd only plunge inside.

Raine moaned, thrusting her hips up at him.

Reaching around her, he fisted her hair and clamped her delicate skull with his fingers. "You'll hold fast to me. You'll not come until I tell you. Do you hear me?"

"Yes, Sir." Her voice was breathy.

As she often did when he commanded her, Raine softened, turning pliant. Submissive. Anticipation zipped through him.

"Good. And you will not look away from me. Not once." He tugged again at the thick strands of her hair to let her know he meant that. He could—and would—keep her stare exactly where he wanted it.

"I won't," she vowed, her stare clinging to his.

"Where are you?"

"Green." Her face showed tinges of apprehension, but she still sounded steady. Strong.

"Good to hear."

He leaned across the bed and grabbed a condom, wishing she'd already been protected with birth control as he sheathed his hungry, waiting shaft. Lifting Raine, he settled her delicate curves against him. Aligning himself against her silky body, his nerve endings ignited in a heated rush. He wanted to be tender with her, but when he parted her slick, wet heat with his ready cock, he plunged home in an endless stroke that sent him deep.

"I'm completely inside you," he groaned. "How does that make you feel?"

Her head fell back, her dark mane spreading across the pale sheets. She rocked beneath him. Her soft kitten moans made his inner Dom howl.

"Look at me," he growled.

Raine did with a gasp, and a jolt of electricity rattled his spine.

"I feel taken," she moaned. "Possessed."

"Do you like feeling owned?" Using the fist in her hair, he cocked her head to one side, exposing her neck. He feathered kisses up the milky column, feeling her pulse flutter under his lips.

"Yes. Every time you touch me, I melt. Every time we're apart, I can't wait for you again. Please, Liam..." She writhed against him with a soft moan, trying to encourage him to thrust.

"Patience. I enjoy your body. Touching you. Commanding you. Making you come when I will it. You intoxicate me. I love to watch you unravel."

A rosy hue crept over her fair skin, and he loved that he could still make her blush.

"I'm not just going to fuck you, Raine." If he showed her how much he loved her, maybe it would take the sting out of all he needed to say.

He pressed a ravenous kiss to her throat, sucking and nipping the heated skin. He burned alive as her cunt consumed him. Her legs wrapped as tightly around his hips as the chains allowed.

"Oh, Raine. You slay me."

"Liam," she whimpered. "More."

"Why?"

"It feels amazing."

It did, and that barely scratched the surface of sensations jetting through his veins. "And?"

"I feel needed." Her body bucked. Her eyes teared up. "I need that. From you."

Clutching her, he stroked her torturously slow, a deep slide into forever. Again. And again. One blurred into the next, her cries filling his ears. She pleaded and begged. Her flesh squeezed him as he plundered her pussy with each thrust. With every retreat, her slick folds tightened, trying to suck him back in.

Baring his teeth with a grunt, he drove up into her tight, velvety passage. Her little feminine sounds boiled his blood and urged him to take her harder, higher, deeper. God, he loved this woman.

He could ask himself why. He could ask himself what tomorrow would bring. But the answers to those questions came back to Raine, as did the biggest question of all: What was it going to take to finally make her understand that peace and happiness lay within her own grasp? All he could do was shower her with his love and be the catalyst.

Gripping Raine tighter, he captured her lips, sliding inside her mouth to take everything—her flavor, her passion, her softness—all the way to her deepest recesses. Everything about her inflamed him. He'd come to crave her, need her like he needed food or water or air.

He pinched her nipples again. Yes, he needed those little cries, too. He needed her to beg. So he slowed his strokes to a torturous drag over every sensitive spot inside her cunt. "Tell me how you feel, Raine."

She writhed all over him. "Burning, aching. I'm dying."

He groaned and nipped the swollen tips of her breasts bouncing in front of him. She bit into his shoulder. With her, nothing was easy, nor would it ever be. He understood that, just as he understood that her love and commitment to them was worth fighting for. He was steeled for the battle of his life, but by god, if she wanted him, she'd have to fight, too. If she did…by the time this was over, she'd feel him beneath her skin and wonder how she'd ever done without everything he offered.

"Give me more," he snarled. "Give me everything."

She cried out at his rough invasion, the sounds of her pleasure only firing him up more as he filled his palms with her swollen breasts and pistoned his hips, thrusting wildly between the wettest, sweetest folds he could imagine on a woman's pussy. Even while his heart bled.

"I feel like…" She panted, struggling, trying to hold the words back.

Liam stared into her eyes, so wide and pleading.

"Tell me!"

"Like you love me." It rushed out almost like a single word, then she drew in a shaky breath, coursing with emotion. "I don't know why. I don't deserve it, but—"

"You feel like I love you because I do."

He grabbed her hips until he felt sure they'd bruise and drove into her using every bit of his breath, every ounce of his strength, shuttling deep with every drop of determination. He'd put his stamp on her the best way he knew how. And prayed that something he'd done had reached her bloody stubborn heart.

"Liam!"

"Take me, lass. All the way inside you, to the places you don't give anyone else. Take everything I've got to give you. Pleasure, pain, joy, sorrow. They're all mine, just like you."

Under him, she whimpered. Her body surged and rolled, swelled and arched. He slid even farther inside of her, her flesh grasping and clutching him.

"Yes!" she cried out. "I'm so close. Please..."

"I love you, Raine. No matter what, I love you today, tomorrow, always. Promise me you'll not forget..."

But her keening cry of impending orgasm was her only answer. He reached between them and stroked her clit to launch her ecstasy. He relished in her trembling beneath him. "That's it, love. Come for me."

Liam closed his eyes and felt her release sweep through him like a shockwave as she wailed out her climax. He tried to hold his own for as long as he could, but his body would not be denied as he pulled free of her, tore the condom from his pulsating cock, and felt the surge of semen burst upward and out, covering her milky white belly and breasts. Liam marked her, roaring as he held on for dear life.

He rubbed his seed into her porcelain skin, determined to have his scent upon her, hoping it meant to her all that it did to him.

Liam had given her everything—mentally, physically, emotionally. He felt spent in every sense of the word as he uncured her sprawled on his back with Raine tangled in his arms. The fan above them lazily spun.

"Do you love me at all?" he asked, unable to stop himself.

Beside him, she tensed. He heard her swallow.

Rolling to his side, Liam pinned her with a stare. Her heart was in her eyes. She wanted to say yes, damn it. He'd felt it in her touch. He could bloody well feel it now.

"I—" Her mouth hung open, but she said nothing else.

Raine sucked in harsh breaths. She paled.

"Be brave."

"I need to go to the bathroom," she sobbed and tried to roll from the bed.

As he grabbed her arm to stay her, agony gutted Liam. Weariness and crushing regret dashed the satisfaction spiraling through him just moments ago. He felt hollow. Destroyed. He gripped her tightly, willing her to look at him. Her whole body trembled. He felt her yearning, damn it. But she wouldn't face him.

Maybe he wanted more than she was capable of giving. Maybe he wasn't enough for her. He swallowed. Maybe she just didn't love him enough.

"Wait," he rasped.

The truth was, she was too afraid to tell him how she felt. Because of her father? No, she'd had no trouble telling Hammer. But his old pal had shoved her love back in her face over and over, bruising her ego. Breaking her heart? Yeah, probably.

His hopes of saving her dissolved. He'd been kidding himself that he could. It seemed he was years too late for that.

How ironic that he'd taken up with Raine to build her confidence a bit and prod Hammer with jealousy. But Macen was having the last laugh. Liam knew he'd never be the same.

With a heavy sigh, he lifted a finger and tilted her chin. The collar at her throat looked so lovely in the light. His heart clutched as he brought her mouth to his for a soft kiss.

As he brushed her lips with his own, he reached behind her neck and slipped the latch on the collar. The precious metal with its dangling ruby was warm from her skin. The catch fell open, and the piece slid into his waiting hand.

She froze—her kiss, her stare, her breath. Raine pulled back slowly, then looked at the collar in his palm, blinking with shock and confusion. Questions clouded her eyes. Anxiety tightened her face.

He dragged in a sawing draught of air. He fucking hated hurting her.

"What are you doing?"

He set the collar on the nightstand. "I told you we needed to talk, Raine."

She tried to jerk away. "You *used* me before you decided to tell me to kiss off."

He held tight, not letting her move an inch. "I made love to you, hoping you'd understand. But you don't." He sighed. "So I'm going to explain myself, and I want you to listen carefully. For this to work, I need you to communicate—"

"If this is about the migraine, I swear that I wasn't keeping it from you on purpose. I just had so much else on my mind that I forgot to mention it."

"If you were thinking of me at all, you'd automatically share something like that with me. It would be second nature. You want my affection. You want my sexual domination. You don't want to do the work necessary to truly submit. Hell, to have a real relationship."

"That's not true." Her blue eyes pleaded, frantic. "I'm working on it. I'm not perfect, but I'm—"

"Still hiding big chunks of your heart and soul to yourself. You're not ready to be collared."

"That's not fair!"

"What's not fair is that I'm your Dom in name only. I won't fight you if you don't want to give yourself freely. Only you can decide how important I am to you—if at all. But I can't keep submitting to *you* while I try to give you what I know you need. I'm not oblivious to your fears, but you either trust me and love me...or you don't. I'm done trying to pry everything out of you, only to discover you've not been bloody honest. I get half-truths and subtle lies designed to make me feel better. Is it because you think I'm too stupid to understand or too weak to handle them?"

Horror crossed Raine's face. "Neither! I told you before; I just don't want to upset or trouble you."

"Or have to risk my wrath, admit you've fucked up, and truly give yourself to me. I know the game, Raine. I've seen it played many times. And I won't play it with you anymore. I want you back...but not until you learn to communicate. Be honest with me. Trust me. And surrender your control to me. I see the real you, no matter how much you try to hide. And I still want you, still love you. I always will."

"You're punishing me for Thanksgiving day," she accused, her voice thickening with emotion.

"This isn't any sort of discipline. But I've finally got your attention, lass. The pickles I fed you back at the lodge to coax you to open up just weren't working anymore."

That seemed like a lifetime ago.

Tears filled her eyes, and she struggled from his embrace again, this time with all her might.

Still, he held strong. "Stop."

"You're leaving me," she accused.

"I'm not. I'm giving you a wee break so you can decide whether you want to go through life alone or open your heart and be loved. I can't make the choice for you." Finally, he released her with a sigh.

She scrambled away and jumped from the bed, spearing him with a teary accusation. Betrayal narrowed her eyes. "I knew you were going to do this eventually. I told you from the beginning that you'd give up on me and leave, just like everyone else. I knew I wouldn't be good enough for you. I told you... I'm so stupid for hoping you'd be different."

As she made a mad dash for the door, his heart sank. He ran after her and slapped his palms against the door on either side of her so she couldn't open it. "Raine, hear me well. I'm not leaving you. I'm giving you some space so you can figure things out. You won't have my expectations hanging over your head to cloud your thoughts. I'm always here to answer questions or reassure you. And don't you dare be thinking about running away. But *you* have to search your own soul. If you're willing to do the work to be whole and want what we could have, come back to me. If not..." His fucking heart was breaking, and he could barely choke the words out. "Then this is the end."

CHAPTER
SEVEN

Raine stood under the hot spray of her shower, sobbing so hard she could barely take a breath. For the last month, Liam had quietly and solidly supported her, keeping her balanced and almost happy. He'd treasured her in a hundred ways. He'd shown her every day that he wanted her.

Until today when he'd left her.

How was she going to survive when she felt as if her chest had been torn open and everything inside yanked out with a few brutally soft words?

She reached for her favorite shampoo. But it was with Liam, in his room, in his shower. He also had her body wash, a bunch of her clothes...and half her heart. He didn't want that half anymore.

And Hammer wouldn't take the other half.

Crossing her arms over her chest, she curled her hands under her chin and bowed her head. The absence of her collar stabbed her with agony again. And remorse. Falling back against the cold tile, she let the tears flow. They mingled with the water, pelting her unrelentingly.

Liam had left her.

The thought razed through her brain again. Her knees buckled. Another sob robbed her of breath. More tears joined the cascade of water. She could barely think past the pain.

On autopilot, Raine shampooed her hair, scrubbed Liam's seed from her body, washed her face, then stepped out. The towel smelled like fabric softener, not Liam. She'd become so accustomed to sharing his, smelling his musk on the damp terrycloth. It made her feel safe. Why hadn't she realized that before now?

Why hadn't she been able to tell him that she loved him when she did, so very, very much? The disappointment on his face had seared itself into her memory.

Maybe it didn't matter. He'd made himself clear that he would welcome her back, but only if she was a different person. Raine didn't know how to be that.

She dredged up an almost superhuman effort to slather lotion on her skin, braid her hair, and apply lip gloss. Raine gave up then. She just didn't care about the rest.

Leaving the steamy bathroom, she wriggled her way into some panties, a bra, a pair of sweatpants, and a sweatshirt. Lying in one of her drawers, she fingered an old T-shirt that had been Hammer's once, long ago. She'd taken it from him and slept in it for months, just to feel close to him. Shortly after turning twenty-one and realizing that he still treated her every bit like a child, she'd tucked it away.

Raine knew now that his attitude had been a front…but nothing had really changed. He would never love her in return. Sure, he might want to fuck her for a night or two—and yes, she could run to his room and seduce him now—but she loved Hammer too much to make him the instrument of her revenge. And regardless of the hurt Liam had inflicted, she just didn't have it in her to stab him in return.

Shoving the shirt back in her drawer, Raine looked around the room she'd called her own for years. She didn't belong here anymore.

So where did that leave her? More to the point, where *did* she belong? Liam had released her because she couldn't be what he needed. Hammer had refused her for so long, and after their torrid night of passion, he'd let her go for the exact same reason.

Her dad had been right all along. She wasn't good enough.

Maybe if she left, Liam and Hammer would finally repair their friendship. That would make them happy someday, and then she could say she'd done at least one thing right.

Of course Raine recognized that running was an old pattern of hers, one both men had chided her about. But in this case, she just didn't see any way for the healing to begin if she was constantly underfoot to provide the friction between them. Besides, if she had to look at them every day and know they'd never be hers, it would eventually destroy her.

Leaving was best.

That would probably seem unfathomable to Liam. He'd been nudging her to leave Shadows with him since he'd collared her because it would be good for her. She hadn't agreed and had refused to go. But everything was different now.

As much as she hated to leave her home, she'd do it for both men. For their friendship, which had deteriorated drastically since they'd torn apart the kitchen on Thanksgiving. She didn't know exactly what had happened, but the tension was tangible and thick between them now. Ugly. The blame for that rested squarely on her shoulders.

Pushing aside dread of the unknown she'd face once she left, Raine grabbed a suitcase from her closet. She had a little money in the bank. She'd find a new place and a new job. After all, she had a college degree and some accounting skills. She was good with people. She'd been an office manager…of sorts. Somehow, someway, she'd figure it out.

Blotting her face with a tissue, Raine sniffled back tears. They were useless. Liam and Hammer couldn't change what they needed, and she couldn't change who she was. It had been destined to end this way, she supposed.

Desolation hollowed her as she tossed most of her belongings into the suitcase. She packed some of her favorite pictures: Hammer dressed as the devil, opposite her angel, last Halloween. She and Liam at their collaring ceremony. One she'd taken of the two men clinking beer mugs the night Liam had first arrived from New York. All happy times. All smiles. So unlike now.

Raine sighed and zipped her suitcase, scanning her room. Sad that she'd packed up most of her life in fifteen minutes. All she had to do was load her car and drive off.

Wait, it wasn't her car. Hammer had bought it for her. The title was in his name. And she'd accepted the gift because it made her feel special to him. *Stupid.* The smarter move would have been to stand on her own two feet. She sure as hell refused to steal from him now.

She fished her car keys from her purse, along with the keys to Shadows, and left them on her dresser. He'd find them at some point.

Dismissing the thought, she dug out her phone, Googled a quick number, and made the saddest phone call of her life. The voice on the other end said she had ten minutes left, but why wait? Why take a chance that Liam or Hammer would come looking for her? It was probably cowardly to just disappear. But so much easier. She'd make sure they knew she was all right and make them promise to let her go.

She backed out of the room, taking one last sweeping look around. Not that it mattered; this place was permanently imprinted in her memories. On her heart. Just like the men who lived here.

No one walked the hall as she slipped out of her room. No one confronted her as she made her way past Liam's door, past Hammer's. She shoved her way into the alley, peering out at the overcast day. Raine couldn't believe this was the last time she'd be at Shadows. Everything had happened so fast. The moment felt so surreal. But she wasn't going to wake up, rub her eyes, and realize this had all been a dream.

Standing in the alley, the wind tugged at her clothes and made her nose cold. It was almost December. Her wet hair filled her with a chill.

She probably should have packed a coat, but the mild discomfort was nothing compared to the torment dismembering her heart.

Right on schedule, her taxi arrived. She turned off her phone and shoved it into her purse, approaching the vehicle. This was it. She swiped fresh tears from her face.

"Where to?" the gruff cabbie asked.

Good question. Someplace familiar—for now. She'd figure out where to head from there.

Raine rattled off the name of a drugstore a few blocks from where she'd grown up. It was in the center of town. Once there, she could begin to settle everything else. The town was relatively quiet, growing so she could find a job and easy to navigate if it took her a while to buy another car. She wouldn't feel safe there—she only truly did under Hammer's roof—but she'd closed that chapter of her life, so moving on…

The taxi driver put his foot on the gas, and the car lurched forward. The scarred dumpster Hammer had once found her hiding behind and the familiar building where she'd learned about love from the two amazing men who had forever changed her life rolled out of sight.

Twenty minutes later, she'd done nothing but stare out the window. She almost felt…numb. It was kind of nice. Raine didn't expect the reprieve to last because the pain lurked just under the surface. But she'd take the daze for now. The minute she found some privacy, it was bound to get ugly.

The cab stopped in the little strip shopping center. She thought about asking him to wait, but he got a call for another fare. And honestly, she didn't know where to tell him to take her. She paid him, grabbed her suitcase, then climbed out.

It started to rain.

Damn it, if that didn't just add to the day. Sighing, Raine dashed into the shelter of the store. She pretended to browse the cosmetics and self-care products. She walked past greeting cards, toys, snacks—and came to something she could really use.

She grabbed the first one on the shelf, paid a goth girl for it, and peered out, hoping for a break in the storm, which probably wouldn't last. But all she had to do was find a place to hang her head for the night. Then the skies could pour down buckets for all she fucking cared.

Except no one was going to rent her a room at ten thirty in the morning.

Crap, she couldn't even plan a departure without fucking it up.

At the end of the road, the sign of a low-budget chain of motels caught her attention. It wasn't fancy, but it was clean and probably pimp-free. Those were her only requirements now.

Fifteen minutes later, she juggled her purchase under her arm and, fingers aching, transferred her suitcase to her other hand as she strolled through the automatic double doors. Securing a room for the night would be no problem. Their computers were down currently, and none of the rooms would be clean for a few hours. The desk clerk agreed to store her suitcase for her, handed her a claim ticket, then told her she could check in officially as soon as the touchy machines all came back online.

Now what? She could hang out in the lobby, but she'd have nothing to do except to think of all she'd lost. Since she was no longer focused on the details of getting from Point A to Point B, the gouging sadness was begging to dig at her again, emptying her of any desire to put one foot in front of the other. It would get better, she knew. In time. A few months, if she was lucky. Maybe a few years.

Maybe never.

Raine shoved the thought aside. "What's the nearest restaurant?"

She'd known once upon a time, but she hadn't lived here in years.

The desk clerk referred her to a pancake house a few blocks away, closer to the freeway. Not that it mattered, really. She wasn't hungry, but pretending to eat would kill time.

As she started for the door, the hotel's little shuttle pulled up.

"The bus will take you anywhere within a two-mile radius for free," the clerk offered helpfully, eyeing her.

"Thanks." Raine didn't glance back, just walked out.

The old bus driver smiled brightly as she stepped inside. His jovial grin was contagious, and she did her best to smile back. He had kind eyes and looked on the brink of asking her what was wrong, but she was sure he'd never been in a BDSM love triangle, so she amped up her plastic expression and commented on the weather.

After handing her a business card with a number to call when she wanted him to retrieve her, the man dropped her off in front of the diner that was way too cheerful for her mood. The thought of eating alone depressed her more.

Shouldering her purse, she wandered up the road instead, crossing a busy intersection. What the hell was she doing? She had no idea where she was going—not just today, but tomorrow. Next week. Next month. For the rest of her life.

Raine rubbed at her forehead. She had to get off the pity pot. Give herself today and grieve, then figure her shit out. All this moping just wasn't going to solve anything.

Vaguely, she wondered if Liam or Hammer had even realized she was gone yet. If they had, would they be searching? Probably. Liam might even feel guilty. Hammer might be ticked off. Maybe she should set them at ease before she did anything else. But if she called there… what if one of them answered?

Suddenly, she looked up and saw the new hospital in town. And she knew exactly what to do.

Hammer stepped from the shower, hearing the senseless droning of the morning talk show host interviewing the latest reality "celebrity" in the background. Exhaustion weighed on him. He yawned and stretched. Was his fatigue the result of another fitful night? The incessant replay of Raine's cries of pleasure earlier this morning? Or the constant spooling in his head of the advice Beck had given him eight days ago that he still hadn't taken?

While punching his pillow and tossing restlessly last night, he'd come to the conclusion that he needed to apologize to Liam. The speech he'd prepared in his head and practiced in the shower felt more stilted than he'd like. But he'd say it. Once that was behind him, he could move onto the second step necessary to take control of his life again. How would Raine react when he confessed that he loved her and always had?

Hammer mussed his hair and threw on some clothes, determined that today he would sit Raine down and utter the three words he'd carried in his heart for so long.

He shouldn't be as nervous as a teenage boy asking his first girl out on a date, but his stomach was in knots. Once he'd told her how he felt, he hoped they could move forward together—just the two of them.

The possibility exhilarated him.

Dressed and ready to vanquish his demons, he strode to the room beside his and knocked on Liam's door. The apology repeated through Hammer's brain as he waited, then knocked again. No one answered.

Frowning, he made his way to the kitchen, wondering if his precious girl was baking. But it, too, was empty. The only sign of life was a freshly brewed pot of coffee that smelled more like tar than anything Raine would make. Still, he needed it.

Hammer poured himself a mug and took a sip as he left the kitchen, grimacing at the warm sludge sliding down his throat.

When he reached the dungeon, he skimmed a glance over the open space. He didn't see Liam or Raine. Had they gone to the gym? Out for breakfast? Or had they just ignored his knock, too wrapped up in their cocoon of bliss to give a fuck about him?

Fighting impatience, Hammer climbed the stairs to the bar. To his surprise, Liam sat on a tall stool, stooped over and nursing a mug of the terrible coffee.

"Good morning," Hammer said stiffly.

Liam barely glanced his way, just nodded and sipped more of the brew, hissing as it hit his tongue. "God, that's shit."

Hammer stared down into his own cup. "It is. Who made it?"

With a grunt, Liam shoved his away. "I did."

It fucking sucked. Hammer abandoned his mug on the bar, too. Then he drew in a deep breath. "I need to say something to you."

Liam glanced to the stool beside him, wordlessly inviting him to sit. Hammer slid onto the seat.

This speech had been ten times easier when he'd been dishing it out to his own reflection. But the fact that he hated apologies and this one felt fucking awkward didn't matter.

Liam shrugged, stared at the steam rising from his cup, his expression heavy and guarded. Hammer couldn't miss the deep furrow between his brows. Jesus, the guy looked desolate.

Another wave of guilt poured over Hammer. "I'm sorry for a lot of things I've said and done. You've always been a like a brother to me. Wallowing in my guilt about Juliet, then assigning it to you while withholding the truth was despicable. But not nearly as unfair as dumping everything on your shoulders years later. I apologize. You deserved better."

He watched as Liam scrubbed a hand down his face. "I'm sorry I wasn't there for you. And I'm more sorry than I can say for the hell you went through. I don't pretend to understand what Juliet did or why you didn't share your pain with me. Maybe you thought I was too young and stupid to get it." Before Hammer could refute that, Liam went on. "Fuck if I know. Doesn't matter now, does it?"

Liam stared straight ahead into the mirror, looking remote, resigned. Hammer bit back a sigh. Had his secretive bullshit irrevocably severed their friendship? *Great.* Wait until Liam realized he not only intended to work his way into Raine's bed again, but claim her once and for all.

"I don't know what to say to that, Liam. I lost a wife and a child in one day, and it eventually cost me my best friend. I might have been wrong to wait so long to vomit out the truth—"

Liam snorted. "Do you think so?"

"Look, I *was* wrong, but I came clean. Everything I said Thanksgiving night was honest." Hammer stared into the mirror, trying to read Liam's reaction. "I'm not even sure what you thought of the revelations about Juliet. You never said."

"I didn't think it mattered to you. Since she died, you shut down and pissed off. So I moved on. Am I supposed to be sorry for that?" Liam finally turned to him with a scowl. "What's the point now? All this retrospective crap doesn't change a thing." Liam made to rise from the stool.

"Wait! I'm not done, damn it."

Rolling his eyes, Liam settled back onto the barstool. "Hurry the fuck up."

Hammer lost his temper. "You got a tampon to change?"

Liam stood. "That's it. I'm done listening."

He clenched his fists. "Damn it, this is not how my apology was supposed to go. Sorry. Just let me finish."

"You've got thirty seconds."

Hammer scrubbed a hand through his hair. *Christ.* Clearly, mending their fractured friendship would require more than words—if it was even possible. The brittle olive branch he'd been trying to extend Liam wasn't reaching far. What he planned with Raine would probably break the damn twig in half.

But Hammer couldn't continue to hurt her under the guise of protecting her. He'd caused her far more anguish by hiding his love. She was a strong woman. After weighing Beck's advice, he realized that. If he took her training slowly, gave her a lot of praise and compromised, she could handle his needs. He would assure her that he didn't expect her to be his slave. Hammer vowed to teach, hold, and love her so he could complete her, just as she would him. But he had to let her decide for herself...even if she chose Liam instead.

That very real fear made his stomach twist. For years, his selfishness had prevented Raine from growing. What if she couldn't forgive him, either?

"Well?" Liam asked into his silence. "Never mind. Why are we even having this conversation? The bloody horse is dead. I think we've beaten him enough."

"He's just in a fucking coma." Hammer tried to crack a smile, but it felt forced and insincere. "Look, I admit that I fucked up. I made the wrong choices. We've both paid a price. I just want you to know that I'm sorry. I never did anything out of malice."

"Got it. Thanks." Liam nodded absently, then looked around the room.

A prickle of unease raised the hairs on the back of Hammer's neck. "What's wrong?"

"It would take me hours to explain, and I just don't have the time or energy now. Besides, I'm not in the bloody mood to hear 'I told you so.'"

They'd only ever really argued about one person. And if she had been here, she would have made far better coffee. "Where's Raine?"

Liam wouldn't meet his gaze. Alarm bells rang in his head.

"Where the fuck is Raine?"

"The last time I saw her, she was in my room. But I'm sure she's left it by now."

His flat reply, coupled with the flash of guilt in his eyes, screamed there was more his old pal wasn't saying.

"Left for where?"

"Her own room? I don't know."

"You don't know where your sub is?" Hammer jabbed, arching a brow.

Liam closed his eyes and sighed. "She's not my sub anymore. I removed her collar this morning."

The words punched Hammer. He felt himself gape at the news, jaw hanging, eyes bulging. A feather could have knocked him off the barstool. Hell, off the planet. "What?"

"You heard me. She's not ready to give what's necessary, and I'm bloody tired of trying to force her submission. I'm not letting her go, just giving her time to think, is all."

Maybe that wouldn't be true of another sub, but this one? She would take it as a crushing rejection, nothing less. In Hammer's book, if Liam had removed Raine's collar, that meant he'd released her. And she was fair game.

The selfish bastard in Hammer wanted to throw a party. Finally, Raine could be his. The Dom in him feared it wouldn't be that simple. Now that Liam had crushed Raine by letting her go, she'd need tenderness and love—two things he wasn't good at—to heal. *Son of a bitch.*

He damn near wrapped his hands around Liam's throat and strangled the life out of him. "What the hell were you thinking? Was it your intention to shove her out the fucking door and push her off the deep end?"

Liam bristled. "I was trying to teach her. Something *you* should have done years ago."

So much for mending fences.

His chest heaved as the last threads of control slid through Hammer's fingers. "If you'd have asked me, I would have told you uncollaring her was the most counterproductive move possible. You should have tried to modify her behavior."

"Not that it's any of your business, but I have—over and over. I was at the end of my rope."

Everything coming out of Liam's mouth blew Hammer's mind. "Raine lived and worked at Shadows, but she's never actually submitted before you. You know that observing and doing aren't the same thing. You should have trained her, not dumped her like yesterday's trash."

"Don't start with more guilt," Liam growled.

Fuck that. "How much guiltier will you feel if she's packed up and left?"

Hammer turned on his heel, Liam stomping close behind, and stormed down the stairs. His cries for Raine echoed through the cavernous dungeon. She didn't answer.

Pounding on her bedroom door, Hammer screamed her name. Terrible silence followed. Breaking out in a cold sweat, he dug the key to her room from his pocket and shoved it in the lock.

"Why are you carrying a key to my sub's room?" Liam challenged.

"I always have, and by your own admission, she's not your sub anymore."

With a curse, Liam shoved him aside. Hammer pushed back.

As the door swung open, their gazes ricocheted around the room. The closet gaped wide. Only a row of empty hangers remained. The dresser drawers staggered open like a mocking smile of crooked teeth. Hammer dashed into the room and looked inside each. He didn't find much…except that old T-shirt of his she used to sleep in. The sight was a fucking stab in the heart.

"Shit! Where the hell has she gone?" Hammer couldn't breathe. His heart stuttered in his chest.

"I don't know." Liam sounded stunned. Lost.

Rage railed through Hammer. He staggered against the dresser. When metal rattled, he looked down to find two keys on a ring. As he picked them up, he recognized both instantly.

"What are those?" Liam demanded.

"This one is to her car." Hammer held up the oblong bit of black plastic, its silver saw-toothed blade sticking out.

Liam gave a visible sigh of relief. "Then she can't have gone far."

"Don't kid yourself. This key…" He struggled to keep it together. "This is to the club."

Liam braced himself against her dresser. He looked as if a wrecking ball had hit him squarely in the chest. "Oh god, she's really gone."

"No shit."

"And she doesn't mean to come back."

Hammer slashed Liam with a seething glare. "Are you happy, genius? Where do you suggest we start looking?"

"I've no clue," Liam muttered. "I didn't think she'd leave before I even had the chance to talk to her."

"What the fuck did you think she'd do, Liam? Sit in her room and ponder all the ways she could change to make you happy?"

"I thought we were important enough to her that she'd want to do the work, that we'd do it together. I told her not to bloody leave." Liam sounded somewhere between bewildered and pissed off.

"Like she ever listens? Fuck." Fear filled Hammer's veins. "We've got to find her, but it's going to be like looking for a needle in a haystack. Wait." He plucked his phone from his pocket. "I have an idea."

He launched the app to search for her phone and quickly tapped out the password. An agonizing thirty seconds passed. The system wasn't finding her phone. Why wasn't he able to locate her, goddamn it? A moment later, the display indicated she was offline. Did he want to be notified next time she came online? *You're damn right, I do.* He tapped the screen to check "yes," gritting his teeth. All he could do was wait.

"The brat turned off her phone. She knows I can't track her unless it's on."

"She thought of everything, didn't she?" Liam shook his head. "What about her bank account?"

Hammer lit up with a smile. "I have access to that." He pulled his phone out again, input her password, and put in a request to alert him as soon as she used her ATM or credit cards. He logged out, then turned to Liam. "There. She may not want to be found, but it shouldn't take long. She'll trip up. And we'll bring her home."

Then I'll straighten her out.

Liam nodded, but anguish tightened his face. "Hell, I can't just stand here and wait."

"Until one of those clues pans out, we need a starting point for our search. I'll check the cameras."

Liam nodded. "I'll help."

In the operations room, Hammer dropped into the chair, sending it spinning across the hardwoods. It rolled to a stop in front of the complex security board. His fingers flew over the keys in a blur. His heart lurched. He prayed he would find what he needed.

Because he couldn't let her go. He wouldn't rest until he found her.

He began rewinding the footage captured by the camera perched above Shadow's back door. Liam peered over his shoulder.

Hammer paused the tape when a taxi appeared. He zoomed in as Raine stepped into view. Fear wrapped its icy hands around his throat and squeezed. All he could do was watch as the woman he loved opened the cab door. Dread that he'd never get the chance to tell her what was in his heart seized him.

Riveted by the images on the monitor, Hammer could only see Raine's back. He studied her body language, as he'd done a million times. Her subtle nuances spoke louder than words. She was decimated.

Raising a hand to her cheek, Raine brushed away her tears. She turned slightly, tossing her suitcase into the back seat. Hammer caught a glimpse of her eyes, swollen and red, along with her nose. He swore to himself this wouldn't be his last image of her.

Liam stared at the screen, barely breathing. "Bloody hell."

Zooming back out, he noted the name of the taxi company, then jotted down the cab's ID number before he snatched up the phone and began barking at the dispatcher.

Two minutes later, he was absolutely nowhere with the woman and her twang.

"Put your supervisor on," Hammer barked. He didn't give a shit about company policy; he needed answers. Every second spent listening to excuses furthered the distance between him and Raine. The clerk put him on hold.

"When did you last see Raine?" Hammer asked Liam. "What time was it?"

"Not long ago, maybe thirty minutes. I left to make coffee and give her a few minutes to get herself together," Liam ranted. "I didn't think she could pack up and flee that fast."

"You don't know her like I do," Hammer growled.

"You're happy as Larry to keep reminding me of that, aren't you?" Liam looked ready to climb the walls—or beat the hell out of him. "I told her I'd be here to help her—always. She didn't hear a bloody word I said."

Hammer couldn't resist baiting him again. "I have no idea why that's a shock."

Liam paced furiously. "Why the hell didn't she come to you if you're so important to her?"

The question brutalized Hammer, along with an avalanche of other crap. Sadness that neither of them had broken through to reach her wounded soul. Fear that Liam might be right. Anger that Raine didn't love either of them enough to stay and heal herself. Just like Juliet.

"Because you ran her off first," Hammer snarled.

"I literally made coffee, then went to the bar to take a breather and gather my wits before I returned to talk to her," Liam explained. "I had every intention of keeping an eye on her so that she wouldn't run. I meant to make sure she understood."

THE BREAK | 119

"Understood what? I still don't know what the fuck you thought you were doing."

Liam waved him off. "I should have tied her to the fucking bed."

"She'd have chewed through the restraints. Once her mind is made up..." Hammer let out a shuddering sigh. If he never heard Raine's sassy remarks or saw fiery challenge light up her blue eyes again, he'd lose it.

"I needed her to commit to me, to us. She's so damn broken. Removing her collar was the only way I could think of to jar her enough to dig deep."

Hammer clenched his jaw, but before he could rail at Liam again, the supervisor came on the line. After wasting precious minutes listening to a guy who barely spoke English, Hammer's patience ran out.

"Look, your driver picked her up at nine forty-three. Either give me the address, or I'll call the mayor," he blustered. "He's a good friend, and I'll have every one of your cabs red tagged for inspection with one phone call. Now give me the fucking address, you sniveling piece of—"

Liam grabbed the phone. "Excuse my friend. He's distraught. Do you have the address, please? This girl is in terrible danger. We're frantic."

Hammer heard the man on the other end talking. Liam scrambled for a pen and wrote down the information.

"Thank you so much." Liam ended the call, then whirled on Hammer. "What were you doing, threatening the only man who can help us? Keep your head screwed on straight." Then Liam shoved the paper in his direction. "The cabbie dropped her here. Where is this?"

Bringing up a map of the city, Hammer nearly choked when he spied the familiar cross streets.

"Motherfucker!" he roared, jumping to his feet. His entire body trembled as he turned to face his friend. "It looks like she's gone back home."

Liam blanched. "Where she lived with her father?"

"No, but close. A drugstore near her old neighborhood." Hammer's blood ran cold. He shoved the desk chair away and marched to the safe in his office, withdrawing an envelope. He turned to find Liam standing there. "We'll start searching there. On the way, you can tell me exactly what you said to Raine when you removed her collar. It might give me some clue where she'd have run." He pulled his keys from his pocket, anxious to follow her trail.

"Don't order me about like I'm one of your bloody subs."

"I'm going out of my fucking head, in case you haven't noticed." Hammer raked a hand through his hair. "We've got to find her."

"Then let's go."

They raced to Hammer's car. When Liam slid into the seat next to him, he peeled out of Shadows' parking lot.

As he watched the busy traffic crawling down the road, Liam buckled up. "Over the past week, Raine has crawled deeper into her shell. Even on a good day, she didn't communicate, she isn't honest, and she doesn't trust. None of that is news to you."

"No," Hammer admitted.

"I've tried 'modifying' her behavior in every way you can think of. I've punished and rewarded. I've coaxed. I've praised. I've demanded and expressed my disappointment. Nothing."

All that? Then again, Liam had never been less than thorough. Why would he have started slacking with Raine? He wouldn't. In fact, as devoted as Liam seemed, he would have tried even harder than usual to reach the girl. And if Raine was truly giving that little... Hammer wondered if he wouldn't have released her, too.

"Are you saying she's more shut down than either of us realized?"

"Now you're getting it." Liam leaned back against the seat, looking exhausted. "I made it crystal clear that I wasn't giving up on her, that I would be there for her. She didn't listen to me."

"All she heard is that you didn't want her," Hammer confirmed.

"Of course I want her. I tried to show her how much. Just because I'd released her didn't mean I'd stopped caring or stopped protecting her."

Who the hell was protecting her now? Hammer's inner voice screamed that he needed to go faster. Hot and urgent, his thoughts raced as he tried to focus on the road. But terror clawed—an ominous déjà vu— back to when Liam had taken Raine from Shadows and sequestered her far away. While he'd nearly lost his mind then, there'd been comfort in the fact that Liam was caring for her. She'd been safe. But now...

"Raine is out there alone, upset, feeling unworthy and unwanted by both of us. I hope to fuck she doesn't do something impulsive, like visit her father. Bill might be an old bastard, but he's still mean."

"Why would she go anywhere near her father? That makes no sense." Liam rubbed the back of his neck.

"It does and it doesn't. Raine will eventually realize that she needs to confront her past. Then it wouldn't surprise me if she paid daddy a visit. But I hope I'm wrong."

Ten long minutes later, Hammer pulled into the parking lot of the drugstore. The two men hurried inside and approached the young cashier. Her nametag read TONYA. The need to find Raine and hold her in his arms rode Hammer hard.

"Excuse me, lass," Liam whispered in a buttery soft lilt. He'd used this verbal seduction on women for years. "Might I have a wee minute of your time?"

"Sure," the young woman sighed with wide eyes and pink cheeks. She looked awestruck.

In unison, Hammer and Liam whipped out their phones, flashing the cashier different photos of Raine. Both turned to scowl at the other.

"Have you seen this woman today?" Liam asked.

Tonya stood nervously, nodding. But she didn't speak.

Fucking hell. Hammer reached for anything resembling patience. "So she was here?"

The blonde with the heavy black eyeliner and nose stud jerked her head in his direction, apprehension flashing in her pale eyes. She nodded again.

He'd had enough of her goddamn bobblehead bullshit. "How long ago? What did she buy? What direction did she go when she left? Was she with anyone, girl? Tell me now!"

"Hammer," Liam growled and shoved him to the side. "As you can tell, it's rather important we find this woman. Can you tell me anything about her?"

Tonya twirled her finger around a chunk of pink hair streaked through her platinum tresses. After what seemed like an interminable lifetime, the young woman stammered, "She, um, b-bought a bottle of tequila. About twenty minutes ago."

Hammer looked at his watch. It was almost eleven. Raine was either planning on getting shit-faced drunk or she'd bought the bottle to ply her father with so he wouldn't put up a fight when she confronted him. Or killed him. Hammer's blood ran cold. He wished to hell he knew where Raine's head was at, along with the rest of her hot little body.

"Did you happen to see which direction she left in, lass? Catch a glimpse of a car or taxi cab, perhaps?" Liam urged, turning on his Irish charm.

"I...I don't know where she went. She wasn't with anyone, just carrying a suitcase and looking sad." Tonya cast her eyes toward the floor. "I'm sorry I can't be more help to you."

Hammer let out a heavy sigh. Damn it, the girl standing before him screamed "submissive." He shouldn't have been so harsh. "You've done well."

Liam reached beneath her chin and tipped her head up, then gave her a warm smile. "Thank you. You've been very helpful, indeed."

As they raced outside the drugstore, both men scoured the streets in either direction, looking for Raine—a hotel, a bar, a restaurant, anything that might have snagged her attention. He saw all of the above and more.

"She could be anywhere." Liam gave voice to his concern.

Hammer pulled out his mobile again. "Raine's phone is still off." He pressed a few more buttons. "No activity on her bank account."

"How much money does she have saved?" Liam asked. "Can't be much. God knows, she likes her shoes and bags and frilly things well enough."

"A few hundred bucks," Hammer said grimly. "She's got no head for money. I took care of her expenses for the most part. I've had a bad habit of indulging her because I knew she did without so much as a child."

Liam's blistering glare said he hadn't known. "We'll discuss that later."

Whatever. Hammer didn't intend to budge. If he wanted to buy Raine something pretty, he would. "Do you think she left in the taxi again?"

"The supervisor said the driver dropped her here and left. Though I suppose she could have called for another one."

"But how? She hasn't turned on her phone."

"And Tonya didn't say that Raine made any phone calls from the store. I don't see a payphone." Liam double-checked with a glance, but shook his head.

"Then let's go. She wouldn't stay here. There's no reason. She'd have a suitcase in her hand. It's probably heavy. So is the bottle of tequila. She couldn't carry them for long."

"Right. And she wouldn't stay on the street." Liam frowned and reached for his phone, too. "Is there a bus terminal nearby? Or someplace to stash the suitcase?"

Hammer shook his head. "We're getting close to suburbia out here. Our best bet is looking for her at a restaurant or motel."

"She didn't eat breakfast. Or much dinner last night." Clearly, that worried Liam. "She's got to be hungry."

"We'll get back in the car and drive around. We can cover more ground that way. We'll stop at all the restaurants and ask a few questions. Maybe we'll get lucky."

They cruised up and down the road once, then peeked into fast food joints, a mini-mart, even roamed the inside of a pancake house. Not a damn thing. Minutes slid into an hour. Where the fuck could she have gone on foot?

"Does the city bus come out this far?" Liam asked, obviously wondering the same thing.

"I don't think so. We haven't seen one since we've been here. Let's stop and think." Hammer raked a hand through his hair as he jogged back to his Audi. "She'd want somewhere to set down her suitcase. I'm betting she's got plans for that bottle of booze."

"Is there a park nearby?"

"Yes, but she could get arrested for drinking in public. If she's the one drinking the tequila, she's going to want to do it in private. But if it's not for her..."

"Who else would it be for?" Liam prompted, following him.

"Her father. He's a drunk from way back. If she wanted answers, bribing him with tequila would be one way to get them. Son of a bitch," Hammer snarled as he pulled the car back onto the main drag. "I hate to say it, but we should pay a visit to dear old dad."

"Then let's go."

Hammer took off, gripping the steering wheel. "I need to prepare you for what you're about to see." Raine's childhood home was the last hellhole he wanted to visit, but if she was there, she needed him… needed them both, to rescue her. "Ol' Bill is a crafty son of a bitch. If Raine went there, there's no telling what he's done to her. And if he's laid a finger on her again, he's a dead man. I trust you'll help me bury the fucking body."

"That bad?" Liam scowled.

Hammer reached into the glove box and handed Liam the manila envelope he'd retrieved from his safe earlier. "See for yourself."

CHAPTER EIGHT

Finally, Raine caught a break. It was Friday. The hospital wasn't a large one, and Beck practiced in more than one location. But she remembered a passing conversation with him about the fact that he'd begun to office here on Fridays. Granted, he might be in surgery, but a roomful of patients in his waiting room gave her hope otherwise.

After Raine introduced herself and pleaded with his office manager, the woman finally agreed to tell the good doctor that she was here.

Beck came barreling in three minutes later in a long white coat and a dress shirt, looking surprisingly respectable. He didn't bother with preambles. "What's wrong?"

The rest of the people in the waiting room stared. Even the office manager didn't disguise her curiosity. She shouldn't have barged in on him at work, Raine realized. He was diligent about keeping his professional and private lives separate.

"Sorry. My mistake. You're busy. Will you just…call Hammer and Liam when you get a break and tell them I'm fine? I'm not in danger, and they don't need to look for me. That's it."

She turned for the door. Beck captured her arm in an unyielding grip, then he jerked her around. His face didn't change much, but his eyes… That was the glare of a disapproving Dom. He didn't say anything for a long moment, just let her feel his concern and displeasure.

"Stay here," he growled.

With a few steps, he marched over to the woman behind the counter. "Cancel the rest of my appointments for the day."

Raine gasped. "Don't do that. Please."

He ignored her. "Call Dr. Martin and tell him I've had something come up. See if he'll take my emergencies. I'm off call."

"Right away, Dr. Beckman," the woman said primly, then looked at Raine with unabashed interest.

Her eyes were probably still red. Her nose, too. She didn't have on a shred of makeup. Her wardrobe was only suited to a couch potato in football season. And she was holding a brown paper bag that couldn't be mistaken for anything except a bottle of booze. Horrifically embarrassed, Raine looked away.

"What would you like me to do about that consultation with the Mayo Clinic? It's in less than five minutes," the manager reminded. "You've already rescheduled on them twice."

Raine could see Beck biting back a curse. Then he stormed back to her. "Listen to me. On the first floor of the adjoining building, there's a cafeteria. Wait there. Give me fifteen minutes. You came to me because you need something, clearly. I'll help you." His stare sharpened as he grabbed her arm again. "Don't. Leave. Or you'll be sorry."

"Don't call them now," Raine blurted. She didn't know why—maybe everything was catching up to her or reality was setting in—but she teared up. "They'll come, and I'm not ready to see them."

"I promise. Just do as I say."

She thought about disobeying, about going back to her hotel room, downing her bottle, and...who knew what then. But she'd already disrupted his day, brought her problems to his office, and prompted him to change all his plans. He'd promised not to call Liam and Hammer in the next few minutes. She owed it to Beck to stay.

"All right. I haven't eaten all day anyway."

He nodded and released her. "Get something in your stomach. Fifteen minutes, princess."

Raine nodded, then left his office, feeling the stares of a dozen patients on her.

It didn't take long to find the cafeteria. They were nearly ready to shut down breakfast to begin preparing lunch. She must have looked pitiful because one of the workers sent her a glance full of sympathy and let her grab a few prepackaged foods before they locked up the counters, leaving the seating area open, with its silent but animated televisions flashing and the chairs empty.

Ignoring the beginning of a talk show, Raine reached into her wallet for cash. Damn it, she'd spent it all on her bottle. She hesitated. She couldn't put everything back after the woman had bent the rules for her.

With a sigh, she handed over her credit card. Maybe the guys wouldn't be tracking her movements. For all she knew, Liam and Hammer didn't care that she was gone. Despite his pretty speech, Liam had washed his hands of her. And Hammer...who knew? She hadn't seen much of him since Thanksgiving.

The woman swiped quickly and sent Raine on her way with a receipt. Setting her purse and the bottle on the table, she plopped into the chair with a cola and a breakfast pastry—and stared at them. She could have cooked something more appetizing at Shadows. Normally, she would enjoy feeding Liam something hot and wonderful. She always made extras for Hammer and left it in the oven. Strictly speaking, she wasn't supposed to, but he'd starve or eat junk otherwise. If she was already in the kitchen, how could it hurt to cook a little extra for someone who needed it? Of course, Liam would have prodded her to eat the something warm and healthy, too. Now?

Raine usually loved sweet things. The Pop-Tarts just depressed her.

What was she doing here? Where was she going? She had no damn clue.

Fighting back more tears, Raine pulled her phone from her bag and gripped it. She fought the urge to turn it on, call Liam, beg him… God, what good would that do? He'd just wanted to know if she loved him, and she'd been too afraid to make herself vulnerable to him.

She had to pick up, move on, grow up, figure it out. And she would. Raine didn't know where to start yet, but it wouldn't be with a teary conversation that would make Liam feel guilty enough to take her back only to have the entire cycle repeat again. Until she changed, that's precisely what would happen.

Dread snaked through Liam as he stared at the envelope Hammer had put into his hands. "What's this?"

"A visual of what daddy dearest is capable of."

With his guts in knots, Liam ripped into the envelope, yanked out the photographs inside, and got his first glimpse.

Oh god. Oh Raine. My poor wee lass. His chest buckled.

The photo was of Raine—much younger, but it was still his Raine. Her innocent face was swollen, colored in a rainbow of unnatural hues: black, blue, purple with shades of yellow and green. Her eyes were closed and so puffy, Liam wondered if she'd been able to open them. The lips he'd kissed so many times were split and caked with blood.

She'd been beaten savagely by a monster who'd meant to destroy her.

His first thought was that he wished he'd been there to protect her. He hadn't known her then, but Liam still felt as if he'd failed her somehow.

His second thought was that he would kill the man.

He took seething breaths to bring his rage under control. "Her father did this to her?"

"Keep breathing, man. It's a shock," Hammer said in a tone meant to soothe a wild beast. "I know."

How ironic. It was the first bloody time all day his old pal seemed to find his control.

"Breathe? Like hell! Answer my fucking question."

"Yes, her father."

The bloody prick they were headed to see. Liam stared down at the photo. There were more pictures he hadn't seen yet. He didn't want to…but he must. If he wanted to understand Raine, this was part of who she'd become. He hoped like hell she hadn't let it define her.

Hammer sent him an anxious glance. "I took those the night I found her. She wouldn't let me near her, even to give her first aid. So I called Beck over, and we slipped a sedative in her Coke. Once she drifted off, Beck made sure she didn't have any injuries that needed immediate attention. The following morning, I took her to a doctor he recommended. She examined Raine. Cracked rib, a couple of stitches, lots of bruising. The rape kit came back negative. She hadn't been sexually assaulted."

Thank god for small mercies.

But from this photo alone, the fact that Bill hadn't raped her might be the only one. Liam wanted to growl at the injustice Raine had endured. He didn't care if the pictures had been taken six years ago or yesterday. The agony her father had forced on her stabbed him with pure fury.

Dragging in a sharp breath, he shuffled to the next picture. Raine's arm, black with bruises in the shape of a man's hand. God, she'd been a skinny little thing. A grown man unleashing all his force on her would have overpowered her quickly. And no one had been there to stop him. How had Raine done it alone?

Another photo revealed a red, angry spot of torn scalp just above her ear, indicating she'd been grabbed and yanked viciously by the hair.

His eyes smarted. She'd been nothing but a scared child, enduring what that bastard had dished out. But by Christ, she'd escaped. No wonder running was ingrained.

The next shot was of her neck and chest. Deep gouges and cuts raked her flesh. More mottled bruises lay beneath the straps of her tank top. Liam could see discoloration around Raine's throat. Her father had tried to strangle her? Fuck killing the man; Liam wanted to destroy him.

At the lodge, he'd pried the girl open with pickles and chocolate. The memories of Raine's words that night rang in his ears. *I found out that I shouldn't mess with Dad's temper... He would never win father-of-the-year awards.* A fucking understatement. *He said he wouldn't go to jail for disciplining his stupidest, most willful...*

Jail was far too kind for Bill.

The Dom inside him wanted to hold her close and protect her. Eventually, he'd turn her over his knee and give her a few loving swats of his own for so grossly understating her past. He intended to make it clear that he wouldn't tolerate her lying or blatantly withholding information anymore.

But wasn't that why he'd uncollared her in the first place?

The enormity of her damage sank in.

All this time, he thought he'd made progress with her at the lodge, convincing himself that he would have dismantled her walls if he'd had more time. He'd blamed Hammer's "need" for stunting his ability to reach Raine. But now he feared that all the pickles and chocolate on the planet wouldn't have been enough for her to reveal the depths of her anguish.

Raine's soul was still torn. She nurtured her pain, using it like a shield to keep anyone from getting too close. He understood that she hid in shame. Her fear of abandonment and difficulty trusting couldn't be more clear. But these photographs proved that she'd rather outright lie than risk revealing her *real* self and letting anyone too close.

As soon as he found Raine, he intended to tell her that he grasped the hell she'd survived, but he would no longer let her use it as a reason to hide from him.

His stare fell upon the final photo. Hammer had pulled the sheet aside to reveal her sleek, supple legs. The bruises and scrapes on them infuriated him enough, but the sickening dark contusions staining her inner thighs ignited his blood. He couldn't contain his wrath.

"Motherfucker!" Liam's fist connected violently with the glove box.

Hammer cast a startled glance in his direction. "Take another breath. It was a long time ago."

"Not for me!" Liam roared. "And now this? I thought you said she wasn't raped?"

"She wasn't. When the doctor examined Raine, she confirmed that there was no trauma to her vagina. Her hymen was intact. But I think Bill sure tried."

Raine must have fought like hell.

Liam's fingers trembled, yet he was unable to look away from the photos. "Why didn't you show me these sooner?"

If Hammer had, he might have understood Raine better, taken a different tactic with her, been more patient. It might have made a difference.

"What was I supposed to do, Liam? Haul you into my office the night you collared her and whip these pictures out for you? She doesn't know I have them, and it wasn't my place to tell you."

No, it had been Raine's. But to Liam's mind, Hammer staying mute on the subject reeked far more of his desire to hoard the girl than to protect her privacy. He would only keep this terrible truth to himself because he believed that he alone should—or could—heal her. How ironic that he'd never even tried.

Liam's mind wandered back to his first day at Shadows, after arriving from New York. He'd known almost instantly that Hammer had far more feelings for the girl than he'd been willing to admit. In fact, their first conversation about her had been eye-opening.

"Tell me about Raine," he'd asked that first night.

Hammer had tensed. Anyone who didn't know the man well might not have noticed, but Liam had. Then, as if Hammer had forced himself to relax, he'd shrugged. "She's a runaway I took in. She works for me."

"Really, now? Is that all? You watch her an awful lot, mate."

"Of course. She's an employee under my roof. I take responsibility for her safety."

And he took it *very* seriously, too much for merely a boss. "I've heard whispers there's a standing edict that no Dom is allowed to touch her. Is there a reason?"

Hammer had drawn in a deep breath and acted as if he'd been gathering his thoughts. Liam rather thought at the time that the man had been fighting his temper. "Raine was abused before she ran away. She's not ready for what any of the Doms here would want or expect."

"Even you?"

"I've never given it much thought, but yeah."

Liam remembered sitting back in his chair, stunned at such a whopping lie. He'd bet money then that Hammer thought of the girl under him every damn day. Why had his best mate felt the need to lie to him?

"What do you think she needs in order to be ready, then? Maybe you ought to help her along."

Almost immediately, Hammer had shaken his head. "Time, space, security, maturity. She's vulnerable. No one touches her, including you. Any other sub under my roof is fair game, but not Raine."

While Hammer had made his rationale sound so noble, Liam had known better. The man might as well have wrapped her in barbed wire and posted a NO TRESPASSING sign around her.

It was then that Liam had realized Hammer was in love with her. Which explained why the man had never once mentioned the girl in the last six years.

As Hammer turned down another residential street, Liam dragged himself back to the present. They had to be nearing her father's house. Liam felt a fresh wave of fury that his old friend had kept so much from him for so long—the truth about Juliet, his feelings for Raine, and the extent of her damage at her father's hands.

Such a bloody fucking debacle. How much time and drama could they have saved if Hammer had been willing to come clean?

Beside him, Macen let loose a heavy sigh. "I'd hoped she would volunteer the fact that her father had abused her. I'm sorry she didn't."

Pot meet kettle.

"Raine mentioned it, but…" Liam held up the last picture. "She never described anything like this. Did she tell you straightaway that her father had beaten her?"

"No. It took months for her to tell me bits and pieces, but I guessed. Why else would she run away from home with nothing but the clothes on her back?" Hammer gritted his teeth. "The private investigator I hired located the violent prick in two days. When I went to visit him, he had fresh stitches on his cheek."

"What does that have to do with anything?"

"She admitted later that she fought Bill off with a kitchen knife. She slept with it under her pillow."

Liam could feel something slide sideways in his mind as the rage and frustration congealed. "Why didn't you kill the miserable wretch?"

"As much as I would have liked to, I had to make a deal with the devil."

"What?" Liam stared at Hammer as if he'd lost all his wits.

"I visited him and introduced myself, explained that I owned Shadows. I told him that his daughter was now under my care and that, under no circumstances, would he ever see Raine again."

"Why the fuck would you tell him all that?"

"I was harboring a minor in a sex club. I had to put all my cards on the table in case he traced her back to me. Then I had to figure out what he wanted to keep his mouth shut and his ass at a distance. Right away, he accused me of having sex with her and threatened to report me as a pedophile."

"You should have just killed him and been done with it," Liam hissed. "Or at least called the police."

"If I had, Raine could have gone to foster care. I refused to risk her being placed in a home worse than the one she'd escaped. And if I'd given into my violent urges, I would have gone to jail instead of being around to protect her."

Liam couldn't deny the logic, even if he hated the explanation. "Then what happened?"

"Bill and I came to an agreement. I promised not to plaster fliers of Raine beaten black and blue all over his neighbors' doors if he kept his mouth shut, didn't report me, and never came near Raine again."

"It couldn't have been that easy to make him agree to all that. What else did it take?"

Hammer tightened his grip on the wheel. "Two thousand dollars a month."

Another shock jolted Liam's system. "You paid that cocksucker for six months, until she turned eighteen?"

"No. I've paid him for over six years," Hammer replied flatly.

"Hang on a bloody minute. That's nearly one hundred fifty thousand dollars!"

"Yes, and I'm sure he's done nothing but drink it away."

"Why the hell are you still paying him? Raine became a legal adult years ago."

"Because I was determined to protect her, and that was the only way I could guarantee Bill would fucking leave her in peace."

Fuck all. Part of him reeled with the extent his pal had gone to protect the woman he loved—even before he knew he loved her. How could Liam not admire Hammer for the care and protection he'd shown Raine so unselfishly for so long? And what did that say about the man's devotion to her?

"I understand you can't be watching her 'round the clock. But you've got me to help protect her now. Between the two of us, we can make sure he never gets close to her again."

Hammer didn't say a word, just glanced Liam's way, his expression considering. "I'd never want to risk her, but… maybe you're right."

"I am." Liam slammed a fist into the passenger door. "I just hate that the bastard is still breathing."

"Yes, but Raine is, too. So the money I've paid him has been worth it."

"Does she know any of this?" Liam suspected he knew the answer.

"Not a fucking thing, and it's better if she doesn't. You need to keep this secret. If not for me, then for her."

Liam didn't like it and wondered if this confidence would come back to bite them both in the ass, but he saw Hammer's point. Raine's pride would sting. "Fine."

Finally, Hammer pulled to a stop in front of a two-story Craftsman-style home in a well-manicured neighborhood. Liam looked out the window. Everything looked so normal, so average. Everyone with their two newish cars and two point two kids. Looking around, he'd never think the people living here had anything more interesting to do than watch the lush grass grow. But Liam knew a brute dwelled within.

"Are you ready to meet dear old dad?" Hammer asked in a tone rife with sarcasm.

No. But Liam steeled himself. "As ready as I'll ever be. I'll try not to murder him. No promises."

Hammer gave him a grim laugh. "I'll keep him busy. You search every fucking room, closet, and cranny for her. Call out her name in case he's got her tucked away somewhere. He'd probably have her gagged so listen carefully."

Gagged? Fuck, holding his temper was getting bloody hard. "I will."

And if she's being held against her will, forget holding back the urge to slaughter him.

Hammer opened the car door. "Then let's get this over with."

"I'm right behind you." Liam emerged from the car.

Hammer knocked on the door. After a curse and a shuffle, it swung open. Liam got his first look at Raine's father.

A shock of snow-white hair stood off his scalp. His eyes were blood-shot and lifeless, but a familiar bright blue. The scar Raine had given him bisected one gaunt cheek with a thin white line.

The man was probably pushing sixty, but looked closer to eighty. A bulbous nose, cheeks full of broken capillaries, and a bloated belly showed the ravages of alcohol abuse. Some might have thought him a sweet old man, but Liam wasn't fooled for a minute.

Bill leaned against the doorframe with a nasty smile. "Well, well. I'm surprised to see you here, Master Pervert. Are you still fucking my daughter?" Then he turned to Liam with a sneer. The old man sized up his designer suit, Italian loafers, and luxury watch. Dollar signs cha-chinged in his gleeful gaze. "You banging her, too?"

That was it. Bill was dead.

Liam surged at the man with a snarl of fury, all semblance of control gone. When Hammer held him back, he fought like a wild man.

"Steady..." his friend warned in a low voice. "Let's find out what the bastard knows first."

Hammer barged his way into the house. Liam followed, ignoring the old man's stench.

Bill stared, and Hammer glowered at the man, his face every bit as threatening as Liam had ever seen it. "Where. Is. She?"

"Who?"

"Raine."

"Why would I know where to find that ungrateful little bitch?" Bill sneered. "Does it look like I have her tucked up my sleeve?"

Killing was too good for Bill. Liam would tear off his head with his bare hands, pour kerosene all over him, then light him on fire. When he lunged at the old man, Hammer held him back again.

"Did she come here?" Hammer demanded.

"You can't find her? That's priceless." Bill laughed.

"Answer the question now or I'll tear you limb from limb!" Liam couldn't contain his rage.

"If I know something..." Bill turned to Liam, eyes crafty. "What's that scrawny piece of ass worth to you?"

"How much do you want to live?" Liam growled, unable to believe this asshole had any genetic resemblance to the woman he loved.

"You going to hit me?" Raine's father challenged.

When Bill least expected it. "Answer us. Do you know where to find Raine?"

Hammer cut him off with a sharp jerk of his head. Right, he was supposed to be sweeping the rooms, hoping against hope that he wouldn't find her lying in one of them, half dead.

"Raine's whereabouts aren't up for sale today," Hammer said. "You get your monthly stipend and that's *all*. You and I are going to have a problem if she's here—or if she came to see you and you didn't call. Do we have a problem so far?"

"Did she run away from you, too?" Bill jabbed.

"Is she here, yes or no?" Hammer demanded. "I'm running out of patience."

"Maybeeeee," Bill taunted.

Liam prowled past the foyer and navigated a path through the piles of old newspapers littering the hall. He recoiled. The manicured façade of Raine's house was an illusion, pretty enough on the outside, but neglect and decay permeated the walls.

He searched the spare bedrooms from top to bottom but found only wrappers, junk mail, discarded boxes, and trash—even in the wide open closet doors. Everything stunk to high heaven. He choked back the urge to retch.

Liam knew the bedroom that had once been Raine's. The walls were a faded pink. A crinkled old poster of Justin Timberlake hung askew off one wall. A big fuzzy "R" dangled from a string above an old twin bed, stripped bare. Now the room had become a ten-by-ten trash can. Somehow, it made him hurt for her all over again.

As Liam hauled into the master bedroom, he coughed, forcing down the urge to heave. Inside, discarded takeout boxes, empty gin bottles, and overflowing ashtrays lay strewn everywhere. Hell, an atomic bomb couldn't have done more damage. He called out for Raine, jerking open the closet. Smelly clothes, stiff sheets, loose change, and old porn magazines assaulted him.

The master bathroom fared no better. Liam tried to ignore the filth of old whisker shavings and cheap aftershave mingling with the black ring of grime in the tub and urine stains on the floor. The linen cabinet was filled with ratty towels and more garbage. The cloying reek of body odor pervaded the air.

"She's not in the bedrooms," he called to Hammer, coming back down the hall and dusting his hand down his pant leg, trying to rid himself of a prickly, crawling sensation. Once he knew Raine was safe, he'd welcome the chance to return to Shadows and scald himself with clean shower spray and antibacterial soap.

How had Raine ever lived here? She wasn't mental about cleanliness, but she liked a tidy space and didn't mind putting in the work to make a room spick-and-span. More than likely, she'd cleaned up after the repulsive old man, and he hadn't bothered after she'd left.

Liam backtracked to the kitchen—and stopped in the doorway. Bill had obviously exhausted his supply of dishes and flatware years before. Paper plates caked with old food cluttered every surface. Cockroaches and rodent excrement mingled with other less identifiable layers of filth. The stench nearly dropped him to his knees.

Again, he opened every door and every cabinet, calling out, but no Raine.

The garage held nothing but a late-model economy sedan that had more than a few dents, a rusted-out washer, and a tilted dryer. Liam checked the interior of all and found no signs of struggle, blood, hair —or anything that led him to believe Bill had inflicted any trauma on her here.

The access to the attic was directly above Liam's head. He pulled on the cord, and the attached compact stairs unfolded. After a brief climb, he discovered the space occupied by insulation and a hot-water heater. Crawl spaces were laid out in plywood. He climbed up. The odors from the house had risen, and it smelled like a landfill. Thankfully, the area was small. His visual check took under a minute. Given the undisturbed inches of dust, Liam realized that Raine couldn't possibly have been here.

It was almost a relief. He couldn't stand the thought of her stepping foot in this grimy hoarder's dwelling again, at the mercy of that spawn from hell.

As he rounded the corner and made his way to the front door, he found Hammer fisting the drunkard's stained T-shirt and shoving him against the wall.

"Don't you keep her tied to the bed or something?" Bill sneered. "I'll bet she likes it."

Hammer growled. "What did you say?"

"I looked your kind up online, Master Pervert. I know all about you."

No, he didn't have a clue.

Liam surged closer. "Hammer, move. I'm going to hit him at least once."

"Believe me, I want to. His sorry ass isn't worth the jail time, and we can't find her from behind bars." But his old friend looked like he thought otherwise for a moment. Then he turned back to the unkempt bastard with thunder in his eyes. "Last chance. Have you seen Raine?"

"The stupid whore hasn't come back here."

Releasing Bill's shirt with a shake of his hand, Hammer stepped back, looking like he, too, was suppressing a murderous rage.

The old man leveled them a taunting sneer. "This is hilarious. She's got both your dicks in a meat grinder. She must mean a lot to you two."

"Not one more disrespectful comment from you," Liam replied in a cold, deathly calm tone. "Hammer, here, may have some qualms with ending your life, but I sure as bloody hell don't."

Bill glared at Liam. "I can't believe she's fucking a mick."

"I advise you against insulting my friend," Hammer said in silky warning. "You'll respect him or I'll shatter your goddamn jaw."

"She'd spread her legs for anything with a dick. Well, except me. Even when I tried to be nice to her, she never showed me any love."

White-hot rage roared through Liam's veins.

"Nice?" Hammer closed in on Bill again like a raging bull. "You tried to rape your own daughter. What kind of sick fuck does that?"

"Don't get all high and mighty." Bill didn't deny it.

Liam's chest heaved. Hammer wasn't faring any better. The old man was either too stupid to notice their fury...or he was baiting them. Liam didn't like it.

"Her worthless mother was gone, and Raine is pretty. But you know that, don't you?" Bill taunted, then looked at Macen. "Bet you enjoyed every minute of popping her cherry."

Hammer drew back his fist fast as lightning.

Liam gripped Hammer's bicep, holding him back. "You're right. We can't find Raine from jail."

But if they didn't leave, Bill would soon be a dead man.

"That's it," Hammer spat. "You're not getting another goddamn dime from me. Do you understand? And don't you dare threaten me. You just confessed to trying to force your minor daughter to have sex with you, and I've got a witness. I've also got a hundred people who can testify that I never laid a hand on her when she came to live with me."

"All deviants like you. We had a deal," Bill protested. "You can't cut me off!"

Hammer stared him down with narrowed eyes. "Watch me."

Macen's phone beeped and he plucked it out of his pocket, pausing, reading. "I just got a bead on her. She used her credit card. Let's go."

As Hammer ran for the Audi, Liam lunged in Bill's face. "I promise you someday, somehow, I will hunt you down like the animal you are and repay you for everything you did to Raine."

The door to the cafeteria opened, and Raine watched Beck march in, minus his white coat, looking grim and worried. He slid into the seat beside her and took hold of her chin, but her pathetic breakfast seemed to distract him. "That's what you chose to eat?"

"They didn't have a lot left."

He spied the receipt and picked it up. "You paid with a credit card?"

She sighed. "Yeah. I know what you're going to say. I doubt they're watching me."

Beck scoffed.

"Seriously, Liam released me this morning."

"Yeah? I can't speak for him since I don't know him as well, but I know Hammer will never let you go, princess. I can promise you that."

"He hasn't spoken to me in a week."

"Doesn't matter. He's been in love with you for six years." He glanced at his watch. "Let's go."

The man was hallucinating if that's what he thought, but Raine didn't argue. "Where?"

"I want to hear this story—without one or both of them interrupting. I want to make sure you eat something better than processed crap. And then I want to give you some advice that you'll probably ignore, but I hope you'll put to good use anyway."

She didn't have the energy to fight him when he grabbed her soda and pastry only to toss them in the trash can. She picked up her purse and bottle with a sigh.

As Beck led her out of the cafeteria, he settled a guiding hand at the small of her back and herded her to a parking garage. He hit a button on the key fob and a bright red Mercedes convertible beeped. Flashy wheels. It figured.

Beck opened her door. "Get in."

Raine slid into the soft seat in silence and watched Beck back out. "I'm sorry for causing you trouble. I shouldn't have come and bothered you here."

"Yeah, you should have. You know they're probably worried out of their minds."

Maybe, and the possibility made her feel a bit guilty. "That's why I wanted you to tell them I'm all right, just in case."

"Well, I'm not a liar, princess. So let's fill your belly and get you settled. Then I'll figure out what to say to those two clowns."

As they rounded the back of the hospital and approached the circular drive at the front, a familiar black Audi screeched into the passenger pick-up zone. Hammer and Liam jumped out, running full throttle into the building. Raine's heart caught in her throat. Guilt gnawed at her composure.

"I'll be damned. They stopped fighting long enough to look for you together," Beck observed, sounding oddly happy. "Want to talk to them?"

Yes. Desperately. But what good would it do? "No."

"Wait, did one of them hurt you?" he scowled, his expression like a thunder cloud.

Beck meant Liam, since he knew Hammer too well to believe that Macen would ever intentionally smack her except in play. But Liam could be so heartbreakingly gentle. Neither would ever bodily harm her.

Just break her heart.

"No." She tried not to cry again.

Why wouldn't this fucking useless sorrow go away?

"God, that face is killing me, princess." He pulled away from the hospital. "Is that all you have, a purse and a bottle?"

"No. I have a suitcase, too." She told him about the motel.

He pressed tight lips together and drove down toward the place. As soon as he pulled up front, Beck held out his hand. "Claim ticket?"

Raine hesitated. "You're not dragging me back to Shadows?"

"Nope. But you're not staying here. I've got someplace better and safer. And no, I won't tell Liam or Hammer until you want me to."

She gnawed on her lip. Beck might have messed with her mind here and there, but he'd never lied to her. She dug into her purse and handed the little scrap of paper over. He hopped out, then emerged two minutes later with her bag in hand.

After tossing it in his trunk, he eased back into the driver's seat. "You know if they ever catch up to you, they're going to spank you bright red. I'll watch. And volunteer to help."

Despite the grim situation, she managed a laugh. "Why am I not surprised?"

"Hey, you have a nice ass." He winked.

"The answer is still no." The last thing she wanted was another romantic entanglement, even if Beck was on the sexy side. She also didn't need more hurt. Physical pain might help her process the emotional agony eventually, but she didn't need it yet. And even if he'd do it, she hated to ask Beck for more.

He nodded. "Just trying to lighten the mood."

A few minutes later, he pulled up in front of a new, industrial-looking building of high-rent condos. He flashed a key card at the parking garage. After the gate went up, they slid inside. Beck parked in a reserved spot, grabbed her things, and helped her into an elevator.

"You don't have to do all this," she protested.

"If I don't want Hammer to kill me, I do. I don't want to worry about you, either."

On the top floor, he emerged and led her inside a corner unit. It was compact and sleek and had killer views that went all the way to the Pacific.

"The bedroom is through that door. Bath attached." He set her suitcase down. "You've already seen everything else."

"I don't want to take up your space. If you live here—"

"No. I crash here sometimes, especially after surgeries that run late. I've got a house about ten miles from here, closer to Shadows. You'll have the run of the place this weekend. The housekeeper just came, so it's clean and stocked with food. Sit." He pointed to the little kitchen table.

Raine sat as he bid, watching him move around the kitchen. "I'm a lousy cook, but I figure as many times as you've fed me over the years, I can return the favor this once."

"I'm not really hungry."

"I don't care. If you're going to get busy with Jose Cuervo, you need something in your stomach to toss up later."

With a wry smile, she waited until he set some eggs, toast, and a bowl of fresh fruit in front of her. "Thanks."

"Dig in. And start at the beginning."

Raine did, confessing everything between Thanksgiving and this morning. When she finished, her food was gone, tears streaked down her face, and her nose was running.

With a curse, Beck grabbed her a tissue from the bathroom, then stomped back. "What did you expect Liam to do, princess?"

"I don't know."

"We're not exactly friends, but I can guarantee that he didn't give up on you. He wants you to think, make some decisions."

"That's what he said."

"Then where do you get off with this bullshit that he's dumped you for good?"

"It's just...where my head always goes." Her mom had left. Then her brother and sister. Her father had never made any bones about his contempt for her, especially at the end. "They're the first people to really want me in their lives. I guess...I have trouble accepting it."

"Or trusting it. You're holding your breath, waiting for something bad to happen. When it doesn't, you create it, even if you don't mean to. It's all you know. And it's up to you to figure out why and how to change. All they want is your soul, princess."

Yes, and that scared the hell out of her. "What happens if I give it to them and neither wants it anymore?"

Beck leaned forward, bracing his elbows on the dark table. "You won't break. You're too strong, Raine. The more important question is, how much happiness are you throwing away because you're too afraid to give either of them a real chance?"

Maybe a lifetime of it.

She looked at Beck with bleak eyes. He patted her hand, then took her plate away. As he set it in the sink, the phone attached to his belt trilled. He yanked it from the clip. "And there are your knights in shining armor now. What do you want to do?"

Raine pulled the bottle from the brown paper bag. "Think. Got a shot glass?"

Beck pulled one from the cabinet and set it in front of her as he brought the phone to his ear. "I'll be back."

CHAPTER NINE

"What do you mean, Dr. Beckman has left for the day?" Hammer demanded of the office manager. "Explain."

Liam glanced at his Calibre de Cartier. It wasn't even noon. "You mean he's not merely breaking for lunch?"

The petite woman stood behind the counter of the empty waiting room, looking at the pair of them as if she'd lost her patience. She shoved her glasses back up the bridge of her nose and straightened her shoulders. "No, he canceled the rest of his appointments about an hour ago and told me to close the office for the day. If you had an appointment, you'll receive a call to reschedule. Now, if you'll excuse me..."

The woman glanced pointedly at the door, jangling the keys in her hand. She made it more than clear that she wanted them gone, probably to enjoy her unexpectedly free Friday afternoon. Liam glanced at Hammer. His old friend knew Beck far better, but playing hooky at the last minute didn't sound anything like the doctor. Beck could be a dodgy prick, but he wasn't irresponsible.

Liam could see that Hammer was a bit suspicious as well.

"You're Vicki, right?" Macen asked.

She looked surprised that he knew her name. "Yes."

"I'm a friend of Dr. Beckman, and he's spoken highly of your efficiency in the past," Hammer explained. "We need your help. We've got an emergency."

"If it's medical, you're better off in the ER." She scrutinized them quickly and frowned in confusion. "Adjoining building, first floor, at the back. I can call and have someone take you on a stretcher or in a wheelchair, if you need."

"No," Liam corrected. "Crisis might be a better word. We have a missing person and think that Beck may have seen her recently. Do you know if he received any unexpected visitors?"

The forty-something office manager set her keys down and looked as if she was weighing how much to say.

"The woman is petite, a few inches shorter than you. Dark hair, blue eyes. She would have looked distraught," Liam volunteered.

Vicki hesitated for a moment, then nodded. "She was here."

Oh, thank Christ! Relief flooded through him, knowing she was safe—or had been an hour ago. Beside him, Hammer looked equally relieved. Liam couldn't fathom for the life of him why she was with Beck, but he hoped like hell the sadist would have calmed her. Unless…

"Was she injured?" he demanded.

"No," Vicki assured, her starch softening.

"And? What happened then?" Hammer demanded.

The woman shrugged. "I don't know."

Liam frowned. "How long was she here? Did she speak to Beck?"

"Yes. Less than five minutes," Vicki said. "Dr. Beckman finished an appointment, then came out here to speak with her. I couldn't hear the discussion, but the doctor seemed somewhat agitated. He canceled all his appointments. The woman you're looking for left. The doctor took another call, then gathered his things and departed. He didn't say where he was going."

"He must have her," Hammer said under his breath.

Liam agreed. He was grateful...but bloody confused. Her reasons for seeking out Beck now didn't matter. He just had to lay eyes on her.

"Thank you, Vicki. You've been very helpful, and we'll not delay you any longer," Liam said.

Turning together, he and Hammer exited the office with its faux-friendly décor. They headed back down the corridor and bypassed the elevator to sprint down the stairs. Hammer was already reaching for his phone, scrolling through his list of friends.

"Why would Raine go to Beck?" Liam questioned. "A month ago, he scared the piss out of her. He bruised her with that fucking rubber paddle. Why would she run to that bastard instead of talking to me? I know she's got a terrible habit of not saying how she feels. But hell, if not to me, why didn't she go to you, then?"

"I could guess..." Hammer sighed and pressed the button to connect the call to Beck. "She must know I'd help her, but she's distressed and thinking with her emotions."

"I suppose she believes she's only 'making things worse' or whatever else runs through her head. Both of us have set her aside in one way or another. But how could she think we don't care?"

Hammer sighed. "She's probably embarrassed about being released or she thinks I would chide her for her behavior. I don't know. Goddamn it, answer," he growled into the phone as they tore out of the building.

In the anemic sunlight, they made their way to Hammer's car and peeled away. Liam didn't know where they were going. He didn't think Hammer did either, but Raine wasn't at the hospital. The cafeteria where she'd given her credit card was closed for now. When they'd checked, only an employee inhabited the gift shop. Raine hadn't been injured, so why would she stay here? More to the point, Beck had gone as well.

The car's Bluetooth system kicked in, and the ringing phone carried over the sound system. Anxiety charged his veins. If voice mail picked up instead of Beck, Liam wondered if he'd bloody lose it.

"Where are you going?" he asked Hammer. "Where would Beck take her? His house? Another office?"

"I don't know. Anywhere but here."

Liam heard a click and tensed.

"Well, it's about time you called, Hammer. I've been waiting," Beck baited on the other end of the phone.

"Where the hell is she, you fucking bastard? Where did you take her?" Liam wanted to charge through the phone and strangle Beck.

Hammer cut him a glare as the doctor laughed.

It took everything Liam had not to pick up Hammer's phone and smash it on the dash. If he didn't need answers so badly, he might. He opened his mouth to say something, not caring much if he insulted the wanker.

Hammer slapped an arm across his chest. "Shut the fuck up and let me talk."

There was little love lost between he and Beck, and Hammer stood a better chance of getting answers. Breathing hard, Liam swallowed down his impatience. "Get some answers."

"Where is she, Beck?" Hammer demanded. "Where did you take her after you left the hospital? And don't give me the bullshit that you don't know."

Beck laughed again. "It's hard to tell which of you has their dick in more of a twist."

Liam stared out the window and tried to block out Beck's mocking tone. His only consolation was that he felt anger pouring off Hammer, too.

"I'm glad we're so amusing," Hammer grated out. "We're not feeling very jovial at the moment since we're worried out of our *fucking* minds because Raine is missing. So maybe you could pull your head out of your ass and help us?"

With another chuckle that made Liam want to punch the arse, he sank deeper into the luxurious leather seat. He could only hope that he'd have Beck by the balls someday and could repay the favor.

"Oh, put your panties back on. Raine is in one piece and perfectly safe. I made sure of it."

"Where?" Hammer growled.

Liam wanted to add his two cents, and it only infuriated him more that every time he talked to Beck, the doctor took delight in poking at him. He'd love to tell Beck exactly where he could go, but that wouldn't help them find Raine. He had to swallow it back—again. He was beginning to feel like his balls were stuck in a bloody vise.

"If she wanted you to know, she would have told you herself, wouldn't she?" Beck heaved a sigh. "She's thinking with the help of Jose Cuervo, and I expect I'll have to check on her in a bit to help her hang her head over the toilet. But otherwise, she just needs space."

"You're letting her drink tequila in the middle of the day?" Hammer demanded.

"You think she's still a minor, scout?" Beck sounded somewhere between amused and exasperated.

"She can't hold her liquor, you stupid motherfucker." Hammer looked like he might grind his teeth into dust. "And you know it."

"Look on the bright side. She's usually a happy drunk, so tequila might improve her mood."

The mock chipper attitude crawled up Liam's back. That vise around his balls tightened.

"Hey," Beck added like he had a grand idea. "Is she a horny drunk, too?"

"Don't you touch her, you fucking wankstain!" Liam railed. "If you lay a single finger on her, I swear to god I'll kill you in the bloodiest way possible and I'll enjoy every moment of it."

Hammer clutched the wheel. "I'll be all too happy to help him if you don't stop yanking our chains."

Beck scoffed. "She's not going to jump off a bridge, guys. Geez, melodrama much? I'm not going to touch the princess. But you two have got to get a grip and back the fuck off. You can't tell her to go away one minute, then expect to keep her under your thumbs the next."

"I just want to bloody talk to her," Liam insisted. "She ran away from home."

"Left her keys to the club in her bedroom," Hammer confirmed. "Did she tell you that part?"

"Not in so many words. Raine is trying to decide what to do next. Neither of you can rush her decision."

"Why can't she think at Shadows?" Liam demanded.

"Really?" Beck asked incredulously. "If this stunning display of calm and logic is any indication, I have no trouble understanding why she left. Look, she's someplace safe, and I won't betray her confidence. I gave her my word and I keep my promises. When she's ready, she'll tell me, and I'll let you know. If it makes you feel any better, she's staying somewhere secure. She can't leave without me knowing. And no, I'm not trying to crawl in bed with her. So back down on the jealousy, lover boy."

Liam didn't have to guess who Beck was talking to. It infuriated him even more. On the other hand, he realized that the doctor had become a brick wall. There'd be no going under, around, or over him for more information. The click of the call ending confirmed that, like it or not, they'd have to wait until Raine decided whether or not to come back to Shadows.

Hammer glanced up as Liam stormed into the kitchen the following morning. He looked as lousy as Hammer felt.

"Did you hear from Beck again?"

Liam's question immediately told him that his old friend hadn't heard from Raine, either. "Just a quick text about midnight to say she'd finally fallen asleep. He emptied the rest of her bottle down the sink and made sure she ate before tucking her in."

"Nothing about what's going through her head?"

Exactly what Hammer had wanted to know. "Not a word."

They both looked at the empty coffee maker. He'd mocked Liam's attempt at making the brew yesterday, but Hammer couldn't do much better. They already missed Raine, but this, just like prowling the dungeon sleeplessly at three a.m., shoved her gut-wrenching departure in his face again. And now that Raine had been gone over twenty-four hours, Liam looked like he was ready to crawl out of his skin. Hammer totally understood.

"Why won't that wanker tell us what she's thinking? She's talking to him, right? What's she saying to him that's so bloody secret?"

"Whatever she wants. He won't break her confidence."

Liam raked a hand through his hair. "I don't like it. I think that prick has always wanted her."

"I know you and Beck got off on the wrong foot, but she's in good hands. The fact that she turned to him is a big fucking relief."

"How do you figure that?" Liam bellowed.

"That means that she doesn't want to cut all ties to Shadows. That might even mean she knows that she needs to listen to someone who won't spoon-feed her bullshit."

"He's a damn sadist!" Liam gawked. "She's not a masochist."

"Get your head back in the game." At least one of them had to remain calm, and Liam needed a rock right now. Looked like it was him. "Losing control isn't like you. You're too smart. Start acting like it."

"Piss off," Liam shot back, but it didn't hold any malice. He straightened up and seemed to pull himself together.

"That's better." Hammer nodded. "Don't worry. I know Beck. He's not going to beat Raine or take advantage of her. He'll do everything possible to help her clear her head and make some decisions. Beck and I talked about her recently. I'm confident he'll guide her back in this direction, if it's possible. But he's right. We can't rush her. If she comes back, we want her to be sure of her choice, not looking for the way out again."

"We don't know what bloody advice he's giving her. He could be telling her to fly off to Timbuktu, for all we know."

"He'll give her the exact same advice you or I would if we knew a sub was floundering."

"What if she doesn't come back?" Liam paced the kitchen, probably seeing Raine everywhere, just like he did.

"Then we have no one to blame but ourselves."

If he'd been honest with Raine eons ago, she'd still be at Shadows, safe and sound. The frustration clawing Hammer's guts would be nothing more than a bad dream. He gave her credit for walking out on her own two feet instead of taking a bunch of sedatives. At least he could be thankful for that. He'd rather have her alive anywhere in the world than cold in the ground.

Guilt crossed Liam's face before he stifled it and glanced at his watch. "A few days ago, Seth promised to come out for a bit. I got a text from him early this morning saying he was leaving LaGuardia and would take a taxi to Shadows."

"Seth, here?" *What the fuck for?* "He said he'd never step on land that might crumble into the ocean."

Liam hesitated, then turned squarely to face him. "I called to ask his help with Raine."

Whoa. Wasn't that a kick in the nuts? In the past, Liam would have come to him, and Hammer didn't have to guess what Seth's visit said about the state of their friendship. He regretted it like hell. Then again, he'd withheld the details of Juliet's suicide. Quid pro quo was a motherfucker.

The one piece of good news? Liam calling in reinforcements said that he was serious about helping Raine.

"I see. As usual, you have a plan. Want to clue me in?"

Liam rubbed at the back of his neck. "I already enacted the plan. It went out the back door when she ran off."

"Let me get this straight. Uncollaring her *was* the plan?" Hammer stifled his opinion of that colossal screw-up. "Got a plan B?"

Liam gritted his teeth. "I'm working on it."

A chime sounded from Liam's pocket, and he pulled out his phone. "Speak of the devil. Seth says he's in the parking lot and will someone open the fucking door."

His friend smiled for the first time since Raine had fled, then left the room. Hammer looked again at the coffeepot, wondering if Seth could do any better than either of them. He remembered the other Dom from his club days back in New York. Smart, firm, fair, funny. If someone from the past had to come back and haunt him, Seth wasn't a bad ghost.

A few minutes later, Liam and Seth rounded the corner. The other man hadn't changed much in the last eight years. He might look a little older—just like Hammer knew he did—but Seth had remained a fit, good-looking SOB. He probably still had subs falling at his feet. Not a strand of gray in that neatly trimmed golden hair. He managed to get sun, despite the New York winters. His green eyes were sharp with wit, as always.

"Hey, man!" Hammer held out his hand. "Good to see you. It's been a long damn time."

Seth shook his hand. "Too long. How the hell are you? You're looking good."

"Well, then it's better than I feel. Thanks for coming." He turned to the coffeepot. "You know how to work this? Liam makes tar, and I brew motor oil."

"That's not true!" Liam protested.

"You're right. That would be insulting tar," Hammer quipped.

Seth shook his head. "You two and your puppy dog faces... There's a fucking donut shop around the corner. Go buy a hot cup."

Hammer's hopes dwindled. "Shit. You can't make decent coffee either?"

"I don't step foot in the kitchen," Seth admitted. "How have you been drinking coffee all these years if you don't know how to make it and aren't buying it?"

"Raine."

"Ah... So she spoils you."

"How are you drinking coffee without making it?" Hammer asked. "I don't remember you being a Starbucks guy."

"I eat pussy really well. It gets me coffee and anything else I want." Seth flashed a cheesy grin. "It's a far more important skill than working that thing." He pointed to the coffee maker.

"We're fucked, then," Liam said.

"Why hasn't Raine made the coffee? Get her out here. I want to meet the girl who's got Liam's balls in a twist."

Hammer and Liam exchanged a glance, then Hammer gave his old pal an expansive gesture. "It's all you."

Liam shook his head and blew out a breath. "Let's go around the corner and buy a hot cup or two. This may take a while."

"Actually, we might need something stronger than coffee." Hammer sighed. "It's five o'clock somewhere, isn't it?"

"In Russia, maybe…" Seth frowned. "What the hell is going on?"

Liam raised a brow. "How many blondes does it take to go around the corner and buy coffee?"

"None, asshole," Seth shot back. "They delegate."

After ten minutes and a bit more teasing, they'd made their way to the donut shop, bought a gallon of coffee, and walked back to Shadows. Hammer poured a mug the second they hit the kitchen and drank half of it down in one swallow. He gave a moan of relief. Liam followed suit. Seth shook his head.

"It's not bad." Liam peered into his cup. "But it's not as good as Raine's."

No, it wasn't.

"Oh, you're both whipped by this girl and her voodoo pussy. Where is she? I want to shake her hand." When neither of them said a word, Seth frowned. "Spit it out. I haven't seen faces this glum in ages. Did you just find out there's no Santa Claus?"

"There's no Raine. We discovered yesterday morning that she'd left." Liam stared out the window.

Seth whipped his head around. "What?"

Liam and Hammer spilled all the gory details about the last twenty-four hours as Seth poured himself a cup of coffee and stared.

"I'll be damned. So the plan backfired." Seth scratched his head.

"And then some," Liam confirmed.

"Would Beck let me talk to the girl?" Seth asked.

Hammer exchanged a glance with Liam, then shrugged. "No offense, but she's closed off right now. She might be talking to Beck, but I don't know that for sure. And if she's not talking to any of us, she's not going to talk to a stranger. I'm going to text Beck for an update."

Liam nodded, obviously liking that idea. "Any news about Raine would be welcome."

CHAPTER TEN

When Raine woke about noon, Beck was there with some ibuprofen and a bottle of water. "You decide yet whether you want to go home or you're running away for good?"

"Good morning to you, too." She took the tablets and the water, then swallowed both down.

Beck grinned. "Just asking. Hammer has been texting me every hour on the hour since sunup. He and Liam want to know how you're doing and what you're thinking."

"I don't know." Raine clutched her head. "Did I fall asleep on the couch last night?"

"Yep. You and Cuervo were all cuddled up."

Raine had a vague recollection of Beck carrying her to bed, and she was more than a little embarrassed. "Sorry."

He shrugged. "I didn't take you for a *Rambo* movie marathon sort of girl."

"I didn't want anything romantic." It would only have made her sadder.

"What do you want to do today, princess? I've already made my rounds at the hospital, so I'm free if you want to talk or head out to the beach…or get a good spanking." He leered.

Raine shot him a quelling glare. "Behave."

"Why, when being bad is so much fun?"

She took another swallow of water. "I don't know what to do. I need to stop licking my wounds and come to some decisions."

Beck pushed a strand of hair from her face. "Those men want to help you be whole. There's no way they don't love you."

Liam did for sure. He'd tried so hard to reach her. The more she'd fallen for him, the more afraid she'd become. The more she'd pulled away. All the vows she'd spoken during their collaring ceremony? Raine knew she hadn't kept up her end of their bargain. She'd given him no choice but to release her.

Hammer? He cared for her in his own way. She hadn't failed him as badly. Mostly because he'd never set expectations or tried to take her in hand. Still, she knew in her heart that he must be disappointed.

In either case, she was going to have to grow or change or something because neither of them would accept her limitations forever. Liam had already made that clear, and Hammer was sure to follow. If she couldn't change, maybe she'd be better off moving on. "I don't know if love is enough."

"Bullshit." He leaned closer and leveled a contemplative stare her way. "I've been thinking about this, and I might have the answer to your problem. Do you realize you could have them both?"

She gaped at him in stunned silence. Had he prescribed himself some wacky pills? He must have because that notion… "You're insane."

He chuckled. "A lot of people think so, and maybe it's a little true. But I'm right. Deep down, you know it. Even deeper down, you want them both, too. Admit it."

Raine felt heat rush to her cheeks. She'd fantasized about that a few forbidden times when she'd let herself. She'd cuddled up to Liam in the middle of the night, thinking how complete it would make her feel to be sandwiched between him and Hammer. She'd always dismissed it as a pipe dream.

"What I want and what I can have aren't even on the same planet."

Beck smirked. "Think positive."

"If I can't even handle Liam's expectations, how do you expect me to please him and Hammer?"

"They'll teach you. Stop fighting and pay attention. Figure your shit out. You're smart, Raine." He leveled her a serious stare. "They've shared before. For the right woman, I think they'd do it again."

And Beck thought that was her? "They shared Hammer's wife, and in case you weren't aware, that didn't end well. Besides, they can't get along for two minutes."

"That's a temporary pissing match. And it's not your problem. Your issue now is helping you. If you do that, all your little dreams might come true. You could heal those two by giving them what they both need most. That's you, Raine."

Raine still thought Beck was a little insane, but her head hurt too much to argue. This mythical threesome wasn't the point of their conversation. "If I go back to Shadows at all, I owe them a whole me. Their feelings are wasted if I can't give either one of them—much less both—everything in return."

"Right. So what's in your way?"

What wasn't? All her emotions were a crowded tangle in her head. The fear of being abandoned or hurt had been carved into her soul. Reacting to them was a reflex. How did she stop that?

Raine had to find a way. The last twenty-four hours had proven that living without them made her utterly miserable. She wanted to go home, wanted the familiar shelter of Shadows, of their arms. Despite what he'd said the last few weeks, Hammer would never commit to her. But that was okay; she could love him from afar. She'd been doing it for so long, she was a pro. She loved Liam so very much. He filled her heart. They could be happy—if she could hurdle her fears and move forward.

The first step was brutal honesty.

"My dad." For starters, anyway. "He had all the power in the house when I was a kid."

"And he abused it, along with you."

Raine resisted the urge to grab the covers up to her chin and protect herself. From what? Beck was only here to help her, and she had to stop hiding from everyone. It only led to self-destruction.

"Yeah. I've avoided really thinking about it, but…I know it—*he*—is a stumbling block."

Beck sat back and stared. "Have you talked to anyone professional about it lately? I know Hammer took you to see a counselor right after you came to Shadows."

She sighed impatiently. "She asked the dumbest questions. 'So I guess your dad's behavior made you mad?' Um, you think?"

He stifled a laugh. "So she wasn't the therapist for you. She wasn't very good in the sack, either."

Raine batted Beck's shoulder. "TMI, dude."

"That sounds a lot like back talk, princess."

The warning was too obvious to miss. She dialed back on the banter. "Sorry. It wasn't meant that way. I appreciate everything you've done. I know you didn't have to."

Beck waved her away. "You haven't seen or talked to your dad since you left home, right?"

"No." She recoiled. "God, no."

For a long time, he said nothing, and Raine sensed that he weighed his words carefully. Finally, he rose from the edge of her bed. "Okay, then. Food? It's after noon, but I figure you're hungry."

"Are you?" She rose and batted down her self-consciousness about her skimpy tank and boy shorts. Despite his half-hearted flirting, the rapport between them wasn't sexual. Besides, Beck had seen most everyone at Shadows naked, including her. He was a doctor. She didn't have any parts different than his patients or the other females walking around the club.

He got a gleam in his eye. "You offering to cook? Bachelor food and hospital cafeteria garbage sucks."

She laughed. "I'll be happy to. Give me a few minutes, and I'll make something divine."

It was the least she could do.

After brushing her teeth and hair, Raine washed her face, then changed into a pair of yoga pants and a faded sweatshirt. Slipping on a pair of socks, she padded into the kitchen. Beck stood on the balcony, looking out toward the ocean.

For years, he'd been a mystery, other than the pain he inflicted on subs at the club. When they'd first met, she'd lumped him in with her father mentally a bit, and it hadn't been fair. The subs asked for his pain— begged for it. But this personable, compassionate side of him surprised her. Why should he be single when he could tempt just about anyone? Raine didn't understand. Even now, his profile looked pensive…unhappy. She hoped he found what he was looking for soon.

In the kitchen, she made herself at home. Beck's housekeeper had obviously found a gourmet grocery store because Raine found all sorts of goodies. She seared him some bacon-wrapped scallops, sautéed vegetables, and whipped up a heap of garlic-parmesan mashed potatoes. He'd left a bottle of sauvignon blanc chilling in the fridge. She brought two glasses and the bottle out to the balcony, along with a corkscrew. She schlepped napkins, forks, and took two full plates next, then set them on the little table.

The day was chilly, the wind blowing. The almost perpetual fog near the coast blanketed the air. Raine hadn't made any decisions about what to do or how to do it yet, but somehow a new peace outweighed the turmoil that had made her a hot mess yesterday.

Beck took a bite of his scallops. His eyes rolled into the back of his head, and he moaned loudly. She'd heard him have quieter orgasms.

Raine giggled. "So you like it?"

"Oh, princess. Forget Liam and Hammer. Come live with me."

"I'll take that as a yes." She rolled her eyes.

"Are there seconds? And dessert?"

"No, and I'll see what I can do."

Beck sighed in bliss. Then they fell into a comfortable silence as he poured the wine and they ate.

Thoughts turned over in her head. And over and over. She'd struggled for so long with Hammer, fought Liam's every attempt to reach her. But Beck asked such a simple question. *So what's in your way?* And when she'd admitted that she hadn't seen her dad in over six years, he hadn't said a single word about it. But his expression had been clear. She should.

Raine's first instinct was to run. God, when had she become such a coward? More to the point, could she ever be happy if she kept ducking and dodging everyone who simply wanted to know her?

"I should face him," she admitted.

"Liam? Hammer?" He shoved another bite of potatoes into his mouth.

"My dad."

"At some point," he agreed.

Why wait? Prolonging this limbo wouldn't give her any way to move forward. "Today."

"That's…decisive." Beck drew in a breath, considering. "Let's talk about that for a minute. Do you know what you're going to say?"

Raine had rehearsed so many speeches in her head, mostly after she'd first gone to live at Shadows. But so many of the words crowded her head now, she wasn't sure where to start. "I'll think of something."

Beck set his fork down. "He's dangerous. I can't let you see him without going, too. I'll give you space to talk to him, but I won't be far off."

Raine considered that for a long moment. She'd pondered storming her father's castle before, but always pictured going with a gun…then rethought it because, frankly, he scared her. At least a foot taller than her and a whole lot meaner, he'd probably take the gun away and shoot her. Or she'd see him, lose her damn temper, and shoot him on the spot. Prison didn't sound like fun. A few times she'd considered that doing hard time might be worth killing the bastard, but something had always held her back.

"I can't put you at risk." She shook her head.

"Well, either you and I can go together, or I'll stick about ten feet off your sweet ass all day, and you can pretend not to notice me. Your pick."

"Amazing choices, Beck." Inside, she turned warm. Who would have guessed that the rubber paddle-wielding sadist would turn out to have a huge heart? His kindness and protection were a surprising but blessed relief. "I guess you can go with me, then. I'd feel better if we had more backup."

"Oh, we will. My friends Smith and Wesson are coming along." He grinned. "I'll clean up the dishes. You get ready. An hour?"

"Thirty minutes. I'm not getting dolled up for that old bastard."

"Good girl."

The plan made sense and sounded so liberating when she'd been tucked away in the safety of Beck's condo. Zipping down the road toward her childhood home half an hour later...not nearly as much. Raine's stomach twisted. She wrung her hands. Her palms started to sweat. Her heart thundered.

Beck put a hand on hers. "It's going to be fine. Say what you need to say. You'll be safe. The most important thing is that you purge as much of your anger as you can."

"I really can't thank you enough." She looked at him gratefully.

"Then stop trying and go get him, princess." He pulled his Mercedes up to the curb at the end of the block and rolled up to the house slowly. "This it?"

Her heart lurched as she nodded. "Yeah."

She'd been more terrified in her life, but not in a long, long time. Hammer had taken her in and given her the safe environment her father hadn't. She'd repaid him by running away without a word. Just like she'd given Liam a brick wall rather than her heart.

With another glance, Raine drew in a deep breath. She was doing the right thing.

Beck stopped the car and killed the engine, then climbed out. She opened her door and looked around. Nothing much had changed in the neighborhood. Mr. Markland's religiously trimmed shrubs stood in a meticulous, straight line. Mrs. Fullsome's garden looked full of color, despite the fact that December had begun.

As she stepped onto the sidewalk, she turned her attention to her father's house. The red front door had faded, but it still looked imposing. Behind that solid surface lay a house of horrors. Each year—hell, each day—had turned exponentially more terrible. Raine stared at the house like it was a demon that would steal her soul.

She clutched her stomach. God, she needed to be unshackled from her past, but she did *not* want to be here. She'd vowed never to lay eyes on Bill Kendall again. For six years, she'd kept that promise.

Now, Raine forced herself forward, determined to take back the parts of herself he'd maliciously stolen.

Beck walked with her to the edge of the property, then he grabbed her hand, squeezed...and let go. She sent him one last stare. He nodded at her. Silent encouragement.

Later, she'd tell him again how grateful she was that he'd come along.

Time now to face down the devil.

Sucking in a bracing breath, Raine knocked.

It seemed like forever before the door jerked open. Her knees nearly went out from under her when her father stood in the portal, glaring when he laid eyes on her.

His stark gray hair stunned her. He'd been salt and peppery the night she'd run away. The grooves around his mouth and chin had deepened, as if he'd been wearing an angry scowl every moment since she'd gone. The faint white scar of her handiwork slashed down his cheek. The sight brought back both brutal memories and deep satisfaction that she'd fought Bill off and marked him for the rest of his miserable life. His blue eyes hadn't changed. They were the same eyes she saw every day when she looked in the mirror.

At the venom there now, a shiver wracked her spine.

The monster still resided inside the old man's frame. He'd once terrified her. Now, Raine refused to show fear. Bill Kendall was the reason she couldn't trust. Couldn't communicate. Wouldn't truly give herself to Liam—or anyone. Since leaving this hellhole, she'd never wanted to heal. Lancing her wounds and leaving them to bleed made it less likely that she'd ever allow anyone to hurt her again. *She* had let this vile asshole strip her ability to love.

Never again.

"What are you doing here, whore? And who's he?" He nodded Beck's way. "I suppose you're fucking him, too?"

She ignored his question and thrust her chin out. "I've got a few things to say to you."

"Why should I listen? I didn't want you here then and I don't want you here now."

"Believe me, I'm not staying. I just came to say that I hate you and you'd better not *ever* speak to me again. Oh, and I wanted to give you this."

Raine doubled up her fist and sent it flying into his jaw with a brutal crunch. Pain exploded through her fingers, zipping up her arm, but she didn't care. When Bill's head snapped around and he clutched the side of his face, it was worth the pain.

"You little bitch!" He stormed onto the porch and seized her arm in a cruel grip. "You're going to pay for that."

With a vicious yank, he dragged her toward the house. Raine dug in her heels. Bill turned and snarled, raising his fist to her. She fought the urge to cower.

Behind her, Beck dashed onto the porch. "Need help?"

"Fuck off," Bill sneered.

"I got this," she told Beck. She *needed* to face her father alone.

Thankfully, Beck let her.

Forcing the tension from her muscles, Raine waited for the old bastard to assume she'd given up and curled into a sniveling ball. He fell for her ruse, swinging his beefy fist toward her with unabashed triumph. Suddenly, she countered, raising her forearm and blocking his attack. She followed that with a jab to the stomach. He roared, the sound booming with shock and hate.

Raine kneed him in the balls.

Lurching and grunting, he doubled over, clutching his crotch. She seized the opportunity and grabbed his hair, then slammed his head against the doorframe.

He screamed.

Beck laughed. "Yeah, you definitely got this, princess."

"I'll thrash you for that." Bill lifted his head to look at her with a stare so furiously blue, his eyes almost glowed. Blood trickled from a gash between his brows, ran down his face, and gathered between his teeth.

He looked every inch like a demon.

"Don't you ever touch me again. I was a girl, and you beat me within an inch of my life."

"Isn't that what Master Pervert and the mick do to you before you spread your legs for them at that kink club?"

She gasped. Of all the things Raine expected to spew from his lips, the fact that he knew where she'd been and who she'd been with felt like a kick to the stomach. Had her father tracked her down...or had Hammer and Liam come here looking for her?

Either possibility made her sick. She swallowed the nausea down. *Later.*

"Shut up! I won't let you desecrate them. They're *real* men, which is more than you could ever say." Raine doubled up her fist again and delivered a quick uppercut to his chin.

"Filthy slut! I'm going to call the cops on you."

"Go ahead, and I'll tell them everything you ever did to me, including trying to rape me as a minor. Want that to get out? Should I shout it louder for the neighbors?"

The anger built and swelled inside her like a volcano. The lava in her veins bubbled over, and Raine hit him again, his nose the perfect bull's-eye. After a sickening crunch, blood spurted.

"Hammer made me attend self-defense classes. If you try to hurt me again, so help me, I'll kill you, you worthless piece of shit, for all the years of misery you caused me. You drove my mother away, then my brother, my sister...and finally me. You deserve every moment of your wretched solitude. Rot in it!"

Raine clenched her fist again, but a firm hand at her elbow stopped her. She turned to find Beck shaking his head—and his gun pointed in Bill's face.

"You've done your damage. He's not worth a trip to jail. Let's go."

She'd love to stay and inflict more pain. It was exhilarating. Empowering. Emancipating. But Beck was right. She refused to imprison herself in any way because of Bill again.

The adrenaline began to bleed from her veins, leaving her slightly shaky. But she felt more together than she had in years. No, ever.

She nodded. "I'm ready."

"This isn't over!" Bill screamed. "Walk away, you fucking cunt, but you haven't seen the last of me."

She didn't bother turning around, just raised her hand and flipped him her middle finger. The bastard didn't deserve anything more.

They arrived back at the condo. Beck let her in quietly. In fact, he hadn't spoken a word to her since they'd left her father, like he'd known that she needed to be alone with her thoughts, replay the afternoon a few times in her head to feel the upsurge of triumph... then the downhill slide into wondering what came next.

Instead of heading straight back to his place, Beck had driven her to the beach and let her walk, silently trailing a few feet behind and keeping an eye on her. The crashing waves had quieted her head some. Not nearly as well as Liam's spanking days before Thanksgiving, but this worked for now.

Eventually, she'd sat in the sand, closed her eyes, and cried until Beck picked her up and put her in the car again.

Now she glanced at the clock on the oven. Ten minutes to six. "You hungry? I saw you had some steaks in the fridge. I can cook those up."

"Would cooking clear your head or would you rather have pizza?"

"I'm actually not hungry."

"Skipping dinner isn't an option. Choose again."

Raine sighed. "I'll cook."

"You want another bottle?"

She grimaced. "No. Hair of the dog doesn't appeal at all to me."

"Good. That's the first time I've seen you be a sad drunk. It sucked."

"Gee, I'll be more considerate of your delicate mood next time." Raine rolled her eyes.

Beck swatted her on the ass. "Sassy little thing. I'll start the barbeque."

"They're better in the oven. I got it."

Forty-five minutes later, they sat down to dinner. Afterward, Beck answered a couple of texts, then swore. "I have to head to the hospital for a bit. You'll be okay here? You won't do anything stupid?"

"Like jump off the balcony?" Raine looked at him like he was crazy.

"Like run off," he said pointedly.

She lost her feisty mien. "No. It doesn't work anymore."

He grabbed his keys, then kissed her forehead. "That's progress. You've done good."

"Should I have breakfast ready in the morning?"

"I'll have to see how this goes. I'm probably headed to surgery. If that's the case, I'll be back tonight, really late."

Then he was gone. He was asleep on the sofa when she woke the next morning.

Raine whipped up some pancakes and set them in the oven with crisp bacon and a note. Then she slipped out to explore the building. Sure enough, the swanky place had snazzy fitness equipment. A circuit of weights and cardio helped clear her mind a bit more, and she returned to find dirty plates in the sink and the word *Thanks!* at the bottom of her note. Beck himself was gone.

She wandered around the little apartment, but she'd already seen it all and exhausted the available movie selection. Cable shows about silly chef challenges and house hunting didn't hold her interest.

Palming her phone, Raine stared at the little device, but like last time she'd pondered making calls, she tucked her mobile away. It wouldn't be fair to Liam if she called just to hear his voice when she didn't have any answers to give him. And it would be equally unfair to ring Hammer for his gruff familiarity. She had nothing to offer him, either.

Raine whiled away the day on the balcony, just thinking. How did she learn to open herself up to the people she loved, especially if those people were at one another's throats? How did she go back to Shadows without tearing everyone apart even more?

Beck dragged in about eight o'clock. She'd been about to open a can of soup, but he took it from her hand and led her out the door. "Mexican and margaritas. Now."

Who was she to argue with that?

"I know a great place." She smiled.

"Perfect." He handed her the keys. "You drive. I'm fucking exhausted."

Wow, the control freak was going to let her drive his ridiculously expensive convertible? She grinned. "You're on."

Fifteen minutes later, they sat with some salt-rimmed beverages and had ordered enchiladas.

Beck sighed. "Ah, chips and booze revived me."

"You're such a man."

"I'm also a Dom. So here's the portion of the day where I ask you to tell me what's in your head. What are you going to do next?"

"I gave that a lot of thought while you were gone."

"Only because you didn't want to watch *Rambo* again. I know it."

Her life was upside down, and Beck still made her giggle. "Okay, that's kind of true."

He winked at her. "So, cough it up, princess. I love having you crash with me. I could get addicted to the food really fast. But I'm back on call starting tomorrow, and you won't like me coming in and out at two a.m., and that couch made my back hurt like a bitch."

Beck deflected the importance with humor, as he often did. But he was also dead-on.

Raine dragged in a breath, trying to decide how to ask her questions. "If I go back to Shadows, what are my obligations?"

"To Liam?" He shrugged. "Nothing. He uncollared you. That makes you fresh meat, and I'm pretty sure all the lions will circle now. Hammer's threat probably won't keep the beasts away for long."

She doubted anyone would want to take on a mess like her after she'd put Liam through the wringer, but it wasn't important. "What are my options?"

"You can do whatever you want. Are you looking for another Dom?"

The bowl of chips suddenly looked really interesting. Okay, so she couldn't meet Beck's gaze.

Raine bit her lip. "I think I need one."

"I think you do, too."

So she'd gotten that part right. The affirmation was nice, but it was the rest that stumped her. "What do I do?"

"Who do you want?" He held up a hand. "Let me rephrase that. Who do you think is most equipped to help you?"

If she could open up, both Liam and Hammer knew exactly how to reach her, but with so much history—and so much of it bad—would they? Obviously, Beck thought so, but…

Sifting through her other options, she forced herself to look at him. "Would you do it?"

"No." His answer was so swift and emphatic, it stunned her.

"Can I ask why?"

"Sure. I like my balls where they are. Hammer would *kill* me. Liam would bury me. I like you, princess, but…no."

"But we wouldn't be sexual. In fact, it's better if it's not."

"It wouldn't matter. They couldn't handle seeing you give your power to me."

And she'd likely drive a wedge between Hammer and Beck, too. "I'm sorry. It was unfair of me to ask."

"No, it was logical. You need help; I could help you. It burns me to say no, but at the end of the day you need someone who doesn't mind losing their balls and who doesn't want to fuck you more than they want to help you."

"You're right."

But who?

"Look, you need to really give yourself in a way you never have. I get that you're going to have a hard time with trust. After what I saw yesterday, I totally get it. And by the way, I wanted to shoot the son of a bitch for trying to rape you. I'm sorry."

"It's ancient history, and I need to put it in the past, but thanks."

Beck nodded. "You already know Dominance and submission isn't about sex, but exchanging power. You, as a sub, give your control over to the Dom, who takes, treasures, and molds it into something that will complete you. When you finally start giving yourself in return, you'll find the beauty. The reward will be worth the struggle. But no one can fulfill your deepest needs until you let them know you inside and out, deep down, to the tiniest recesses of your heart."

"I'm not so good at that." She winced.

"Think of it this way… I wouldn't go to the tire store and buy half a tire because I wouldn't get anywhere on it. With submission, if you're not willing to give your all, then like that tire, you'll be at a standstill, princess. It's all up to you."

Their waitress delivered the enchiladas, and they dug in. Beck bought dinner. Raine chewed on his advice. As they walked to the parking lot, the crisp wind whipped through her hair. But it was good to feel alive and finally have direction. "I know what to do."

Liam sat at the bar with Seth and Hammer, barely listening to their chatter. Another pointless day of waiting and worrying weighed upon him. If he had to spend another hour twiddling his thumbs, he'd go stir-crazy. Why hadn't Raine returned? Or at least contacted him? It was driving him batshit mad.

The numerous texts Hammer had exchanged with Beck hadn't shed a speck of light on her location—or her thoughts. The fucking evasive wanker just kept saying that he wouldn't break her confidence. What gave him the right to keep Raine away? Liam ached. Five minutes alone with her—that's all he wanted so he could figure out what rolled around in her head.

He sighed and eyed the bottle of water in front of him. Ten thirty. Night had long ago fallen. The club was closed on Sundays, and the unsettling quiet scraped him raw. Raine probably wasn't coming back tonight. The agony of being shut out of her heart and life wrenched him, and it looked like he had another day of hell coming.

Liam's only consolation was that Hammer obviously shared his pain. That didn't give him the satisfaction he'd imagined. The man wore his worry in the lines of his face and the dark circles under his hazel eyes, which matched the baggage under his own. Liam drained his water. There was no hiding the fact that neither of them was getting much sleep.

He gazed up at the illuminated glass shelves behind the bar, eyed the rows of colored bottles that called to him, promising sweet oblivion. But he couldn't risk it. He needed to keep his wits in case they got a lead on her whereabouts. There was too much at stake to have his brain muddled with booze.

Still, remaining on the tall barstool and not pacing the floor like a lunatic was a bloody chore. Shadows felt haunting and empty without Raine. Every moment clawed at his composure.

Over and over, he kept reliving their last morning together. He'd seen the love pouring from her eyes. He'd felt it. Hell, he'd nearly been able to taste it in the air. In that moment, he'd believed with every fiber in his being that he had finally, unequivocally reached her.

The unadulterated bliss had vanished when Raine had been unable to tell him how she felt. She'd backpedaled behind her walls and shut him out. Why had her love for him frightened her so badly? She hadn't trusted in their bond, despite his painstaking effort to build it. Surely she knew he'd never let her fall, that he would be her safety net, no matter what.

Then again, maybe she didn't know.

His visit to the Kendall house rolled through his brain like a bad horror film. Her vile excuse of a father, coupled with the pictures of her frail body beaten and bruised, had gouged out a chunk of his soul. And he'd only witnessed the heartbreak. She'd lived it, and he could only imagine what that had done to her psyche.

If he'd known then what he knew now, he'd never have removed her collar. He'd change everything, wrap her in his arms and reassure her that she'd never have to feel lost and alone again. He'd promise her that she could reveal all the secrets she hid deep inside, and no matter what, he'd still be by her side, protecting, nurturing, and loving her.

Seth said something and Hammer laughed, drawing Liam's attention back to their conversation. He smiled as if he'd heard the comment instead of being lost in the dream he'd let slip through his fingers.

A strange creaking from the vicinity of the front door broke the hush of conversation. Hammer snapped to attention. Liam didn't recognize the sound, but Hammer tensed, braced his hand on the bar. The lines of worry on his face gave way to something like anticipation. Liam didn't know what the hell was going on, but he turned to the sound, damn near holding his breath.

"Anybody home?" a deep voice echoed from the entrance.

Beck.

Liam's heart stopped, then started pounding ninety to nothing against his ribcage. He shoved away from the bar, and his stool crashed to the concrete floor with a deafening boom. Hope soared. If Beck had come, maybe he'd brought Raine. Right on the heels of that thought came the worry that the prick had stashed her somewhere and simply meant to rub more salt into their wounds. If so, Liam vowed he'd beat the bloody crap out of the bastard.

Heart chugging, blood surging, Liam charged for the front door. Hammer dashed beside him. They rounded the corner. Beck slid past them and headed toward the sleeping rooms, holding a familiar suitcase as he and Hammer both stopped and stared toward the portal.

With raven hair pulled away from her bare, pale face, wearing a sweatshirt that nearly swallowed her whole, there Raine stood.

CHAPTER
ELEVEN

H er blue eyes said she was both wary and contrite. She looked spent.

For a split second, he wondered if he were dreaming, but there she was, meeting his stare with a pensive expression.

Relief gushed through Liam's bloodstream. The gods had finally granted him mercy. "Raine."

"Thank fuck." Hammer barreled toward her. "Where the—"

"Bloody hell have you been, love?" Liam finished Hammer's question and raced toward her, trying to beat Hammer. "Do you have any idea how—"

"Wait." Raine held up her hand, forestalling them both. "Please."

As confusion pelted him, Liam's steps stuttered. She didn't want to talk to him? His brows furrowed. Hadn't she come back to him?

"I..." Raine swallowed tightly, casting her eyes down for a heartbeat before she raised her chin and licked her lips.

"What the hell's wrong?" Hammer barked. Concern stamped itself all over his face. "Precious?"

"There's something I need to say...to both of you." Raine's voice held an edge of unease. She cast a vaguely questioning glance to Seth, who'd followed them into the foyer and lingered behind. Then she dismissed him and carried on.

Liam could tell she was nervous. The suspense gripped him by the throat. "Speak up. We're listening."

His directive seemed to make her even more nervous. *Fuck!* He watched her gaze travel first to him, then to Hammer, before she sucked in a deep breath.

"I'm sorry. I should never have left you both the way I did. I know you've been worried, but I..." She hesitated, then cast her contrite gaze at Hammer. "You've done so much for me over the years. I owed you more than just running off without saying thank you."

"Then why did you?" Hammer pressed.

"Please. Let me finish." Her voice cracked.

"All right." Hammer nodded. "But be prepared, Raine. We have some things to say as well."

"I'm sure you do." She gave the man a faintly wry smile.

Whatever weighed on her mind was heavy. If her every expression and gesture hadn't made that clear, her unusual lack of sarcasm and sass did.

"Liam..." She clung to him with her hypnotic eyes, making him want to crawl deep inside her. But she'd walked out on him so easily, and he couldn't push the strangling hurt aside. "You tried so hard to make me understand that you loved me and wanted me to grow. What I've done to you is beyond unfair. I'm more sorry that I can tell you." She teared up. Regret twisted her face. "I hope someday you'll be able to forgive me, but I don't expect you to."

"I tried everything I could think of to reach you." He sighed heavily. "But I was out of options."

"I know. The last few days, I've done a lot of thinking. I know I have to change. I can't ever be happy if I keep pushing everyone away. I have to learn how to say what I'm thinking and feeling. I have to stop twisting the truth to avoid something uncomfortable." She drew in a shuddering breath. "And I have to learn to believe that not everyone will hurt me. I don't have any illusions. That won't be quick or easy. I'm not even sure it's possible. But I need to try."

Even as she looked at him with sorrow in her eyes, her speech blew him away. Liam didn't think he'd ever heard her be that honest. But her fluttering hands and downturned gaze made it clear that something more lurked in her head.

Liam turned and looked at Hammer. Frustration rolled off his old friend. He knew what Macen was feeling, as he was mired in it himself.

"So…I have a favor to ask," she went on. "I know I've done nothing to deserve your compassion, but I'm asking if one of you would suggest a Domme who might be willing to help me learn."

Liam felt his jaw drop. A Domme? What the bloody hell was she thinking?

"What?" Hammer growled, a look of disbelief etched on his face.

"I'm standing right in front of you, Raine. And you want some woman —a bloody stranger—instead?" Liam didn't bother masking his shock or anger. "I've been trying to teach you for the past fucking month! I told you if you were willing to do the work that I'd be here for you."

"I am more than aware of everything you did to help me, Liam. I wish I'd been able to appreciate it more. And maybe someday…" She shook her head. "But right now, I have to fix me before I can be worthy enough to wear your collar, much less actually devote myself to you in the way you deserve." Her voice shook.

Hearing that Raine thought she wasn't deserving of him broke his heart.

"Please don't be angry," she begged.

Angry didn't begin to cover it. He understood her need to bury the old Raine and resurrect a new one, but her choice to shut him out was unacceptable. "Damn it, Raine—"

"I'm not done yet. I want to come home because Shadows is familiar. If I'm going to get out of my comfort zone in every other way, I don't want to be out of my element, too. I can't afford to make learning any harder." She shrugged. "Maybe it would be easier to trust a female. It's something I've never tried and...I'm willing to do almost anything to be whole."

Except learn to open herself up and submit to him. His jaw clenched.

"I'm asking for your help. I'm pleading for mercy."

Liam held in a curse. She'd barely given him a hello before she asked for someone else to guide her. Torn between pride that she'd returned to do the work and the devastation to his ego, Liam didn't know whether to wrap her in his arms or take her over his knee.

Didn't Raine understand that she was the kind of woman who would only kneel happily for a man she loved? She might find some ease in learning to be more open and honest with others, but she'd never find fulfillment.

"A bloody female Dominant? That's not mercy. That's ridiculous." He cast a stupefied glance at Hammer. The man's expression conveyed the same disbelief.

"Never going to fucking happen," Hammer confirmed. "Did you dream up this idea because you think Liam and I won't be jealous?"

"Well...yes," she admitted.

So Raine meant to sacrifice her chance to truly surrender so he and his old friend wouldn't fight anymore. Obviously, she didn't realize that it didn't matter who else touched her. He wanted her for his own. And he knew Hammer felt the same.

Liam scrubbed a hand down his face.

"One of my greatest guilts, besides leaving you both, is the wedge I've driven between you," she went on. "I won't be the cause of that anymore."

"I've told you that guilt isn't yours, girl." Hammer scolded her.

"But it is. You were friends before me." She pressed a hand to her chest, passionate and tearful. "I'm the point of contention. If I get out of the way, you two will eventually repair your friendship."

Beside him, Hammer shook his head. "That's not your fault, and there's no way I'm letting a Domme teach you shit."

"This is for me, Macen. Don't you understand?" Her expression willed him to. "I didn't expect either of you to be thrilled, but I'd hoped you'd at least support me."

"Oh, I support your need to grow," Liam growled. "But excuse me for not dancing a jig at the happy news that you want to do it with a Dominant you don't even know. I need a fucking drink."

Raine watched Liam storm away from her, breaking apart inside. She hadn't expected him to accept her request for a Domme right away...but she'd expected him to understand at least a bit. Hammer was the one she'd imagined would blow his temper and rail.

Now, she was almost afraid to look at him. But she forced herself to. Barely leashed fury brimmed in his hazel eyes.

Obviously, he hadn't liked what she'd said. But if he restrained himself from saying more, that meant that she'd pushed him so damn far, he'd chosen to say nothing rather than voice something incredibly ugly. Raine had rarely seen him this angry. When she had, he usually cut that person from his life.

The thought that she would lose them both forever crushed her. Her first instinct was to wonder if she should leave Shadows after all. Raine checked it. Eventually, she would be better. She would keep communicating with them. Even if Liam left, she would write or call or text—whatever it took—to mend fences.

And hopefully, with her out of their way, they would be friends again someday.

"I'm not doing this to hurt either of you," she murmured to Hammer.

He clenched his jaw. Veins bulged in his neck. He still didn't utter a single word.

Leaning with one shoulder against the wall, the tall stranger she'd noticed earlier hovered a few feet behind Macen. He peeled away from his perch, his watchful green eyes sizing her up. "Don't be a prick, Hammer."

Temper mottling his face red, Hammer shook his head. Then he cut a stare in the other man's direction, his eyes narrowed with fury. "Do *not* let her leave."

Then he was gone, his broad shoulders disappearing around the corner, carried away by his long, angry stride as he followed Liam to the bar.

A pang crushed her chest. She'd never really had him, but to lose him now totally devastated her.

The stranger, who looked like a Hemsworth brother, sidled up to her and eased his hand around her elbow. "Hello, Raine."

She shifted her gaze to him, trying to hold it together. "Who are you?"

"I'm Seth, a friend of Liam's and Hammer's from New York. I haven't had the pleasure of meeting you until now, but I've heard a lot about you. I'd like to talk to you for a few minutes."

About what? She'd just vomited out some of the most intimate things she'd ever said in her life. What more did he want?

He began to lead her away. She dug in her heels.

With a gentle but firm grip, he tugged her forward. "How do you feel?"

"I've just hurt the two men I love more than anything. How am I supposed to feel?" She sighed, shoulders slumping.

"You're trying to do the right thing."

"I am. God knows I have a long history of screwing up, but this is the only plan I see."

"You look exhausted." Despite his strong, angular face, Seth came across as surprisingly compassionate.

"It's been a long few days."

"You want to turn in for the night?" he asked.

Raine bit her lip. She doubted she would sleep much, but she also didn't think that following Liam and Hammer to the bar would do anything except make the situation worse. Maybe the best thing to do was let them chew on her idea and find the logic so they could all move on...wherever that led them.

"Maybe I should."

"Show me your room. I'll make sure you get tucked in all safely."

Raine rolled her eyes. "I can find my way down the hall. I'm not going anywhere."

"I wasn't asking." He raised a brow.

She couldn't miss his Dom face. Of course.

For a moment, she thought about balking, but why? Tumult rolled through her, and she couldn't very well go crying to Liam or Hammer anymore. Beck... He'd been nice, but he'd unloaded his responsibility for her. She had to buck up and handle things on her own. Frankly, she'd rather do that in the privacy of her own room in case that meant tears.

Besides, she couldn't claim to want a Dom, male or female, and be bratty about such a simple request. From the look on Seth's face, he only had the best intentions at heart.

"Yes, Sir."

"Very good."

Turning away, Raine led him out of the entry and through the cavernous structure, down the hall, finally to her room. The door opened without a key. Everything inside looked almost exactly as she'd left it except that Beck had set her suitcase by the door.

Nothing had turned out the way she'd intended, but she still felt ridiculously glad that she'd be putting things away in the place she called home.

Stepping aside, she let Seth follow her in.

"Get ready for bed. Then we'll talk," he instructed.

Picking up her little case, she dragged it into the bathroom. She washed her face, brushed her hair and teeth, changed clothes, then padded back out.

Seth eyed her and drew in a deep breath. "No wonder. Okay…"

Raine frowned at him. What was he going on about?

"Why don't you have a seat?"

Again, it wasn't a request. Since she had no chairs in her room, she crawled into bed, scrambling between the sheets.

He sat on the edge beside her. "I know you don't know me, and this probably seems awkward, but you were so honest in the foyer. I need you to continue that. I came here to help Liam straighten a few things out, but I think you might need my ear just as much. Like Beck, I won't betray your confidence. I just need to get to the bottom of this so I can understand how to help."

Crossing her arms over her chest, she beat back mortification. "This is totally awkward. Everyone knows my damn business."

She didn't really want to talk to Seth about all this, but he'd heard her whole speech in the foyer. It wasn't like she had many secrets at this point.

Seth tsked at her. "Liam likes *ladies*. I know he wouldn't appreciate you swearing, would he?"

"No," she conceded. "But he let me go."

"Did it seem that way to you just now? He threw a tantrum over losing you, which I'll totally rib him about later. He admitted that he'd given you his heart. You can't think he's done with you."

She shrugged. "When Liam uncollared me, he told me that I wasn't ready for what he had to offer. He was right. I can't keep hurting him. And I can't keep coming between him and Hammer. If you know them both, you know they used to be friends."

"The best."

"Exactly. And now they can't stand one another. I can't pretend that's anyone's fault except mine." She covered her face with her hands. "The guilt has been eating me alive. I think they want me to choose...and I can't. I love them both too much. And it could ruin their friendship for good."

Seth tilted her chin up and stared at her, studying her every nuance, pinning her against her headboard with an almost dissecting gaze. "If you were whole, as you put it, and they were on good terms, would you have any qualms about letting either one into your life again?"

"No."

"Would you let either of them be your Dom?"

"If I knew I wasn't going to hurt Liam again, yes. Hammer..." She sighed. "He puts on a big show, but if he didn't want anything to do with me for six years, I don't think he truly wants me. And now that he's not speaking to me anymore, I'm sure that will never be an option."

"If you believe that, you're fooling yourself. How about both of them?"

She reared back. "Beck, the guy who brought me back here, suggested the same thing. I think you two are nuts."

"Or it's possible we're the only sane ones in this mess." Seth shrugged. "If Liam and Hammer agreed to it, would you have them both?"

Why was he trying to crawl in her head? "In a perfect world, of course. It'll probably happen on the twelfth of never as hell is freezing over, but I've fantasized about it."

"Because you love them?"

She sighed, wishing she could tell Seth that she didn't want to play Twenty Questions anymore. "Yes."

Seth smiled smugly. "Why don't you get some sleep?"

Raine didn't want to, but she probably needed it. If it made Seth and his questions disappear, even better. "Sure, but would you please make sure they don't get too drunk? Hammer will down tequila and he'll have a terrible hangover that will make him a bear tomorrow. Liam is probably drinking Scotch. He really needs a friend now. He and Beck don't get along. If Hammer turns his anger on Liam, he'll be outnumbered and—"

"I'll take care of it." He squeezed her shoulder. "Get some sleep. Things should look brighter in the morning."

Raine certainly hoped so because everything looked damn bleak now.

S torming into the bar, Hammer grabbed a bottle of Patrón. He tore off the cap and slid onto an empty barstool, tipping the bottle to his mouth for a long swig. Beside him, Liam tossed back shots of Scotch. Beck sat around the corner of the L-shaped bar. The big pussy nursed a bottle of beer and looked at him expectantly.

"Don't I get a thanks for bringing Raine back? And she's even in one piece," Beck drawled.

Hammer really tried not to punch him.

"Shut the fuck up," Liam snarled and shot back more Scotch.

"What he said." Hammer glared.

"You're not happy to see her?" Beck mocked.

Happy? Laying eyes on Raine again had been like Christmas, Valentine's Day, Easter, and a kick-ass New Year's Eve all rolled into one. He'd never been so damn relieved in his life. But now that she'd returned, his latent rage boiled up. She'd run off without saying a fucking word. And when she'd returned, had she wanted his protection or comfort? Oh, no. Instead, she'd warded him off by shoving a hand in his face. While still reeling from that silent "fuck you very much," she'd had the balls to ask him for a Domme.

Not on your life, precious.

"Of course I am," he finally managed.

There. That didn't sound like he wanted to rip Beck's face off. Or give in to the impulse to snag Raine by the arm, haul her ungrateful ass over his lap, and paddle her backside. Sucking in a breath, Hammer cordoned off his anger. If he punished her now, that would make him the worst sort of player. No real Dominant should *ever* punish a sub who asked for help. Raine might not have come back for him—or Liam—but someday she would understand the depth of her betrayal. Then... Well, his hand itched for that day.

"It doesn't show. She decided to come back all on her own and ask for help. That's a big step for her."

Tossing back another gulp of tequila, he shrugged. "Huge."

The small part of him that wasn't horrifically pissed off felt proud. He'd never seen Raine so resolved to grow and blossom. The rest of him? Downright furious at her version of "help."

"Just drink your beer." He didn't want to talk to Beck. Or anyone. He had to figure out what the hell to do.

"Stop soaking your brain with tequila and use it for a minute. Raine has a good idea. A female Dominant could teach her the basics."

"Raine has lost the bloody plot! A Domme?" Liam shoved his tumbler aside, opting to swig from the bottle instead.

Yeah, this was going to get down and dirty. Hammer was *so* there.

"It's a terrible fucking idea, Beck." Hammer glared. "Until Raine feels the connection with a Dominant who commands her body, heart, and soul, she'll be like a race car with a compact's engine. She'll run, but not like she should."

He slammed back more booze. The tequila burned, but he welcomed it, hoping it would numb the sting of Raine's desertion.

She needed more than another woman could give her. Goddamn it, she needed him—his guidance, his boundaries. His love. Fuck if he didn't want to banish everyone from Shadows and wrap Raine in his arms until he'd bound her to him in every way possible. But damn it, her little speech tonight had tied his hands. Yeah, he could still tell her that he loved her. He probably should. But then he'd have to stand back and let the chips fall.

The control freak in him hated that idea.

"Exactly," Liam agreed, leaning onto the polished wooden surface and looking past him to stare at Beck. "What the fuck did you do to her these last few days? Brainwash her?"

"Good question. I never thought I'd live to see the day that Raine sought out a woman." Hammer shook his head.

"Pull your heads out of your asses," Beck complained. "She just wants happiness."

"I can make her happy," Liam countered. "But I don't think I could bear to see her give her affection to anyone else. How did everything get so fucked up?" Liam tipped his bottle back once again. "I've gotta figure out how to win her back. I need a plan."

"In case you haven't been keeping score, you're batting a big fat zero with your last two grand ideas," Hammer jeered.

Liam flipped him off. "At least *I* tried."

"Yep." Hammer nodded. "You're the most *trying* man I've ever met... Just saying."

"Ha fucking ha," Liam sneered.

Beck nearly fell off his barstool laughing. "You two are hopeless, you know that?"

"What the hell do you know about love?" Hammer bristled. "Someday, somehow, Raine is going to choose one of us...then, of course, the other will have to die."

Slugging back another drink, he wondered if Raine would ever let him love her the way he should have all along.

Liam peered at him. "I might be tempted to beat you ugly so that she'd never want you, but I swear I'd never kill you. That's just bad form." Liam frowned at Hammer. "There's only one person that I'd like to unload a forty-five on, and that's her dad."

"Here. Here." He agreed, raising his bottle and clinking it against his old friend's.

"Neither one of you paid attention to her hands when she came in, did you?" Beck piped up.

Both he and Liam turned. The burly sadist wore a grave expression.

"Her hands?" he asked, wondering what part of the conversation had slipped past him.

"Yeah. She went to visit her father yesterday."

Hammer's heart nearly stopped.

"What the bloody… You're serious?" Liam blinked.

"You'd better not be," Hammer warned.

When Beck gave a curt nod, he felt as if he'd been blown clear to the other side of the room. Anger burst in his veins. Raine had gone back to that shithole, to see that animal, without him. She could have been hurt. Or Bill Kendall could have killed her.

With cold precision, Hammer turned his head, leveling Beck with an icy glare. "Why?"

"Do you really have to ask?" Beck sent him a mocking stare.

No. Hammer had known she'd eventually seek out Bill for answers, vindication…closure. But damn it, he'd imagined he'd be beside Raine, supporting and protecting her. "You didn't fucking let her go alone, did you?"

"Of course not, ass-hat."

"Tell us what happened before I beat the truth out of you," Liam demanded.

Beck shook his head. "Whatever. You're so… what is it you guys across the pond call it? Pissed. Yeah. You're so pissed drunk, you couldn't beat yourself off."

"I'm Irish, not English, you bloody twit," Liam growled. "And yes, I could, if I wanted to." He scoffed, drinking down more Scotch. "But I don't. And don't change the subject."

"Did Bill touch her?" Hammer added. "If he did, you're taking me there right now so I can plant a bullet in his miserable head."

"Settle down, Lone Ranger. I already covered that contingency." Beck gave him a condescending pat on the shoulder. "I had my gun out and sited right between the son of a bitch's eyes every fucking second. But she didn't need me. You remember those self-defense classes you enrolled her in years ago?"

"Yeah." It took him a minute for the puzzle pieces to fall into place, but when they did, Hammer grinned. "She kicked his ass, didn't she?"

"Like a ninja." Beck grinned.

"Fuck, yeah!" Hammer cheered. "That's my girl."

"She's *my* girl, motherfucker," Liam insisted, slurring.

"She *was*. And she could kick your ass, too. 'Cause *I* got her lessons," he preened.

"Jesus, I wish I was recording this. All the fet folk we know would howl." Beck laughed.

"Shut up and tell us what happened when you took her to see that fucker," Hammer snapped.

"She slayed her dragon, more or less. It was good for her. You know, you two aren't the only ones who care about her."

Liam stood, wobbling, looking ready for a fight. "You better not have fucking touched her!"

"Yeah." Hammer felt his skull about to explode and reached out to throttle Beck.

The other man shoved him away. "I didn't. Jesus, you idiots… Give it a rest. I'm tempted to lay you both out cold, but you're both too drunk to fight."

Hammer glanced at a weaving Liam. Sadly, Beck was right. Besides, unloading all the fury roiling inside him onto the doctor wouldn't help anything. He'd already seen vividly that displacing his guilt and anger led to bad things. He had to buck up and fly right.

"Sorry, man. Thank you for keeping her safe. Now tell me what happened. Details!" Hammer slammed his bottle on the bar.

"Did you hear what she said to that sniveling douchebag?" Liam prodded.

"Oh, yeah. Raine let old Bill know, in no uncertain terms, that he was a steaming pile of dog shit." A smile tugged at the corners of Beck's lips. "You two would have been proud."

"Good lass," Liam whispered. "But what the devil would we have done if he'd hurt her?"

Something clogged Hammer's throat. Maybe it was too much anger, or the booze talking, or simply relief that Raine had come home, where she belonged. His eyes stung.

"Don't even think that. But I can guarantee they'd never find a single part of Bill's body." Hammer reached up and gave Liam's shoulder a reassuring squeeze. "The question we should be asking, since Raine's plan sucks, is what's the best way to help her?"

When he felt a slap upside his head, Hammer turned to find Seth delivering the same smack to Liam.

"Good to hear you say that, Macen," the other man announced from behind him. "Because after talking to Raine, I know."

"How?" Hammer bristled. "You've known her all of five fucking minutes and suddenly you can read her mind?"

"Pretty much."

Liam turned and steadied himself on the bar, wagging his finger at Seth. "If you fucking touched her..."

"Chill, Conan. As much as I wanted to introduce her to my most amazing skill..." Seth licked his tongue over his teeth, slurping nosily. "We just talked."

"Damn good thing because I would have cut your tongue out," Hammer vowed. "You should have asked her to teach your pansy ass how to make coffee."

"Busting my balls isn't going to help Raine, so zip it. Would you rather the girl stayed fucked up? Or do you want to help her?"

"You already know the answer," Hammer grumbled.

"I've been trying for weeks now. You're not leaving me out, damn it!" Liam insisted, looking up with bleary eyes at Seth.

"Good to see you both agree." Seth looked between them. "How long do you think you can act like big boys and play nicely together?"

"About five more seconds," Beck piped up with a mocking grin.

"Get stuffed, you bastard," Liam barked.

Beck just shook his head as he laughed.

"We're getting along fine right now." Hammer glared. "Spill it before I lose my patience."

"Here's the deal..." Seth began. "Raine is about the most torn woman I've ever met."

"It's that asshole father of hers," Liam blurted.

"No, I don't mean broken, though I suspect she's that as well. I mean she's in love with you lug nuts, and your constant, hellaciously annoying bickering has torn her heart in two." Seth shook his head. "Can't imagine why she loves you both, but..."

Liam plunked down on his barstool, grabbing the bar to balance himself and stay upright. "Because we're dashing and handsome and—"

"Good in bed, goddamn it," Hammer added.

"That, too." Liam raised his bottle, and Hammer clinked it again.

"And so modest," Beck drawled.

"Do you think you two could sober up so we can discuss this?" Seth arched a brow.

"Hang on. I'll be back. But don't say too much," Beck announced, then sauntered from the bar. "I don't want to miss this."

"I'm not dunk. I mean, drunk." Liam thrust his shoulders back and raised his chin.

Hammer elbowed him and tried to decide which of the two images of Seth swimming in his vision was real. "We'll keep up."

"Just a guess here…" Seth said wryly. "But neither of you wants Raine with a Domme, right?"

"Absolutely not!" Liam pounded his fist on the bar.

"The whole idea is bullshit," Hammer agreed.

"Congratulations. So far, you've both scored a hundred percent on the quiz."

"Quiz?" Liam blinked, then looked at Hammer, his eyes wide. "Shit, we didn't study, mate."

"If Seth is giving the quiz, we're good. He can't be smarter than us," Hammer said in a stage whisper.

"Spare me sloppy drunks." Seth shook his head in disgust. "This will wait until tomorrow."

"Nah, this might help." Beck set down two steaming mugs of coffee.

Hammer pounced on it and took a sip, moaning long and loud. "Son of a bitch! You know how to make good coffee?"

Beck scowled at Hammer. "You're so helpless that you don't?"

"I used to like you," he muttered.

He and Liam sipped their steaming brews as fast as they could. When they'd drained their mugs, Beck refilled them. Staring at his watch, Seth waited impatiently.

Before long, Hammer's thoughts turned right-side up. The glazed look in Liam's eyes began to dissipate.

"We're sober enough. Get on with it," Hammer demanded.

"Finally... Here's the deal," Seth said, staring first at Hammer, then Liam. "Like I said, Raine is in love with you both. If her heart is torn in two, how do you expect her to heal with just one of you?"

Hammer froze. *Share Raine?* That's what Seth was suggesting. Beck had, too. It wasn't a foreign concept. Hell, he'd had a woman between himself and Liam. But the thought of sharing Raine... *Hell no.* The possessive caveman in him wanted to drag her off by the hair and keep her for himself.

Then again, Seth asked a really good question, and there seemed to be only one answer. He turned to look at Liam.

"We have to work together?" His old pal grimaced.

"You don't have to like it, but yes," Seth answered. "I came because you asked me to help you reach the girl. I think this is the only way it will work. If you can't handle that, take your bottle and stumble on down to your room. I'll help him instead."

"The hell you will!" Fury thundered across Liam's face.

Hammer couldn't stand the thought of being shut out of her recovery either. No way would he roll over and play dead.

"Then fucking agree and get along already," Seth insisted. "It's what she wants. You'll have to figure out specifics, but if you would stop thinking with your pride—" he glared at Hammer "—and your jealousy—" he shot Liam a pointed look "—you'd know I'm right." Seth rolled his eyes. "I told you this shit a month ago."

"Exactly. I talked to Raine about this, too" Beck said. "She didn't hate the idea at all. So stop pissing on her like she's a damn hydrant and do what real Dominants do. Help her."

"It's up to you." Seth rose. "But if you don't, she's a pretty girl. She won't be alone for long. In fact, feel free to keep fucking this up. Once she leaves your sorry asses, I'd be *so* happy to tap that."

CHAPTER TWELVE

I f Liam hadn't felt exactly sober ten minutes ago, he did now. Work with Hammer to heal Raine? After a month of arguing, it boggled the mind, really. Hammer had been part of the problem for so bloody long, crushing her fragile spirit with his indifference, then dragging her to his bed and fucking her within an inch of her life. Liam didn't see this working.

But nothing else he'd tried had helped, either. Though he hated to admit it, no one knew her background, habits, and tendencies better than Hammer. After nearly a month with Raine as her Dom and her lover, Liam knew her better sexually, maybe even emotionally in some ways. More importantly, together they knew her inside and out. And they probably needed every bit of knowledge to reach her because he feared Seth had a point that a heart divided couldn't heal without both parts.

Beck and Seth's conversation drifted through the bar, becoming more faint as they headed out of the room. The meddling fucks had left him alone with Hammer. Seth, the last of his good friends, had thrown him to the enemy. Or it felt that way. He sighed.

"They're right," Hammer said into the solemn silence.

"About what?"

"Everything. She only wants a Domme because we're too stubborn to get along."

Yes. Because Raine wanted them to be friends again, she had given up on the sort of Dom she needed. It was his duty to put her needs first.

Fuck.

"Our bickering has torn her apart," Liam conceded.

"Yep." Hammer tapped the rim of his coffee cup. "All we've done is put her between us in all the wrong ways and made her life difficult."

"I don't like this idea."

"I don't, either," Macen agreed. "The other thing to consider is, if we don't offer her a choice between us and a Domme, we're not being fair. And she might dig in her heels."

"A choice? Who could we bloody offer to give her to? And what if Raine picks that option?"

"It's a chance we have to take," Hammer pointed out. "She'll only do the work with us if she chooses to. Seth says that's what she wants… and I believe he's right."

"Finally! First smart thing you've said all night," Beck called back, peeking around the corner with a grin.

"Fuck off!" he and Hammer both shouted in unison.

Liam waited until Beck disappeared again, then turned back to Hammer. "I don't suppose helping her together could be any worse than what we've already done to her separately."

"Well, I don't know about that." Hammer sighed heavily.

Juliet. Of course that tragedy would plague Macen's thoughts. It had for over eight years. "I think I do. She loves us both, according to Seth, but is eaten up with guilt. If we took that off her shoulders and focused on her…"

Nodding, Hammer stared into his coffee. "At least she wouldn't have to worry about us anymore."

Liam couldn't dispute that. Still, Hammer had been twenty kinds of asshole over the past month. He knew why now…but that didn't make this idea more palatable. His old friend could be a damn good Dom, but Hammer had never been a demonstrative partner with his wife. Sexually, yes. Where his heart was concerned? Liam couldn't remember more than a handful of occasions when the man had told Juliet that he loved her. Raine needed those words. She needed a man who would both show her and tell her how he felt. When Hammer didn't, she would likely distance herself from him.

And Liam would have her all to himself again—the way it should be.

He smiled, rather liking that plan.

Of course, they had to fulfill her needs and heal her first.

"I can't disagree." Liam nodded the other man's way. "Let's say, for argument's sake, that we intended to work on helping her together."

Hammer leveled him a stare. "All right. Let's do that."

"What do you think are her most pressing issues? We can't overwhelm her too quickly with too much. If you had to pick a few of her worst habits to focus on, tell me what you'd choose."

"I'm sure you have ideas, too. But one thing I know—that we've just seen in the past few days—is the way she retreats into her head. She doesn't share what she's thinking. If we'd known, I wouldn't have had to pry from her how late her period was. You would have known about her migraines. I don't think she would have ever left home if she'd been able to talk through her problems with one or both of us."

"I agree. Raine not only has difficulty saying how she feels, she's not always honest. She's given me a lot of half-truths. She's quite good at telling me what she thinks I want to hear."

"Or what will keep her ass out of trouble."

Liam sent him a reluctant grin. "She's good at that, as well."

"That has to stop," Hammer insisted.

"It does. One of her biggest problems has been that she can't purge her hurt, share her fears, or tell me what she bloody wants. I've been trying to drag it out of her and guess along the way. Raine is afraid I'm going to tell her that she's too much trouble or something."

"She's also afraid to be too vulnerable with anyone, and it didn't help that I turned her away the one time she worked up the courage to be honest about her feelings."

No, it hadn't fucking helped at all, but taking out his irritation on Hammer now, while satisfying, would be pointless.

"So we're agreed?" Liam asked. "Communication and honesty. But I think there's more."

"No question. Raine has other issues."

"The biggest must be trust." Liam hated to say it, worried that Hammer would see it as an indication of the weakness in his relationship with her. "You may not agree." The other man probably didn't have half the problem with earning Raine's trust since she'd been there for six years. But after barely a handful of weeks with her, Liam was struggling to catch up. "But I know it's true."

Hammer didn't hesitate. He simply nodded. "I think she probably trusts me more than about anyone, but there are chunks of her past and her feelings that she still won't share. I've asked, pressed, insisted, demanded, threatened. Nothing."

That made sense. All the way until her last moment as his submissive, Raine had never trusted that he meant to stay. To hear that she lacked trust in everyone, even Hammer, set him back on his heels.

"Do you think she's really ready for this?" Liam asked.

"Yeah. I could hear it in her voice."

Liam shrugged. "I've heard that before. Her resolve doesn't always last. The minute she gets scared..."

"We won't let her falter or hide."

"We can't, I know. But what if she quits on us?" Liam hated to voice the question, but that possibility was too real to ignore.

"That's another chance we take. We'll have to monitor her constantly."

"True." He looked Hammer's way to find the man staring back at him.

"So we're on the same page. Communication, honesty, and trust?" Macen asked.

"If I had to pick three, yes. I think they feed into most other issues she's struggling with."

"Absolutely."

And hadn't that agreement come easily? They'd never quarreled as fiercely as they had since Liam had taken Raine for his own. But now? It felt like old times...but better.

Liam stood and paced from one end of the room to the other. Why was that?

"Would you sit down?" Hammer complained.

"I'm thinking." He traveled the length of the bar a few more times. "You know, we never talked about what Juliet needed this way."

"You hadn't been with Juliet as long as I had."

"I haven't been with Raine as long as you, either."

Hammer shrugged. "You were young, still in your early twenties and having fun."

"Give me a break, Hammer. I'm only five years younger. And I wasn't immature or stupid."

"No, you weren't. I guess...I didn't want to burden you."

"I didn't want to step on your toes."

"I thought I had it all under control," Hammer admitted. "I probably would have resented your suggestions at the time. Besides, I knew you didn't love her."

He'd enjoyed her, sure. And he would never have told Juliet that truth. Her spirit had been too breakable to hear it. He'd wondered now and again if she'd known and that was part of the reason she'd committed suicide.

"I still wanted to give her something she needed," Liam said. "I just didn't know what that was."

"In retrospect…" Hammer sighed heavily. "Neither did I. If I had, she would never have chosen the silent way out."

"But Raine isn't Juliet. Granted, she may have one or two issues, but surely, if we put our shit aside for a bit and do what we should, they're nothing too difficult to handle."

"The question is, *can* we put our shit aside?" Hammer asked with brutal honesty. "We haven't done a good job of that for a while."

Liam couldn't disagree. If someone would have told him on his flight from New York to Los Angeles that he and his best friend would soon be at one another's throats, he would have laughed himself silly. Looking back over the past month, they'd said—and done—things to hurt the other. He regretted the sad state their friendship had fallen into. Hammer must also or else the man would have simply ceased speaking to him altogether.

"We've been friends for much longer than we've been enemies."

"And we've shared before." Hammer let out a tight breath. "We know some of the warning signs to watch for."

"True. If we're at all serious about this, we have to negotiate a few things."

"We'll definitely talk to Raine about our intentions, ask her for her hard limits and whatnot. But I don't want to give her too much up front. The less she knows, the less she can prepare ways to sidestep us."

"Can't argue with that. And I already know Raine's hard limits. I asked her before I collared her. But that's not what I meant. You and I need to negotiate our behavior."

"For instance?" Hammer's voice turned chilly.

Liam refused to let the man's tone change his agenda. "First off, we can't help Raine if we start fighting in the middle of a scene."

"At this point, I think that would be the worst thing for her."

"Right. I also think you and I should have a word or phrase that will pause everything so we can discuss whatever's happening."

"A safe word?"

"Something like that, yeah." Liam nodded. "I still find Raine's hidden triggers now and again. We have to be mindful."

Hammer relaxed, seeming to see the train of his thoughts. "Yes. She's probably a damn landmine. The night I spent with her, I thought about doing so many things that I didn't because I worried I might step on some hot spot." He gave a self-deprecating laugh. "I've known Raine for so long, but I don't know this side of her. How does she do with restraints?"

"She loves them." As Hammer reared back, Liam shrugged. "After seeing what her father did to her, I'm a bit blown over too. But she hates gags."

"Does that surprise you?" Hammer laughed.

Liam joined in. "Not much. If you let her, she'll try to tell you what she wants in a scene. Of course she sometimes talks herself out of a panic, too. You don't always know what you'll get with Raine. She's seemed leery of whips, so I haven't given that a go. I think riding crops are a big 'no' for her, which is fine with me. She loves a good spanking."

"Does she ever reach subspace?"

He nodded. "Surprisingly well, given her trust issues. It wasn't easy at first, but over time, she's become more comfortable."

All this talk about Hammer partaking in her submission was making his guts churn. But if he was going to give Raine what she needed, he would have to grit his teeth and stifle his jealousy.

"Good to know." Macen swallowed down more coffee. "How about if either of us says it's time for a breath of fresh air, that will be our signal to pause and find another solution to the scene?"

"That will work."

Hammer hesitated for a long moment. "You know, I think that's a good idea. When we were with Juliet, I sometimes took her further than you thought I should have, right?" At Liam's nod, he went on. "I wish like hell I'd asked your opinion and listened. She and I probably would have wound up divorced, but maybe she'd be alive."

"You've got a hard head, Hammer. I don't know that you'll listen now, either."

The man blew out a rough breath. "I've grown since then, but you're right. I'll do my best. Sometimes that dark side of me wants to take over. Having you to reel me in when that happens might be best. I don't want to scare Raine or damage our progress with her."

Since his old friend often seemed to think he knew best, that was a big admission for Hammer. It shocked the hell out of Liam—and made him look inward as well.

"I've been a bit too guilty of letting Raine have her way more than I should. I enjoy coddling her sometimes, and god knows she could use the tenderness. But she also needs firm guidance."

"So I won't let you shirk that. Got it." Hammer smirked. "Look at us getting along and shit."

"Don't jinx it," Liam scolded.

"What else?"

He paced the length of the room again. "We don't know how long her progress will take."

"It sure as hell won't be overnight, but I'm willing to stick it out. What about you? If you had any intention of going back to New York after the winter, and she's not ready…"

"I'm not leaving L.A. without Raine. I'd decided I was staying indefinitely, so I bought a house here. I'd planned to give her the key wrapped in a box the morning the shit hit the fan."

Hammer stared, blinking. "You were planning to move *her* to this house?"

Liam squared his shoulders. "I was."

"Holy shit." Hammer sounded floored.

"Raine needs a steady home."

Guilt flashed across Hammer's face, and he raked a hand through his hair. "Goddamn it, I know."

"You did the best you could at the time. Let's not get off track. Raine won't be moving on with her life at all if we can't help her."

"True," Hammer agreed.

Another thought occurred to Liam, and he winced. "I also think it would be best if you were discreet with your other subs. I'm not suggesting you give them up, but it would help her if you hid them better than you did Marlie."

Hammer cringed at her name. "Actually, I already gave them up."

"Did that plastic whore give you a disease I don't know about?" Liam sent him a sideways glance.

"No." Hammer scoffed. "I haven't scened with anyone in weeks. I haven't fucked anyone since Raine. I don't want to."

That took Liam totally aback. Hammer loved sex, and he'd never imagined his friend would give it up, even temporarily.

"That's bloody near a month, mate—a record for you. Your balls must be blue."

"Yep, and my hand is damn tired of getting a workout. But no one else is Raine."

As much as Liam wanted to, he couldn't argue with that.

Hammer cocked his head and sent him a questioning glance. "Are we agreeing to do this? For her?"

Liam hated it, but saw almost no way around it. "I think it makes sense, but..." He scrubbed at his face. "Making it work is going to be...complicated."

Because one topic could turn this truce back into a war.

Raine wasn't his anymore—at least not technically. That meant Hammer was free to say or do anything to her, as long as she consented. Macen had already vowed to get her into bed the moment he could. Liam had few illusions. Raine loved the man. If she said "no" to him, it wouldn't be for long.

"You mean, figuring out who gets to fuck her will be complicated," Hammer drawled.

"Yes." Liam spit the word. "But hell, after her speech today, maybe she won't want either of us."

"Don't kid yourself, O'Neill. If she cares about us both, she's going to want us. Maybe together...maybe apart. If she needs us, how can we refuse?"

Liam bit his tongue hard enough to taste copper as he fought to dial down a sudden red rage. The memories of Raine's scent in his nose and her cries in his ears as he sank into the hot, soft depths of her body clawed need through him. But Hammer was right. If they wanted Raine to grow and be happy, they both had to do the right thing for her, even if it bloody killed them.

"All right," he managed to choke out the words.

They stared at one another for a month of Sundays before Hammer cocked a brow at him and finally broke the silence. "Anything else?"

"To be clear, once we're in a session, we have to be dedicated to it."

"Yep. Whatever it takes."

"No arguing."

Hammer nodded. "No bullshit."

"No putting your pride first."

"No doing the same with your jealousy."

Hell, Liam wanted to punch Hammer, but what was the point when he was right? "Fine. We present a united front to Raine. Whatever's happened prior doesn't make a damn bit of difference once we enter a room and begin to work with her. If we disagree, we do it calmly, rationally, and out of her earshot. Raine comes first."

Hammer nodded. "We'll make it work. We have to."

"If we don't want to leave her growth to someone else, yes. We come at her together. Strong. Focused."

"Willing and able to give her what she needs—no matter what that is. United in coaxing her into giving us what *we* need."

"Agreed." Liam hoped to hold Raine again, happier and more whole— and eventually all his. But after this conversation, he wasn't so sure. If Hammer helped shape her today, where did that leave their tomorrow?

Hammer held out his hand. "I'm in."

Liam could do nothing but shake it.

A s much as the man inside Hammer disliked this idea, the Dom in him saw the logic. He'd utterly failed Raine for years. He couldn't put his guilt above her needs and fail her again—even if sharing her with Liam would chafe him raw.

Getting his wife between him and his best friend used to make Hammer's dick as hard as steel. The power of their bodies claiming her as one and driving her to screaming orgasms and exhaustion had been the headiest rush he'd ever experienced. Maybe he and Liam had too much animosity between them now for that. But any chance to fuck Raine again was a chance Hammer intended to take.

Still, one concern kept gnawing away at him.

"I'm not sure Raine understands how much work is ahead of her."

Liam shrugged. "I'm not sure, either. I want to reach her more than I want to breathe. But neither of us can force her to grow faster than she's ready to."

"If she hasn't thought this through and isn't serious, we'll find out real fast. But she's strong enough."

"And stubborn enough, that's for damn sure."

"That she is." Hammer chuckled. "We'll need to praise her for every speck of progress. Once she tastes success, we'll have to hope it motivates her to keep growing."

"She'll need more than praise," Liam said. "She'll need reassurance, too."

"Naturally." Hammer nodded. "But the one thing in our favor is that she aches to please. We've both seen it."

"Her submission can be bloody amazing. But she can shut it down so quickly, you get damn near dizzy."

Hammer grunted in understanding. Drawing out the submissive inside Raine wouldn't be simple. He was a demanding Master—and he knew it. Pushing a sub to her boundaries and beyond under his hand —and his body—had always given him a thrilling sense of control. If Raine were truly willing to cast aside her cloak of security, the freedom and beauty she found would blow her mind.

But taking a sub that far fed something dark in him. He always wanted more and more. The need to believe that he'd owned every part of Juliet and to make her prove it every way he could conceive had been their downfall. Maybe it was a blessing, after all, that he'd have Liam there to balance him. His old friend hadn't loved Juliet, and he hadn't thought of her as his responsibility, so he'd seen no reason to curb any of Hammer's more extreme demands. But Liam would watch over Raine and protect her with every cell in his body.

With Liam added to the equation, however, the expectations on her would double. They'd have to remain vigilant, delving deep and bolstering her often, to keep Raine from crumbling beneath the strain.

"I'm worried that Raine's lack of experience in sharing her feelings could leave her overwhelmed and frightened," Hammer said finally.

"I think that's why communication is so critical. It's the first point we have to drive home with her. If she'll just share, we can erase some of her fear."

Yes, and Hammer knew that if he expected her to trust him, to communicate openly and honestly, he would need to do the same…no matter how uncomfortable it made him.

"Replacing old patterns with new ones will take time." And he hated that for a million reasons, too. His own impatience. His concern that he and Liam couldn't get along indefinitely. Mostly, he hated to see her so miserable and lost. Nor could he risk losing her. Granted, she wouldn't take Juliet's way out, but she'd proven that she would pick up and leave if driven to flee.

"It will," Liam agreed. "One of the first patterns I want to break is her bloody bad habit of trying to misdirect with sex."

Hammer heard Liam's words, but he better fucking not have heard them right. "What did you say?"

"When I'm displeased with Raine, her first instinct is to lose her clothes and rub against me. I hate to admit how often I let her distract me before I realized what she'd done." He rubbed at the back of his neck with a wry grin. "She's really damn good at it, too."

"Son of a bitch!" Hammer grabbed the mostly empty bottle of tequila from the bar and zinged it across the room. The violence of the shattering glass startled Liam—but it didn't do a damn thing to improve his mood.

"Have you lost your bloody mind?" Liam stared at him like he'd grown a second head. "Or do you just like to break things?"

"Raine uses sex as a distraction? I heard that right?"

"Yes." Liam frowned. "Calm down. We'll deal with it and anything else she throws at us. She won't be allowed to instigate."

"Goddamn right she won't be. That behavior will fucking stop. Immediately. The first time she tries, I'm going to put her over my knee and beat the hell out of her ass."

"Why are you getting so bent over this? It's not a major issue. We're aware and we'll deal with it. But your hot button isn't her problem."

Hammer jumped off his barstool. "It's my problem, your problem, and her damn problem, too. That kind of distraction is just one of the ways Juliet hid from me. She avoided telling me how she felt about anything by sidetracking me on her knees. I was stupid and selfish enough to let her. By god, I won't let Raine do that. Why do you think I push her so hard when I want an answer?"

"So we'll be watchful."

"If we're not, she'll slip through our fingers."

Juliet had taught him a valuable lesson he couldn't fail to heed. If he did, her death would mean nothing.

"So...we'll begin tomorrow morning?" Hammer prodded. "We can clean out the liquor supply room and—"

"No." Liam shook his head. "She's too comfortable here."

"You said that she returned to Shadows because she wanted to be in her element."

"Because it would be easier on her, yes." Liam sent him a weighty stare. "None of this should be easy."

"You're right. If it is, she won't learn anything. Too many familiar people and places here to hide behind. We can't have her dodging us instead of doing the work."

"Precisely. I think we should drive her up to my lodge in the mountains."

"Why not the house you bought?"

"I've got plumbing work and painting going on. We want to be alone with her, not surrounded by contractors. Besides, at the lodge there'll be no taxis to shuttle her back to the city if she gets the urge to run away. And I've got the perfect room there to suit our needs."

"Go on," Hammer urged, seeing the benefit of keeping Raine off-balance.

"Though she's been to the lodge before, the surroundings aren't nearly as familiar to her."

"She has?"

Liam sent him a sheepish grin. "It's where I brought her when I took her from Shadows."

So that's where the son of a bitch had spirited her away after she'd spent that mind-blowing night in his bed? He'd wondered more than once.

"It's quiet there?" Hammer asked.

"Very."

"Secluded?"

"Extremely." Liam smirked.

"Then it sounds ideal. We'll talk to her early, then. If she chooses us, we'll pack her up and head out at dawn, before the traffic gets bad. I'll call a few trusted club members to see if they can watch the place for a few days. But before we do any of that, I think we should agree on exactly how we'll get her to learn these three lessons."

Liam flashed a mischievous smile. "Now you're talking."

CHAPTER
THIRTEEN

The following morning, Raine woke to a warm hand cupping her shoulder and a deep voice in her ear. A familiar scent wrapped around her, instantly transporting her back to happier times and comfort. Love. *Liam.*

With a lazy smile, she rolled over, bleary-eyed, and faced him. Hammer stood at his side. Both men wore tense expressions.

The jolt of surprise shoved away her vestiges of sleep. Raine blinked. Why were they here and dressed before a single ray of sun had brightened her room? And why were they together, watching her?

Pulling her blankets to her chin, she pushed her hair from her face and sat up. "What's going on? Is something wrong?"

"No, love," Liam assured. "We came to tell you first that we're glad you decided to come home. I know you were upset when you left."

And they didn't seem angry that she'd fled. They had every right to be. Instead, they looked resigned. No, decisive. Their odd demeanor confused her.

"It's good to have you home, precious. Now, on your feet." She couldn't miss the command in Hammer's voice.

Liam wasn't trying to tear his head off for that? Or objecting to his dominance? She stared at the pair of them, blinking.

"Raine?" Liam prodded. "Hammer asked you to do something. Acknowledge him and obey."

Was he serious? She frowned, Liam's words not fully computing. But the two of them were looking at her with the same expectant expression and standing side by side. Together.

"All right, Sir." Tossing the covers back slowly, she climbed from the bed. They stepped closer, crowding her against the edge of the mattress. She trembled. "Did you wake me up to say that you found a Domme for me?"

Neither answered. Their silence made her nervous. She looked up to find them exchanging a glance. If she didn't know better, Raine would swear they were in on some conspiracy together.

"We woke you to tell you that we discussed your request at length last night," Liam finally began. "We agree that you need to learn—a great deal, in fact."

She would have loved being a fly on the wall for that conversation. "And?"

"You've asked for a Domme, and we're willing to grant you one." As a bittersweet relief began to slide through her, Hammer went on, his stare unwavering. "But we have another possibility for you to consider."

A silent tension gripped them both and squeezed her lungs. Whatever they had on their minds meant something to them. They wanted her to say yes. Their impatience must be the reason they'd woken her up so damn early.

"What is it?" she asked cautiously.

"We'll get into the specifics in a moment. Before we do, we have a few questions to determine if this alternate option is right for you." Hammer glanced at Liam like he waited for the other man to begin the next part of this rehearsed speech.

What the hell?

"No doubt you'll want someone who will devote their time and knowledge to you. Yes?" Liam prodded her with a watchful stare.

"I think I'd make more progress that way," she admitted. "I'd like her to be understanding and compassionate. Like Mistress Hillary, maybe?"

"Unfortunately, she's out of town for the next two months." Hammer didn't look at all unhappy about that. "But let's not talk about any certain individual until we've identified all your needs."

"This isn't as easy as plucking a name out of a hat, love," Liam chided. "There should be a special bond between Dominant and submissive. If you don't click with the first choice, you'll soon be back to square one. So you should choose cautiously, agreed?"

"Yes, Sirs." They were right. If she gave her all to the wrong Domme, then had to start over with someone new, it would waste time and cause her frustration. At the thought of opening herself up to a stranger, a sludgy lump of vulnerability caught in her chest.

"Good. You'll want someone you feel comfortable with." Hammer raised a brow at her as if daring her to contradict him. "A top you can talk to, who understands you."

"Of course. It's one reason I asked Beck, but he said no."

"Beck?" Liam bit out.

Raine raised her chin and nodded. "Yeah. He's not a stranger and he helped me realize that I needed to come home and start fixing myself."

Hammer looked almost smug now. "You do, but the Dominant who trains you will inevitably claim a piece of your heart. Beck can't do that. And you won't learn any other way. It's how you're built."

Raine sighed. She hadn't thought of it that way, but he was probably right. Who did that leave her?

She frowned as suspicions took shape. "I expect a deep rapport would grow in time. Where are you going with this?"

"Time is the key word." Liam's lips curled up in a self-assured smile. "You'd be starting at square one with a stranger. It could take weeks, or even months, to establish the sort of trust necessary for your journey, assuming it's a good fit at all."

Suspicions dive-bombed her brain now. He and Liam had some shit up their sleeves. Neither of them ever did a damn thing without some lesson or expectation attached.

"Of course, trust will be critical." Raine wedged enough space between them and her to cross her arms over her chest. She tapped her toe. "Everything you're saying is common sense. So what's this other option you have in mind?"

Would Liam take her back? Or did Hammer mean to step in? Because this definitely had something to do with one—or both—of them.

Liam leaned in before delving deep into her eyes. "If you want to learn about opening yourself to someone and giving your submission, no one knows you better or wants you to grow more than me and Hammer. Give yourself over to us. We'll guide you down your path."

For a long moment, Raine just stared. Had she heard that right? "You two? Together? Is that a joke?"

"Do you see us laughing?" Hammer stared disapprovingly with piercing eyes.

They'd offered her her wildest, most impossible desire. Sadly, it would probably end in someone's murder. And it would be her fault.

"It's fucking insane. It'll never work."

"You know I don't like that language, Raine." Liam's brows slashed in disapproval.

She was completely stunned, and he wanted to worry about her cursing? "The three of us together are a time bomb. It won't take long to explode, and we'll all get hurt. I can't do that. I can't open myself up when I'm going to spend at least half my time waiting for you two to come to blows. I'd love to say yes, more than anything." That admission would probably put Liam on edge or spur Hammer's temper—and they'd start fighting any second. "But it's a fantasy, like world peace."

To her shock, neither one of them lost their cool. In fact, they didn't seem ruffled at all to hear that she wanted them both. *Whoa.*

"It's not a fantasy, love. It's what we're offering you. And before you answer, listen to what we have to say."

Their whole conversation this morning had been laced with "we" and "us." Had running off been a wake-up call for them? Or had Seth bashed their heads together until they'd decided to play nice?

Liam and Hammer weren't perfect, but they usually had her best interests at heart. She owed it to them to at least listen because she could only imagine what sort of compromise they'd ironed out to even make her this offer together. And it was *so* enticing. Raine tried to ignore the rush of heat thrumming in her blood and think logically.

"All right. I'm glad you two are speaking again. I'll listen."

"We've put our differences aside to help you." Hammer cupped his chin in a thoughtful gesture. Damn if she didn't want him to reach out and touch her. "We've agreed to devote our time to you. I can safely say there aren't any Dominants at the club who, combined, have more experience than us."

"Make no mistake, we want you to have the best instruction available. Mistress Hillary can't provide you half the understanding and compassion we will," Liam added gently but firmly.

Raine couldn't deny how much she'd missed the affection he showered on her. Even Hammer never failed to show his caring—in his own silent way.

And the thought of having them both made her entire body light up like a Fourth-of-July spectacle.

Maybe they had really thought about this outlandish scheme. They were doing their damnedest to persuade her to accept. But no matter how badly she wanted to throw caution to the wind, doubts still crowded her mind.

"We already know your secrets." A hint of a smile curled across Hammer's lips. "You can't argue that we know what makes you tick."

"You've already established a bond with us." Without missing a beat, Liam's words fell in behind Hammer's. "No one understands you better than we do. Let go of your fears and put yourself in our hands. Let us take you on the journey."

His sincerity tugged at her heart. God, she wanted to say yes.

"We'll do everything we can to give you what you asked for." Hammer frowned. "You haven't changed your mind, have you?"

"No."

"We're completely united on this," Liam added. "We know you're worried we'll start arguing and tossing fists, but it won't happen, love. Tell me, is there another reason you're hesitating?"

"It's a huge decision," she insisted. "I need time to think."

But about what? Aside from their quarreling, it would be heaven having the two men she loved molding her. Hell, it would be a dream come true.

Hammer reached out and pulled her close to his chest, his warm breath caressing the shell of her ear. She felt herself melt.

"Do you really need time to think about being the center of our world, precious?" he challenged in a low, hungry voice.

Liam pressed in behind her, and his lips skimmed a path up her neck. "Open up and let us in. We won't let you fall."

A quiver of need slammed down her spine. She had no trouble envisioning what it would feel like to be at their mercy. Desire hummed.

Pressed between them, the fantasy that had spun through her head for weeks paled in comparison to the decadent reality. She sucked in a ragged breath.

They were trying to put aside their differences for her. No way to think otherwise or overlook that fact. They were giving her the chance to grow. Hell, the chance of a lifetime.

Her fantasy come true.

"I accept—on one condition." Negotiation was part and parcel of BDSM. No way was she entering into this without them hearing her concerns.

Liam eased back from behind her before sidling next to Hammer. Shoulder to shoulder, the two most important men in her life stared down at her, waiting.

Hammer slowly released her. "We're listening."

"You two have to get along. The minute there's any arguing, name calling, backbiting, jealous rants, or strife of any kind, I'm done. I mean it. I refuse to come between you two again."

They exchanged a glance, then Liam shrugged.

"Done." Hammer sent her a sharp nod.

"Our disagreements are over," Liam vowed.

She wanted it to be true. Whether they could make that stick remained to be seen, but short of calling them liars, Raine had to believe them. "As long as we're clear…"

"Crystal, love," Liam assured.

"Thank you."

"You're welcome. Now you'll hear our terms." Hammer nodded. "You will not question the methods we use to help you achieve submission," Hammer warned in his deep, growling Dom voice. If the man knew what that did to her girl parts, she'd be toast. "They will not always be easy, but they will be effective."

Liam picked up. "You will never doubt that we want anything but the best for you. And every time you curse, we'll add it to your list of infractions."

"Your little f-bomb has been duly noted." Hammer glared. "You will also never try to pit one of us against the other. Ever. Your training starts..." He looked at his watch. "Now. Raise your hand if you have any questions or do not understand our terms."

Their dual expressions of determination told her they were deadly serious. Though she couldn't help but worry their idea was doomed to fail, she was so damn touched.

"No, I understand."

This was really going to happen. God, she didn't know if she should be terrified or thrilled. More than a little of both swirled inside her.

"Good. Shower now. We will pack your bag. I'll come collect any toiletries you'd like to take and give you additional instructions then."

She blinked up at Liam. This wasn't the Dom she knew. She'd expected this sort of strict control from Hammer. But right now, Liam was all demand and no cajoling. It was sexy. Raine bowed her head for a moment, trying to wrap her thoughts around this morning's events. But there was only one answer in her heart. "Yes, Sir."

"Then I suggest some action," Liam urged. "If you dawdle, we'll add that to your list of infractions, too."

"And I guarantee you won't like it," Hammer added.

Then in unison, they turned toward the door.

That was the end of the conversation in their minds? "Wait!"

They turned back, Liam with a dark brow raised in warning, Hammer with an impatient stare.

"Why are you packing me a suitcase? Where are we going?"

Liam smiled. "You'll find out. Time's a wasting, Raine. I suggest you move."

Then they walked out. With a quiet click, the door shut behind them.

R aine shut off the water, anxiety humming through her veins. Liam's badass Dom mode earlier had been arousing as hell, but she'd found herself more than a bit intimidated. He'd instructed her to get herself ready quickly, but for what? All the uncertainty zipping through her was making her damn near dizzy.

Shoving the shower curtain aside, she shrieked, startled to find Liam standing before her with her towel draped over his arm. His stare raked her possessively, as though he meant to devour her in one big bite. Her nipples pebbled. Heat erupted deep in her womb. Just one look from the man and she was aching. This imposing side of him only served to make her more nervous about the surprising scheme he and Hammer had cooked up.

After last night, Raine had no doubt that Liam was mad—and hurt— that she'd run away. She adored his sweet side. His tender, nurturing compassion made her turn all gooey. But now he'd reverted to the reserved control he'd used with her at the lodge. It was effective and disquieting.

"Come here." His voice was thick as he opened the towel, inviting her into his arms.

A flutter of excitement scurried up her spine. Oh, she'd missed his warm embrace. Fighting the need to surge into his arms, she tiptoed closer. He enveloped her against him. Closing her eyes, she inhaled his spicy, familiar scent. She loved it every bit as much as she loved him.

"I can't begin to tell you how good it feels to hold you again." His silky Irish lilt slid over her like warm honey. "I've missed you."

She snuggled deeper. She could feel every hard inch of his body pressed against hers as he squeezed her tight. "I missed you, too."

Reaching up, he dislodged the clip in her hair and feathered his fingers to loosen the strands. All the while he stared down at her, not uttering a word. As he captured her with his gaze, the worries that had plagued her for the past few days faded into the background. But her guilt and insecurities still niggled her, seeping past the comfort of his embrace.

"Why?" Her unguarded question slipped out before she could curb it.

"Why what, love?"

"Why are you doing this for me after the way I left you? When you removed my collar, I panicked. I ran. I-I'm sorry. I didn't think you wanted me anymore." She hadn't planned to open up and show him her vulnerabilities. Now that she had, Raine searched his eyes, desperate to know what he thought, felt. His unreadable expression left her feeling more exposed than her nudity.

At Beck's condo, she'd believed that she'd cried all she could, but new, hot tears threatened, proving Liam owned something deep inside her.

"Shh. There now, love. Of course I want you. I never stopped." He stepped back and pulled her down with him as he sat on the toilet lid. "I'm trying to help you in the ways I know you need. This isn't about me; it's about you."

Raine curled up, sliding her arms around his steely shoulders as he placed a sweet kiss on her forehead. She sank into his embrace with a sigh. Being here felt so right.

"I didn't mean to snap at you last night," he murmured.

"You had every right to."

Liam gently rocked her, smoothing her hair back from her face. "You surprised me with your request. Just know that I love you. I'd do anything for you. Well, except watch you give your submission to a Domme."

Despite her anxiety, she laughed. So gentle, so loving...so Liam.

"Come on." He smiled down at her. "Stop your worrying and show me that you missed me."

With a sudden shyness, she leaned up and pressed her lips to his, feeling small and treasured in his arms. Liam moaned as he took her lips with a fierce tenderness that made her toes curl and her body dissolve with arousal. She squirmed, but he held her in place with firm fingers on her nape. With his free hand, he gripped her hip and pulled her tighter against him.

He was like a drug shooting straight into her veins, and the surge of "instant Liam" made her heart thump wildly. God, how she'd missed him. Missed this.

Their tongues tangled. A moan of desire bubbled and rolled up from her throat. Though the days she'd spent apart from him were painful and empty, they'd been healing, too. And coming back to him—to the comforting fire he roused—centered her.

Easing back, she saw a gratified smile sparkle all the way to Liam's eyes. Then he plucked her from his lap, tore away her towel, and swatted her bare ass.

"Now get a move on. We're waiting." With a wicked grin full of promise, he turned. "Bring me your toiletries after you're dressed. And make sure you wear a skirt. Something short."

With that, Liam left the bathroom.

Nerves jumping, Raine dashed to her closet and dressed, then applied some tinted moisturizer and lip gloss. Pausing to look in the mirror, she noticed her lips were swollen from his kiss. All the energy buzzing inside her merged with the joy she felt at being with him again.

As she stepped back into her room, she noticed Liam sitting patiently on her bed. An empty suitcase lay open beside him. He stood and accepted the items she held out in offering. After unloading them into the bag, he led her to the door.

"I'll finish packing for you, love. Right now, it's time to eat breakfast. Hammer is waiting for you."

Raine's eyes widened. Liam was voluntarily sending her to Hammer? Yes, they'd both agreed to be her Doms, but everything seemed surreal.

"And you want me to find him?"

"Yes. He's waiting in the kitchen."

That made Raine's heart stutter again. Lord, if Hammer was cooking, she hoped he was preparing dry cereal. Anything more complicated could be catastrophic. Absently, she kissed Liam, then darted out of the room, almost dreading what she'd find. Hammer had proven he could set the kitchen on fire.

As she scurried down the hall, Raine felt a tingle roll through her and glanced back to see Liam watching, his seductive stare promising more than a kiss—soon.

As she rounded the doorway to the kitchen, Hammer stood at the stove, cursing as he hissed and shook a splatter of hot bacon grease from his hand. Raine bit her lip, trying not to laugh.

Remembering the last time he'd attempted to cook, her thoughts wandered years back, to the third morning she'd awakened at Shadows. The scream of a smoke alarm had sent her racing down the hall, panicked that the entire building was going up in flames. What she'd found instead was the sharply perceptive man who had taken her in. He fanned a dish towel at the shrieking alarm. Flames flickered behind the glass window of the oven as more noxious smoke rolled from its door.

With a gasp, Raine had raced around the room, turning off the oven and searching numerous cabinets until she found a box of baking soda. Yanking the door open, she dumped the powder over the flames, snuffing out the fire from the frosting-laden Danishes he'd tried to broil.

Hammer, despite seeming so tall and intimidating, had given her a smile of pride. "Thank you, precious."

She hadn't known why at the time, but her heart had soared and her stomach had flipped over completely.

Her heart nearly melted in from her chest now as she watched him attempt to cook for her again. Raine hoped that meant he was on the road to forgiving her. She sure hadn't thought he would be last night when he'd refused to speak to her. Hammer cutting her cold would be like losing a limb. This morning, she still wasn't exactly sure where she stood. They weren't strictly friends. But they weren't exactly lovers, either. Like Liam, he wanted to help her. That had to mean something.

She wondered if he knew that Liam had pulled her naked into his lap minutes ago and kissed her. Or if he'd care. Would Hammer kiss her, too? Do more? Or had the only way he and Liam been able to stop arguing and make her this offer was to take sex off the table?

Damn, she should have asked what boundaries they'd set for themselves before she'd agreed to let them guide her. But she intended to ask as soon as she had them alone again.

Easing toward the stove, she placed her hand over his and reached for the fork in his grasp, looking up into his face. For recognition. For approval. Would he push her away or welcome her?

"Do you want me to take over?" she asked softly.

"It would be safer for us all. Here." He handed her the fork with a grin.

Instantly, that set her at ease. She took over at the stove with a wistful smile. "Remember the last time you tried to set the place on fire?"

"I might take that for sass, precious."

But he wouldn't, and his teasing tone made that obvious. She chuckled as she nudged his shoulder to move him away from *her* stove. "I've got this. Grab yourself a cup of coffee and relax."

Skewing up one side of his mouth, Hammer lifted the coffeepot from the counter. "Um…"

He tipped the pot over, revealing that it was empty, and sent her a hopeful smile, thrusting it toward her.

She giggled. "You're so helpless."

Shaking her head, she stepped around him and filled the pot. She could feel his eyes watching her every move.

"Not at everything," Hammer refuted in a rough drawl. "But you know that."

Raine remembered. Every moment of the night she'd spent in his bed was seared in her memory.

"Like barking out orders and growling?" she teased to match his mood.

Suddenly, his smile disappeared. Hammer's commanding Dom face took its place.

Uh-oh. Fun time is over.

"I have one question for you," he said.

Raine held her breath anxiously. "Yes?"

"Are you absolutely sure this is what you want to do?"

Despite her earlier reservations, she'd never been more serious about anything in her life. The past was where it belonged, behind her. The present was winding itself before her, albeit on a unexpected path. The future...who knew? But she refused to give up on tomorrow simply because it scared her.

She lifted her chin with conviction. "Positive."

"I hope you mean that." Hammer's stare held hers hostage for a long, silent moment.

Then his attention drifted toward the coffeepot, and he sighed.

So big and bad...until he had no coffee. She grinned. "It will be ready soon. *Patience.*"

"Watch yourself," Hammer warned with an arch of his brow. "Don't forget, your lily white backside is going to be in our hands soon."

Their broad, strong hands. And the visual of them all over her blasted through her brain—of them stripping off her clothes with those hands, binding her to their bed, dragging their lips across her skin, driving their cocks deep inside her, pounding, claiming, overwhelming... God, she hoped they'd give her that chance.

The room felt hot, or maybe it was just her cheeks. Biting back a moan, she zipped her gaze down to the bacon sizzling in the pan, hoping Hammer couldn't read her thoughts. Raine ached for something that might never happen, and she had to accept that. Or did she? The question that had haunted her earlier roared back with force. They'd said they would both top her...but what exactly would that entail?

Raine gathered up her courage and changed the subject. "Can I ask *you* a question?"

"Of course."

"Why are you trying to bury the hatchet with Liam and help me?"

Hammer moved in behind her, his warm breath caressing her ear. He pressed every hard inch of his body against her back, and his cock prodded her backside. No mistaking that he wanted her. Though she tried not to shiver, his closeness made that an impossible feat. He wrapped his big hands around her hips in a commanding hold and pressed into her. Raine gasped and melted into him. Desire flashed over her skin. God, he felt so good.

She wanted more—of both of them.

"Because you're worth it, precious. You've asked for help, and no one on the goddamn planet is going to lead you down your path except us."

Twisting from his hold, she turned and met his solemn stare. "But why? I mean, I know why Liam wants to guide me. He says he's in love with me. But you…you've already gone above and beyond taking care of me for years. I would have thought that you'd be happy to cut me loose and let Liam teach me what I need to know."

Resolution stamped across his face an instant before Hammer slid a hand around her back and skimmed it up her spine. Then he gripped his fist in her hair and tilted her head back, his stare intent. He meant to get some message across to her.

"Whatever you think, whatever has happened in the past, you belonged with me the minute you walked in the door."

Hammer swooped down, his lips capturing hers. Impassioned. Reverent. The kiss branded her with fire…and something almost desperate. She'd never felt him so ardently gentle. Hell, she'd never known he was capable of it.

Beneath her tank top, her nipples drew up hard and ached as every muscle in her body went soft. The potent claim of his mouth soon had her dropping the fork to grab his shirt in her fists with a sigh.

Hammer poured himself into this one euphoric kiss. It held all the markings of a silent confession, and Raine wondered if she were imagining this touch to be Hammer's nonverbal proclamation of love. Was that even possible? Or was he simply trying to provide caring so she'd let him "fix" her? After he had, would he slam the door shut between them again?

Immersed in his raw emotion, Raine stopped trying to answer the questions swirling in her head and gave herself over. She lost herself in his kiss, pouring out all the longing she'd barely had the opportunity to release in six years.

Hammer growled in approval. She savored each exalted second until he slowly pulled away. Still, he allowed his lips to linger on hers for another bittersweet moment.

Then she jerked away. Could she return his affection without Liam's permission? Should she have kissed Liam without consulting Hammer? What were the rules of their new partnership?

As if he could peer into her soul, as he so often had, he sent her a reassuring smile and took her hand, pressing a delicate kiss in the center of her palm.

"Everything is fine, precious. Finish fixing breakfast. Then we'll start fixing you."

CHAPTER
FOURTEEN

As the sun hid just below the horizon, Liam led Raine outside toward his SUV, with her hand tucked in his. Hammer trailed close behind, his palm resting at the small of her back. The guys were so quiet. Tension hovered in the air. Now wasn't the time to ask questions—but she wanted to.

Liam opened the back door. "Get in."

Raine frowned. Two men occupied the front seat. Were they letting someone else take her somewhere? That didn't sound like Liam and Hammer at all. She sent Liam a questioning gaze, then bent to see who sat in the car.

Beck swiveled in the driver's seat and grinned. "Hop in, princess. Your chariot awaits."

"Why are you going...wherever it is we're going?" she blurted. "Aren't you on call?"

"Hammer, you want to teach her some manners?" Beck suggested.

"I've got it." Liam swatted her ass.

She yelped, then glared at him. "It was just a question."

"Yes, a nosy one," Hammer said archly, digging into his pocket. "If you can't mute your curiosity, I'll be happy to help."

He dangled a ball gag in her face. Raine's eyes widened. She shook her head.

Seth roared with laughter. "This is going to be so entertaining."

She gave a little huff and sent Seth a stare that let him know he wasn't helping one bit. He just laughed more.

With her butt still stinging, Raine jumped into the back, as far from Hammer's ball gag as possible. Liam stopped her from sliding past the middle when he eased into the back seat on the driver's side. Hammer entered on the passenger's side and shut the door, sandwiching her between them. She still hadn't recovered from Liam's kiss in the bathroom or Hammer's in the kitchen. Now they pressed in tightly on either side of her. As Beck eased out of the parking lot and headed for the freeway, her heart raced. Perspiration dampened the skin between her breasts.

She had no idea where they were going. But with Hammer and Liam pressing their body heat into her, she prayed the drive wouldn't be far. She sensed their gazes straying toward her, could feel their hunger. They even smelled fantastic. *Damn!* Raine closed her eyes and squirmed, looking for some space. There wasn't any. Her pussy clenched.

Everyone relaxed into their seats, and Beck sipped coffee from a big travel mug. Raine held in a curse. She had a hunch this wasn't going to be a short trip.

To her left, Liam planted a hand on her bare thigh, just above her knee. She tensed and blinked up at him. It wasn't an overtly sexual caress, but he still made her heart race. She shifted and tried to cross her legs.

"None of that, love." Liam stayed her, tightening his fingers on her.

"You never cross your legs around us," Hammer growled in her ear.

Their deep voices caressed her. Raine pictured her legs open and them touching her intimately, possessively. A flash of arousal burned an electric supercharge hot through her veins. Blood rushed to her nipples, swelled her folds. God, she couldn't breathe. Dizziness swamped her head.

Before she could recover, Hammer took her hand and slung her wrist over his thigh. His thumb whispered across her forearm in slow, sensual circles. No mistaking the heat rising from his crotch, maybe an inch under her palm.

And Liam didn't seem to care. What the hell was going on here? He and Hammer were actually touching her simultaneously. Yes, they'd sworn to shelve the animosity between them and operate as one to help her, but Raine hadn't entirely believed it. And they surely hadn't discussed sex. Now, with her body on fire, need overtaking her and their hands on her, she felt more confused than ever.

Seth turned on the radio. The band coming through the speakers began singing about their sex being on fire. Yeah, she could relate. The man turned to her and grinned.

Asshole, she mouthed.

His smile disappeared. "Did you say something, Raine?"

Oops, he wasn't in the teasing mood. *Traitor.* She shook her head.

Beck chuckled and caught her glance in the rearview mirror. She'd smack him upside the head for being an asshole too if she wasn't sure she'd get in more trouble for it.

"Problem, Seth?" Liam asked.

Between the two men, she tensed and sent Seth a pleading glance.

"If there is, I've got a ball gag *and* nipple clamps." Hammer patted his pocket. "Just say the word."

Raine zipped a stare over to him. Was he trying to goad Liam's temper? Or just drive her over the edge of desire? God, she'd been dropped into the *Twilight Zone*.

She drew in a deep breath and closed her eyes. *Find your damn Zen.*

Yeah, that shit wasn't working. And it wasn't even seven a.m. yet.

"No problem so far," Seth finally said. "I've had a cup of Raine's coffee. I get the big deal now. I'm feeling generous…at the moment."

Kings of Leon were still screaming about their sex, and she sang along in her head, hoping it would distract her. It worked until Liam sidled even closer, his thigh plastered against hers. Hammer turned to ask Liam if he had enough room...and breathed on her neck.

Raine bit back a moan. How much more sensual overload could she take? As Beck had pointed out back at his condo, BDSM wasn't about sex. But Hammer and Liam sure were making it hard for her to think about much else.

The sun began to spill into the car as Liam's hand inched up her thigh. Every cell in her body held a collective breath, along with her, just waiting...

If she slid down and tried to get Liam's hand closer to her aching clit, would he notice? Yes, and he'd never give her what she wanted. At this point, she suspected Hammer would back him up, too.

She dared a peek at Liam. He stared straight ahead, but wore a smug little smile. Damn it, he knew exactly what he was doing to her.

His fingers crawled up her thigh again, this time taking her skirt with him an inch or two. A little gasp slipped past her lips as her clit began to throb, begging for his attention.

On her right, tingles screamed up her arm with every little circle Hammer drew on her wrist. She could imagine that pattern around her nipples before he drew them into his mouth, sucking, laving, nipping. She blew out a shaking breath. That visual wasn't helping.

The temperature in the car rose. All she wanted to do was arch to Liam and Hammer, straddle one or the other—or both—and plead with them to fuck her.

As the song finally wound to its screeching conclusion, the singer screamed that he was consumed by what was about to transpire. She wished to hell something would transpire here, too. If it didn't soon, she might lose her damn mind.

"Seth, can you, um…turn the heater down?" she managed to choke out.

"Gee, I think it's really comfortable." Beck shrugged. "You hot or something, princess?"

"I think it's fine, too." Seth turned to her. As his stare fell to Liam's hand on her thigh, a grin crawled across his face. "But the sun is coming up. It'll warm the car up more, so maybe we should. She's looking really flushed."

If she wasn't so turned on, she'd be totally embarrassed. And Seth was enjoying her discomfort immensely. She wanted to punch him.

"It's a bit chilly back here," Liam drawled. "But if you're hot, you could take off your sweater, love." He tugged on the edge of her cardigan.

So that she'd be wearing nothing but a tank top and a very short skirt? "I'll be fine."

Hammer squeezed her fingers. "Remove the sweater."

She gave him a long-suffering sigh. They were determined to expose her for reasons unknown. Beck and Seth were getting a huge kick out of seeing her all flustered, but she didn't imagine Liam and Hammer considered this a joke. They had to be loving the ego stroke of knowing they aroused her. The bigger question was, why did being on display while the guys touched her turn her on?

Raine was loath to part with her sweater, but Hammer had given her a direct command, and she'd agreed to submit. So she struggled out of the little red button-down garment and handed it to Liam. She stifled the urge to ask him if he was happy now—barely.

"Thank you." Liam draped her sweater over his knee with a smile, then put his hand on her thigh again, higher this time.

"And now your underwear," Hammer demanded in her ear.

"What?" she gasped at him.

Hammer glowered back. "Did you not hear what I said, Raine?"

Her heart stopped. She blinked at him. A glance around the car told her everyone waited, watched. As much as this made Raine uncomfortable, every nerve ending in her body leapt with life and need.

"I heard, Sir."

He sent her a stern scowl. "Don't make me wait."

God, she must be crazy. Her insides jittered. Her pussy clenched. And damn if his words alone didn't make her soaking wet.

"Something smells really sweet," Seth commented, almost in passing.

"Yeah. My mouth is watering." Beck smacked his lips loudly. Then he shot her a leering grin from the front seat.

This was not happening.

Raine closed her eyes for a moment and forced in a calming breath. Liam's fingers slid up her knee again, playing along her inner thigh. And Hammer still stared, expectant and impatient.

"You're stalling," Liam murmured, sliding his hand completely under her skirt. His fingers passed over her clit, pressing for an electric moment before they curled around the waistband and tugged. "I'll help you."

Wow, thanks so much.

"Lift up," Hammer demanded, grasping the other side of the waistband.

Together, they tugged down, and off the panties came. Then even she could smell how wet she'd become.

"I'm suddenly hungry," Seth commented.

Liam gripped her panties with a dark, satisfied smile. "Find your own bloody meal."

Raine wondered if she could die from chagrin...and unfulfilled need. Quick glances at the men on either side showed hard cocks straining against their slacks. They were enjoying winding her up and exerting their control. Why did she like it so damn much, too?

She dug her nails into her palms and pressed her lips together tightly. Otherwise, she'd give into the temptation to ask them the point of this little exercise. If she did, Hammer would surely drag out the ball gag, nipple clamps, and who knew what else was in his pockets. If she had to bite her tongue off, she'd shut up.

Beside her, Liam lifted her panties to his nose and inhaled deeply. As she watched, her eyes widened. Hammer's wicked laugh rumbled in her ear. Liam reached across her body and brushed her sensitive nipples, causing her to moan, as he handed her undergarment to Macen.

"Problem, precious?" Hammer challenged, lifting the panties to his nose, then closing his eyes as if savoring her scent.

Shit! She stared straight out the windshield. "None, Sir."

"Excellent." He sniffed again.

Liam glided his fingers to her inner thigh once more. "You smell divine, love."

"Definitely delicious," Hammer murmured into her ear, then passed the panties back to Liam.

Could a girl self-combust from sexual frustration?

Beck worked his way through the thickening rush-hour traffic, but she had no idea where they were going. At the moment, she almost didn't care. If it contained a bed big enough for these two men to put her out of her misery, she'd be thrilled as hell. If not, she hoped for some privacy soon so she could take the edge off this need.

"How long did you say it would take to get there?" Beck asked from the driver's seat. "We'll probably need to stop for gas if it's more than another eighty miles."

Hammer leaned forward and clapped Beck on the shoulder. "Plan to, man. With traffic, I'm expecting this to take…three or four hours." He swiveled a stare back at her. "But don't rush. We're in no hurry."

A t just past noon, they arrived at the lodge. Liam breathed a sigh of relief. Beck had taken Hammer at his word and hadn't rushed the drive a bit. During those five hours, he and Macen had never stopped touching Raine—but they also hadn't stimulated any part of her that would grant orgasm. They'd controlled her—every moment, every mile—and it had been heady. The sweet, salty scent of her arousal had filled the car and swirled in Liam's head, damn near making him drunk. He'd barely managed to restrain himself from pulling her onto his lap, burrowing his rigid cock—hell, his bloody soul—into her completely, then listening to her scream for him as he came like a fucking volcano.

As much as Raine had to learn, Liam wasn't sure how long it would be before he could indulge in any of that.

Beck stopped the car, and Liam opened the door, turning to help Raine out. She emerged into the brisk afternoon looking flushed and unsteady and completely off-kilter—exactly the way they wanted her. This Raine couldn't possibly be thinking about ways to dodge him or Hammer, much less scurry behind her walls.

"Are you feeling all right, love?" Liam asked.

"Fine." But her voice shook. Her breathing wasn't quite under control.

Taking Raine by the hand, he repressed a smile and led her toward the lodge. Approaching her other side from the vehicle, Hammer claimed her free hand. The scent of her skin lingered on Liam's clothes and in the air. He wanted to hoard that sweetness for himself. But he no longer had the luxury of being her only Dom. For this "fixing" to work, everything had to be about Raine. And the simple but irritating truth was, she needed Hammer, too.

It hadn't been easy to watch his old friend touch her, but Liam couldn't deny that he'd loved the way she responded to them so readily. Her squirming little pants and aroused gasps had filled him with power. Liam had no doubt Hammer felt the same.

Their shared hunger for the same woman had been so familiar—yet utterly different. Unlike their bond with Juliet, this felt strong, raw, insatiable. Connected. Even Beck's and Seth's occasional comments had filled him with a strange possessive pride he'd never felt with any other woman.

A few feet from the car, they reached the front door. Liam opened it. Raine eased inside the foyer, gazing around the big open lounge with its blazing fireplace. "I recognize this. It's your lodge."

"Yes," Liam confirmed. "You were a wee bit tired and distraught the last time we arrived."

Raine cut Hammer an assessing glance before walking into the room. "I like it here. It's cozy."

"Good. We want you comfortable," Hammer said, then addressed Liam. "Gorgeous place, man."

"It's peaceful," Seth added, a couple of steps back as he grabbed some luggage. He closed the back of the SUV, then fell in behind them.

"Amazing views," Beck put in, juggling a couple of suitcases. "Best of all, no one will hear you scream for miles, princess."

Raine gasped. "Beck!"

Adam, the caretaker, rushed from the back of the house to meet them. He took the bags from Seth and Beck, then turned to Liam with a smile. "Welcome back. Ngaire has prepared lunch for you. I've followed your instructions, and you'll find everything as you requested. We'll be just down the hill. Ring if you need anything."

Liam thanked the older man, then nodded to his pleasing, plump wife. As soon as Adam distributed the luggage to the bedrooms, the pair disappeared out the back door, to their little cottage.

"I'm starved!" Seth complained, prowling toward the kitchen. "Where's lunch?"

Everyone trailed behind him. Collectively, they began pulling out plates, silverware, and napkins to set the table. Someone found a bottle of wine and a few cans of beer. Fresh baked rainbow trout came from the oven, sprinkled with delicate herbs. Potatoes and asparagus followed, along with a loaf of crusty sourdough. In less than five minutes, everyone dug in, praising Ngaire's cooking between bites. But Raine picked more than ate, still wriggling in her chair. A glance around the table told Liam that everyone else noticed, too.

When the meal concluded, the whole gang pitched in to do the dishes. Once the kitchen was clean, he and Hammer escorted Raine upstairs while Seth and Beck left to prepare the room in which her training would begin.

Liam pushed open the door to the master suite. With a hand at the small of Raine's back, he led her inside. Her suitcase sat near the picture windows overlooking the mountains.

With a glance at Hammer, who nodded back, Liam made his way into the bathroom and began to fill the sleek tub with hot water and bath oils. He found scented soaps, shampoo, razors, and shaving cream all laid out on the nearby counter beside fluffy white towels. His cock jerked just thinking about what they planned next.

Satisfied that the caretakers had tended to every detail, Liam stalked back to the bedroom. Raine stood beside Hammer, looking more than a little shaky. But she wasn't balking or quitting. He'd take little victories like that and hope they added up to bigger ones soon.

Raine glanced his way, and he saw the questions rolling across her face.

"Spit it out, love," Liam said. "What's got you worried?"

She fidgeted, shifting from one foot to the other. Whatever bounced around in her head, she was reluctant to say it—a bad habit they'd break her of shortly.

"It's just... I noticed only my suitcase here and I was wondering..." She sighed. "Do you mean to leave me alone?"

"This is your room, but we'll have access to it twenty-four seven. You won't really be alone," Hammer assured.

"But neither of you will be sleeping here?"

He and Hammer exchanged a glance. She hadn't asked them to stay with her outright. But it surprised them both that she'd voiced her question because having them beside her was something she obviously wanted.

"We're not," Liam answered softly.

As her shoulders sagged and she looked down, Liam lifted her chin with a soft smile. "Now don't look so crestfallen. At times, you'll be happy to see us go so you can have a bit of peace. But that will only come when we think you need to reflect or rest."

"Even then, we'll be nearby and in your head, precious. We'll be surrounding you. We won't let you feel lost or abandoned," Hammer promised.

Liam caressed her cheek. "As you progress, we can discuss sleeping arrangements again. Does that answer your question?"

Understanding—with a hint of regret—flickered in Raine's eyes as she gave a tentative nod.

"There'll be none of that." Liam released her, glowering. "You'll use your words from now on. Understood?"

"Yes, Sir," she whispered.

"Good." Hammer reached up and trailed his knuckles down her cheek.

She closed her eyes, clearly finding reassurance in his touch. Watching a delicate contentment fill her face, Liam's hope brightened. Such a challenge, Raine was...then sometimes she could be so giving and soft.

Hammer dropped his hand suddenly. "Strip."

Liam heard the man's impatience. Macen was eager to start testing Raine and having her under his control. Liam shared the feeling.

Her eyes flew open. She blinked between them while they waited for her to process the demand. Finally, she pressed her lips together, resolution overtaking her expression. *There was her backbone...*

Her fingers trembled, but Raine peeled off her flimsy tank top. Then she reached around to unfasten her bra, thrusting her breasts toward them. It was all Liam could do to keep from gliding his tongue up the soft valley of her cleavage. She wriggled out of her short skirt next, and he watched the sway of her hips, captivated, as she exposed the dark tuft of hair striping her pussy and revealed her creamy thighs. Blood rushed to his cock.

Raine stood naked before them, beautiful and tense, looking like warm ivory velvet. Liam clenched his fists, resisting the urge to put his hands all over her.

Beside him, Hammer caressed her bare curves with his stare and sighed roughly, struggling to hold back. Liam knew it not only by the erection tenting his trousers, but the tick of his clenched jaw.

Bloody Christ, this series of tasks would challenge their control.

Finally, Hammer reined himself in and stood tall, stance wide, hands behind his back.

Liam watched Raine's gaze fall to the floor as he paced around her, stopping when his chest brushed her back, a mere breath from her skin. "Tell me what you're feeling, love."

"Nervous." She drew in a shuddering breath. "Unsure."

"Good girl," Hammer praised. "Are you afraid of us?"

"No." Her gaze bounced up to them both, reassuring. "I'm afraid I'll lose my courage, clam up, and disappoint you."

It wasn't the answer either wanted but both had inherently known. Still, for Raine, that was bloody honest. Liam met Hammer's glance.

"You're doing a fine job now. Just keep trying your best. We'll work through everything else," Liam promised. "Take a deep breath."

Raine drew in a shaky inhalation, then let it out, looking calmer. "Thank you."

Hammer eased closer, standing in her personal space. "I'm sure you're nervous because you don't know what we expect. So we'll explain now. You will address us as 'Sir' when you respond. Do you understand?"

"Yes, Sir." Her gaze lowered again.

"Very nice." Liam kissed her bare shoulder. "You will kneel when we enter a room and remain there until we tell you otherwise. Is that clear?"

Raine began to nod, then stopped herself. "Yes, Sir."

"Wonderful, love," Liam murmured. "Let's get you in the tub. We'll talk more then."

"Why?" She frowned. "I had a shower this morning."

With a sigh, Liam bent down and lifted Raine over his shoulder, then turned, putting her ass directly in front of Hammer. Right on cue, Macen whacked both cheeks, one after the other. She yelped.

"We didn't ask you if you're clean or if you wanted a bath," Hammer pointed out. "*We* want you in the tub. That's all you need to know."

"And you didn't address me properly, Raine," Liam reminded as he strolled into the bathroom and dropped her on her feet. "What do you say?"

"Yes, Sir. Sorry, Sir." She swallowed, and he could see the worry twisting her expression.

They couldn't let her self-doubt fester, especially this early in the process. Time to put her at ease.

Each man took one of her arms to steady her as they helped her into the tub. When the warm water enveloped her feet, she sighed. The scents of rosemary and lavender rose with the swirl of steam.

"Sit," Hammer directed.

Raine lowered herself into the soft, inviting water and sat unmoving as they stripped out of their coats and shirts, then draped them over the back of the vanity chair.

"Lie back. Close your eyes. We'll take care of you now," Liam promised as he knelt beside the tub.

He waited until she complied and a little sigh escaped her. Some of the tension left her body.

"You look beautiful," he whispered in her ear. "Now spread your thighs and tell us what you think submission is."

Her eyes flew wide open, and she stared at him as if he'd asked her to explain quantum physics. "Excuse me, Sir?"

"Okay, let's try one command at a time." On the opposite side of the tub, Hammer reached into the water and wrapped a hand around her ankle. "Do you have any trouble interpreting what we meant by 'spread your thighs?'"

The heat of the water had turned her cheeks pink, but she flushed something close to red now. "No, Sir."

When she didn't move, Hammer raised a brow. "Do I need to tell you to do it now?"

"No, Sir. But it's a little embarrassing. I know you've seen it all. It's just... even though this is a common request for a Dom to make of his sub, it feels odd to flash you both."

Liam grabbed her chin and turned her toward him with a frown. "There isn't a single part of your body that I'm not intimately familiar with and hasn't pleased me. I've no doubt it's the same for Hammer. You're not flashing us; you're showing us what's ours. Now do as you're told."

"Yes, Sir." Her voice shook, but she raised one leg to the rim of the tub. Hammer guided the other up until she lay splayed wide. Raine tensed, her blue eyes begging silently for approval.

"So fucking beautiful," Hammer said roughly as he skimmed his fingers up to wrap around her inner thigh. "Now answer the second part of the question."

She gasped softly, watching Hammer edge closer to her slick folds. Her gaze swung back to Liam's face, anxious and tight.

"Say what's on your mind, love," Liam coaxed.

"Um...Sir. He's touching me, and you're watching." Raine looked like she searched for words. "That's okay with you?"

"Did I seem upset when Hammer touched you in the car?" he asked.

"No, Sir."

"Didn't we promise you no fighting or disagreements?"

Understanding dawned in her eyes. "Yes, Sir."

"Good. If you think you'll learn to submit and open up without us touching you anywhere and everywhere, Raine, you're mad."

"Oh." Her breathy exhalation went straight to his cock. "So…there will be sex, Sir?"

"That option isn't off the table, but it's up to you. Your behavior and progress will dictate our decisions."

Relief and excitement fluttered across her face, and a sense of triumph that she wanted them so much chugged through his veins. Yes, that meant sharing her with Hammer, but he welcomed the chance to touch her again. He was desperate to see how far they could send her spiraling into pleasure.

"Now answer the damn question," Hammer demanded. "If we have to ask it again, you'll come out of that tub and over my knee."

"Submission…right." Raine nodded and hesitated, clearly gathering her thoughts. "I know it's a power exchange. I get that I'm supposed to give myself over to you and trust that you'll both praise and punish me when I need it." She frowned. "I've felt the need to please you both, though in different ways. Disappointing either of you hurts something inside me. Liam, last time we were here, I felt something both painful and amazing. When we talked about my childhood, remember? Blurting all that out was hard, but I knew it would damage us more if I refused to talk. I remember looking at you and hoping that you'd catch me. I was so grateful when you did. And I felt like yours."

"I'm sensing a 'but' here. Go on," Liam urged.

"But I've looked around Shadows and watched the others scene. It's confusing. So many different types of Doms and subs. I've seen brutal punishment for the tiniest infraction. And I've seen almost no discipline for incredibly bratty behavior. And I've seen a lot of sex—tender, rough, odd, beautiful. But I have a hard time adding those things up in my head and figuring out how it's all submission. I know my wants and impulses, but I don't know if they're wrong." She frowned, then seemed to remember herself. "Sir."

Liam exhaled. Her view was so scattered. Why hadn't he asked her that question sooner? If he had, he would have started at square one when he'd collared her. Of course, he hadn't known her well then. Since then, Raine hadn't talked to him or opened up like she should. But he'd assumed her understanding of the power exchange was far deeper.

"I know putting that into words was difficult for you. Thank you, love." He leaned in, cupping her face in his hands, and took her mouth in a searing kiss.

Raine yielded her lips to him, opening and allowing him to sink deep inside her. She clung, wrapping her arms around his neck, so welcoming. Her sweetness intoxicated him. Liam moaned, some part of him wishing he could spend all day just worshipping her mouth. The other part of him realized they had work to do.

Easing back, he kissed her nose, then reached for the shampoo.

She blinked up at him, then slid her gaze over to Hammer. "What I said…that wasn't wrong?"

"No, precious. Today, there was no right or wrong answer. You have a lot to learn, but that's why we're here. I'm proud of your honesty."

He leaned in and tangled his hand in her hair, tugging gently until his lips hovered just over hers. They shared a silent moment before Macen took her mouth, devouring and rewarding at once.

Liam couldn't afford to think now about how that made him feel. If he did, his heart might break. Instead, he watched, focusing on how Raine was opening, blossoming under their attention. This bath was serving its purpose—showing her how good it could be if she let it. To dwell on the love she might never give him would only be borrowing tomorrow's trouble today.

As Hammer eased back, Raine smiled softly. Then she looked Liam's way, and his heart caught when their gazes tangled. She sent him a searching smile, and he gave her the reassurance she sought. He answered in kind. Damn if she didn't glow, bask in their affection, seemingly at peace.

As she lowered her gaze, that grin brightened even more. Then she looked up at him through her dark lashes, her blue eyes sparkling.

Liam hoped like hell she was truly ready to open herself and be whole —and that she'd still want him afterward. "Tilt your head back so I can wash your hair."

"Yes, Sir." Raine complied, closing her eyes.

He plucked at the bathtub's nozzle and pulled the attached hose up from its base. The spray of water jetted from the head. He urged her to scoot down, then eased her back, supporting her neck in his palm. Slowly, deliberately, he soaked her raven mane, then squirted a dollop of floral shampoo at her crown. Liam plunged his fingers into the strands and kneaded at her scalp until she moaned in bliss. He couldn't deny how much he enjoyed having Raine put herself in his care.

Meanwhile, Hammer whisked a soapy loofah up her legs, over her belly. He lathered her shoulders, her breasts, dragging it slowly over her nipples. Her breath caught.

Liam watched, thumbing away the suds that drizzled onto her fore-head. She groaned as he rinsed the shampoo, then spread conditioner through her hair. Again, he worked it through, this time massaging her neck, rubbing the tension away before he rinsed her hair clean.

Not once did she flinch or open her eyes. In that moment, she gave them total trust. Liam burned for more of it.

"You did so well, love." He kissed her forehead.

"Thank you, Sir. That felt good," she purred.

"Now stand up, precious. It's time to shave that little landing strip you've left unwaxed." Hammer extended his hand.

She frowned. "I thought it would be fun. You don't like it?"

"No."

"Why not?" Confusion knit her brows.

"Because when I rake my tongue up your pouty cunt, I want it bare. Is that a good enough reason for you, precious?"

"Oh. O-okay, Sir." Raine blushed and slipped her slender fingers into Hammer's wide grasp, rising like a goddess from the water.

Her long, dark hair dripped over the swell of her backside. Drops mingled down her thighs. Swallowing tightly, Liam skimmed his palms over her pert ass and gripped her hips, steadying her.

He watched Hammer squirt a cloud of white foam onto his fingers before painting her dark pubic hair. The man's stare riveted on the sweet pussy, inches from his face. Liam had no doubt Macen wanted to slide his fingers between Raine's silky folds and stay.

Hammer's nostrils flared as he glided the razor over the cottony foam. "Such a pretty pussy, Raine. So soft and slick. It's wet from more than the water, isn't it?"

Liam felt her tremble. He soothed her, caressing down her thighs, brushing his fingertips across the sensitive flesh behind her knees. "Answer him, love."

"Yes, Sir," Raine choked out, not meeting their stares.

"Good girl. Don't be embarrassed. We like you aroused." Hammer dropped a kiss on her hip before he rinsed the blade in the water and shaved off another strip of foam. "Spread your legs wider."

Gliding his hand up the inside of her thigh, Liam nudged her legs apart, helping her balance her foot on the rim of the tub.

Hammer soaked the swollen pout of her pussy with the nozzle. She gasped as the spray grazed her clit. A moment later, he smoothed his thumb over her now bare mound, so close to her sensitive button.

"We're done, precious," he said thickly.

But no one moved. Christ, Liam felt the heat pouring from between her legs and leaned in to brush his lips across the firm globes of her backside. The scent of her pussy filled his nostrils and made his mouth water. Fuck, she crumbled his restraint. He'd last been inside her a mere three days ago, but it felt like forever.

Liam could see that Hammer wasn't faring much better. His stare still hadn't left her cunt. Beads of sweat had broken out across the man's forehead, at his temples. Raine panted, little catching breaths that told him exactly how much she desired them. Liam glanced at the nearby bath oil before staring again at Raine's ass, remembering all too well how snug and perfect she felt around his cock.

And if they stayed crouched here much longer, he had no doubt they'd be balls deep inside her in the next two minutes. While he'd love feeling Raine tight and hot around him, they couldn't let her believe their time at the lodge was about anything other than her growth. Sex, if it came, would be the bonus they all reaped for her open, honest submission—nothing less.

"I think it's time we let Raine dry off," Liam growled between clenched teeth as he backed away.

Hammer jerked his head in Liam's direction, and he could see the man visibly fight for control before taking a step back. "Yeah. Time for a breath of fresh air."

"Couldn't agree more."

"Good. I'll get her damn clothes."

Liam hands shook as he unfolded the towel and tried to cover Raine.

"Thank you, Sir." She took it from his grasp, then bent over and wrapped it around her dripping hair—leaving her body entirely bare.

Well, hell. Liam almost envied Macen the task of digging through her suitcase.

"Hurry up, man!" he shouted.

"I'm working on it," Hammer barked back.

Raine tried to smother a giggle and failed.

"Do you have something to say?" Liam asked her sharply.

She pressed her lips together, suppressing her amusement. "No, Sir. I enjoyed my bath. I hope you did, too."

"Minx." He swatted her ass. "Out of the tub you go." Drawing in a deep breath, he took her hand and cupped her elbow to help her step free. The second she padded onto the fluffy bath mat, he released her. "Hammer, where are you with those clothes?"

The man stormed into the bathroom. "I'm right—" Macen let out a deep breath, devouring the sight of her from head to toe. "Fuck."

That's where this was headed, all right. Liam reached over to the counter and snagged another terrycloth sheet, thrusting it at Raine. "Dry yourself off. We're going to step out for a moment. You're free to do your hair and makeup. Leave the bathroom door open. There'll be no touching yourself."

"Yes, Sir." A smile flirted at her lips as she grabbed the towel and shook it loose.

Hauling in a shuddering breath, he turned away and grabbed Hammer by the arm. "Let's go."

His old friend didn't argue. He dropped a handful of black lace on the vanity, then raced him out of the room. Hammer beat him into the bedroom by a fraction, but Liam spotted the door to the balcony first, rattling it and cursing at the lock until it fell open.

With a groan of relief, he stepped outside. Macen followed. Instantly, the winter chill blasted them in a mighty gust as they looked across the sweeping vistas of the pine-dotted mountains. It was wintry enough to snow, and right now that felt damn good.

"This is better than a cold shower," Hammer said.

"It is. I won't miss my shirt for an hour or two."

"It will take that long for the blood to leave my cock," he grumbled.

"This won't be easy. She laughed at us, mate. Giggled like a girl."

"We'll add that to her growing list of infractions."

Liam slanted Hammer a dubious stare. "And which of us is going to spank her without losing control?"

Hammer grimaced. "Beck?"

"That dodgy prick isn't touching her."

"I know. We'll be more collected after dinner."

Liam rested his arms on the railing beside his friend, bowing his head. "We have to be."

Hammer snared his gaze. "She's responding."

"Can't deny that." And wasn't that a double-edged sword?

"Are you all right with that?"

"If she learns to open up, then it's best for her." Liam shrugged. "There's nothing else to say."

Macen clapped him on the shoulder. "I know this is hard on you, but I respect what you're doing for Raine."

A couple of ugly replies came to mind, almost like a knee jerk. Liam shoved them down. Petty had no place here now. If he was being honest, as hard as it was to watch Hammer touch Raine, he also felt deep comfort in having his friend back.

"Thanks. Let's find a cup of coffee. Once she's dressed, we'll send Seth up to make sure she doesn't let her fingers put out her fire."

"Best idea you've had all day. Because this bath..." He shook his head.

"It was a bloody hard exercise in restraint." Liam grinned. "Shut your whining mug and let's go."

U nder the vanity lights in the master bath, Raine guided the little brush through her lashes, applying her mascara in a daze. To say that today had been mind-blowing was like saying the North Pole was cold. Liam and Hammer had both topped her—and touched her—at the same time. No one was bloody or bruised, screaming, shouting, or throwing punches. The next World War hadn't commenced. In fact, they'd seemed to enjoy taking care of her together.

Liam and Hammer had once been friends, but she'd mostly seen them mix as well as oil and water until today. Sure, they'd behaved civilly enough before Liam collared her, but Hammer's aloofness had even extended to his best friend, and she'd witnessed Liam's frustration and hurt. Today everything had been different, and Raine couldn't put her finger on why. Yes, they'd agreed to put aside their differences to help her, but their rapport now didn't feel like a forced compromise. It felt more like a kinship, like they'd fallen into a comfortable brotherhood.

Absently putting the wand back in the tube of mascara, she wound it closed and glanced at her appearance. She'd pass muster for dinner. Dark curls framed her flushed cheeks and trailed to her breasts. Red gloss sheened her slightly swollen lips.

In the mirror, she looked the same, but everything inside felt raw, confused, yearning. Different. The need they'd incited breathed just under her skin, lying in wait to hurtle her into aching desire again with their next touch. It was a miracle she hadn't begged them for relief.

What would it be like to spend every day between them, wrapped in their care, the center of their lives? It sounded ludicrous—mostly because it was—but it was her fantasy. No way she could deny how perfectly happy and whole everything they'd done today made her feel. She'd better enjoy it because it probably wouldn't last.

"Raine, time for dinner!" Seth shouted up the stairs.

"Be right there," she called back, shoving her makeup in its case and turning off her curling iron.

She wasn't really hungry, but when the watchful Dom had left her a few minutes ago to check on the meal, Raine figured she wouldn't have long to sort out her thoughts alone. Nice to know that something about this day had been predictable.

Raine dashed out of the bedroom, her bare feet padding down the stairs. The scent of something delicious wafted in the air, and the little growl of her stomach surprised her. Then again, she hadn't eaten much the entire day—too bewildered to consume the big breakfast she'd cooked and too confused to do more than nibble at lunch. The anxiety and arousal simmering inside her would probably kill her appetite for dinner as well. But if she spent the evening surrounded by Hammer and Liam, wrapped in their affection, she really didn't care.

From the kitchen, she heard Beck's boisterous laughter and sighed. So dinner wasn't going to be a quiet evening for three. She had no idea what was on the agenda, but since Hammer and Liam had "requested" she wear this sheer black baby-doll, Raine had her suspicions. *Great, more sexual teasing.* How the hell was she going to survive even another minute of feeling like an orgasmic time bomb?

Tugging at the lace tickling the tops of her thighs, she shoved back her self-consciousness. Why hadn't they given her some damn flannel pajamas?

Drawing in a deep breath, Raine rounded the corner into the kitchen and stopped. The four Doms stood, their chairs scraping the hardwood floor. She felt every eye on her, eating up her exposed flesh, and forced herself to stand with her head up and shoulders squared—and ignore that fluttery feeling inside her.

Raine raised her chin. "Hi."

Liam arched a brow at her.

"Sirs," she added hastily. She'd behaved casually for so long, she had trouble remembering her protocol.

Liam smiled at her before extending his hand and leading her toward the empty chair between him and Hammer. "You look lovely, lass."

"Scrumptious," Macen whispered in her ear as she sat. "I know what's for dessert."

As the other men resumed their seats, heat rushed up her face. She sent him a delicate scowl. "Hammer…"

He chuckled.

The men had set the table and laid out the meal the caretaker's wife had prepared. Everything looked fine, but Raine still frowned. "I would have been happy to cook."

"We enjoy when you do," Hammer said. "But we need you focused, not disappearing into the kitchen."

"Besides…" Liam glided his hand up her thigh, his fingers inching breathlessly close to her silky thong. "You'll need to save your strength."

Raine's breath caught. She zipped a questioning glance his way. He leveled her a smoldering stare. She shifted in her chair, wondering how she was going to make it through this meal.

"So, princess, did you enjoy your bath?" Beck asked with a wicked grin. He was being a jackass.

She answered with sticky sweetness. "It was nice, Sir."

"Just nice?" Hammer baited as he set a crusty dinner roll on her plate.

She resisted the urge to throw it at him. "Fine. Lovely. Enjoyable."

Trailing the pads of his fingers down her arm, Liam grinned as goose bumps peppered her flesh. "I'd call it amazing. An experience worth repeating."

"Very soon." Hammer smirked as he loaded her plate with chicken and rice casserole.

The men ate with gusto, chugging back a beer. Raine scooted her food across her plate with her fork and sipped at her wine, the appetite she'd had minutes ago now an afterthought. What would the next few days bring? And how would she get through them? Would there be an orgasm in her future?

"I didn't know you had this place, Liam," Seth said into the silence. "Do you come up here much? Ski in the winter, hit the lake in the summer?"

"I just inherited it last year, but I hope to visit more often."

Raine only half listened until Liam grazed his fingers over the silk covering her pussy. An electric arc danced through her body. A vicious ache followed. She grasped the table.

Damn, she'd been on edge all day. She struggled for a breath. A moan clogged her throat, and she barely managed to swallow it down.

"You're not eating, precious." Hammer smiled her way, mischief in his eyes. "Something wrong?"

"No, Sir." Under his watchful gaze, she speared a chunk of chicken and forced herself to chew.

Liam caressed down her thigh, then scooted back from the table. Without warning, he hoisted her onto his lap. "I'm not sure I believe that, Hammer. Do you?"

Raine swallowed tightly, feeling wired and flustered. They were going to dissect her thoughts, and all she could focus on was their touches and hot stares undressing her, with Liam's heat enveloping her and his steely erection prodding her thigh.

"No. Let's help her." Macen glided his fingertips up her calf.

She tried not to whimper.

After tearing apart a steaming roll heaped with melted butter, Liam lifted a piece and coaxed her to open for him. When she did, he slid the morsel into her mouth, his fingers lingering on her lips, urging her to lick them clean. His dark stare held hers captive, and Raine drowned. He anchored her in his steely arms, both giving her tenderness and oozing sex. She clung in return, sucking on the slightly rough pads of his fingers, tasting the salt on his skin.

Hammer moved her plate next to Liam's and slid closer, occupying her chair. As his body heat assailed her, he reached into his salad bowl and plucked up a thick slice of cucumber, slathered in dressing.

"Open for me, precious," Hammer commanded.

As she leaned in, lips parted, a drop of the creamy sauce splattered on the swell of her breast, trickling down the pale flesh. His eyes flared with heat as he eased the vegetable onto her tongue. Then he bent and licked the dressing from her skin, his lips brushing down the curve of her chest until he nipped her turgid crest through the lace and sucked hard.

Liam swallowed her moan by fusing his lips over hers and dominating her mouth, tangling his fingers in her hair.

Raine's body burned. Her heart roared in her ears…but she could still hear Beck groan from the other side of the table.

"Holy shit," Seth muttered.

Hammer turned his attention to her other nipple, leaving the first hard bud aching and clinging to the fabric. She arched to him, then wrapped her hand around Liam's nape, drawing him closer and losing herself in his kiss.

He jerked away, then elbowed Macen in the shoulder. "She needs to eat."

Food was the last thing on her mind.

With a jerky nod, Hammer pulled her into his lap. His erection prodded her backside, every bit as hard and demanding as Liam's. Meshed against his broad chest, Macen pressed close, his feverish heat surrounding her. She still shivered.

Raine blinked up into his hazel eyes. His breathing was rough. He looked at her as if she was the treasure he'd never expected to find.

Liam cupped her chin and tilted her gaze to him. "Take a nibble, love."

As he held a chunk of pineapple between his fingers, Raine opened, biting the plump fruit between her teeth. The juice seeped past her lips, dribbling onto her chin as Liam bent forward, sliding his tongue along the sweet path before he claimed her lips in another demanding kiss.

Hammer cupped her hip, his fingers skating over the curve of her ass. She could feel his stare burning into her as he watched. "That's it. Give yourself to us. Feel me. Open for him. Let us take care of you."

"Please," she whispered as Liam eased away. "More."

God, they couldn't leave her like this. But apparently they planned to because they spent the rest of the meal passing her back and forth. In between bites of chicken, salad, bread, and fruit, they caressed her, whispered to her, aroused the hell out of her. She gulped down her wine and her mind raced, circling on one thought: how perfect this felt.

When the men's plates were empty, and she'd eaten enough to stop her stomach from rumbling, Liam stood and lifted her, then set her on his vacant chair.

Beside him, Hammer rose to his feet. "Stay with Seth and Beck. In a few minutes, they'll give you instructions."

"Yes, Sir." What else could she say? She suspected they meant to start the work they'd brought her here to do. Raine wanted and needed to finish it. But she'd be lying if she didn't admit the whole idea made her nervous as hell. Still, she refused to disappoint them or continue existing as an emotional cripple.

As she watched them go, Raine bit her lip nervously.

"How you doing so far, princess?" Beck leaned in and rested his elbows on the table.

"I'm all right." She heard the unsteadiness of her voice.

Seth shook his head, then sent Beck a look of annoyance.

"Let's start again, Raine," Beck growled in his badass Dom voice. "What's going on behind those pretty blue eyes? You're here to open up. Let's have it."

Beck and Seth both sent her intent stares, and she couldn't help feeling like a bug under a microscope. "I'm not sure where to begin. I have all these feelings and questions...and crazy notions. And they're driving me nuts."

"Those two haven't exactly given you a lot of peace today so you could think things through." Beck grinned. "Of course, that's on purpose."

"Of course," Raine said wryly, rolling her eyes.

"How did you expect it to feel?" Seth asked.

"I don't know. Everything happened so fast this morning. When I agreed to their bargain, I didn't have time to picture much. But this is like a dream. I keep expecting to wake up and find myself miserable and alone again. Because when I'm with them, everything is right in my world."

"It should feel that way." Seth smiled. "Tell us your questions."

A million of them circled in her head. "I don't exactly know why they're doing this. They've told me what they think I want to hear, but... Liam says he loves me, and I guess he wants me back someday, but Hammer treated me like his sister for six years, so—"

"You mean except the night he fucked you endlessly?" Beck cut in.

Raine crossed her arms over her chest and sighed at him. "Except that one. But you've seen him do it. You know what I mean. How many other women did he take to bed while I stood there in plain sight? He acted like I was invisible until Liam took an interest in me."

"Oh, princess. You were a lot of things to Hammer, but never invisible. That man loves you."

She reared back and scowled. "No, he—"

"*Loves* you," Beck insisted.

Equal parts joy and terror sparked through her at the sadist's emphatic comeback. Still, that familiar self-doubt managed to worm its way back in.

"He cares, but—"

"Cares?" Beck snarled. "Do you think Hammer is the sort of man who goes all out for every waif who crosses his path? Do you think he shelters every lost girl by providing doctors and help, money, time, and support? He gave you almost everything you ever needed, princess." He laughed gruffly. "Shit, when Liam brought you here the first time, you should have seen Hammer curl up in bed with your clothes and inhale your scent, like that would bring you back. When you ran from Shadows a few days ago, he sounded prepared to burn down the world to find you. And you think he merely cares? Grow up, Raine."

"Liam loves you, too," Seth said quietly. "If you're having trouble believing it, stop. I've known O'Neill a long time. It took me less than two minutes of seeing the man with you to know that you're everything to him."

Their words hit her squarely in the chest. Maybe they were right. Liam and Hammer wouldn't talk out their strife and drop everything to help her if they didn't more than care.

Raine released a shaky breath and closed her eyes. Tears threatened. "I don't know why they would love me. I've made their lives really difficult. Hammer practically had to finish raising me, and Liam has tried so hard... I've fought. I've hidden. I've lied."

"Stop beating yourself up." Seth took her hand. "You're doing the right thing now. That's what matters."

"I hope it's not too little, too late. Up until today, I was convinced that I'd destroyed their friendship. But seeing them together like this..." Raine groped for the right words. "That's what their bond should be."

Seth nodded. "You're right."

"Couldn't agree more," Beck added. "All that bickering bugged the shit out of me, especially since I think, deep down, they want the same fucking thing. You should have seen the kitchen after Thanksgiving."

"I did. What the hell was that?"

"Language." Seth raised a brow at her.

Raine dropped her gaze. "Sorry, Sir."

"I think that was them beginning to work it out." Beck shrugged. "Throwing dishes is for pussies, and if Hammer hadn't been so wrenched, I would have told him that. But their friendship wasn't right even before you came along, princess."

"Hammer told me not to take all the responsibility on my shoulders, but he never explained. So—"

"You didn't believe him," Beck filled in.

"No," she admitted. "But what I saw today... It stunned me. Before now, I would have said it was impossible for them to share a woman again. But their actions together are so seamless. One picks up where the other leaves off. They're so in tune, it's like they can read each other's minds. They operate as if they're two halves of a whole. Like… they were born to be together in this way. The guilt that I've somehow kept them at one another's throats for so long—"

"Stop there," Seth demanded. "That's both their doing and their problem. Focus on you for a minute. How does being with both of them make *you* feel?"

"Centered for the first time in my life. Secure. Protected. Happy." She shook her head, still looking for the right words to express herself. "Don't get me wrong. Every look, touch, and whisper has me completely off-balance. But being with them is so perfect. I don't ever want to give it up. Juliet must have felt like the luckiest woman in the world."

"I don't think so. She had issues." Seth paused. Something bitter passed over his face. "Hell, she *was* an issue."

"You didn't like her?" That surprised Raine. Hammer had loved Juliet enough to grieve for years—in his way. Liam…she wasn't sure exactly how he'd felt about the woman.

"Not much." Seth didn't hesitate. "She didn't have a spine. Not like you."

"Sometimes I have too much spine," Raine grumbled and shot a guilty look Beck's way.

The doctor just laughed. "That's actually a good thing, princess. Trust me."

"You'll need it with these two," Seth drawled. "What's your end game here?"

"What do I want out of this?" At their nods, she sighed. "I started down this path just to grow, to learn how to be open with someone and not try to protect myself all the time."

"You're being pretty damn honest now," he pointed out.

"Because I can't go back to being miserable. And no offense, but I can talk to you because my heart isn't on the line."

"None taken." Beck shrugged.

"Besides, I'm guessing they left you here as my sounding boards."

"Smart girl," Seth said.

"Yep." Beck nodded. "If you need help, we're here. And we'll be happy to whack Hammer and Liam upside the head if they need it. But we'll also talk you through anything you're unsure of or hesitant to address with them."

"I'm really grateful for the help, guys. Thanks."

"So your goal is simply to not be miserable?" Beck prodded. "You don't want anything else out of your time with Liam and Hammer?"

"Yesterday, no. Today...I'm afraid what I want is a little more pie in the sky. I know you said it was possible, Beck, but I'm still thinking I should go buy a bridge from someone on a street corner."

"It's not farfetched. Say it, princess."

"I want them. Always," she admitted softly. "I still think it sounds crazy. But today, they seemed happy. I'm happy. Part of me insists that it can work. But they tried with Juliet and it didn't."

"Apples and oranges. You're different than Juliet. They're not the same men, either. Liam and Hammer are stronger and more in sync now."

Raine digested that information. "They weren't like this with Juliet?"

"No. Not this...intimate. Hammer is more gentle. Liam is more possessive." Seth searched for words. "I don't know how to explain it, but it's definitely not the same."

She believed Seth, but struggled to pin her finger on why Liam's friend would be right. They must have cared deeply for Juliet. She frowned.

"Tell me what's running through your head, princess," Beck cut in.

"So…how did everything end badly?"

"She didn't communicate." A mixture of sadness and contempt crossed his face.

Beck snorted. "That's an understatement."

"Um, you know I suck at it." She tossed her hands in the air.

"You're doing a great job now. And you can do it with them," Seth assured. "You've got what they need. Juliet was simply the wrong woman for them to share."

"What makes you think I'm the right one?" Raine held her breath. "I'm not any better than her at communicating, I'll bet."

"Well, since she committed suicide without giving either of them a damn clue that she was even unhappy, much less contemplating ending her life, I'm going to disagree."

Raine backed away in horror, clapping her hand over her gaping mouth. "Are you serious?"

"Yes." Seth winced. "Shit. I thought you knew. Sorry."

Which of them had found Juliet's body? Where had she done it? Where had Hammer and Liam been when she'd taken her last breath? What had they done afterward? The shock and the pain they must have felt—and lived with all these years… Raine's heart splintered for them. Both would have shouldered so much guilt. But it explained why Hammer had kept his distance for so long. And why Liam had been so determined to fix her.

She blinked at Seth, shocked. "I knew she was dead. I wondered if it was something tragic, like a car accident or an illness. The possiblility that her death had been self-inflicted crossed my mind, but… Oh my god."

"Anyway, it's safe to say she didn't communicate at all." Seth clenched his jaw, then let his gaze wander out the kitchen window as if he was wrangling his own regrets.

Obviously.

"Can you picture yourself doing that to them?" Beck asked.

"Never. Ever!" she vowed. "I want to be with them without tearing their friendship apart. More than anything, I want to be the right woman for them."

"Perfect. Now tell me why you've come here," Seth barked.

"To be whole. To be worthy." That meant she had to learn how *not* to be like Juliet. She must figure out how to communicate.

Ouch.

"Yes. Everything Hammer and Liam are doing now is to teach you what you need to know. Communication is a part of that, princess," Beck pointed out.

"A very important part." Seth agreed.

"Amen, brother."

"I know," she said softly.

"Make no mistake, Raine. What Hammer and Liam are doing for you is difficult. You're the first woman they've attempted to share in any way in the decade since Juliet died. Hell, I think you're the only reason they're really talking now. So when your demons come to haunt you, and you fear they can't possibly love you..." Seth growled. "You better remind yourself that their love is what's motivating them to see this through."

"Exactly," Beck chimed in. "Their animosity isn't just because of you. They shared a woman who *killed* herself. But they've put everything aside to help you. If that's not love, what the hell is?"

CHAPTER
FIFTEEN

With her head a tangle, Raine allowed Beck and Seth to usher her upstairs. No idea why they were leading her this way. But unlike the informal chat in the kitchen minutes ago, the Dominant hum rolling off them didn't exactly invite conversation.

Making their way down the long hall, Beck softly squeezed her elbow as he stopped in front of a closed door.

"This isn't my room," she pointed out.

Seth sent her an amused glance. "We know."

Okay… They had to be bringing her here to begin the work now. Raine glanced at the portal. What awaited her on the other side wasn't just important. It could change her life. She dragged in a deep breath.

Liam and Hammer had persuaded her to accept them as her Doms, and she understood now what that had cost them. Whether they meant to or not, they would teach her their expectations and wishes. She would learn—and maybe figure out how to be the right woman for them. If she succeeded, maybe she could have her castle-in-the-sky fantasy. And if not…she'd still be in a better place.

Seth opened the door, and with a jerk of his head, he silently instructed her to enter. As she did, a handful of candles illuminated the mostly empty room. Frowning, she squinted to adjust to the scant light.

There was no trace of luxurious furnishings, like inside the master suite, not even a lamp or chair, just two stark items: a mattress covered in a simple white sheet and a dark wooden St. Andrew's Cross in the corner shaped in a giant *X* with several eye bolts attached to the sides at both top and bottom. Absently, she noticed a carved wooden box that nearly blended in with the carpet next to the cross. It looked benign enough, but knowing the two Doms she dealt with, it could contain almost anything.

The significance of her austere surroundings didn't escape her. They didn't want her distracted by anything. They could please or punish her at will. And they probably wanted her to rely on them for every-thing—food, comfort, companionship.

This room put her on notice. They meant business.

Turning slowly, she pinned Beck with a questioning gaze. Raine didn't want to second-guess herself, but...could she really do this?

"They're giving you what you asked for, princess," Beck pointed out. "It's yours for the taking. So are they, if you do this right."

"I'm scared," she whispered. "What if I fuck this up?"

"Language." Seth scowled.

"Sorry, Sir." She had to watch her tongue. "But you know what I mean."

"Yep." Beck pulled her closer and cupped her shoulders. "Princess, you can do this. You know what you want. You know the stakes. You have the strength."

"We'll be here after...if you need us," Seth promised.

"Got it." Raine nodded resolutely, trying to ignore the way her stomach flipped. "Thanks."

"Good. Wait here. Don't leave this room," Beck commanded.

"Yes, Sir."

He shut the door, leaving her very much alone. The temperature was as cold as the décor. The air blowing from the ceiling fan overhead caused the shadows cast by the candles to dance on the walls. She turned in a slow circle, studying the room. She saw no closet, no bath-room, no window, just a strangling quiet that poked at her anxiety.

Raine paced. The urge to run and hide swamped her. The insecurity pumping through her veins was uncomfortable but deeply familiar. And she was growing weary of being off-kilter, but she knew that wasn't going away anytime soon. Above all, she had to stop fearing that she would never be what they wanted and start learning how she could be everything they needed.

As she nibbled on a ragged nail, the snick of the doorknob stopped her in her tracks. Spinning toward the sound, she held her breath. Her heart stuttered.

Hammer and Liam prowled into the room.

Let the games begin...

They eased the door closed in a whisper and stepped toward her, inches away. Almost in unison, they clasped their hands behind their backs and widened their stances as they squared their broad shoul-ders. Identical solemn expressions filled their stern faces. An absolute sense of their command rolled through the room, sliding over her body. Her breath caught. She shivered.

Her Doms—at least for now—were united.

"I'm glad—" Their lips tightened in displeasure, and she stopped in mid-sentence. *Right... On your knees.*

Raine swallowed tightly, then lowered herself to the carpet. Resting her backside on her heels, she drank in one last glimpse of the men she loved, then cast her gaze to the floor. Cool air swirled around Raine's shoulders as the tips of four Italian loafers came into view. She waited, her entire body tense. Vulnerability and yearning washed over her. What did they see? What did they think? Why didn't they say or do something? Despite all the worry and uncertainty, a joy she'd only ever experienced once, here at the lodge with Liam, resurfaced. The sense of rightness that seemed so familiar with them settled over her.

"Such a lovely sight," Liam praised, trailing his fingers through her hair. "Thank you for remembering our instructions. You make us proud."

"Very pretty, precious." Hammer cupped her shoulder.

She drew in a relieved breath and smiled to herself. "Thank you, Sirs."

Then Raine bit her lip. Was she supposed to speak? They'd never told her that she couldn't, thank goodness. She wanted no part of Hammer's ball gag.

"Welcome to your first task." She heard the challenge in Hammer's tone. "Lie on the mattress for us."

Task? Her mind whirled with possibilities as she rose and padded to the bed, sliding onto her back and looking up at them. What would they expect her to do?

With a curious stare, she watched Liam ease down onto the mattress on her left, Hammer on her right. Both men watched her intently.

"Do you like your new room, precious?" Hammer asked.

He was joking, right? But since there wasn't a hint of playful in his tone, she knew better.

"It's… um, different from the bedroom you put me in after lunch, Sir."

"I didn't ask for a comparison," Hammer pointed out. "I asked if you *liked* it."

"Not really." Raine saw the subtle shift of their expressions and hastily added, "Sir."

Liam leaned closer. "Tell us why, love."

She stared between them. Now that they loomed closer, their dominance pressed in, thick and overpowering. Raine could almost taste it. Her pussy fluttered. She sucked in an uneven breath.

"There's almost nothing here, Sir," she replied, shivering. "It's bare."
And freezing.

"That it is." Liam caressed her cheek.

"Are you moving me in here?" she asked.

Hammer shrugged. "That's up to you."

"This isn't really a bedroom." She frowned.

Liam nodded. "I converted and expanded a closet into a playroom for the two of us since we were last here. I intended to surprise you for Thanksgiving."

Right on cue, guilt pelted her. And she'd screwed it all up by not communicating about dinner or asking his plans or... Raine winced. "I'm still sorry about that."

"Not the point now." Liam propped an arm over his bent knee. "We've moved most of the equipment out of the room for this exercise."

Which explained why it was bare. "I understand, Sir."

"You don't yet, but you will," Hammer vowed. "So it's bare. Is that the only reason you don't like it?"

"It's chilly in here, too, Sir."

It was December, after all. And unless she missed her guess, it would probably snow overnight. The room itself felt subarctic. Liam and Hammer wore suit coats, long-sleeved shirts, trousers, and shoes. They had her dancing around in a transparent nightie and a thong, damn it.

"Oh, so you're cold?" Hammer's tone both patronized and confused her. "I'm sorry to hear that."

"A shame." Liam added with an arch of his brow.

That's all they have to say? Raine frowned, looking from one to the other. They stared back expectantly. What the hell were they waiting for?

Hammer gave her a superior smile, then a sudden gust of even colder air blasted her from above. Somehow, the ceiling fan began to spin faster. What in the world…? She glared at Macen. How had he done that?

Raine wrapped her arms around herself. "Can we turn the fan down, Sir? Or off?"

"Of course." From his pocket, Hammer withdrew a remote and pointed it at the fan. It clicked off, then the blades wound down slowly until they stilled. Liam rose and made his way to the thermostat on the wall near the door. The moment he adjusted it, Raine felt warm air begin to seep from the vents. "Better, precious?"

"Getting there, Sir. Thank you." *Butthead.*

"You're welcome." A roguish grin curled Hammer's lips. Liam wore the same expression.

They were setting some sort of trap, waiting for her to open her mouth and put her foot in it. This cat-and-mouse game confused the hell out of her, but Raine was determined to figure it out and beat them.

"So what do you need me to do for this task, Sirs?" she asked, wishing they'd let her sit up. Looking at them hovered above her only made her feel at a disadvantage. Then again, that was by design, no doubt.

"We'll get to that, love," Liam assured. "So you're comfortable now?"

Damn it, they knew the heater would take a few minutes to warm the room. Their little smirks told her that. Why didn't they offer her a blanket to help warm her? Was she supposed to learn something from discomfort? She was more likely to focus if she wasn't shivering, and this was too important to mess up.

"Actually, could I have a blanket and some socks, please?"

Proud smiles stretched across their faces at once.

"Absolutely," Hammer praised. "I'll be right back."

As Macen left the room, Liam edged closer. "All you had to do was ask."

But if they knew she was cold, why didn't they just give her a way to fix it? Unless… Hell, they wanted her to say it. They wanted her to *communicate*.

And she could just guess what they'd "work" on for the rest of the evening.

Oh, shit. She was doomed.

Raine turned on her side, curling into the fetal position, and faced Liam. No. Somehow, she had to get over this hurdle. In order for them to take another step with her, they must believe she could give them more than Juliet. They had to trust they weren't headed for tragedy again. She had to open her head or give up the desire to be with them both.

What's it going to be? she asked herself.

No contest.

"You want me to communicate, don't you?" she whispered, looking up at him.

Liam sent her a wry glance. "I've been wanting that for weeks now, Raine. But I think I've made that plain."

He had. She just hadn't wanted to understand the importance of spilling her guts. But knowing about Juliet now… Lack of communication could tear them apart, and Raine knew she was the only one who could prevent it.

"I know, Sir. I'm sorry."

Before he could reply, Hammer returned with a soft cotton blanket draped over his arm and a pair of fuzzy black socks in his hand. He bent and drew the blanket over her before kneeling at the foot of the bed. Liam joined him, and together they slid the warm socks over her icy feet.

"Is there anything else you need?" Hammer asked, his warm hand lingering on the back of her calf for several long seconds.

"No, thank you, Sir."

Liam trailed his wide palm along her thigh. She warmed at first, then melted a little.

Then he turned to Hammer. "She's figured it out, mate."

"Good." Hammer looked incredibly pleased. "I knew it wouldn't take long. Are you warmer now?"

"I am. Thank you."

"Glad to hear it. Let's begin."

They hadn't yet? From the anticipation on their faces, she guessed not. Her tummy knotted. "I'm ready, Sirs."

"Stand up, love," Liam instructed.

Raine did, biting her lip as she watched them walk toward the tall wooden cross.

"Strip and come to us, precious," Hammer ordered. "You can leave the socks on if you'd like."

Questions swirled through her brain. They'd centered this task around communication, so she would have to talk. That probably meant she would have to give them some painful truths before they rewarded her with their touch.

Shoving down her tinges of disquiet, Raine dropped the blanket and pulled at the silky ribbon tying the baby-doll together just under her breasts. The sheer fabric parted. She shrugged it off her shoulders, letting it caress her arms before it pooled on the floor. Cool air brushed her nipples. A quiver of anticipation sailed up her spine. Her thong turned damp, and she peeled it off, tossing it aside. She'd warmed enough to ditch the socks. Not an inch of her remained hidden. Raw and hungry, Liam's and Hammer's hot stares scraped over her flesh.

The sense of her utter nudity filled her, making her aware of every breath, every heartbeat, every step as she crossed the room.

Neither said a word as Liam clutched her shoulders and pressed her back against the cool, glossy cross. It towered over her. The wooden slabs intersected beneath her shoulder blades.

She trembled as Hammer bent to the box on the floor and pulled four fleece-lined cuffs free. He tossed two of them to Liam. In silence, they bound her wrists and ankles, surrounding them in softness. Then they worked in tandem, attaching long, slender carbiner clips to her cuffs before aligning her with the cross and securing her to the lowest eyebolts. She had to stretch her legs a bit wide to reach.

Liam smiled. "You're such a wee thing."

Raine frowned up at him. "Hey, I'm over five feet tall, thank you."

Hammer trailed his fingers down the sensitive flesh under her arm. "By a whole quarter of an inch."

She huffed. "Half inch—and it's an important half inch."

"That it is." Liam brushed a kiss over her lips. "I hope to have the chance to feel every inch of you again."

"So do I." Hammer nipped at her ear.

Her breath caught. If she'd been wearing panties, they would have melted. Though they'd just affixed her to the cross, Raine wondered how much more sensual torture she could endure before she screamed. She'd almost rather talk.

"Now that you're strung up nice and pretty, we're going to ask you some questions," Liam instructed. "You'll answer every damn one of them, too."

That made her nervous; Hammer was usually the more demanding of the two.

"We'll give you a choice. We can do this the easy way..." He looked in Liam's direction.

With a grin, Liam bent to her breast and licked one nipple with a teasing flick, then sucked the bud deep into his mouth. She felt the jolt all the way to her clit and gasped in a startled breath.

"Or we can do this the hard way." Hammer gave her a tight smile and bent to the wooden box again, withdrawing a TENS unit.

Her eyes went wide. She'd seen a sub jolt and twist and scream attached to the electrical device. She'd also seen them moan and beg and come. Everything depended on where the electrodes were attached and how intense the Dom made the impulses. Raine didn't have many illusions; Hammer didn't know her body exactly, but he knew what to do with the unit itself. It wouldn't take him long to figure out how to get the reaction he wanted.

Macen left the room for a brief second and returned with a folding chair, which he opened directly beside her. But he didn't sit, just set the device on the padded seat, within easy reach. He attached one pad to her bare pubic bone, then another right on top of her clit. As he turned the thing on, she tensed, but still couldn't precisely brace for the tingling jolt that crept across her skin and up her nerve endings. Logically, stimulation there should give her pleasure. This felt like a whole bunch of ants crawling where they didn't belong.

Raine tossed her head back and clenched her fists. "Shit!"

"Tsk, tsk, love. We haven't even started and your mouth has turned foul. I won't have it." Liam slapped her thigh. "Hammer?"

"On it." He turned the device down to something bearable. Just as she took a deep breath, he turned it back up, a smidge higher than before. "What's it going to be?"

"Sorry, Sir," she managed to say. "It slipped out. Please turn it down."

They stared at her, watching her writhe for a long moment before Hammer slowly reached for the unit and turned it off. "You're aware of your two choices?"

"Very much, Sir."

"Excellent. Because we can do this all night long." His superior smile looked every bit smug. "Your safe word?"

She turned her gaze to Liam. He knew it, but clearly he meant to make her say it aloud. "Paris."

"Duly noted." Hammer's fingers hovered over the dials on the TENS unit, as if he just waited for the opportunity to light her up again.

"Did you have a favorite teacher in school?" Liam asked.

Raine frowned. She'd run away. When she'd returned, she'd given them a pronouncement she thought was life altering: She wanted to learn to open herself to them. And this is what they wanted to know? "Um...yeah. Third grade. Mrs. Denton."

Hammer rewarded her with a caress of her breast, a thumb across her nipple, and a hot kiss just below her ear. "Are you comfortable having Beck and Seth here with us?"

"Yes, Sir," she managed to answer, despite the distraction. "They're easy to talk to."

"Why?" Liam caressed his way up her thigh, then glided his fingertips along the cheek of her ass.

"Because..." Focusing with their hands caressing her bare skin was more than a little challenging. "They don't have any expectations. They just listen and offer advice."

"You're doing a fine job, Raine." Liam bent to her nipple and took one in his mouth.

As he sucked hard, Hammer toyed with the other. "What's your favorite ice cream?"

"Caramel Caribou."

Liam frowned, backing away to stare at her. "What the devil is that?"

"Another necessity to have on hand for that time of the month," Hammer teased. "After the migraine, she turns into a sugar fiend."

"That's not true," she protested.

"Oh, it's not?" Hammer reached for the TENS unit.

"Okay, maybe so," Raine rushed to say. "Yes, I like ice cream then, Sir."

Hammer chuckled and his hand drifted away from the device. "Tell him what's in it."

"It's toffee ice cream with caramel cups and ribbons. There's a chocolate flavor, too." She sighed.

"That's right, precious." He looked at Liam. "Another favorite of hers."

"Would you rather have ice cream now or..." Liam brushed his fingertip up the insides of her thigh, caressing into her folds before easing two fingers inside her. "This?"

Raine swallowed back a gasp. "Definitely this."

Hammer chuckled. "Right answer."

She basked in pleasure, then Hammer added to it, pressing himself against her chest and looking straight into her eyes before he took her mouth, demanding everything clear down to her soul.

When Liam rubbed at a sensitive spot inside her, Hammer swallowed her moan.

Liam eased his fingers deeper. "Are you wet for us, love?"

With a last peck, Hammer lifted from the kiss and braced his elbow on the cross above her, still watching her intently. "Yes or no?"

Raine wanted to point out that Liam had his fingers up her pussy, so he'd be the first to know. Just a guess, but a flippant response would only halt the bliss they'd been heaping on her, and Hammer would turn the TENS unit on again. She hated feeling like ants crawled in her cooch.

"Yes," she admitted. "I have been since you first put me in the car. I've wanted you two all day."

"Lovely answer," Liam crooned. "Even more than we asked for."

"So good, precious." Hammer bent to scrape his teeth over her nipple. A flash of pain mellowed quickly and coalesced into a pleasurable hum.

Liam circled against the sensitive spot high and deep inside her. "We're talking. It's not terribly painful now, is it?"

Answering—hell, speaking at all—was becoming difficult. Desire gnawed at her, stealing breath, robbing thought. Raine wanted nothing more than to melt against them, beg, do anything to keep these sensations coming.

"No, Sir. It's heaven."

The smirk rolling across Hammer's face was her only warning that her task was about to become much harder. "Why did you give your virginity to Zak?"

Raine jolted. Liam withdrew, and they both stepped back. There it was, the blindside. This was the same damn game Liam had played with her last time she'd come to the lodge, but instead of punishing her with pickles, they'd devised something more physical and sinister.

Blurting the answer to this question opened up that vulnerable place inside of her that always made her want to shrink back and hide, but she had zero doubt that if she didn't at least try to get it out, they would not only turn that little dial and make her suffer, but she'd fail them.

"To get your attention," she admitted.

Hammer neither rewarded nor punished—yet. "You had it. I saw you every day. We talked about school, work, your friends, the club. I answered questions, ate meals with you, took you shopping. You had most of my attention."

Looking back over those years, Raine realized Hammer was right. "That's not what I meant. You spent every day with me, yes." She bit her lip. Now, it was going to get painful. "You spent every night with someone else."

"You were barely eighteen, Raine."

"But I *was* eighteen, a legal adult. I was tired of you treating me like a child. I thought having sex would prove to you that I wasn't a kid. I didn't think you wanted my virginity."

"I would have killed for it."

The gravity in his tone quieted her. She'd done something she deeply regretted, and it had hurt him. What if she'd learned to communicate years ago? "If I had told you that I wanted to give it to you then...?"

"You never made me that offer, so we'll never know what I would have done. Did Zak make you feel special and treasured that night?"

Damn it, he knew the answer to this question. Regret poured hot through her. The shame she'd felt that night scalded its way inside her veins again, black, ugly, devastating. "You know he treated me like trash."

"Because he was a player. And an asshole. I banned him from Shadows after I beat the fuck out of him."

"So you tried to manipulate Hammer into giving you what you wanted instead of communicating?" Liam questioned. "Sex was the last thing your fragile heart needed at the time, but you took matters into your own hands and had a terrible experience. Do I have that right?"

Humiliation scraped at her as fat tears burned her cheeks. "Yes. But I didn't know what to do. Growing up, anything I made the mistake of admitting I wanted was immediately taken away, destroyed, or killed. If I didn't want any more broken CDs or dead puppies, I had to keep my mouth shut. In my head, if I told Hammer how I felt, he'd only spurn me. Or worse, kick me out and never speak to me again."

Both men stood staring at her for a long, silent moment, as if absorbing her words. Then they moved in quickly, surrounding her, their hands and lips soothing her freshly opened wounds. Hammer kissed away her tears, his broad fingers stroking her hair, offering comfort. Liam enveloped her and tilted his head to capture her lips and swallow her sobs. When he lifted away, he gripped her so tenderly, as if trying to keep her from shattering in his hands.

"I would never have cast you aside, sweet girl," Hammer breathed as he caught her gaze in his. "You're the most precious gift life has ever given me. I may not have shown it, but I've treasured every single day you've been with me."

She saw love in his eyes. It was there, just like Beck had sworn. At that moment, it didn't matter if Hammer could say the words or not, she saw it, felt it, drank it in, and filled herself with every ounce of it.

How many years had she convinced herself that he didn't care? How many ways had she tried to coerce his affection because she simply hadn't asked? So much wasted time, energy, and heartache. It was too late to change the past. All she could do was move forward, knowing she had his love now. And that if she wanted to keep this connection growing, they had to talk.

Liam's soft lips peppered her cheeks, her nose, her mouth. Looking into his gentle brown eyes, Raine saw compassion and devotion reflected back at her. He had never stopped believing in her, never stopped trying to open her up, never stopped steeping her in his love.

She didn't know how it was possible, but Raine was falling even more for these men.

"You're doing beautifully," Liam murmured. "We've got you. You're safe. Keep being brave. We're not going anywhere."

She sniffed and nodded as he reached up and wiped her tears with his broad thumb.

"We're so proud of you," Hammer added. "We know this isn't easy. It's hard for us at times, too. But until we open all the wounds and purge what's inside, we can't begin to help you heal them."

"I know." Raine nodded as she slumped against the cross. She had to dig through the past if she was going to embrace her future. Now that she knew she could draw strength from their unwavering tenderness and understanding, she could go on.

Liam traced his fingertips over her lips. Gazing into her eyes, Raine could see something heavy weighed on his mind. Remembering all the ways she'd dodged his questions in the past, whatever he was about to ask, she owed him nothing but honesty now.

"When I brought you here the first time, we talked about your father. Or rather, I asked and you gave me an abbreviated version of events that basically told me almost nothing. If you'd given me the whole truth, I would have understood you better. I could have helped you more. But you tied my hands with your silence."

"I didn't know how to give up my control or let down my walls, Sir. I'm trying to learn now. Saying I'm sorry isn't enough, but that's all I can say."

"I don't understand, Raine. Why did you hide the truth? I was listening. You had to know I wouldn't punish you for being honest." Confusion furrowed his brow. "If I'd known the truth, we might not be here having this bloody inquisition. Tell me why you kept it in."

His words drowned her in guilt. She seemed to be a never-ending pool of it today, as they pointed out all the ways she'd screwed up and she had to take responsibility. But she couldn't let the shame she'd dragged around like an anvil for years take her under for good.

She could give Liam excuses—she had plenty—things like she hadn't known him that well at the time or she hadn't realized that he'd been so serious about helping her. But they were lame and pointless and would only get in the way.

Instead, Raine fought for a ragged breath and returned his stare as regret poured from her. "I was afraid to be that vulnerable to you. My father took my power from me. Anything he knew I liked or wanted, he made sure I never got. Then he would crawl into my head and tell me all the ways I wasn't good enough for those things. He manipulated me and he crushed me." Tears fell, and she had to force herself to whisper, "I wasn't strong enough to stop him."

God, she was so afraid to hear either of them agree with that.

"Stop. I need a minute. I can't…" She turned her head away. "You know my most hurtful secret and…"

"Stay with us, precious. Are you worried you're still not strong enough?" Hammer asked, nearly pressing his face to hers. "Or did beating the shit out of him change that?"

Raine choked back a sob. She even hated the tears running silently down her face. More weakness. But if they were going to spend this much energy helping her, she owed them the ugly truth.

"In the moment, I felt so strong. I'd let what he said roll off my back. I'd vanquished him and made him bleed for a change. Then…" She sagged on the cross as a sob took her. "Beck drove me to the beach, and I realized his insults were coiled up in my brain. I thought I'd taken the head off the snake, but I could still hear him hiss. I worry I'll never be strong enough to block him out."

No one moved for a long moment, then Liam and Hammer rushed to unfasten her cuffs from the cross, as if they couldn't get her down fast enough. Macen peeled away the pads of the TENS unit. Was this it? Had her ugliest truth finally broken their will?

She risked a peek at Liam. Heartbreak was all over his face as he gathered her in his arms and carried her gently to the bed. Hammer followed close behind, sorrow etched into his expression. Almost as one, they melted to the mattress on their knees.

Liam settled her on her back. His fingers shook as he cupped her face and kissed every tear away. "We've got you, love. I'm so sorry for all that monster put you through, but he can't hurt you now—or ever again. Even if you don't believe it, you're too strong to let him. He may have taught you to expect the worst in others, but we will always be here. I'll always protect you. And if I get the chance, I'll fucking slice the bastard. I'll make him bleed."

"You can't. He's dangerous. I don't want him near either of you. Somehow, he knows where I've been all these years. He told me—"

"It doesn't matter if he knows where to find you." Hammer stretched out behind her, stroking her with such uncharacteristic tenderness. "If he ever comes near you again, he's a dead man. That's a promise."

"That it is, my brave, beautiful lass." Liam brought her head to his chest. "Don't worry about us. Just let it out and know that I love you. I'm amazed by the way you've carried on so well for so long."

"I haven't. That's why we're here." She sobbed.

"Give yourself a bit of credit. You've been through more than most, Raine," Liam whispered. "I saw what you endured. The brutality of it blindsided me. Getting flattened by a truck would have been easier, I think. I can only imagine how you felt. I truly wish I'd known sooner so I could have helped you."

On the one hand, Raine completely saw Liam's point. Maybe if she'd told him everything earlier, she could have started healing and saved them all so much pain. But the more important he'd become to her, the more frightened she'd been to be vulnerable with him. On the other hand, how could he know the extent of her father's cruelty?

She froze. "What do you mean, you saw it?"

Hammer exhaled heavily, then eased back. Something—guilt, maybe, or regret—flashed across his strong face. "There's something I should tell you. You wouldn't allow me to call the police after I'd found you. But I needed ammunition against Bill in case he came back for you."

Raine's heart drummed in her chest. "And?"

"I was worried about you. All those bruises, the gash in your lip... Hell, I didn't know whether or not he'd broken your damn eye socket." As he spoke, he turned both angry and ashen. "I called Beck into your room after you fell asleep. He checked you over to make sure nothing was broken before we could get you to the hospital that next morning. Maybe it wasn't the right thing to do, but while we were there, I took pictures of everything that prick had done to you." He hesitated. "I showed them to Liam when you went missing."

Raine felt as if he'd yanked the floor out from under her. She fought and struggled, elbowing wildly until she sat up and scurried back, staring at Hammer in horror. "You took pictures? And kept them for all these years?" She swung her gaze to Liam. "You saw them?"

Liam nodded solemnly. "It's all right."

"The hell it is!" She jumped to her feet and glared at Hammer. "You betrayed my trust and didn't tell me for six fucking years?"

He leaned in and grabbed her wrist, tumbling her back down flat on her back between them. "Watch your goddamn mouth. I took them to protect you, so I'd have something to show the police if they ever came knocking. They've been sitting in my safe all this time, and I only showed Liam because one of us needed to reach you. If it wasn't me, then he needed to know what demons you were fighting. Blame me and hate me all you want. It doesn't change what I did. I'd make the same choice again."

Something between sincerity and determination filled his face. Raine closed her eyes. Logically, she saw his point, but that didn't make her ache less. "I didn't want anyone to see me like that. I wanted you to forget. I didn't ever want Liam to know." She tried to curl up into a ball and hide her face. "It's the reason I wandered the streets for two days before you found me. The second anyone saw me, I ran. By the time you discovered me, I was in so much pain. I meant to leave the next day, but..." Together, he and Liam held her down, not letting her hide. Feeling like that scared girl again, stripped and defeated, she stopped struggling. "Can I be alone?"

"No, precious. I will never forget, and whether you wanted Liam to know or not, he deserves all your truths. The good. The bad. The ugly. Didn't he already make that point with you?"

Yes, he had. Raine couldn't do more than nod.

"It's not going to make him love you less, but until you start believing that, you will always want to curl up, close off, and hide. We're not going to allow that anymore." Hammer's voice was calm but stern.

"Exactly. You'll not be squirming away from my questions ever again," Liam vowed. "And I'm not giving up on you. If you're still thinking that, don't."

"Besides, the truth is out and see?" Hammer said. "We're still here. We think you're fierce, a survivor. We're fucking not walking away. Neither are you."

She'd walked into this task knowing she had to learn to tell them everything. She couldn't do that if she hid. "No, I'm not. I'm sorry. Stay..."

Liam rubbed a soothing palm on the small of her back. "Good. I don't think you grasp yet how much you mean to us. Whatever happens when this is over, don't think for one minute that you're not treasured by us both. I never expected to fall for you, Raine. I just wanted to help you along, but you surprised me and stole my heart. Now..." He paused. "There's nothing you could ever say or do to change that."

They were forcing her to be cuttingly honest, but they were also giving her their truths. It was costing them to admit their secrets and feelings. They'd both been so reassuring and giving—and far more understanding that she'd ever expected. "I needed to hear that. Will you both kiss me?"

CHAPTER
SIXTEEN

Hammer stared into Raine's pleading blue eyes. She looked more fragile than he'd seen her in years, but the courage she'd shown in embracing their task and divulging her worst fears revealed such strength. And commitment. Tonight, she'd come so much further than he'd expected. And she'd blown him away.

As she lay before him with her soul exposed, his heart swelled. She radiated a need for reassurance, and Hammer ached to give it to her. She deserved a reward. But goddamn it, if his cock didn't throb in demand, too.

"You've earned a kiss and so much more, precious. But not here. Back in your room."

"Precisely, love," Liam crooned. "Kissing you will be our pleasure."

The way she smiled up at them pumped Hammer full of more power than he could ever recall and stuffed his lungs until he felt ready to burst. Being a part of her progress—watching her blossom—gave him such a profound sense of accomplishment.

He and Liam shared a glance, then he scooped her up in his arms. Liam opened the door, then dashed back to blow out the candles before trailing them down the long hall, into the master suite.

Wall sconces on either side of the bed glowed. Ambient light spilled over the golden silk duvet. Liam surged ahead and shoved the mountain of pillows from the bed with a wide sweep of his arm. He'd have to remember to thank his old friend later. No time now.

Hammer eased Raine onto the bed and covered her with his body. He pinned her to the mattress with a knee between her thighs, cupped her nape, and slanted his lips over hers, taking complete possession.

Under him, she arched and whimpered, throwing her arms around his neck, open and welcoming as she swallowed in all his hunger and gave it back tenfold.

Lost in the sweet sea of her mouth, Hammer barely noticed the sounds of clothing rustling in the background—until Liam appeared at his side, pressing kisses across Raine's shoulder and down her arm. He was bare from the waist up.

After one more stroke inside her mouth, Hammer pulled away. Raine wasn't exclusively his, and he couldn't hoard her. Besides, he wanted the opportunity to press his naked skin to hers as well.

Rolling to his feet, Hammer toed off his loafers, watching Liam pull Raine beneath him. The man pressed his forehead to hers. They shared a breath, a silent, suspended moment. Hammer had seen the two of them together before, but now a new intimacy flourished. He could almost see how bare she'd laid her soul.

"I'm desperate to touch you, love," Liam murmured as he smoothed the dark hair from her face.

Raine clung to him, gripping his shoulders, then gliding over the tops until she thrust a hand in his hair. "Please."

Liam took her chin in his hand and tilted her to his descending lips. Their kiss was somehow raw and tender at once. Hammer couldn't ignore the devotion flowing between them. He'd been completely against the two of them at first...and now he couldn't deny that Raine had grown immensely because Liam had nudged and demanded that she emerge from her shell. Hell, he'd all but walked through fire for her. And she'd finally responded, giving them both the chance to see the stunning submissive just under her skin. But Raine had also been good for Liam. He'd never seen the man so centered, committed...in love.

Tearing off his coat and shirt, Hammer littered the carpet with the garments, then stalked back to the bed, drinking in the sight of Liam and Raine tangled together. Maybe it should bother him, but he knew she hadn't given him any less of herself. She'd climbed an emotional mountain for them tonight. As much as he hated to admit it, Hammer wasn't sure he could have managed this much progress with her this quickly if he'd been working alone. He knew Liam couldn't; it was why he'd uncollared her. If they both truly held a part of her heart, then nothing short of working together to make her whole would do.

Raine gripped Liam's neck as he began to ease away. "Don't leave me."

"I'm not going anywhere," he promised, propping himself on his elbow beside her. "We're both here."

Hammer crowded along the other side of her body, pressing his lips to hers again. He closed his eyes, and she put her small palm to his chest. He groaned. So sweet. And when he looked into her eyes again, she smiled with her soul. Damn it, the girl had always touched his heart, but now he could feel her holding it, squeezing it, feeding it.

"So beautiful," Liam said thickly before he took her mouth again and cupped her breast, flicking the hard pink nipple with his thumb.

Something between a groan and a gasp fell from her lips. Her body trembled. So delicate, so eager... Hammer covered her neck in kisses, then dragged his lips down, laving his way over the full swells.

"You are, precious," he whispered into her skin.

Her eyes slid shut, and the look of utter bliss on her face went straight to his cock. She arched, and her nipple brushed his lips. Fuck, he wanted to suck her in and take her deep, hear her moan, feel her scratch at him for more. With a shuddering breath, he barely managed to refrain.

A glance up showed Liam watching, poised, tensed. He dragged his thumb over her other nipple again. Another of Raine's little feminine cries slipped free.

Hammer hung onto sanity by the barest of threads. "If you want more than a kiss, say it."

"Use what we taught you today," Liam seconded.

Her eyes flew open. Her gaze pinged between them both. "I need more. My nipples ache. *I* ache…"

"Do you?" Liam whispered right over the bud. "I might need to hear you beg for it."

Hammer licked a path just around her nipple, not yet giving Raine what she wanted. "Plead sweetly, precious. Tell us what you want—in explicit detail."

"Please put your mouths on my nipples. Suck them," she panted. "I'm dying…"

He and Liam exchanged a glance. His friend grinned, then down they went, their heads descending to her breasts together. The most delicious sense of conspiracy filled him. And as they drew her hard tips into their mouths, Raine gasped in desperation, curling a clinging hand around each of their napes. An abiding sexual thrill plowed through him. Jesus, she was going to burn them alive.

Her nipple hardened even more against his tongue. Under them, she moved restlessly, her hips lifting, her legs spreading. God, what he wouldn't give to lower himself down there and lick her juicy cunt before he fucked her senseless. He could smell her. Surely Liam could, too. But somehow, they were going to have to hold themselves at bay. This was *her* reward, not a chance for he and his pal to get off. Besides, as naked as they'd stripped her psyche today, they couldn't push her too far. Despite Raine's strength, her spirit would be breakable tonight. They couldn't risk her when they still had so much work to do. The sex would happen another day—at least he hoped and prayed so. Because the idea of sinking his cock deep inside her again in any way absolutely lit him on fire.

Right now, he just didn't know how much further he could push his control.

"Yes!" she cried out. "You're both sucking and it's…oh, it's jolting straight to my clit."

"Do you like it?" Liam tormented her with a rough whisper. "Do you want more?"

"Do you need more?" Hammer added, stroking a hand down her belly, his fingertips playing where he'd shaved off her landing strip just hours ago. The heat rising from her cunt left him no doubt how needy she was.

When she shifted and tried to tempt him to touch her slick folds, he delivered a little slap to her pussy. "Are you supposed to manipulate or communicate, Raine?"

"Communicate. Sorry, Sir," she gasped. "Please touch me."

Hammer dragged his palm back over her stomach. "I am, precious."

"As am I," Liam added, pinching and twisting her nipples. "You'll have to be more specific."

"Touch my pussy, Sirs. Both of you. Please," she choked out. "*Please…*"

Across her body, he exchanged another glance with Liam. But they were on the same page; he saw it in the man's midnight eyes. Neither of them could deny her now.

Scooping his hand between her legs, Hammer petted her drenched pussy, then worked a pair of fingers into her tight opening. Goddamn it, she was so swollen. Instantly, she clenched down on his digits, and he could just imagine how fucking good it would feel to bury his cock there.

Dragging in a breath and praying for restraint, he filled her, rooting around for her most sensitive spot. He found it in seconds, thrilled to feel her sink her little nails into his arm as she gave them a long, dazzling groan.

Liam cupped the pad of her pussy and began rubbing a slow, torturous circle. As soon as he did, she looked up at him with an imploring stare.

"What is it, love?" he prodded.

"I've been on edge all day," she squeaked out.

"As have we." Liam pressed and kneaded the flesh just above her clit. "Touching you is a beautiful hell."

"Burn for us," Hammer demanded. "Ache, need, writhe, and whimper so we can soak it in."

Raine did. She flushed and cried out, tensing, body bowing, hips wriggling. Around his fingers she swelled and clenched, squeezing even tighter. The flutters of her cunt rippled along the digits. He sent a warning glance at Liam, but his friend was already pulling back.

"No! No, please..." She breathed so hard, her words were broken.

"Ask us for it," Hammer growled.

"Please... Let me come, Sirs." She squeezed her eyes shut. Tears of need leaked from the corners. Her breathing was shallow. Her whole body yearned.

He'd never seen anything so fucking gorgeous.

"All right, then. Come for us." Liam's smoky whisper warmed her breast before he took her nipple deep between his lips again.

"Look at us, precious." Hammer plunged his fingers deeper. "And scream."

In seconds, her eyes flashed wide. Every muscle in her body sat poised on the edge. As Liam rubbed at her clit once more and Hammer grazed his fingertips across the smooth bundle of nerves, Raine opened her mouth and let loose a high, belting mewl of satisfaction. It filled the room, jerked at his cock, and provided the most amazing soundtrack to the epic bucking of her body as orgasm gripped her, endless and incredible. Her blue eyes glowed with desperate love.

Raine's ecstasy jolted a shaft of heady satisfaction through him. They had done this for her. He felt every inch like her Dom. A glance at Liam told Hammer that his old friend felt exactly the same.

A long minute later, the bliss released its hold on her. Raine sagged back to the bed, eyes closed, panting, shaking, and spent. Moments later, tears began to fall. Then sobs wracked her, dredging up emotions he suspected she'd long buried and wrenching them from deep inside.

He and Liam closed around her, each trapping one of her thighs under their own, wrapping an arm around her middle. Liam pressed soothing kisses to her lips gently as she wept.

"Beautiful, love. You've given us everything we've asked for and more. I'm so proud of you."

"Perfect," Hammer breathed, wrestling his urge to claim her. "I've never received that much raw honesty. It's a gift I will never forget."

"I'll never forget it, either. Thank you both." Her voice shook.

He cradled her cheek and pressed his lips to her temple, her nose, her lips, then circled back again. Liam whispered to her, taking turns at her mouth as she clutched them like they were her lifelines.

Slowly, her crying quieted. Peace began to settle into her. With the sweetest touches, she stroked their faces, shoulders, arms, sending them tremulous smiles. God, he wasn't even going to come close to fucking her now, and yet he would count this as one of the most meaningful nights of his life. Raine just moved him. She always had. Even if she went back to Liam after she healed, she always would.

The thought was a machete to the heart. Never feeling her again…it just wasn't an option.

"It's our pleasure to take care of you," Hammer assured Raine. Then before he could give into the urge to yank his zipper down and seat himself deep inside her, he rolled away and stood. "I'm going to bring you some water. I'll be right back."

As he shrugged on his shirt, Liam stood as well and bent to recover his clothes. "I'll run you a fresh bath. Do you need anything else, love?"

Raine rose to her hands and knees and scrambled off the edge of the bed. Hammer watched with a frown as she dashed toward them, staring up with the most earnest plea. Submissive need oozed from her pores. She glowed with it. Trembled with it.

Then she sank to her knees. "I don't need water or a bath. I don't need anything except to give back to you, Sirs."

She bit her lip. The pulse at her neck fluttered. Hammer couldn't stop himself from tangling his fingers in her hair.

Beside him, Liam cupped her chin. "What is it you want?"

"To give you pleasure." Her voice shook. "I want to touch you…make you come. Please, Sirs."

Hammer looked Liam's way. He'd yearned to see her willingness to submit, but he'd been afraid to hope that she would need to yield herself so totally. For a long moment, he couldn't breathe, couldn't speak. Liam looked as bowled over as he did.

"Say something?" she begged.

Liam bent and caressed her cheek. "Oh, love…"

"Please. I need to be needed." Tears shimmered in her eyes. "I have to give you the pleasure you gave me. You don't have to say a word or even touch me. Just let me…"

Raine reached up. Through the material of his trousers, she fitted her hand over Liam's cock, curling her fingers around his length. He almost stumbled as he tossed his head back and groaned. Then she did the same to Hammer, stroking his length through his pants. Blood rushed to his dick like a flash flood.

"Do you need a breath of fresh air, mate?" Liam managed to grate out as Raine's delicate hand clutched at him.

"Me? No." Hammer shook his head and arched into her other palm. "Fuck no. You?"

"Air is the last thing I'm thinking of." Liam pressed his hands over hers and made her grip him tighter.

The relief on her face was excruciating—and sexy as hell.

"Yes, you can please us, precious." Hammer's voice turned rough. "Open that sinful little mouth and take every fucking inch we have to offer."

He peeled her hand away from his cock. Liam did the same, then they extended a hand to help her from the floor. Raine's slender fingers curled around his, sending a jolt of demand through his veins. Together, he and Liam sat her on the edge of the bed. He could almost feel the anxious hum rolling off her.

In unison, they unzipped and released their swollen erections. Liam fisted his thick shaft as he stepped between her legs, kneeing her thighs wide before cupping her chin. With a rapt stare, Hammer nearly groaned as Raine looked up, begging Liam in a silent, blue-eyed plea.

"Oh, love…" He slipped his swollen cock between her waiting lips.

They moaned together. Hammer could almost feel the silken fire of her mouth as she suckled the head of Liam's cock, then worked down and laved the shaft in a slow push to the base. She filled her mouth, hollowed her cheeks.

Hammer stroked himself and bit back a growl of demand. Fuck, even watching her tongue dart around Liam's cock before she sucked him deep again made Hammer grit his teeth. His blood pumped with fire. She made little noises and gripped Liam's thighs, looking lost in pleasure as she worshipped his stiff length. Christ, three weeks of desire churned in his heavy balls, and he needed to be inside her in some way, stake whatever claim he could.

Liam's eyes rolled back in his head as a low moan rumbled from his chest and he shoved his fingers in her hair, tugging lightly until she whimpered and swallowed him whole again.

Son of a bitch, if that wasn't one of the hottest things he ever witnessed, not because he'd never seen a woman give another man a blow job. Because Raine ached to give. Liam needed to take. Love bound them together, brought them closer. They both looked so damn fulfilled.

Hammer couldn't resist reaching out and gliding his knuckles along the delicate hollows of her cheek. "That's it, precious. Suck him down deep. So pretty. Fuck, I can't wait to feel your mouth." Needing to be closer, he wrapped a hand around her nape, choking back a rumble as he watched her take Liam even deeper. "Yes, that's it. Worship his cock, Raine. Take everything he gives you."

"You're not helping, fucker." Liam grimaced as he thrust fast and deep for a blissful, teeth-gritting second. Sweat lined his brow as he panted and pulled away. "I need a minute."

Hammer wanted to laugh, but the need bubbling inside him screamed for the feel of her tongue trailing over his sensitive crest, cradling his cock. As Liam gasped for breath, Hammer took hold of her mane and turned her head to him.

Gazing down at the woman who haunted his dreams, he drank in her hard, dusky nipples. Her creamy flesh glowed with a pink, aroused hue. Wet and swollen, her lips all but begged to be fucked. It took every ounce of strength not to pound at her like an animal. He wanted what Liam had just felt. The desire, yes. But the connection, the completion. He fucking needed those.

As Hammer gazed down at Raine, her big blue eyes spoke the silent words he'd forever longed to hear: *I give you my soul, Sir. I'm yours.*

I'm yours, too, precious, he vowed.

Clenching his jaw, Hammer rattled in a breath, then drew his leaking crest over her lips. "Part those pretty lips and show me how you yearn to please."

"Yes, Sir."

Raine glided her tongue over her bottom lip, swiping at his offering. A groan ripped from his chest. She was killing him, and she hadn't even begun.

His stare never wavered as he wrapped a fist around his aching cock. At the rush of breath spilling from her lips over the sensitive head, he jerked, then pressed into her willing mouth. Hammer's heart clutched as she closed around him. As she licked her way down his throbbing length, a moan escaped him. It turned to an agonized roar as she danced back up to drag her tongue across the sensitive rim and glide over his swollen veins.

"You look stunning, love," Liam praised. Crouching in front of her, he nudged her legs even wider. "Show us your cunt, Raine. We can smell your hot spice, but we want to see your swollen slickness." He ran a finger through her folds. "Yes, you like Hammer's cock gliding down your throat, don't you? I can tell. He likes it, too."

She writhed and whimpered, splaying herself even wider as she rolled her hips in need. Hammer drank her in, their gazes still locked, wishing to fuck this could go on forever.

"Seeing your lips stretched around me, feeling you take me all the way down..."

Raine did it then, swallowing on him. He grunted a curse, trying to keep himself together.

Clawing for control, Hammer found his rhythm. Her soft throat constricted around his crest again, and he rocked, fucking his way into her mouth, loving the feel of her nails in his hips and her teeth grazing over the head of his cock before she paused, made him wait, and started all over again.

Jesus, she was dismantling him without a word.

Liam skimmed his palms up her torso, then plucked and pinched Raine's nipples. Her mewls vibrated up Hammer's shaft, all the way to his aching balls. Sweat dripped from his forehead. The familiar prickle of release slammed down his spine. With a curse, he jerked away from Raine's seeking lips and tried to calm the tremors wracking his body.

Without hesitation, Liam stood and thrust between her lips once more as she took him deep, again and again, until he looked staggered and on the edge. With a curse, he withdrew once more, and Hammer resumed.

Seamlessly, each took up where the other left off. For long minutes, they each filled her mouth, riding the edge of control and prolonging their pleasure.

Hammer's skin felt too tight. He struggled for breath as he watched Liam command her once again, recognizing the moment ecstasy peaked and he began to spiral out of control.

"That's it. Don't stop," Liam roared, locking stares with her. "Ohhh-hffffuck, Raine!"

"Drink him down," Hammer urged her.

"Harder! Suck harder," Liam gasped. "Take it all."

Hammer watched him buck furiously. He grunted and growled while Raine's slender throat worked to swallow every drop. Her feminine little moans went straight to his cock. And as Liam pulled out, she kissed the man's hip, then stared up at him, her eyes begging for reassurance.

Their give and take hadn't just aroused Hammer; it moved him. Hanging by a thread, he barely resisted the urge to shove his friend aside, grab her by the hair, and launch deep.

"Thank you, love." Liam struggled to recover his breathing as he dropped to the bed, sliding in behind her. "That was perfect. Give Hammer the relief he needs now. Open for him, Raine."

She glanced up as Hammer finally positioned himself between her legs. A coy smile turned her lips up as she cupped his sac in her palm and gave a gentle tug. "Did you want something, Macen?"

His restraint snapped. He plunged his fingers through her tresses and shoved into her mouth, to the back of her throat. Her silky heat surrounded him as she hollowed her cheeks and sucked hard, the ride fast, furious. Hammer burned with the shocking jolt of pleasure. He refused to look away from her for even a second. She was his for now, and he intended to burn this one glorious moment into his brain.

As he fucked her lips with hard, demanding strokes, his breathing grew labored. His body tensed as tingles sizzled under his skin. Every nerve ending blazed. Absorbed in the rightness of Raine and the silky heat of her mouth, his need to mark her drove him. He breathed like bellows, gritting for air between clenched teeth as orgasm brewed at the base of his spine.

"Good," Liam breathed against her ear. "Watch him. See what you're doing to him. Open wider. Let him fuck your mouth like he's ached to for years, love. Show him how much you need him, too."

Raine whimpered. Her gaze beseeched him. That was all it took.

A thunderous growl ripped from Hammer's chest as he exploded. Spasms gripped his shaft, cradled by her fiery tongue, as he jettisoned down her throat. His ears buzzed. His limbs numbed. He watched in awe as Raine gulped and swallowed, her gaze still clinging to him.

When the room stopped spinning, Hammer eased from her mouth and collapsed onto the bed. Raine curled up between them, exhaling a sigh of contentment. With a shaky hand, Hammer smoothed a palm down her arm. She wore a little smile.

"Thank you, precious, that was…" A smile tugged one corner of his mouth. "Amazing."

"You're welcome, Sirs." She beamed and blushed all at once. "I enjoyed that."

Liam eased her to her side, wrapping an arm around her and cuddling her back against him. Her eyes drifted shut as Liam glided his hands over her body, bathing her in gentle affection. Raine purred like a sated kitten as they nestled her between them.

"We're so proud of you, Raine," Hammer murmured in her ear before he brushed his lips over hers. "So beautiful."

With a little moan, she smiled up at him. "Thank you, Sir."

"So generous," Liam crooned. "And so fucking sexy."

She peeked over her shoulder at him. "When I'm with you both, that's exactly how you make me feel."

"Sleep now, darling girl. You've more than earned it." Hammer cupped her head and ran his fingers through her hair.

Liam traced indiscriminate patterns over her stomach with his fingertips. "*Is breá liom tú, siubhail.* I love you, sweetheart. Now dream of us. We'll be here when you awaken."

Hammer's heart was in his throat. Liam made it seem so easy, almost natural, to tell Raine how he felt about her. Soon, Macen vowed, he would have a chance to say those same three words to her. He just prayed it wasn't too late.

"**S**he's asleep," Liam whispered. Tenderly, he stroked her delicate face.

He loved watching Raine sleep because she gave herself over completely. It was the only time she let go of all her fears and trusted him enough to protect her. It was the only time she really let go.

At least before today.

What she'd given of herself to him and to Hammer earlier had gone above and beyond his every expectation. He ached with love.

"Precious?" Macen called in a low voice.

She didn't move a muscle, drugged by the blissful respite.

Christ, Liam wanted to stay in bed with her and hold her tight, breathing in her heady scent all damn night. But he knew they needed to debrief, prepare for tomorrow, and find a fucking drink.

"She won't wake now. We're good to go. And we won't be far if she needs us."

Carefully, he rolled to the side of the bed, stood on legs still shaking, and zipped his trousers. He heard Hammer do the same before they walked to the door. At the doorway, they both peered back at her. Raine's dark mane spilled over the white pillow. She looked so small and vulnerable, all but swallowed up in the big bed.

With a faint smile, Liam ambled down the stairs, his body still humming with the sensations of her soft mouth engulfing him. After spending all day with a cock that could have pounded nails through concrete, they'd watched as she'd climaxed so beautifully under their hands. Under their control. It had taken every ounce of restraint not to fuck her mouth like a wild man and shoot his seed down her throat in two seconds flat. It had helped knowing Hammer suffered in equal measure.

Neither said a word as they made their way to the great room. At the liquor cabinet, he passed Hammer a bottle of tequila as Liam accepted the Scotch offered in return. They knew one another so well, and Liam took comfort in that.

After pouring their drinks, they settled into matching armchairs before a roaring fire, each taking a few silent moments to reflect. He stared at the flames, then shifted his attention to the wall of windows along the front of the lodge. Gazing out into the wide vista, he saw the cotton-like hue muting the moon and shrouding the snowcapped mountains. No doubt, snow was on the way.

Hammer raised his glass, a satisfied smile spreading across his face. "To a hell of a job well done."

"To good beginnings. *Dea-shláinte.*" Liam raised his glass. He couldn't help but grin, too, before they both tossed back a healthy swallow. After a fiery gulp of the alcohol, he sat back in his chair, content for the moment. "We did it. We reached Raine."

"And managed to set aside our jealousy for a whole day," Hammer drawled.

Liam nodded. And didn't that shock the fuck out of him? Though he couldn't lie to himself; the first few miles in the car had been excruciating. As Raine had cued into them, listening, obeying, becoming aroused… Somehow, he hadn't thought as much of his jealousy then.

"We did. I think, in part, because she's an amazing woman. And we're giving her exactly what she's needed."

"No doubt about it. But I also think it's because we've done this before, even though Raine responded so differently."

"Than Juliet?" Liam finished. "Yes, she did."

"Fuck. I know I shouldn't, but a part of me feels guilty. The connection with Raine feels ten times deeper and more powerful than it did with my own wife."

That didn't surprise Liam. Now that Hammer wasn't trying to hide it, even Raine should be able to see the love Macen had for her.

"Something about all this feels... Shit, I don't know." Hammer scrubbed a hand through his hair.

"Familiar but not. So it wasn't just me, huh?"

"No." Hammer looked at him long and hard before he spoke again. "What just happened upstairs was... It blew my mind. Do you think that's what it was supposed to feel like before?"

Liam swirled the liquor in his glass before taking a sip. "I don't know what I expected, but I'm not sure I've ever felt that sort of bonding or connection with another person."

"Compared to Raine, I see now that Juliet only went through the motions. I guess she thought it was what we wanted. No. What *I* wanted. No wonder her heart wasn't in it. God, I was so fucking full of myself."

"Let it go, Macen. It's ancient history. I don't know what was going on in her head and neither do you. But now, we've got to put all our focus on Raine."

"You're right, man. In my wildest dreams, I didn't think she'd respond to us like she just did. Raine did more than peek around her walls; she tore them down before our eyes." A look of wonder spread over Hammer's face before a smirk curled his lips. "And you didn't throw a right hook all damn day. I appreciate that."

He cocked his head with a faint smile. "I could say the same to you. You're not going to try and convince me that you didn't want to take a swing too?"

He grunted. "I wasn't going to give her any reason to stop what we were doing."

Liam raised his glass again. "To self-restraint."

Hammer chuckled and lifted his tumbler.

"I guess we know that she's serious now about opening herself." Liam stared at the fire licking over the logs, recalling how Raine pushed ahead and persevered to meet their every demand.

"I've got to tell you, I thought we'd spend at least the first few days trying to pry most everything out of her."

"I thought the same."

"Just because she's done well so far, we can't give her any wiggle room," Hammer warned. "Now we've got to make sure she leaves her defenses down for the rest of the tasks."

"Agreed. Otherwise it will be too easy for her to slip back into old habits. But it's a hell of a start."

"It gives me hope, man. Definitely gives me hope."

"Christ, I'm sorry about the photos. I didn't mean to walk right into that one." Liam grimaced.

"Don't sweat it. She needed the truth sooner or later. But fuck, I hated hurting her that way. Betraying her wasn't at all what I'd intended. I should have told her about them long before now."

Liam sent Hammer a speculative look. "Why haven't you ever told her that you're in love with her?"

"Where the hell did that come from?" Hammer barked.

If they were mending fences, Liam was tired of tiptoeing around his friend. The time had come to lay everything out in the open.

"Seriously, mate. You should have told her. She's never held back how she feels about you."

"Everything that happened today tells me that you're right. I should have confessed my feelings a long time ago. I just let all the other fears and bullshit get in the way. Fuck me." Hammer shook his head. "Now that I'm ready to say it, it's not the right time or place. There's no way I'll distract her from what we're trying to accomplish here. Besides, her telling me that she loves me is only a recent thing. I may have suspected but…"

"I'd give anything to hear her say those words to me."

Hammer's mouth hung open in shock. "She never has?"

"Not once."

"Just because she hasn't said the words doesn't mean… Christ. You're joking, right? Can't you see the way she looks at you? You have to know she loves you."

He hoped. Wanted. Pined, even. But he didn't know.

Liam stood and walked to the windows. "She feels something for me, but I still need to bloody hear it."

He felt Hammer stroll up behind him and put a hand on his shoulder.

"I can see it's tearing you up. But trust me, she'll tell you. Be patient. She'll sort things out and say the words you want to hear."

"I wish I shared your confidence. I sure as hell don't want her learning how to share her heart by your example," Liam poked.

"Fuck you, asshole." Hammer laughed, then sobered quickly. "I did the best I could at the time with both you and Raine. The hiding and evasions snowballed somehow. The truth hurt too much. Before I knew it, the avalanche of hurt and confusion buried me."

"Don't shut me out again, Macen. I would have been there for you. I still am, you bloody wanker."

"I know, man. Thank you." Hammer gripped him in a brotherly hug and smacked him on the back.

"So, are we done measuring our cocks now?" Liam asked. "Because mine is still bigger than yours."

"In your fucking dreams." Hammer chuckled.

"See, I told you they were idiots," Seth grumbled as he and Beck strolled into the room. "They're even talking about whipping them out and comparing."

"Obviously, there's nothing wrong with their size or mojo. I think everyone who lives on the mountain overheard Raine's screams." Beck smirked.

Liam and Hammer exchanged a smug look of pride.

"Which brings me to my next question." Seth groaned and adjusted the swell beneath the zipper of his jeans. "Are there any available women at this godforsaken altitude?"

"Oh, bugger off. There's a bottle of lotion under the sink in your bathroom. Have a grand time with your fist."

"Just jack off quietly," Hammer instructed.

"And clean up afterward. I don't want Ngaire having to mop up behind you." Liam laughed.

"You two made a Raine sandwich, I take it?" Beck asked with a leering grin.

"You perverts." Hammer scoffed. "We didn't fuck her. We rewarded her for a job well done."

"Like it's any of your bloody business," Liam growled.

"Well, technically it is. You brought us up this mountain to help, so... yeah, we need to know if you gave her a good reward or a mind-blowing one. By the sound of her screams, I'd say she definitely got her mind blown." Seth grinned. "Wish I could have seen it."

"Shut the fuck up and get a drink," Hammer grumbled. "We've had a hell of a breakthrough you need to hear about."

As the four men settled in near the fireplace, he and Macen told the others about the inroads they'd made with Raine. Liam was still in awe at how she'd burst open and shared her soul with them both. They'd worked as a team, like they had in the past—but better, more naturally. It reassured him that he and Hammer were on the same page. Same page, nothing. It felt as if they'd started writing a new chapter in their friendship. After the chasm that had so recently divided them, mending the fracture felt damn good.

"I'm not trying to play devil's advocate here," Beck began. "But are you sure you two didn't have her so revved up, she responded that completely just to get off?"

Liam shook his head. "No. I'm well versed in the ways she maneuvers from the truth. There wasn't even a whisper of that today."

"Don't get too cocky yet," Seth warned. "She's still got a hell of a lot of work ahead of her."

"We're not," Hammer growled as if taking offense to the other man's words. "We know what we're doing."

"I know you do." Seth raised his hand, staving off Macen's glare. "All I'm saying is tomorrow might not be as easy as today. I'm just trying to prepare you both."

"We never said it would be easy," Liam agreed. "But then I was mostly thinking for her, not us. Seems like she's not the only one learning a few things."

"What do you mean?" Beck leaned in to study first Hammer, then Liam.

"Her home life." Hammer slammed back a gulp as if steeling himself to continue. "Bill did a number on her emotionally and physically, far worse than we'd known."

"The sick, fucking prick killed off anything she coveted. Her dreams, goddamn puppies she wanted for pets... The son of a bitch needs to die a slow, painful death. And I'd love to be the one to do it, too." Liam felt his anger boil again.

"Get in line, man. I'm right there with you." Hammer nodded with a tight set of his jaw.

"Sounds like she's going to need the first part of tomorrow's task even more." The look on Beck's face revealed the depth of his concern.

Liam had harbored contempt for Beck almost from day one. He'd noticed the friendship between the brash, tattooed Dom and Hammer when he'd first arrived. It had crawled under his skin that another was privy to his best mate on more than a surface level. Even though the resentment made him feel like a girl, it scorched him. But after the day they'd spent working with Raine, Beck had grown on him. And Liam himself had a new understanding; he and Hammer still shared a bond deeper than brothers. Far deeper than Beck or any other could imagine.

"It sounds like she's needed what you both have to offer for a long time." Seth tossed back a shot of bourbon with a hiss. "I'm glad you two didn't make us drag out the two-by-fours."

"That's a last resort." Beck chuckled. "They'd just try to shove them up our asses."

Seth scoffed. "Good luck with that."

The sling of insults continued a few minutes longer before they all buckled down and got back to business. They discussed strategy and collectively agreed to a plan of action.

One by one, the other men left for their beds while Liam sat before the dying embers. Pondering all he'd once had with Raine, praying he could have it again…but better than before. He could see a future with the girl so very clearly, and he ached down to his marrow for it.

Placing his empty tumbler on the side table, he thought about Hammer. He didn't want to focus on how deeply they both loved

Raine. But it was a fact he couldn't deny. Facing the reality that the dream of ever having her for himself again might be nothing more than fantasy chilled him. He hated the way his jealousy made him feel, but he owed himself the same honesty and openness he and Hammer demanded of Raine.

It seemed much longer than a few short weeks ago that his life had been uncomplicated and predictable. The struggles he now faced were nothing compared to her ultimate happiness. Come what may, it satisfied something inside him to see her blossom beneath their hands. Their voices. Their will. She became something more with them both, some*one* more... He had no words for it yet, just an inkling of something not quite free of the shadows. But when it revealed itself, when they could see all of her soul, it would be the most priceless gift he'd ever received.

Climbing the stairs, he reached her room. With a soft snick of the handle, he peeked inside. She lay just as they'd left her, buried deep beneath the covers, only her nose and dark hair peeking free.

The need to go to her damn near overwhelmed him. It surprised him, too. But it shouldn't have. Raine had always had that effect on him, from the very first time he'd seen her. He'd been so torn, never sure whether to beat her ass black and blue, fuck her senseless, or hold her against him and feel their hearts beat together—none of which she'd minded too much. And always to protect her, to keep her safe from whatever frightened her that he couldn't see. But he knew what she feared now, and something inside him raged for the injustices she'd endured. He couldn't have helped her as a child, but he could love the woman now. Liam hoped it would be enough.

CHAPTER
SEVENTEEN

C oaxing voices drew Raine from the inky depths of sleep. The heat of two solid bodies surrounded her. Crisp soap and a familiar mix of male spices filled her senses. A little smile played at her lips before she even opened her eyes.

"Time to wake up, love."

Liam. She'd grown to love the sound of his voice first thing in the morning. When she'd worn his collar and slept in his bed, she had often drifted off anticipating what his first words would be the following morning—and how much they'd make her shiver.

"You're not sleeping the day away, precious, at least not alone."

Hammer. The rare times he'd awakened her in the past had usually been about Shadows, but business sounded like the last thing on his mind now.

She opened her eyes and saw them each leaning over her, already showered, dressed, and immaculate. Definitely sexy. She sighed happily. "Morning."

Contentment warmed her. Happy, safe, and sheltered, Raine felt sleep tug at her again. She snuggled deeper under the blankets and closed her eyes.

"Oh no, you don't. Up with you, wench!" Liam pulled back the covers. The cold air blasted her skin and pebbled her nipples as he rolled her to her side to swat her bare butt.

It startled far more than hurt. At her yelp, Hammer chuckled.

"If you don't move, I'll take that as a sign you'd like to be spanked again," Macen murmured in her ear.

Raine giggled. "And what if I would?"

"Demanding little brat." Hammer shook his head with mock concern.

"A pretty one, though. But we'll have to do something about that saucy mouth, however." Liam's eyes glittered with mischief as he raked her with a hungry gaze.

"I've been a bad girl," she teased.

Their touch would be a great way to wake up, and if orgasm came with it, even better.

Raine couldn't miss their hot stares riveted on her. With a sultry smile, she stretched, arching her back—and thrusting her naked breasts up to them. Her legs fell open, and both men's stares zipped immediately down to her pussy. An exhilarating sense of power filled her. She might kneel and call them Sir, but she could definitely get their attention.

A big smile broke across her face.

"Look at her, all full of herself," Liam chided, but his voice sounded rougher than usual.

Hammer's eyes darkened. "I see that. Do we need to start the morning by reminding you who's on top?"

Pretty please? "Whatever you think is best, Sirs."

"That is a stunning piece of manipulation." Hammer watched her, his gaze almost impressed. "I can see I'm going to have to up my game and stay on my toes."

She blinked up at them, resting her hands on her stomach just beneath her breasts, plumping them up. "What? I'm merely offering myself in whatever way pleases you."

"Because you flashing me those pretty nipples and showing me your cunt is all about my pleasure, I'm sure. It has nothing to do with yours." He sent her a skeptical smile that told her the jig was up, but she didn't care. After the difficult task yesterday and their emotional exchange last night, the banter felt good.

"Precisely," Liam added, tongue firmly in cheek. "We've got an agenda that doesn't allow for a morning romp. So get up, love. Into the bathroom with you. We'll give you a few minutes to see to your business, then it's on with the day."

Raine pouted and glided her hand down the front of Liam's dress shirt. "Are you sure I can't serve you in any other way?"

She reached deliciously closer to his buckle when he grabbed her wrist and lifted her hand away. "You can start by not topping from the bottom and doing as you're asked."

"Bathroom," Hammer ordered. "Now."

She shivered at his deep command, then scurried from the bed with a come-hither glance back, grinning when she heard them groan as she shut the door.

Raine hurried to relieve and tidy herself up. When she returned, both men waited on the edge of the bed, their watchful stares sweeping her from head to toe. A thrilling sense of anticipation gripped her. They wanted her submissive and eager. Despite her teasing earlier, she felt alive and beyond ready to give them exactly what they sought.

Sucking in a deep breath, Raine crossed the carpet, then bowed her head and knelt before them, naked and ready.

"Gorgeous, love," Liam praised in a whispered rumble.

"Stunning as always," Hammer added in silky approval. "Raise your gaze to us, precious."

She lifted her head and took in the two men who owned her heart. Their polished exteriors hid hungry, commanding Doms. They focused on nothing but her. Everything about their demeanor said they couldn't wait to get their hands on her again.

Memories of the previous evening flashed through her mind, so vivid she could almost feel their hands on her pussy, stroking her to ecstasy. She could almost taste them on her tongue, both giving her their power and pleasure with guttural male groans.

It could happen again.

As soon as the thought whispered through her head, her pulse quickened and heat slid up her spine. Anticipation made her heart skitter. Need throbbed and tingled beneath her clit. Only one emotion fueled all that: love. So much love it was hard to contain.

Liam patted the mattress, silently demanding that she sit on the bed between them. "Come here."

They eyed her every move as she rose. Before she even settled herself, they positioned her with her back against the headboard, arms at her sides, legs slightly spread.

"There. Now we can look at all of you." And Hammer's hot stare said he appreciated everything he saw. "Tell us how you slept last night."

She sighed happily. "Very well, Sir. I crashed."

"I don't think she'd mind if we tucked her in like that every night." Something wicked flashed through Liam's eyes as he stroked her thigh gently.

"Her sweet mouth could become addicting, but it would be worth every moment." Hammer growled, cupping a breast in his hand and lightly thumbing her nipple. "I take it you enjoyed yourself, too?"

"I did, Sir," Raine gasped out. She had no idea how long they were willing to work together and fulfill both her and her fantasy, but she intended to take advantage of every moment.

"Look. Her cheeks are already flushed," Hammer pointed out, tormenting her nipple with his thumb again.

She struggled to focus on their words. Liam's fingertips skated against the sensitive skin of her inner thigh, dancing so close to her aching pussy. She shuddered in a breath and closed her eyes.

But she could still feel Liam's stare. "Feeling bashful, love?"

"Aroused," she admitted. "Everything has happened so quickly, the sensations are magnified. It all feels wonderful but surreal."

"Why?" Hammer asked.

Despite their provocative touches, they were digging into her psyche. It didn't put her on edge as it would have only days ago. They'd coaxed her to peel back her barriers and examine how her behavior had affected her relationships and her happiness. They'd dredged up some of her most painful hurts. Revealing her vulnerability and giving them the power to wound her had been so damn hard. But they'd taken her apart and put her back together with such care. Her psyche might still be a little scratched and bruised, but Raine felt the healing under her skin.

"We can't hear you, Raine. Stop filtering," Hammer interrupted her internal musings, sounding displeased. "All that stuff running through your head—the things you don't want us to hear—we need you to say."

"I'm not sure how to put it into words that will make sense. I've barely had time to analyze it myself." The urge to express the changes she felt was almost suffocating, but blurting it out probably wouldn't make sense.

"Then take your time." Liam tucked her hair behind her ear before smoothing a hand over her knee. "There's no judgment here. No right or wrong answers, love."

She nodded, falling back on the familiar comfort of sarcasm while she gathered the rest of her thoughts. "Can I just say that I'm shocked neither one of you ended up with a broken nose?"

Hammer arched a brow, leaving her no question they meant to have a serious conversation.

"Sorry," she murmured. "You two *were* the biggest shock, though. I really did expect an argument or a fight. I'm so relieved and impressed that you gave me something much better instead. God, it was perfect, all of it. So were you. Thanks for that."

"You're welcome." Liam's words were stiff and didn't invite further commentary.

Raine realized they didn't want her to examine their behavior, just her own.

"I learned some things about myself yesterday." She hesitated for a moment before continuing. "At the end, I really felt like I'd achieved something I thought impossible."

Their twin smiles of encouragement were a balm. Now she was giving them what they wanted.

"What was that?" Liam coaxed.

"I stepped out from behind my walls and the world didn't end. No one attacked me or tried to take advantage of my vulnerability. I told you exactly how I felt and I was still safe."

"You'll always be with us," Liam pledged.

"You shared so much of the gorgeous woman inside with us." Hammer caressed her arm and settled her shaky composure. "Beyond our wildest dreams, in fact."

Liam took her hand. "How did opening up to us make you feel?"

"Empowered. Terrified, too, but in a good way because I felt better knowing I could just be me. Letting go of some of those insecurities made me feel stronger."

"We're both proud of you, Raine." Liam tucked his hand in hers, strumming his thumb along the inside of her wrist.

"Very." Hammer cupped her cheek, and she couldn't miss the approval in his eyes.

A sense of triumph filled her. "I needed to hear that. Thank you, Sirs. It's nice not feeling like an eternal screw-up."

"You never have been, precious. That was in your mind, not ours," Hammer pointed out.

"Don't you think it might be time to let that pretty little head of yours start listening to your heart?"

Liam's soft question hit Raine in between the eyes. She smiled his way gratefully. "I think so. I'm definitely going to try harder now. It's like you've shown me there's light at the end of a dark, awful tunnel. And I want that. It's been lonely and scary in here these last six years. You two give me hope that I am finally on the right path."

"You definitely are." Hammer smiled at her before brushing his lips over her cheek.

Liam moved in for a kiss, too. "Yes, love. You did so beautifully yesterday. Today, we'll be asking you to give us more."

Even yesterday, that would have scared her. Their reinforcement just now steadied the ground beneath her feet. While it felt foreign, a confidence she'd never known surged inside her.

"Are you ready for your next task?" Hammer queried.

"I think so. I'm just a little anxious."

"Anxious? As in scared or excited, love?" Liam probed her with a curious stare.

"Some of both. But I'm eager to start."

"That's what we want to hear," Hammer praised.

Liam nodded. "But before we carry on, tell us how it feels to have us both beside you?"

"Analyze your feelings out loud. Talk it through with us. You're as safe as you were last night," Hammer promised.

"When you touch me and tell me I'm doing a good job, I feel... relieved. I feel complete. You make me want to do you both proud."

"Hold on to that feeling while we take you through the day. Lean on us, Raine. We're right beside you all the way," Hammer insisted.

"We're not going to leave you half done," Liam promised. "You've learned that your growth is worth the bits of pain now, haven't you?"

"Yes." She bit her lip. "But there's always that little voice in the back of my head... I'm terrified of failing you two."

Liam cradled her face in his hands. "The only way you can fail is if you give up."

"Just keep trying. As long as you keep reaching for us, we'll be there to hold you." Hammer rose and headed for her suitcase, plucking up a little red silk robe. He turned with a mischievous smile. "Time for breakfast, precious."

That was it? They were done picking through her soul? Funny, it hadn't hurt a bit. But Raine knew they'd only been assessing her mood and progress. No doubt they still had plenty of difficult hurdles for her to overcome. Butterflies in her stomach dipped and fluttered.

"I'm starved!" she admitted.

"I imagine so. You didn't eat much yesterday." Hammer helped her to her feet and slid the robe up her arms, settling it over shoulders.

Neither Hammer nor Liam said another word for several long moments, just stared at her as if they expected something Raine didn't understand. As the uncomfortable silence dragged on, she swung her gaze between them. Liam's expression all but screamed: *Didn't we just have a lesson about communication?*

With a cocked head and a raised brow, he leveled her with a slightly menacing stare. "I assure you, love, Ngaire has a cupboard full of pickles."

Raine winced. "Ugh, no pickles. You know I hate them."

"Indeed, I do." Liam's voice was cool and told her he expected more of an answer.

With a frown, she stared at the man. What the hell did he want her to say?

"There might be some of that trout leftover from yesterday's lunch," Hammer suggested.

"For breakfast? Gross!" Then she understood the game. Not just communication, but *complete* communication. "I'd really like two eggs over easy with salt and pepper, please. With that, I want one piece of lightly buttered toast, a banana, and a glass of orange juice—without pulp, if you have it—Sirs."

Hammer chuckled as Liam flashed a broad grin.

"Much better." Hammer cupped her chin and held her in a passionate gaze before he bent and pressed a hungry kiss to her lips.

Raine longed for him to devour her whole. She shoved away the tinge of disappointment when he released her.

"I'm sure you'll earn exactly what you want," Hammer responded as if he could read her mind. "Now hop into the shower and get cleaned up. We'll meet you in the kitchen."

Liam stood and pulled her into his arms, laying a lingering kiss on her lips. "When you come down, be wearing this, love. This—and nothing else. Do we make ourselves clear?"

"Yes, Sir." Liam's commanding mien filled her, and Raine felt the jolt of it all the way to her toes as she bowed her head. Warmth and excitement melded with her love for him. "I won't be long. I promise."

"Good lass." Liam lifted her chin to him and kissed her one last time. "Don't make us wait."

Watching them walk away, she felt almost giddy to get on with the rest of the day. Her soul overflowed with serenity. As she made her way into the spacious bathroom, Raine was determined to hold tight to the tranquility that filled her.

Raine fidgeted with the belt of the silk robe Liam and Hammer had instructed her to wear. As she descended the stairs, the panoramic view from the windows in the great room revealed a fresh layer of white powder blanketing the ground. The spindles of bare trees rose up to the blue sky. Everything looked hushed, peaceful.

From the kitchen, she heard male voices and laughter, along with the clatter of dishes. The aroma of fresh coffee and bacon filled the house. Her mouth watered and her tummy growled in response.

She smiled as she entered the room and spied the four men seated around the massive wooden table, looking impossibly handsome and thoroughly male. Catching sight of her, they rose in unison. She paused, startled by their intent stares. Testosterone saturated the room. Her nipples pebbled hard and tight against the silk. A flush warmed Raine's breasts and rose up her neck to heat her cheeks as she glanced from face to face. She saw nothing but welcome in each. Raine marveled that such busy, sought-after men cared enough to give her their time and energy.

Despite the fluttery, female sensation, Raine felt safe and lovely as they suffused her with unswerving attention.

Dropping her gaze to her toes, she greeted them softly. "Good morning, Sirs."

"Hey, princess. How you feeling?" Beck asked as he plucked up his dirty plate and took it to the sink, along with his utensils.

"I'm fine, thank you. Just famished," she replied as Beck rinsed the plate.

"Come. Sit beside us, precious." Shifting forward, Hammer wrapped his hand around her elbow and eased her into the chair between him and Liam.

The rest of the men took their seats and resumed eating.

Settling back, Raine couldn't forget dinner the night before. Were they planning to spend another day touching and tormenting her? It would be worth it if they ended the night with sizzling pleasure again.

Beside her, Liam wrapped a hand around her thigh and sent her a seductive smile that made her tingle.

"I'll rustle you up some breakfast." Beck smiled before filling a plate near the stove. He'd looked out for her for years, long before she'd realized he wasn't just a sadist, but a friend. He'd been a godsend when she'd sought him out at the hospital. His easy care now filled her with gratitude.

"Thank you."

Seated across the table, Seth sipped his coffee. "You look well rested, Raine. How confident would you say you feel about completing your task today, on a scale of one to ten?"

Darting a quick look between Hammer and Liam, she tried to decipher their expressions, get some read on their plans. Nothing. "They haven't given me a clue what to expect, so I'll say a six for now."

Beck chuckled as he set her breakfast, exactly as she had requested, on the table in front of her. "And not knowing is eating you up, isn't it?"

Raine really wanted to stick her tongue out at him, but managed to refrain. Instead, she ignored his question and focused on her food. "Everything looks great. Thanks."

That only made Beck laugh more.

"Go ahead, precious. Eat," Hammer encouraged. "Liam and I need to head upstairs and get your room set up. It will only take a few minutes. Beck and Seth will keep you company."

"And Raine?" Liam leveled her with a formidable stare. "Remember, they're here for you, too. We expect you to follow their instructions and give your obedience. Is that understood?"

She hesitated. A dozen questions sat on the tip of her tongue, but she silenced them. They'd asked for her trust, among other things. Yesterday, they'd more than earned it. "Yes, Sirs."

"Good girl." Hammer brushed a finger across her cheek. Her heart skipped a beat. "Enjoy your breakfast. We'll see you shortly."

She nodded, watching as they rose and took their plates to the sink before leaving the room. Nearby, Beck stood facing her, ankles and arms crossed as he leaned against the counter, watching her eat. Normally she'd hate that, but he was on her side. Besides, nothing fazed her too much this morning.

She moaned in appreciation at the first bite, then quickly devoured everything on her plate. Afterward, Raine relaxed back and sipped her orange juice, wondering what Hammer and Liam were preparing for her and if Beck and Seth had more questions this morning.

They didn't make her wait long.

"Full, princess?"

"Stuffed. It was delicious."

"Good, then let's get started." Seth smiled tightly. "Stand in the center of the room and remove your robe. Fold it neatly on the floor and kneel.

Then she'd be naked. And the looks on their faces told her they knew it. "I, um... Hammer and Liam..."

"What's the matter, princess? Is nudity a hard limit for you?" Beck challenged.

"No, Sir. I just…" *Respect their instructions and give your obedience.* Liam's edict echoed in her head.

Neither man so much as parted their lips to explain their intent. They merely waited for her to comply.

Slowly, she rose and moved to the center of the room. Obviously, this exercise was meant to shove her off-balance. Again. She took a deep breath and focused. Hammer and Liam had devised this task, and Raine understood their intentions. *Open up for the men you love. They've asked you to peel away the layers and allow yourself to be vulnerable.*

After she unknotted the belt, she slipped the robe off her shoulders. Swallowing a lump of nerves, she eased it off. Nudity may not have been a hard limit for her, but without Hammer and Liam—her life-lines—she found it more than a little uncomfortable. But she pressed on.

Carefully folding the robe, she placed it on the floor, then gracefully sank to her knees. Palms resting upward on her spread thighs, she straightened her spine and thrust out her chest before bowing her head respectfully.

Beck lingered at the counter. She felt his assessing gaze. She heard the scrape of Seth's chair again before he approached, the tips of his shoes visible as he stood in front of her.

Bending low, he cupped her chin and lifted her face to meet his gaze. "Don't shy away, Raine. You're a beautiful woman and you have nothing to fear from us. Think of me and Beck as your mentors, arbiters in case of dispute, and your chief cooks and bottle washers."

Beck pulled away from the counter and handed Seth a piece of paper, which he promptly passed over to Raine.

"Read everything on the page aloud to us, princess," Beck drawled, sidling up to the other man. "One by one."

Raine stared at the handwriting, recognizing Hammer's familiar scrawl. She scanned the page, blinking.

"Affirmations? Really?" She spit out the questions, recoiling as if they'd placed a sour pickle on her tongue. "Ugh."

Beck just grinned. "Get busy."

She exhaled something just shy of a scoff. They expected her to say this aloud? She shuddered at the thought. Focused on the paper fluttering in her hands, she ignored the meaning behind them.

"I will open myself up and share, not only my needs, but my emotions." The phrase spilling from her lips sounded monotone, the sentiment hollow.

"Continue. A little more enthusiasm would be nice," Beck chided.

"I will be totally honest at all times without fear of embarrassment or reprisal. Nor will I hold back for fear of hurting someone's feelings." Raine sighed and stared up at the two men eyeing her with critical gazes. "I get the value of communicating. You two made that really clear. So did they. But I'm not used to sharing every little thought that pops into my head." She gave them an exasperated frown. "I'm really supposed to say, 'Oh, I think I'll wear a pink thong today? No wait, Sirs, can I wear the blue pair instead?' Or, 'When I brush my teeth, is it okay if I start with my molars first and work my way forward?' And, 'Should I eat the ice cream or the bran muffin?' I mean, seriously?"

"That's *not* what the affirmation means," Seth barked, his brows creased in anger. "No wonder they always want to spank your ass."

"What they're asking is impossible. If I just blurt everything out, they'll be hurt or pissed off all the time. I don't mean to, but... Why is being sensitive to others suddenly bad?"

"They are grown men who can deal with their feelings, Raine," Seth scolded. "That's not your concern."

"*Totally* honest," Beck stressed. "If you're truthful about your thoughts and emotions as you experience them and express them in the non-brattiest way possible, you shouldn't have any problem."

"What does that even mean? I'm not trying to be bratty, but—"

"Let me make this black and white for you." Seth scowled at her. "You could have saved yourself a hell of a lot of pain if you'd simply leveled with Liam. Instead of avoiding him, you should have said, 'Sir, my period is late. I'm scared. Talk to me. Hold me. What happens with us if I end up pregnant with Hammer's baby?'"

His words gouged her deep. Guilt that she'd hidden nearly everything from Liam all but crushed her beneath its weight. Even more debilitating was the realization that she hadn't trusted that he would stick by her side, despite the fact that he'd asked her to repeatedly.

A sob caught in her chest as she launched to her feet and spun away. How many times had he told her he loved her? How many ways had he tried to prove it? God, she'd been such a fool. Raine had spent so much time convincing herself that her slightest misstep would send Liam running for the door. She should have shared her fears and worries, but instead, she'd cut him off and severed the very artery that could have given their relationship life.

Seth's warm hands cupped her shoulders as he moved in behind her. She felt his warm breath against her ear.

"I'm sorry, Raine. I didn't mean to upset you." She couldn't miss the depth of remorse in Seth's whisper. "I was trying to explain the difference between the mundane and the important. If there's something you feel you need to hide, that's a red flag, and you need to say those words aloud. Sharing your feelings is the only way to maintain a healthy rapport with your Doms. Do you understand?"

Raine swiped the tears away and sniffed before she gave a shaky nod. "Yes, Sir."

"Good," Seth praised as he turned her back to face him. "Let's continue."

She glanced toward Beck as she eased herself down to the robe again. Raine could see the sympathy in his eyes, but his expression was resolute. She needed to find the same determination and see these affirmations through.

Looking down at the list, she inhaled a steely breath. "No one has control over any aspect of my life unless I choose to give them my gift."

"What comes to mind when you say those words, princess?" Beck urged.

"You know." She tried to give a nonchalant shrug. "My father."

"You took back your power from that animal in no uncertain terms. I'm glad I got to see that." Pride glowed from Beck's face.

"What does that affirmation mean to you in terms of Hammer and Liam?" Seth asked.

Raine paused, sorting through her thoughts. "That I have the choice whether or not I give myself over to them."

"Excellent," Seth praised. "You're doing that right now, and they thrive on your power. It's what fulfills them. But how does it make *you* feel?"

"Centered."

"I think she's getting it." Beck sounded pleased.

"Okay, sweetheart. Last one." Seth nodded to the paper in her hand.

"I deserve…" Raine stumbled over the words, rereading them again. She felt Seth's assessing stare. The longer she stalled, the stronger she felt his impatience.

"Keep going. Tell us what you deserve." Seth's tone was soft but teemed with Dominant command.

She swallowed the lump of reservation in her throat. "I deserve happiness." The next words were harder to get out. "And love."

Did she? Maybe the better question was, why *didn't* she? She wasn't a bad person. She'd never intentionally hurt people. Why shouldn't she have some happiness? Some love? So many cracks marred her soul. She'd spent her life striving to feel worthy. But the past was behind her, and if she kept her courage intact along this journey, maybe Hammer and Liam would work their magic, and she'd finally smooth away every jagged hurt and be whole.

"You do," Beck reassured. "I know you doubt that from time to time, but deep down, you know it's true."

Seth crouched down in front of her again. "Raine, look at me."

He waited silently until she mustered the courage to raise her head and show him her uncertainty, her insecurities.

He smiled. "I know this is hard, but we're proud you got the words out. Next time, convince us that you're not just reciting these words, but that you *believe* them."

It sounded as much fun as being waterboarded, but she knew they only meant to help. "I'll do my best, Sir."

"That's all we're asking. Now, tell us why you're having trouble accepting that statement as fact."

"My father convinced me I wasn't good enough." She shrugged self-consciously. "If you hear it enough, you believe it. Liam told me that it was time for my head to start listening to my heart."

"I think Liam is a very wise man. And he loves you very much. You should listen to him." Seth smiled gently.

"They're ready for you upstairs, princess." Beck extended his hand to her. "Slip your robe back on and they'll meet you on the landing."

Raine let Beck help her to her feet. "Thank you, Sirs, for helping me sort everything out."

Seth watched as she wrapped the sash around her waist, then he took over, tying it into a loose knot. "Think long and hard about your affirmations while you do your task today. They'll help."

And with that, Seth placed a sweet kiss on her forehead before he shooed her out of the kitchen.

At the top of the stairs, Hammer tapped his foot impatiently, watching Raine ascend. The little red robe swished around her thighs, cinched her waist, caressed her hard nipples. He squeezed the length of silk rope in his hand. Beside him, anticipation rolled off Liam.

Today wouldn't be easy, but if it went well, it would be satisfying as fuck.

As she drew closer, her gaze bounced between them, her expression looking a little shaken—definitely more nervous than she had before breakfast—but determined.

Liam took her elbow and led her between them, down the hall, to the playroom. Once inside, Hammer shut the door, watching Raine. She stared at the padded table they'd outfitted in the middle of the room, again lit only by the array of candles, and drew in an audible breath.

"Something wrong, love?" Liam asked.

She seemed to gather herself, then shook her head. "No, Sir. I'm a bit uneasy. I'm not sure what to expect or what to do. But I guess you'll tell me, right? Should I be on my knees or on that?"

When she pointed to the bondage bed, Hammer stepped in front of her and looped a finger under her belt. "We appreciate such a complete answer. But I want you to focus on me for a moment. Keep what you learned yesterday in mind. Communication will be critical. Today's task is about honesty."

Raine blanched. "I know it's important, but sometimes the truth hurts people. I try to avoid upsetting anyone."

"There's a difference between saying something gently and lying. No one wants to be lied to, Raine," Hammer pointed out. "Didn't you have an affirmation about that earlier this morning?"

"Since you wrote them, you know I did, Sir. Seth pointed out that I can't be responsible for how others feel, but I just don't know how to look someone in the eye and upset them."

His gaze softened. "Seth is right. Your responsibility is to communicate the truth, not to worry about how it affects us."

He let that sink in and waited until acceptance flitted across her face. "I'll do my best, Sir."

Liam took her hand. "Talk to us throughout this exercise and do what we tell you. All will be well."

"Let's begin." Hammer brushed a soft kiss over her lips, then slipped the knot around her waist free.

Liam moved behind her and took the robe from her slender shoulders. He hung it from the doorknob, then together, they led her to the side of the raised table.

"Climb up, precious."

Casting a quick glance between the two of them again, she braced her palms on the padded surface. With his hands gripping her hips, Liam helped her up. Hammer waited on the other side, wrapping his arms around her torso to steady her.

Once they laid her supine, he and Liam both bound her wrists with cuffs built into the sides of the table. "These restraints aren't to hold you down, but to hold you open for us. We're going to ask you questions. Each time you answer honestly, we'll place a new fastening around you."

"We won't be binding you to the table, love," Liam added. "We'll be binding you to us."

Her gaze flipped over to Liam. "Do you mean that?"

"With all our hearts," Hammer promised.

Liam smoothed the hair from her forehead. "Don't you feel it?"

"Believing is really hard for me, but I'm trying, I swear."

Not the answer he wanted to hear, but Hammer understood and accepted it—for now.

He finished tying off the first restraint. Under his hands, Raine trembled, but resolution filled her face.

"We see that and we're proud. Today will be more difficult, Raine," Hammer warned. "Yesterday showed the value of good communication. Honesty is a big part of that. I haven't always been honest with you, and I'm changing that. You have to do the same." Her silence made the hairs on the back of his neck stand up. He refused to make the same mistake twice. "Raine?"

She hesitated for a suspended moment, apprehension flashing in her eyes, but there was no point in moving on unless she committed to the rules and the process. "Yes, Sir. I understand."

Liam gave a visible sigh of relief. "We have faith in you, Raine. Now put your faith in us."

They had to get on with the task. Hammer knew giving her time to worry would only let her doubts sneak in.

"I trust you more than I trust myself," she admitted.

Hammer rocked back on his heels. His heart jumped to his throat. He and Liam exchanged a glance. He saw his own shock reflected back in his friend's dark eyes.

"Follow your instincts. We'll help you through," Liam vowed, then pressed a lingering kiss against her mouth.

As soon as Liam pulled back, Hammer kissed her, too, a slow brush of lips. He nudged them apart, tasted her for a sweet moment, then pulled away.

She looked at them with her heart in her eyes.

It was time to begin.

Liam leaned over the table again, hovering directly over Raine's face. "Tell me, when you were collared to me, did you continue to cook and clean for Hammer after I told you not to?"

"Can I get in trouble for my answers?" She bit her lip.

Vixen. Hammer didn't know whether to shake his head or laugh.

"Only if you're bratty or dishonest," he quipped.

With a chuckle, Liam caressed her arm. "If you're honest, you'll earn nothing but praise. Answer my question."

Her eyes slid shut and she winced. "Then, yes. I did."

"Why?" Liam prodded.

She cracked an eye and looked Hammer's way. She'd never once told him that his dinner was in the oven or that she'd changed his sheets. Just like he'd never openly thanked her. Instead, he'd had the oil changed in her car and left squares of her favorite chocolates where only she would find them. It had been their secret.

"How did you know?" she asked.

"I'm not blind," Liam said. "Why?"

Raine took her time answering. A fist of anticipation gripped Hammer's stomach and squeezed hard as she collected her thoughts and focused on Liam again.

"I'd taken care of him for so long, I didn't know how not to. And, no offense..." She glanced at Hammer before redirecting back to Liam. "He's pretty helpless in the kitchen. As long as I was cooking for us, it didn't make sense to not make a little extra and leave it warm for him. The thought of him going hungry or eating takeout all the time bothered me. Ditto with the cleaning."

"Thank you for being honest." Liam grabbed a length of rope and attached her to the table again, this time binding her upper arms.

"Did that make you mad?" she asked, apprehension evident in her voice. "Because I never wanted to upset you. It wasn't meant to."

"What upsets me is that you did things for Hammer behind my back." Liam tightened the binding. "You didn't trust me enough to be honest."

Raine nodded like she understood completely. "Somewhere during our last trip here, I become so attached to you that I was afraid to say anything that might drive you away. Me caring for Hammer wasn't indicative of any disrespect or disloyalty to you. I just didn't know how to say it."

Liam peered down at her, his face tightening as if he repressed a hundred different thoughts. As if he wanted to wrap her up in his arms and never let go. "You just did, love."

"And thank you for not letting me starve," Hammer added, fastening his own rope around her opposite arm. "Focus on the silk, precious. Each is a line of trust between us. Feel it on your skin, in your blood, deep down."

"I do," she murmured as he tightened the knot.

Hammer couldn't miss the arousal in her voice, and fuck, it turned him on.

"When did you first start thinking of Liam as something more than my friend?"

Raine's eyes went wide. She pressed her lips together, then cut her gaze over to Liam. Hammer didn't have to guess that she wasn't keen on this question.

He tugged on the rope across her biceps. "Trust."

Nodding, she blew out a breath. "When you first introduced us, I, um…thought he was very attractive. He asked a lot of probing questions during our first few conversations. He asked me about you. Then he asked me about me. I didn't say much in either case. But I knew he was watching me a lot. I couldn't figure out why exactly." She let out a breath, then grasped for her fortitude. "The morning I broke the cup at your doorstep, the morning Marlie stepped from your room—"

"She was a mistake," Hammer cut her off.

That made Raine smile. "She was a 'see you next Tuesday.'"

"Excuse me?" Liam frowned, clearly confused.

"A cunt," Hammer supplied. "C. U. Next… You get it."

Liam burst out laughing. "That she was. Very clever, love."

The new lightness in the room seemed to give her some confidence. "Anyway, Liam came to see me in the kitchen that morning and offered to train me. At first, I thought he just felt sorry for me. Then he kissed me. Then I knew he wanted me."

Hammer flashed Liam a shocked glare, then with a grimace, he forced himself back on track. Water under the bridge. Ancient history. Not important right now—even if he wanted to give his old pal a piece of his mind.

As she watched him, uncertainty passed over her face. "Did I say something I shouldn't have?"

"No, precious. You did well." He wound another length of rope through the fastening in the table, then draped it over her shoulders.

Liam took the end and joined it on his side, pinning her down more. "Very honest, just as we asked for."

Raine looked visibly relieved. "I'm trying."

"We know," Liam soothed. "Tell me why you think I uncollared you."

"Well...I know you weren't happy that I didn't tell you about the migraine," she began.

"Not happy at all." Liam raised a brow. "But do you really think that's why?"

"I didn't say that," she defended. "I knew it didn't help, but...I guess I did a lot of things. I didn't always tell you what was in my head." Her gaze skittered away. "My only defense is that I'd never really had more than a one-sided relationship. I didn't know how to believe you when you said you'd be there or that you cared."

Hammer winced. Her words stung. Honesty was brutal, but he couldn't hide from the truth. He'd kept her at arm's length for years. From the moment she'd begun to blossom under his roof, he'd been scared fucking shitless at how much he cared. He'd wanted to protect her more than he had any other woman. At first, he'd told himself it was because she'd been so damn young and vulnerable. Then Hammer thought his feelings had grown because he was determined to save her, since he hadn't saved Juliet. Finally, he realized that he'd simply fallen for Raine.

Funny how he hadn't figured out that he loved her or that she alone could heal him until Liam had stolen her away.

"Did you or did you not actively avoid conversations you'd find uncomfortable?" Liam asked.

"I did." She sent him a sad, penitent stare. "But I didn't mean to shut you out."

Liam leaned over the table, his face turning foreboding. "You refused to tell me about your argument with Hammer just before Thanksgiving. You gave me some cockamamie story that it was about the menu."

"We did talk about it," she offered.

"That wasn't what we argued about." Hammer scowled.

She sighed in defeat. "I know."

Liam grabbed her chin and redirected her. "So do I. And instead of being honest, what did you do?"

"I tried to be close to you. And you didn't want my affection." The hurt in her voice was unmistakable. Her lower lip trembled.

Hammer caught Liam's gaze. His friend looked as confused as he felt.

"No," Liam corrected. "You tried to end the conversation with sex. Frankly, that's how you ended a lot of arguments."

Fingers wrapped around the edge of the table, Hammer fought for his temper. Juliet had used that tactic on him so often. He'd fallen for it just about every fucking time, and look where that had led. He took in air between his teeth, resisting the urge to rail. But there was no goddamn way he would allow Raine to open her body to avoid doing the same with her heart.

Raine blinked. "You were angry, and I knew it, Liam. I wanted to soothe you. I needed your reassurance. Your touch is one way I could feel your caring."

Really? That's what she thought? Hammer released his grip on the table. He'd seen Juliet use her body to end conversations. But he'd never seen Raine use her wiles in that way. Sure, she'd tried to seduce him once, but he'd been dead asleep. She hadn't wrapped her lips around his cock to stop a fight. When he'd all but fucked her in the bar, she hadn't tried to stop the argument. In fact, she'd done her best to walk away. Maybe Liam had assumed that she'd meant to distract him and he'd mistaken her intent?

Maybe. But Hammer intended to make himself very clear either way. "Listen to me, Raine. You will never, ever use your body to sway either of us from asking you questions, prying you open, or digging in your head. If you need reassurance, you will ask for it, not lose your clothes and rub up against us. Is that crystal fucking clear? This is *not* up for negotiation."

Raine stared, blinked, clearly confused. "Okay. I didn't mean to distract Liam that day, just…" She sighed. "I can argue with you, and I know that no matter how angry you are, since it's your club, you're not going to leave. Besides, you like a good argument. Liam isn't the same. He seemed genuinely upset, and I hated that."

Hammer growled. "You think I enjoy arguing with you?"

She looked up at him as if the truth were obvious. "It's your foreplay, and since we rarely did anything else… I mean, if you hadn't liked it, you wouldn't have picked so many fights."

"You're wrong." Hammer all but lunged at her. "Picking a fight and pissing you off was the only way you'd stop protecting yourself and give me the truth."

"And maybe I picked fights because it was the only way I could get you to pay attention to me." She pursed her mouth and sent him a little frown. "I still think you liked arguing with me. It was difficult not to notice you were always hard."

"That's my constant state around you, fight or no."

Liam cleared his throat. "So you didn't mean to distract with sex. All right. But the truth is, you tried everything else to avoid telling me why you argued with Hammer."

Then she cast those blue eyes back to Liam. "If I told you about the argument, I would've had to tell you how late my period was."

"And you thought that if I knew I'd leave you, right?"

"Yes."

"Even after I said I wouldn't run out?"

"But you did," she argued, tears filling her eyes.

"Am I standing here now?" he challenged. "Have I gone anywhere?"

She sighed. "No."

"I uncollared you, love, not because I wanted to leave you, but because you were never truly with me."

Raine fought against her bonds, straining to get off the table. Her legs flailed and she lurched up from the surface as much as her ropes allowed.

Hammer thrust a fist in her hair and tugged, jerking her face to his. "Stop. When you fight the ropes, Raine, you're fighting us."

"Don't do this," she sobbed.

"Don't avoid our questions," Hammer growled. "There's no right or wrong answer, just the truth."

She cut a glance to Liam, looking both accusing and hurt. "I told you. I tried. You expected more than I knew how to give. You scared me to death."

Grabbing another length of rope, Hammer attached it to the table and tossed it over her hips, then thrust the other end at Liam. He took it grimly and tied it off at her other hip with a scowl.

"How did I do that?" Liam demanded incredulously, finishing the knot. "Because I loved you and I wanted you to love me back?"

"Yes." Her entire body shook as she cried. "I didn't know how I could be so afraid of something I wanted so badly. The fear paralyzed me." She dragged in a jagged breath. "Every time I'd let go a little, I'd be so proud of myself. Then you always seemed angry that it wasn't more. I felt so out of my element."

"You shut down," Hammer supplied.

Raine nodded.

"You never said any of this," Liam pointed out softly. "How was I supposed to know?"

"How could I give you what I didn't know how to give? Love seems so easy for you. The words just pour out. Me?" She shook her head. "What I knew was that if I wanted something too much, it would be taken and destroyed. You were so good. I wanted more. I didn't dare tell you."

"So you destroyed it yourself?"

She closed her eyes as sobs wracked her again. "See, I fuck everything up."

Liam caressed her cheek. "Shh. No. Falling in love with you was so easy. From day one, I wanted to protect and guide you. I wanted to reach you. You made me laugh. You made me mad. You twisted me up in knots. But you made me feel alive. My vanity was believing my love was enough for us both. I never meant to make you feel unworthy."

"I know you didn't. I'm sorry I haven't been honest. The last thing I ever wanted to do was hurt you." Her lashes fluttered open and her gaze clung to Liam. Everything about her face was a plea for acceptance. "I love you."

The air left Hammer's lungs in a rush. It didn't surprise him that Raine was in love with his best friend. Deep down, Hammer had known it, but hearing Raine's sweet words wrapped in such earnest need... Fuck, he wanted to scream, rage, tear the room apart. But he couldn't breathe, couldn't move, couldn't speak. Liam had waited for weeks, hoping she'd declare her feelings. Now that she had, Hammer just clenched his jaw, grateful the others were so engrossed in each other they didn't notice he was quietly coming undone.

"Oh, god." He cradled Raine's face. "You don't know how long I've waited to hear that. Thank you for being brave. And here's my heart, bound to yours." Liam grabbed a stretch of rope and fitted it under her breasts before he handed it to Macen to complete.

Hammer stared at it mutely, seeing the overwhelming love in his friend's eyes. With numb fingers, he took the silken length and wrapped it around the bolt on his side of the table as Liam bent to Raine and covered her mouth with his, delving deep, mastering her lips. Telling her without a single word that he loved her, too.

As Liam lifted away from Raine's kiss, Hammer couldn't do a damn thing except paste on a stoic expression.

Immediately, she looked his way, soft concern on her face. Yeah, she didn't want to hurt him. Too late.

"How long have you been in love with him?" Hammer whispered.

Raine paused. He could see her thoughts turning, watch her scan memories.

"I think…" She smiled wryly. "When Liam fed me pickles. It was the most tender yet terrible way imaginable to tell me that what I said mattered." She turned to Liam. "That night at dinner when you wanted to know about my childhood and finally persuaded me to tell you, do you remember? It was then."

"I do. I made dessert out of you after that, love." Liam grinned.

Raine blushed prettily, and they shared a memory Hammer knew he'd never precisely understand. It fed every insecurity he possessed. But he forced himself to swallow it down, along with his wounded pride.

"You're doing so well, precious. He's waited a long time to hear how you feel." Hammer murmured to her.

How the hell could he be happy for his friend and so enraged at the same time?

"It doesn't change the way I feel about you, Macen. Nothing ever would." She glanced up at the ceiling and drew in a deep breath. "And that's what I really didn't know how to say, that I love you both."

"I knew. I've known for a while. That's hugely honest. You're doing great," Hammer choked out.

He grabbed some rope and handed Liam another piece. Together, they bent her knees, then secured the silk around her ankles and tied the lengths off to the table. Hammer checked her circulation along his side.

Liam did the same on the other with a shake of his head. "You might have told me, mate."

"I tried, you stubborn fuck. You weren't listening." Hammer turned serious again and pinned her with a stare. "One more thing stumps me, Raine. I understand why you felt you couldn't talk to Liam after he uncollared you. Why didn't you come to me?"

"And say what? I couldn't ask you to fix my boo-boo, Macen. I worried that if I went to see you that we'd..." She closed her eyes, looking tense and uncomfortable. "Fall into bed, and that I wouldn't have the strength to say no. Then you both would have thought I'd chased you down for revenge sex. It's even an ugly thought, and I didn't want that."

"I half expected you to," Liam admitted. "But I'm glad I meant enough to you that you didn't like the thought of seducing him just to hurt me."

"I've never wanted to hurt you," she swore, then sent a pleading stare Hammer's way. "Or you. The last thing you wanted to hear was me crying about Liam. Besides, I thought that without me there, you two might fix your friendship. I didn't want to be in the way anymore."

Hammer didn't like it…but he understood her point.

"Look at me." He didn't say another word until she did. "No matter what's happening in your life, Raine, if you need anything, I *always* want you to come to me."

"But you couldn't fix it, Sir. No one could." She sent a remorseful stare Liam's way. "It was my doing."

"You have *no* idea what I'm capable of, precious. So don't imagine that I couldn't have helped. You didn't give me a fucking chance."

"You really didn't give me one, either. You just left, even after I told you not to run away," Liam pointed out. "Did you not believe we'd worry about you?"

"I thought you might," she confessed softly.

"Might?" Hammer barked.

"That's why I went to Beck. I told him to let you two know that I was okay."

"And you thought Beck should be your messenger boy instead of calling us yourself?" Liam glared her way. "Did you honestly think we wouldn't be frantic to find you? Bloody hell, we were out of our heads."

"I know." She grimaced, and Hammer could see the worry on her face again. "I saw you. I was in Beck's car, and you two were running into the hospital."

Hammer's jaw ticked and he fought like hell not to lose his mind. "And you didn't make him stop? Turn around and flag us down?"

Liam shot him a fierce scowl, and Hammer figured he must not have done a great job at hiding his anger.

"I needed more time to sort things out. I wasn't ready to talk to either of you. But I picked up my phone at least a hundred times to call. I missed your voices." She sniffled. "I missed you."

"Then don't put any of us through that again," Liam demanded. "Tell us that you'll stand and fight and face your problems when things get tough."

"Say it." Hammer leaned into her face, teeth clenched.

Liam bent to her ear. "We want to hear it, Raine. Promise us you'll never run again."

She hesitated, seeming to wrestle with her thoughts. Fear gripped her expression, then she gathered herself, dug up courage, and nodded. The play of emotions entranced him. His triumph spiked.

"All right," she whispered. "I won't run again. I promise."

Hammer felt the tension drain from his body. He sighed with relief. Liam pressed a kiss to her forehead, then nuzzled her cheek. Hammer kissed her shoulder, her neck, her lips for a soft moment. "Thank you, precious. We needed to hear that."

"We did." Liam agreed and sent a stare his way, reaching for Raine's ropes. He wanted her free.

Fuck, yes. As much as he enjoyed her bound, Hammer wanted to hold her more. Clearly, Liam did, too. Raine had given them so much today. Her honesty—even when it hurt. Her promise—even when it cost her. Christ, she was stunning.

Together, he and Liam worked the knots, starting at the rope across her shoulders. The first binding slithered free and fell to the carpet with a soft thud. A soft pink pattern with the rope's imprint embossed her skin. For the first time, he saw Raine wearing the marks of his dominance. Not the bruises he'd given her when he'd fucked her mindlessly that drunken night, but the stamps of his possession dancing over her flesh when he'd worked with Liam to control her. Holy shit, the sight made his cock throb.

"Hammer?" Liam prodded him, already untying the binding across her hips.

With a nod, he rushed to catch up, unknotting the silk around her upper arms, under her breasts, then releasing the cuffs holding her wrists before finishing at her hips and ankles.

Raine sat up, reaching for them as quickly as they lunged for her. She pressed herself against Liam's chest and buried her face in his neck even as she reached her free hand to him, and Hammer used it to draw himself closer, meshing his back to hers. So small, so fragile. So brave.

He loved her.

"You did so good today," Liam said. "Your promise to stay and work things out means the world." He pulled back enough to search her eyes. "I'm going to hold you to it, love."

She smiled softly. "After seeing how quickly you tracked me down, I believe you. But I'm here now. I'm staying. I feel like…we've all walked through fire. I don't know what will happen tomorrow. But today, it felt really wonderful to just say what I thought and for you to be okay with it. Everything I said today was honest." She stared deep, conveying the truth of her words. "Everything."

Liam kissed her softly. "Oh, Raine. I love you, too."

After a soft press of lips, she turned his way, and Hammer's heart stopped at the love in her eyes. No coyness. No anger. No hiding. It was just…there.

Hammer didn't even try to stop himself from grabbing her and covering her lips with a frantic kiss. And he didn't hold back an ounce of his burning love. Now wasn't the time to tell her, but he damn well intended to before they left this mountain.

At the moment, he settled for wrapping his arms around her. Liam did the same. No one said anything for a long moment. The silence conveyed everything they'd accomplished—and didn't speak a word about what came next, as if the hush of now was sacred.

"Did I pass the test?" She grinned at them.

Liam's grip tightened. "You did. Let our arms hold you to us every bit as securely as our ropes. We've got you."

And Hammer didn't intend to let go. He wanted to inhale her, meld her against him. He wanted to own her. He'd almost had the chance. If his timing had been different, if she'd been fertile that night... Not that he wanted to force her into becoming his, but would she have fought it that hard? Or would she have been happy? Honestly, he didn't know.

And he was desperate to.

Hammer gripped her face and brought her gaze to his, searching her eyes. "Raine, you were crying on Thanksgiving day. Because you were relieved you weren't pregnant? Or disappointed because you wanted to be?"

CHAPTER
EIGHTEEN

L iam felt her body stiffen against him as his gut churned. What would Raine say? He could pretend it didn't matter, that it was all history now and best left there if he—they—intended to move forward. But Hammer wasn't going to rest until he got answers.

"Tell you what," Liam suggested. "Let's settle you in your bed where it's warm and comfortable, then finish the conversation there."

"No." Hammer shook his head. "Liam, I've waited. A few days ago, I thought I'd never see her again. This is the time for honesty. Let her answer first."

Then Hammer turned back to Raine, pinning her with a stare that demanded the unvarnished truth.

"I…" She sighed, bringing her hands up to cling to Hammer's wrists as he held her face. "Oh, what does it matter now, Macen? I wasn't pregnant, just late."

"You know damn well it matters. I need your honesty. I need an answer," he demanded, even as she tried to break his hold and hide. "Don't hide from me. It's another form of running away."

Liam gritted his teeth, but Raine couldn't be allowed to retreat—even if he didn't want to hear the truth. "Answer him, Raine."

Wrapped around her side, he felt her trembling, heard her hitch in a sobbing breath. Liam opened his mouth to calm her and defuse the tension.

"What do you want to hear, Macen? That I was devastated not to be pregnant? That I wanted to be the mother of your child? That something inside me had entertained the impractical hope that maybe I would carry the life you'd created inside me and have a part of you always?" Slow tears slid down her cheeks.

Hammer gripped her tighter. They locked stares. His eyes looked as glassy, as haunted, as hers.

"Goddamn it, I want the truth," Macen insisted.

"Fine," she wailed, her back straightening. "Of course I was disappointed. I love you. I've wanted you for so long that I don't remember what it feels like *not* to want you."

Each word hacked at Liam's heart like a knife, slicing him to pieces. *Fuck. You wanted honesty. You got it. Enjoy that bitter pill.*

Raine swiped at her tears and bowed her head, dropping her voice to a whisper Liam had to lean in to hear. "But I wasn't pregnant, so it's all moot now. It would have been an impossible situation, anyway. Not carrying your child in my womb meant I could have a life with Liam, and..." She drew in a shaking breath. "And in the end, I was happier about that. Oh god, I'm sorry, Macen."

Her face crumbled as she reached blindly for Hammer. He gathered her close and held her, rocking her gently.

"It wasn't planned, I know. But I *wanted* that child with you so damn bad." Hammer confirmed Liam's greatest fear. "Christ, I kept picturing a daughter as beautiful as her mother."

Raine laughed through her tears, clinging to Macen's shoulders. "And I'd hoped for a boy, just like his father."

The earth's axis shifted beneath Liam. She'd wanted Hammer's baby. But she'd wanted him more? Raine's sorrow, along with the heartfelt confessions she and Hammer shared, told Liam that she wasn't at peace. But damn it, he wasn't, either.

There was no sense in trying to convince himself that his world hadn't just blown up in his face, that his dreams of sharing a life with this woman, just the two of them, lay dying around him. A vise gripped his heart. He couldn't bloody breathe as he swallowed the urge to roar out that any life growing in Raine's womb would be his— and his alone.

But instead of erupting with the injustice of it all, he had to put on an act worthy of a goddamn Oscar and watch sobs shake Raine. He had to see Macen cradle her as they shared grief. And he couldn't say a damn thing or he'd risk destroying her.

As they clung to one another, Liam felt fucking invisible. And that broke his heart more than anything.

He reached beneath Raine, lifting her gently so he could move back and stand apart.

She whirled on the table, bracing herself on the padded surface, and turned devastated eyes to him. "Don't. Please… This is the biggest reason I never wanted to talk about how late my period was or whether I was pregnant. No matter what I said, someone would be hurt. You've done so much for me, sacrificed your feelings so I could break through my barriers. Whatever you believe, I do love you. And I knew the minute I opened my mouth, I could do more damage to you than we might ever recover from."

"No, it's fine. I'm just giving you some room, is all." He lifted her hand to his lips and kissed it, hoping she wouldn't notice his shaking fingers. He couldn't even look at Hammer. "Of course you were disappointed. Why wouldn't you be? I know you want children someday."

"But, I—"

"You don't have to explain." Liam forced himself to keep his voice even and calm. "Hammer is going to carry you to bed, love. Rest up for a bit. It's been a big morning, and you were so brave. I'm proud of you, Raine."

How bittersweet was it that she'd finally given him exactly the answer he'd sought two long weeks ago. And just as she'd feared, it had annihilated him.

"Stay with me," she begged.

"I'll be here. Go on with Hammer. He needs time with you. I think you need it, too. If you're up for it, we'll take a walk outside after lunch, maybe throw a snowball or two. But for now, get some rest. You've earned it."

Raine gave him a sad, watery nod, then turned back to Hammer. The other man scooped her up in his arms and waited while Liam opened the door to the playroom. He followed them to her bedroom. Inside, Liam inched back the covers and watched in helpless fury as Hammer lay beside her and drew her into his arms again.

Liam bent to kiss her before leaving, but her tears and Hammer's tender endearments began again. This time they were too much for his crumbling composure. Silently, he retreated and went in search of solitude to ease his torment.

As the day wore on, Liam fought the acid brewing in his gut. With a controlled smile firmly in place, he'd managed to scrape through lunch. Even Raine and Hammer had been subdued, so sitting back and letting Beck and Seth try to lighten the mood had been easy. Hammer hadn't fucked Raine, so he could be grateful for that one small mercy. If Macen had, Liam would have heard it as he paced in his room next to hers.

After lunch, he'd survived the hike with Hammer and Raine in the newly fallen snow, giving them stilted smiles and monosyllables. Liam had hoped breathing in the frosty air would cool his simmering anger or that taking in winter's beauty might ice his pain. But Hammer's presence only added fuel to the slow burn inside him. He'd held her hand, knowing that his "pal" held the other. It added some nasty kindling to his blaze.

Dinner had been a complete misery. Raine looked positively stunning in something tiny, white, and lacy. Liam hadn't chosen it, so he could only presume Hammer had. Of course, he'd absolutely loved being cut off at the balls about Raine's attire. He snorted. Macen hadn't noticed his mood or cared. To Raine's credit, she'd sat in his lap through part of the meal and tried to soothe him with kisses. He'd accepted her affection, taking her sweet mouth time and again, and trying to smother his ire.

Since tucking Raine into bed an hour ago, the temperature of Liam's fury had risen. Now seated on the great room's sofa, begrudgingly engaged in another debriefing session, he struggled to keep the conflagration under control. But the fuse burned shorter and hotter with every minute he had to endure Hammer's presence.

Tossing back a second shot of Scotch, he sighed, focusing on Beck and Seth. He appreciated all they'd done to help Raine. They'd devoted their time and understanding, with a collective goal to aid the girl in finding some peace. He and Hammer were supposed to be her *ultimate* choice of Dominants. At the moment, Liam felt more like a bloody fool.

When his glance settled on Hammer, who detailed Raine's achievements for the day, Liam felt the anger that had been roasting all day—hell, for the last month—blaze into an inferno and spread like a flash fire through him. Undeniably proud that she'd exceeded their fiercest expectations once again, he should have been high-fiving Macen. But the fear that Raine would never be just his again wrapped a fist around his balls and squeezed tight. If he wanted to have her in his life, in his arms, or in his bed again, would he have to share her with Hammer? That worry axed him like a vicious blade, cutting him where he sat.

He clenched his fists as Hammer divulged Raine's confession to the final question of the day—the powder keg his old pal had set ablaze, finally igniting Liam's fury.

"That had to be damn hard to hear, man," Seth sympathized. Concern lined his face.

All eyes turned expectantly toward Liam. The best he could do was nod and try not to spear Hammer with an accusing glare.

"Go ahead. You've been itching to say something about it all day. So get it off your chest and out in the open," Hammer barked before emptying his glass of tequila in one gulp.

"What the fuck is there to say, Macen?"

"You tell me. You're the one sitting by the fire, pouting like a bitch."

Hammer's condescending remark, coupled with the patronizing brow, set Liam's temper razing through the room. All the grievances he'd been swallowing since he'd first taken Raine for his own sat like bile in his throat, waiting to spew.

"You're the bitch here, Hammer. But I've got to hand it to you. You almost succeeded," he spat before raising his glass in a mock salute. "Aces to you."

"Succeeded at what?" Hammer growled as he turned in his seat. Face-to-face, Liam could see confusion and anger narrowing Macen's eyes.

"At totally fucking up Raine's life," Liam jeered. "It wasn't enough that you stunted her emotional growth for years by locking her away in your ivory tower. You had to top it off by trying to impregnate her, you selfish prick."

"What?" Hammer roared as he launched to his feet. "That's not what happened and you damn well know it."

"Okay. Everybody take a deep breath," Seth instructed as he situated himself between them, trying in vain to keep them apart.

Slamming his glass on the table, Liam surged out of his chair. Eager to go toe-to-toe with the man he used to call his best friend, he set his shoulders and clenched his fists. "Are you enjoying making Raine your substitute for Juliet?"

"What the—" Hammer screeched. "You need to get your goddamn jealousy under control, Liam, and think about what you're saying. If Raine had been pregnant with your child, she would have wanted it, too. You're too smart to be this stupid, asshole."

"Time out," Seth bellowed, slashing an angry scowl first at Liam, then at Hammer.

"Jealousy? Look in a bloody mirror. The minute I showed the least bit of interest in Raine, you suddenly turned on me like a rabid dog."

"Christ, here we go. You're not really going to start whining about that again, are you?" Hammer snarled. "Damn it, I know what she said up there cut you deep. But you're out of line, man. *Way* the fuck out of line. Deal with the shit Gwyneth put you through before you destroy yourself and any chance of happiness."

"Don't start psychoanalyzing me, you bastard, especially when you've done such a bloody fine job on yourself. You don't know a damn thing about what I went through with Gwyneth. You were too busy banging subs a dime a dozen, so shut the fuck up."

Hammer scowled. "I know you can't stand that the fucking bitch cheated on you, but you're not the first guy to find out his wife was unfaithful. Stop being a damn martyr because you're about to screw up the best thing that's ever happened in your life."

"What? A fake friendship with a man who's kept me in the dark about everyone and everything that ever mattered? Thanks, but no thanks, Hammer. You've shown me your true colors and they're uglier than fuck."

"I'm not talking about me, asswipe. I meant Raine. She *loves* you."

"Oh, so you're suddenly concerned about salvaging my relationship with Raine? This from the man who bragged just days ago that he'd get her back in bed. Isn't that just your way?"

"And what's your way, Liam? Ripping the collar from her throat and shoving her out the fucking door? You're goddamn lucky we found her because I would have killed you if she'd left me for good."

"Left *you*, is it? She's *mine!*" Liam growled.

"Not now, dumbass." Hammer smirked.

"That's enough, you two," Seth barked.

"Shut the fuck up," Liam snarled at Seth before glancing over the man's shoulder to pin his anger on Hammer once again. "You know, I tried hard to forgive you from keeping secrets from me. I even managed to feel sorry for you. After Thanksgiving, I'd hoped you'd gotten over your shit so we could finally put our differences to rest. But no. You buried the only worthwhile pieces of yourself with Juliet."

"Stop!" Beck roared, sidling next to Seth. "Sit the fuck down, you two."

"Butt out." Hammer scowled at the other two Doms before he turned back to Liam. "You leave Juliet out of this."

"How can I? You can't let it go. Instead of dealing with your guilt, you've hurt me. You've hurt Raine. And you don't give a bloody fuck."

Liam couldn't miss the flash of pain in Hammer's eyes. *Good!* The bastard needed to feel how much it hurt to have his heart ripped from his damn chest—exactly the way Liam had.

"This is about your sorry ass. Don't pin this on me. I thought you'd be a man about helping Raine grow. But obviously you'd rather shit in your diaper than pull your head out of your ass." Hammer leveled him a glare of contempt.

"Take off your rose-colored glasses, Macen. Did you honestly think the three of us were going to set up house and live happily ever after just because you had a boner to do it ten years ago? Hate to burst your bubble, mate. But when we leave here, Raine will be mine again," he blustered, knowing he had no way to make that hope a reality.

"Over my dead body," Hammer fumed.

"For fuck's sake. Shut. Up," Beck howled as he glanced toward the stairs.

Liam turned.

There stood Raine. Dressed in jeans and a dark sweater, she clutched her suitcase as tears streamed down her face.

"Fuck," Hammer groaned in regret.

Swiping a careless hand across her cheeks, Raine burned them both with a stare steeped in pain. She took Liam's knees out from under him. His heart clutched, and a wave of dread tingled through his limbs.

As he and Hammer both started toward her, Raine pinned them with a scathing glare, shaking her head and halting them in their tracks. Liam longed to scoop her into his arms, hold her tight, and tell her he was sorry for breaking his vow.

As she descended the stairs, she gave off a near-palpable blast of arctic air that rattled his bones. He could almost feel her reconstructing her walls, building them tight and impenetrable. His guts seized. All the progress they'd made was now destroyed because he and Hammer hadn't kept a lid on their shit.

"I agreed to do this with you both under one condition," she spit out through clenched teeth. "Just *one!*"

The agony in her voice slammed Liam with guilt.

Hammer tried to take another step closer. "Raine, listen. We—"

"Shut up!" she snapped as she seared him with a fierce scowl. "Don't you dare come near me."

For once, Hammer was stunned silent.

"I let you both bring me here so I could try and fix myself, to finally have a fucking happy life. And I'd almost been convinced that my dreams would come true. But Liam just admitted that you two can't share me. How naïve I was to think you could." Raine's voice cracked on a gut-wrenching sob. "Even knowing that it didn't work with Juliet, I fooled myself into believing it would be different with me—that *we* were different. I bought into the fantasy." She looked at Beck. "Didn't you tell me to grow up earlier? You couldn't have been more right."

Liam shook his head. *No. No.* "It can work, love, if—"

"Don't you talk to me, either," Raine choked. "I appreciate all the ways you both helped me. But I thought that today's task about honesty would run both ways. I see now it was a stunt. While I was ripping my heart open, you two were beating your chests over which of you got to slide into my panties again. Whatever. I thought you two were everything I ever wanted. But I finally understand that you're both so fucking broken, I'm not sure you'll ever be what I need."

"Bullshit!" Hammer growled.

Raine's words utterly demolished Liam. Her truth about the baby earlier today hadn't cut his soul as wide open as her words now. Even walking in on Gwyneth's adulterous ménage hadn't charred him this completely. He had to make this up to Raine. But first, he had to force her to hear his apology and pray she accepted it.

"Wait a minute, Raine," Seth interjected as he moved alongside Liam.

She shook her head. "There's no point. I can do a lot of things, Seth. But I can't continue to love two men who don't love me enough to keep one promise."

"That's not fair, precious," Hammer implored, his voice broken.

Liam turned to stare at the man. Macen looked pasty and shaken. He'd never seen Hammer so afraid.

"Don't start, Macen." She wagged a finger at him. "You don't know the first thing about fair."

"Raine…" Liam started, not sure what to say—what he *could* say—to make her listen.

She shook her head, looking right through him and Hammer as if they weren't there, and held back a sob as she turned to Beck.

"Forgive me, love. I'm sorry for everything." The inevitable loss threatened to crush Liam.

"Get me off this fucking mountain," she choked. "Now."

"No!" Hammer barked, leveling a frantic gaze at the tattooed Dom.

"Raine," Beck soothed as he wedged between Hammer and Liam before closing in next to her. "Let's talk about this for a minute."

"I'm done." He'd never seen more resolution on her face.

"You promised you wouldn't run away again," Hammer reminded her.

"You're going to talk to me about broken promises?" she challenged. "Your turn to choke on disappointment. Can we go, Beck?"

Glancing over his shoulder, the tattooed Dom grimaced in apology to both Liam and Hammer before wrapping an arm around her waist. "Come on, princess."

Helpless and wrought with contrition, Liam watched as Beck led her toward the door. Hammer took a step forward, then stopped.

"Fuck." Macen scrubbed a hand down his face. "This can't be happening. Precious…"

Liam strode toward her. "Stop, love. Let's talk—"

She opened the door and didn't turn back.

"Wait!" Hammer screamed at the top of his lungs. "Don't leave. I love you!"

She froze, dead in her tracks.

The entire room stood still.

Slowly, Raine turned, focused solely on Macen as her chin trembled. A mournful sob escaped her lips. Beck seemed to support her dissolving frame.

Liam gaped at Hammer in stunned silence. And what he saw made his eyes burn. Macen's face was etched in pain while he watched help-lessly as the woman they both loved stood ready to walk out the door. She'd wrenched Hammer's heart open. A trail of tears wet his harsh cheeks.

Raine's face twisted as her brows drew together. "Goddamn you, Macen. You wait until I'm ready to leave to tell me? Or are you just saying anything to make me stay?" She shook her head. "It doesn't matter anymore. I wish this had turned out differently."

Raine stormed out, slamming the door with a thunderous boom.

"I'll do what I can for you, dumb fucks, but I'm not making any promises." Beck sighed in disgust before he opened the door and followed Raine out into the night.

Hammer closed his eyes and palmed the tears from his cheeks. The second Raine walked out, she'd shredded his heart. For years, he'd wanted to declare his love. He'd never imagined that she'd believe his admission had been a disingenuous ploy and reject him. He might not have been the best at showing her how he felt, but he knew what love meant because of her. For Raine, he'd always cared and been concerned in a way he hadn't for anyone else.

But you haven't always put her needs first.

THE BREAK | 359

"Fuuccckkk!" Liam roared. "She's gone again. Bloody hell!"

"Calm down, you two. Let's talk," Seth ordered with a scowl.

"I think we've said more than enough, don't you?" Liam mocked.

"What's talking going to solve?" Hammer sounded at the end of his rope. "In case you missed it, she *left* us."

Seth just shook his head. "So you're going to stand there like whipped puppies and take it? Beck will reason with her, but if you want her back, we need to iron this out."

Liam scoffed. "I don't see how."

"You two are friends, remember?" Seth arched a brow. "Friends fight, like you just did. Now it's time to move on."

Hammer narrowed his eyes. "Are you fucking blind?"

"No, but you two are. Raine needs time to cool down. Then Beck will bring her back, and you clowns need to be ready when she gets here. You have an hour, maybe two, to lick your wounds and practice groveling. With your egos, neither one of you have a minute to waste."

"I doubt that's enough time to patch everything up," Liam muttered. "I'm not sure a decade would be."

Hammer saw the accusation in Liam's eyes, and it pissed him off all over again. "Probably not. If you'd just get over your jealousy—"

"You're blaming *me* for Raine leaving? I was fine until you started baiting me. If you'd kept your bloody mouth shut, we wouldn't be in this fucking mess."

"Oh, you've got some big fucking balls. In case you didn't notice, we both had to hear some goddamn hard truths today. Imagine my surprise to discover that you were sucking face with Raine when I told you to keep your hands off her. But then we both know the real reason you hooked up with her in the first place, don't we?" Hammer could feel his blood pressure rising.

"Because you weren't giving her what she needed," Liam tossed back.

"Because you wanted to yank my chain." Hammer shoved a finger in his face.

"For the record, I was trying to help someone I cared about, you bloody wanker."

"Yeah, so you could see if I'd get jealous. And if not, well, why not just get in her pants? After that, do you think I enjoyed hearing her tell you that she loved you? That was a Hallmark moment I could have lived without."

Liam rolled his eyes. "Oh, I've had a bloody party listening to her tell you she loves you for the last month! All that time, I've had to hear your insufferable whining about how I stole her from you."

"Shit. I finally get the courage to tell her I love her, do I get sweet kisses and cuddles? No, she thinks I'm fucking lying."

"What the fuck did you expect? You wait until she's running out the goddamn door. Face it, Macen. You're an idiot. Why didn't you tell her in the bedroom this morning when you had her alone? That's when she needed to hear it. And she might have let you fuck her, too."

"You're right. I was an idiot. Silly me for trying to honor our pact. So much for our strong, coordinated effort. Remember, she wasn't supposed to be yours or mine? Or did you have a secret agenda in mind all along?"

"You've lost the plot, mate." Liam shook his head in disgust.

"Jesus, you two." Seth sighed as he opened the door. "Let's get this out of the way before we go any further. You have five minutes outside to beat the fuck out of each other. Get it out of your system. When you come back, your heads up north better be ready to take charge."

"With pleasure." Liam stomped toward the door, shucking his jacket, tie, and shirt before tossing them onto the chair. "Are you coming, old man? Or are you afraid?"

With a glare Liam's way, Hammer stood and tore off everything he wore above the waist, unceremoniously dumping them onto the same chair, then he barreled toward the door. He stopped as he passed by Seth. "You're buying me a new pair of Louis Vuitton loafers, asshole."

The other man just laughed as he slipped on his coat.

Stepping off the porch, Hammer sunk to his shins in the thick snow. He suddenly realized he should have told Seth that he'd need to replace his Armani trousers, too.

Liam hopped in the snow, his breath making clouds in the frigid air, fists pumping like a boxer's. Hammer wanted to laugh, but the rancor glowing in O'Neill's eyes told him this wouldn't be a polite spar.

Before Hammer could get his footing in the slick, fine powder, Liam bounced in close and caught Macen's jaw with a right hook. His head snapped back. A low growl tore from his throat.

"It's on, asswipe," Hammer bellowed.

Crouching low, he slammed a shoulder into Liam's midsection. A grunt exploded from Liam's throat, filling Hammer with satisfaction and sending the two men tumbling to the frigid snow.

Liam hissed as the frozen precipitation hit his bare back. Hammer snarled and straddled O'Neill's chest, then hauled back a fist.

From the stoop, Seth stood wrapped in a woolen coat, rocking back on his heels and shaking his head.

Hammer ignored him and watched as Liam struggled to sit up. He launched his fist straight at Liam's nose, making contact with a satisfying crunch. Blood sprayed in a perfect arc, landing on the Irishman's chest and chin.

"You ready to give up yet?" Hammer baited.

"Concede to you, you fucking bastard?" the other man scoffed. "In your dreams."

They panted heavily, and Liam struggled to push Macen off, then gave up with a curse. Instead, the man wiped at his nose, then reared back and punched him in the stomach. The air left Hammer's lungs in a rush, and he felt faintly nauseous—and not for anything would he admit it.

"What are you doing, O'Neill? Trying to tickle me?" Hammer taunted before connecting another shot to Liam's cheek.

"Get the hell off me. Christ, I can't breathe with your weight on my gut," Liam grunted as he twisted his body and heaved upright, unseating Hammer and tossing him onto his back. Rising to his knees, Liam hovered over him and plowed his fist into Macen's nose. Pain exploded in his skull.

Hammer managed to grit his teeth and hold it together, even as blood ran into his mouth. "Stop hitting me with your purse."

"You fight like a fucking girl. Planning to scratch me next?" Liam goaded before driving his fist into Hammer's gut.

Macen groaned but managed to give Liam a mighty shove and send him tumbling.

Sprawled out in the snow side by side, the two men panted as they stared up into the twinkling night sky. The freezing temperature cooled his temper. Hammer realized he didn't want to kill Liam, simply vent the years of pent-up fury once and for all. His nose hurt. His stomach felt sore. He spit out a mouthful of blood. His only consolation was that he didn't think Liam had fared any better.

"Had enough of me kicking your ass, gramps?" Liam quipped.

"Fuck off," Hammer turned to scowl at his friend.

Blood still seeped from his nose, but Liam grinned at him like a loon. In that moment, he prayed his friend only wanted to blow off steam, too. They'd taken their argument—hell, themselves—far too seriously.

This was what they should have done after Juliet's suicide. Yell. Fight. Get fucking drunk. And cry. Macen had done all that alone and resented Liam for it. He knew now that his old friend would have happily joined him, if he'd only asked.

"I can go again. Just give me a minute. I need to catch my breath," Hammer groaned.

A hint of smugness resounded in Liam's low laughter until he palmed his jaw and cursed.

"Time's up, ladies. Let's go back inside. We can sit by the fire, hold hands, and sing *Kumbaya*," Seth called from the front porch.

"Fucker," Hammer muttered.

"I think we should beat his ass next," Liam murmured conspiratorially.

Both men cracked a knowing grin. As if they'd read one another's minds, they raised their right arms and flipped Seth off, laughing. It felt good.

Liam stumbled to his feet and held out his hand to Hammer. "Come on, you old fart. Let me help you up."

"Who are you calling old? If our mommy over there on the porch—" Hammer thumbed in Seth's direction "—had given us five more minutes, I'd have kicked your ass."

Liam dropped his hand. "Yeah? Who's on their feet first?" He grinned. "Or should I just let you drag your own half-dead carcass up alone."

"Hey, I didn't say I was turning down your help." As Liam held out his hand again, Hammer laughed and latched on, rising to his feet.

Seth waited for them on the porch with a sour expression. "You two look like you fell face first into a meat grinder. When Raine comes back, she won't like looking at either of you."

"We'll turn off the lights. She doesn't need to see us, anyway. Just feel." Hammer smirked.

"Or Beck and I could just take her off your hands," Seth teased.

"You wanna die?" Hammer asked.

Liam suggested something anatomically impossible as they marched inside, grabbed their dry clothes, then hurried to the fireplace.

The heat felt good on Hammer's stinging skin. Using his shirt to wipe away the blood that dripped from his nose, he eyed Liam. Would they be able to salvage their friendship and love Raine together? He wasn't sure, but Raine blurting out her fantasy—her hope—had sharpened his. He wanted her. But he wanted her with Liam, with the best friend who'd tried to stand by him through thick and thin. Hammer might not always agree with Liam's choices, but he knew the man never had less than good intentions. It was a place to start.

Seth joined them a minute later, tossing towels at both of them before he refilled their glasses with liquor.

"First things first, we need to discuss whether you can continue guiding Raine together or if you need to call it quits."

"I'm not giving up," Hammer growled.

Liam didn't answer.

Seth swiveled a gaze in O'Neill's direction. "You?"

Pain tore across Liam's face. "I'm giving serious thought to chucking the whole fucking nightmare. It's like a train wreck that keeps rolling over the same broken rails. Every damn time I think we're getting on track, something causes it to derail again. I'm bloody tired of it."

The desolation in Liam's voice felt like a kick in the gut. Hammer wiped more blood from his nose on his shirt, silently staring as the drops expanded on the silk in a starburst of crimson. "Look, if it's about the conversation today..."

"It's not just her pregnancy scare." Liam glanced up. His expression was unreadable, which worried Hammer even more. "That was just the straw that broke the camel's back. I honestly didn't think you cared whether she'd be pregnant or not. I know now, what with Juliet and all, that it's a touchy subject for you. But you never wanted children in all the years I've known you. So I'd decided to adopt the kid and raise it as my own, if it came to that. I had a whole fucking fairy tale all laid out in my head. What a joke!"

Liam sank wearily into the chair next to Macen and mopped the blood from his face with his towel. Hammer hurt just seeing his pain.

"Think of me what you fucking like, but I want you to take her and be happy," Liam murmured, defeated. "I'll go back to New York. I won't stand in your way."

"You can't do that! You'll crush her," Hammer insisted. "Remember? She *loves* you. There's no way you can tell me that you haven't seen how much she's grown because of what we've done these past two days."

"I've seen it," Liam admitted. "But—"

"But nothing." Hammer shook his head. "Raine needs us both. She loves us both. I think what's got you so fucked up inside is the reality that nothing you or I can do will change that. Am I right?"

Liam sighed. "I had it in my head—in my heart—that she was going to be mine."

"We both did, but there's something you need to think about. If you walk away, I'm left with a woman who can only give me half her heart. The other half belongs to you. I couldn't spend my life knowing I'd never be able to make her whole."

"I'm not trying to leave you with half a woman, Macen. But I don't see—"

"Then open your eyes. Raine is the one we've always needed," Hammer insisted. "We not only have the chance to fix her, but us. You know it as well as I do. Goddamn it, surely you can feel it somewhere in there, just like I can." Liam still didn't say anything, and Hammer wanted to shake him. "Could you imagine never touching her again? Ever?"

Liam's face twisted up as he tried to hold back. "No. I love her too much to leave her half empty."

"Then don't."

After a long silence, Liam drew in a deep breath. "It could be worse, I suppose. I'll have to be grateful that she didn't fall in love with a complete asshole like Beck."

Hammer couldn't help but grin as he sighed in relief. Even Liam cracked a wry smile.

"I want you to know that earlier today, I didn't just pull that question out of my ass. It had been rolling around in my head for days. I had to know if she would have been happy if she'd been pregnant." Hammer scrubbed a hand through his hair. "Didn't you want to know?"

"I was too afraid I wouldn't like the answer," Liam confessed.

"What if you'd gotten her pregnant? Would you have asked then?"

Liam reared back. "Of course. I'd want to know if she would be all right..." He sighed, giving Hammer a little grin. "You sly bastard."

"You see, I had to know, not for an ego stroke. For *her*. And she gave us the honesty we asked for. She's blown me away with how far she's come." Hammer couldn't conceal his pride.

"That she has. But today came with a price I hadn't expected."

"We couldn't shy away from hearing the truth, no matter how it stung. We just weren't fully prepared for the fallout," Hammer mused. "I seriously thought about taking Raine aside and asking her feelings about being pregnant. But in my head, you and I were in this together. No matter what she felt, it affected us both."

"I understand why you wanted me there. Honestly, I do" Liam nodded. "But it caught me off guard and stabbed deep."

"Not my intent, man. Hell, the two weeks I was counting the days of her cycle, I didn't know if I was scared or happy with the possibility of being a father. It wasn't until Thanksgiving, when fate decided for me, that I realized I wanted a family. And if anyone was going to be the mother of my children, I wanted it to be Raine."

Liam gaped at him as if he were an alien. "Bloody hell, I never thought I'd hear the words family and father out of *your* mouth."

Hammer shrugged and grinned sheepishly. "Yeah, well…the first time I have to change a dirty diaper, I'll probably be singing a completely different tune. But hopefully you'll be there to help me out." Hammer held Liam's gaze.

He wanted his friend back on board. Even if the train had a bad track record, Macen knew he'd never be able to make the journey with Raine half as meaningful without Liam.

"I vote we leave the dirty nappies to the wee one's mum." Liam grinned.

"Fuck yeah," Hammer breathed out, then stood. "She needs us, man. Together. Through thick and thin. And I have a sneaking suspicion that we're going to need each other even more. The girl's a fucking handful." Hammer sobered quickly. "I just hope we can get her back."

They sat in silence for a long minute as Hammer wondered if he'd ever be able to prove to Raine that his words of love were sincere. He'd simply have to wait until Beck cooled her down and brought her back to find out. For now, one bridge was on the mend, and it relieved the hell out of him.

Macen stood and wrapped Liam in a brotherly hug, grateful to have another chance at a new beginning with his old friend. Liam slapped him on the back in return.

"We'll just have to convince Raine that we're her best options." Liam chuckled.

"And grovel," Seth piped up. "You two will be kissing ass till the next millennium."

Hammer laughed. "God, I hope you're right."

Seth applauded like the sarcastic ass he was, then bowed. Straightening, he dusted off his palms. "My work here is done. Now let's have another drink."

CHAPTER
NINETEEN

Raine let Beck guide her into the sleepy little bar, decorated in early log cabin Americana. A startling collection of game heads were mounted to the walls. Their dead, glassy eyes stared back at her.

The place wasn't crowded on a Tuesday night. In the corner, a jukebox played a happy country-western ditty that scraped her raw. A few people at nearby tables laughed and chugged back beer. They looked happy.

The hollow feeling in her stomach and the ache deep in her chest served as painful reminders that her life had fallen apart.

Beck seated her in a corner, then grabbed the chair across from her and dragged it around the table until he sat right beside her. He took her shaking hand and pulled her closer. Without a qualm, she laid her head on his beefy shoulder and let out more tears. He smoothed a palm over her crown and murmured soft assurances.

God, she was so tired of crying. Of being upset and disappointed, confused and…torn between two lovers.

She lifted her head and looked at Beck. A month ago, he was the last person she would have called her friend. Tonight, she thanked goodness he was in her life.

"I don't know what to do," she confessed.

"Start by talking to me. They've taught you how to communicate and be honest. Those lessons aren't less meaningful because of what happened tonight."

Raine dragged in a breath as she sorted through her thoughts. Finally, she nodded. "You're right."

"Break it down. Tell me exactly what about their argument upset you most."

"They weren't supposed to fight. That was my only condition for agreeing to their proposition. It makes me wonder how much squabbling they've been doing behind my back."

With a shrug, Beck considered her words. "Princess, you're talking about two strong-willed alpha Doms. And they're human beings. They're going to fight. It's unrealistic to think that just because you coerced a promise out of them to get along, they could do it twenty-four seven."

She sat back to consider his words. A waitress in a short denim skirt and an eye for Beck came over to take their drink orders. He asked for coffee. *Fuck that.*

"Bring me tequila shots. Let's start with five of those and—"

"She'll have a glass of white wine," Beck cut in.

Raine glared at him. "What the hell?"

"You have to go back and face them. Don't you want to do it sober?" He glowered, trying to guilt her into sobriety.

"No, I don't." She crossed her arms over her chest. "They broke their promise."

Beck ignored her and addressed the waitress. "Coffee and white wine."

"Chardonnay or Moscato?"

Grimacing, she peered at the waitress. "No Pinot Grigio or…"

"Honey." The waitress worked hard not to roll her eyes. "It's a beer bar. We get vacationers who want to get drunk for cheap and locals who don't care how highbrow their buzz is. That's all we got."

Point taken. Raine sighed. "Chardonnay, please."

The woman shot Beck a look of both sympathy and interest before she turned away. He dismissed the waitress immediately and shifted in his chair. "They're gonna fight. Liam and Hammer are damn good, but they're not perfect. You're expecting them to be."

She pressed her lips together, seeing his point even when she didn't want to. The sight of them tearing into one another, the ugly things they'd said…

"Focus here." He pointed between his eyes. "You're talking to me, remember? You're not in a world all by yourself."

"Okay," she conceded. "So they're people who aren't going to get along all the time. Why can't they argue about football or the best car or who takes out the trash? That's normal guy stuff. They could rib each other, then toss back a few and laugh. But they always fight about *me*." She thumped her hands against her chest. "I'm always squarely in the middle. I feel like I need to referee more than submit."

"They fight about what's important to them." Beck chuckled. "But feel free to blow a whistle on them and call time out. See what happens."

She'd get her ass spanked for sure.

Raine shot him a quelling glance. "You're supposed to be helping me."

"You've got the answers. If they'd fought tonight about football or cars or whatever, if they'd gotten every bit as riled up about that as they did about you, what would you have told them?"

"To calm down. To take a step back." She bobbed her head as she sifted through the possibilities. "To be reasonable. To communicate and compromise."

"Exactly. This isn't any different. They lost their tempers. I'm sure they've simmered down and are drowning in a whole pile of 'oh, shit' right now."

"I've damaged their friendship."

"*They've* damaged it," Beck corrected. "You're too busy worrying about how they feel to think about what you need. I've listened to them debrief after the last two sessions. You've made amazing progress. That isn't because Liam was there. It isn't because Hammer topped you, either. It's because they did it together. You love them. And they love you. You can't really have expected this to just—" he snapped his fingers "—work overnight."

But she had, in a way. Not that she'd come to the lodge expecting happily ever after, but she'd wanted it. Beck and Seth had both encouraged the idea. And after the beautiful lesson on communication and the stunning intimacy that followed, she'd awakened this morning full of optimism. In the back of her head, she'd already been clasping their hands, putting on a white dress, and enrolling in childbirth classes. They'd just been trying to help her grow.

The waitress set down Raine's wine. A dribble sloshed over the rim because she was too busy making time with Beck to care. She settled his coffee in front of him with a smile. "Sugar? Cream?"

The woman made the two words last about ten syllables each, and Raine lost her patience. "Thanks. If you didn't notice, he's trying to straighten out my life. He's single, but he doesn't live around here. And unless you like welts with your spanking, you're barking up the wrong tree."

The mousy brunette recoiled and looked at Beck as if he'd turned into Satan. "Let me know if I can get you more coffee or wine."

Then she scurried off. Beck turned to Raine. A smile played at his mouth. "I should beat your ass for that, but it was damn funny."

Raine winced. "I'm glad you're not mad. Sometimes I lose my temper. Sorry if you were interested in—"

"Not her," Beck assured. "Let's get back to you."

She knew damn well he'd given her a reprieve. "After fighting for a month, maybe I was unrealistic to think they wouldn't ever have a dispute about me again. I guess I just didn't want to feel torn anymore. I want them to get along. I want them to be adults, damn it."

"If you ever repeat this, I'll deny I said it. But men can be large children. They fight and draw lines in the sand and need time outs…"

"They were trying to hurt one another," she pointed out.

"Sometimes guys do that. It's the verbal equivalent of whipping it out to see whose is bigger."

Raine shook her head. "But they were using *me* to hurt each other. It really pisses me off that they push me to break through all my barriers to communicate and to be honest with them when they're not doing the same with me."

"That's valid," Beck agreed. "I'm sure they've realized it by now. But I think today was their first step toward being truly honest with one another. It got ugly because they got everything out in the open. They needed it, in my opinion. I know you didn't want to hear all that, but I think it's good you did."

As much as she hated it, Beck was probably right. "Hammer didn't *try* to get me pregnant. He just didn't try not to. He was drunk, and everything happened fast. But I don't think it was intentional. Liam is wrong about that."

"So tell him."

Gnawing her lip, Raine nodded, filtering back through the verbal war she'd heard. "Do you know everything that happened between Liam and his ex-wife?"

"Nope. He's always kept me at a distance. I don't think he liked my friendship with Hammer much. It's been better the last few days, but we'll see what happens. If you want to know more about Gwyneth, ask him, not me. I'm not the one who can tell you."

Beck was just full of good points tonight, damn him. Raine sipped her wine and watched him grimace at his coffee.

"Do you think Hammer thinks of me as a substitute for Juliet?"

Without a second of hesitation, Beck shook his head. "No. I think whatever he once felt for her died not long after she swallowed those pills. He finally saw her as she was—and it wasn't the woman he'd convinced himself he loved, in my opinion. You..." He pointed at her. "You are what he's needed. That's why he's in love with you. Ditto for O'Neill. I don't know his troubles, but I know he's got them. Just like I know you're a balm for them."

He made all the disaster in her life sound so simple to fix—love. And she'd kill to know what secret Hammer kept that Liam had to forgive him for...but even if Beck knew, he wouldn't spill.

Raine choked back another sip of her vino. "I think what hurt me most was the moment I realized that Liam never had any intention of this threesome lasting beyond our time at the lodge. And I know we didn't talk about that or agree to it on a permanent basis, but...I love them both. What did he think was going to happen? I could kneel for them and be complete for a few days, then give it up? Being here has made me realize this is what I *need*. You tried to tell me that back at your condo."

"You thought I was a little insane, didn't you?"

"Maybe a touch." She rimmed her wineglass with her finger and smiled at him.

"But now you know."

"I do," she agreed, taking another sip.

"So the issue isn't really the words they exchanged tonight. The more important thing is what happens next. What do you think you should do? Be smart here..."

Raine stepped back from the situation as much as her emotions would allow. If she were giving a friend advice in this situation, what would she say? "Sit them down and be completely honest about the fact that I love them, that I hate it when they fight, and that I want them always. But that sounds unrealistic, too. If they can't get along today, there's no tomorrow. And with that argument tonight, I can't imagine them trying to climb in the same bed with me together—ever."

Beck shrugged. "There's an important thought in there. Keep digging. You want another wine?"

She looked down to see that she'd drained the glass and shook her head. "I've had better wine from a convenience store. No offense."

"None taken. I've had better coffee from a hospital cafeteria, and that's saying something. Ready to go?"

When Beck made to stand, she grabbed his hand. "One more question."

He settled in his seat again. "Shoot."

"Did they have more tasks planned for me?"

"One," he admitted grimly. "It revolved around trust."

"They wanted me to give them my trust?" she clarified.

"They wanted a show of it, yes."

Something about the way Beck tensed put her on alert. "Okay, cough it up. What were they going to do?"

He hesitated, looked at his coffee, lifted it, and set it aside with a scowl. Then he drew in a deep breath. "Tomorrow afternoon, they intended to take you into the playroom and put you entirely in Seth's hands. No options off the table. They wanted to see if you trusted them enough to extend your trust to someone you didn't know well because they asked you to."

That startled Raine. "Sex?"

Beck shrugged. "They wanted to see if you would put your faith in them enough to keep you safe."

"That's the stupidest thing I've ever heard." She sighed.

"Tell me how you really feel, princess." Chuckling, Beck leaned closer. "I have no doubt they never would have let him lay a finger on you. They just wanted to see what you'd do."

"I'm familiar with the tactic. I've seen other Doms use it at Shadows. Liam and Hammer are crazy if they thought I wouldn't see through that. If they can barely stand each other touching me, they're not going to let Seth do it."

"Oh god, you're going to keep them on their toes. I'm going to enjoy this ringside seat."

She swatted his shoulder. "Seriously!"

He grinned. "Just out of curiosity, is the idea so stupid because it's transparent?"

"Besides that..." She waved his words away. "Trust, like communication and honesty, should run both ways. Or in our case, all three ways. None of it works unless everyone is doing their best. Gosh, listen to me. I learned something!"

Beck nodded. "Yes. So you have to tell them what you need and trust that they'll communicate honestly in return. It isn't more complicated than that. Well, except the part where you have to trust them to take care of you."

Individually, she really did. She hadn't always been good at showing it. She'd never had to submit to Hammer. And she hadn't really let go with Liam like she should. In the end, though, they had done so much to make her whole. She trusted that they wanted what was best for her. But could they do that together?

"You're right. I think I have an idea." She hopped up from her seat, eager to return to the lodge.

"All right." He threw down a twenty and turned to wink at the waitress who was pretending not to spy on them. "Let's blow this taco stand so you can go wrangle those men."

Ten minutes later, they walked through the door of the lodge into the cheerful great room with its blazing fire. Seth stood near the hearth and turned when Raine entered. But she barely noticed him.

Dressed in jeans and freshly showered, Liam and Hammer stood, both tense. Then they stepped toward her, and she got a good look at their faces.

She gasped. "What happened to—" The truth hit her between the eyes, and Raine threw her hands up in exasperation. "You two fought? What the hell? And don't talk to me about language right now, Liam. I have every right to be ridiculous if you're going to be."

They both had the good grace to look sheepish.

Liam rubbed at a mottled, red-purple spot on his jaw. Both their noses looked swollen. Hammer had a bit of a goose egg on his chin.

Behind her, Beck chuckled. "God, you two are funny."

"Fuck off, Beck." Hammer scowled.

"I deliver her back to you twice and that's the thanks I get." He shook his head. "We need to talk about the concept of appreciation, man."

"Where's her suitcase?" Liam snapped.

"Still in the SUV." Raine made her way across the room and sat in one of the overstuffed chairs adjacent to the sofa.

Beck followed and patted her on the shoulder before he took his place beside Seth. "Hand them their balls, princess."

She turned to stare at her friend over her shoulder. "Can you behave?"

"We're sorry, precious," Hammer began. "We never meant to upset you."

"No," she corrected. "You never meant for me to hear. If you expect me to be honest, you should be as well."

He and Liam exchanged a glance before he nodded. "You're right."

"Good." She leaned forward, bracing her elbows on her knees. "Tell me, are you two done fighting?"

"We are," Hammer promised.

She nodded, then turned to stare at Liam. He was too quiet, and that worried her.

Her tender Irishman hesitated, then nodded. "We talked through a lot of things tonight. We're back on the same page, love."

Raine sincerely hoped that was true. "In order for me to stay, I need to put that to the test. I understand the final task you had planned for me was about trust. No offense, Seth, but I'm not bottoming for you. I'm definitely not sleeping with you, either. I love them, but right now trust is a little thin, and I don't think I could respond in a way that would please anyone."

Seth looked impressed. "That's honest. Fair enough. By the way, they weren't going to let me touch you."

"Told you," Beck put in.

She sent him an impatient glare.

"Sorry," the doctor murmured. "You're doing good. Carry on."

Raine gave him an absent nod, then addressed Liam and Hammer again. "I came here wanting you both in my life. After two days here, I realize that's what I need. I also know I can't stop you from fighting, and making you promise to get along was never going to work. But I don't think it's too much to ask that you not hit one another."

"You're right," Hammer admitted. "We're done."

"I threw the first punch. I'm sorry," Liam added.

They both looked so contrite with their proverbial tails tucked between their legs. It wouldn't last long. They'd soon be big bad alpha Doms again. But at the moment, it was nice to see that distressing her had unsettled them deeply.

"So, here's what I'm thinking: We should all work on our trust. I have a proposition for you."

"We're listening." Liam's eyes looked sharp, his body taut.

Hammer lounged against the back of the sofa, but he was no less attentive. "Tell us."

"For us to work, you two have to trust one another, believe that you'll do the right thing, and have my best interest at heart, right?"

They both nodded.

"I have to trust that you'll take care of me and give me the experience I need."

"As always," Liam answered.

"But now we have a new component. You need to trust me not only to submit myself totally, but to love you equally. You have to believe that I will come to you openly and never choose one over the other. And I assure you, I won't, not ever again. Do I have any of that wrong, Sirs?"

They looked at one another in a seeming silent moment of communication.

"You're right." Hammer nodded at her. "Go on. What's your plan?"

Now the conversation got more difficult. If this didn't work, she could never try to love just one of them while cutting the other out.

She'd have to walk away from them both. Raine understood the huge gamble she was undertaking...but didn't see another way. If this plan didn't work, they would never last.

"Before I get into that, I need your promise that communication and honesty also run not just from me to you, but from you to me. If I have questions, you'll give me answers."

Another hesitation. Another glance. Then Liam nodded. "Of course."

"Later, I'll want answers about some of the things I overheard tonight. If you're not prepared to give me those answers, then I'll know you're not ready for this level of trust and Beck will take me down the mountain."

"And then what?" Hammer challenged.

"Nothing." She shrugged. "Because we'd have nothing. You both made it very clear how important communication, honesty, and trust are. It's so clear that I get it now. We have nothing real without them. I won't settle for less."

Hammer scrubbed a hand down his face. Liam shifted in his seat. Neither looked very comfortable with her request. Beck and Seth didn't move a muscle. The sense of anticipation turned thick in the air.

"All right," Hammer said finally. "I'll answer your questions in the best way I can."

"I will, too." Liam nodded her way.

"Good. I'm trusting you to keep your end of the bargain."

"But why later, love?" Liam asked. "Why not now?"

"Because I want to do it after our show of trust. If we get through that, the answers will mean more. If not...then none of it will matter. Okay?"

"Whatever you need to feel comfortable," Hammer promised.

Liam nodded. "We want you happy."

They were willing to give back to her, and that fact alone made Raine's heart soften. She wanted to fling herself in their arms, but now she had to say the most difficult words of all.

She stood, pacing around her chair. To her right, Liam and Hammer both edged toward the front of the sofa. Tension gripped the room.

"Go on, love," Liam prompted.

There was no easy way to say this. They would either agree or not, and stalling wouldn't change that.

Raine sucked in a bracing breath. "I need you both. I want to give myself completely to you with a fully open heart. I know what I'm asking won't be easy for either of you, and you can say no. But I'd love the fantasy just this once. If you want that, too, come find me. I want you to make love to me. Together."

After Raine mounted the stairs and disappeared into the master suite, the door shut. Seth grabbed her suitcase and ran it upstairs. A moment later, he heard the water running through the pipes to her bathtub.

Liam let out a breath he hadn't realized he'd been holding and turned to look at Hammer. "Well, mate. I think her balls are bigger than ours put together. I'm not sure either of us would ever have been able to handle her on our own."

Hammer laughed. "Amazing woman, isn't she? Others pale in comparison. I've got to admit, Raine is the only one I'd ever let hand me my balls on a platter."

"You two are so pussy-whipped, it's fucking hysterical." Beck snickered.

Seth jogged down the stairs with a sly grin at Liam. "I remember asking if she'd put a spell on you with her voodoo pussy. At least you didn't lie about the fact that she has."

That made Beck laugh even harder. Hammer joined in, too. Liam tried to keep a straight face, but he couldn't hold back a smile.

He elbowed Macen. "Hey, I'm not the only one."

"Absolutely not," Hammer admitted, glancing up the stairs toward the master suite. "I can't wait for her to put another spell on me."

Beck rolled his eyes. "This is like hearing about my little sister getting down and dirty. Come on, Seth. Let's raid the kitchen."

As the other two Doms left, noisily emptying the contents of the refrigerator, he and Hammer stared into the fire. Neither man spoke for a few minutes, each sipping their drinks, wrapped in their own thoughts.

"If she thinks it's only for one night," Liam groused, "she's out of her pretty little head."

"I guess the only question left is whether or not we're in this together," Hammer murmured. "You need to be clear on whether you're staying or going now."

Hammer was right. Liam nodded. "I know."

"Because neither of us will ever be satisfied with just half of her. There's no way I'll settle for just one night. I can't imagine you being happy with that, either. If we go up those stairs, we show her it's not a one-time shot, that we're in it for the long haul." He pointed up toward Raine. "We make her feel it."

"You're right. She needs to know we mean it."

A grin crawled up Hammer's face. "Exactly. Because she just topped us, and we can't let that fly."

"Damn straight." Liam rose for another swallow of Scotch, then headed toward the stairs. Something about the uncertainty on Hammer's face stopped him. In his friend's shoes, he'd want to know that his partner was committed. "You know, I wasn't really serious about throwing in the towel earlier. It was frustration talking. And I've worried that my jealousy was just hurting us all. I can't promise it won't come back. You might have to give me a kick or two."

"What are friends for?"

Liam grinned. "Indeed. But I know Raine needs us." He took a sip of his drink. "And frankly, we need her. I'm in all the way."

Hammer let out a breath of relief. "Thank god."

"If we're discussing more than a night, what about later? What will you do about other subs?"

"If I'm with Raine, there are no other subs. What about you? You always had a little black book back in New York," Hammer reminded with an arch of a brow.

"I don't think I'm going back. I bought a house here, remember? I'm planning to stay here for her." He cleared his throat. "For all of us."

Hammer nodded. "What about you and me? Are we good? Anything else we need to sort out? 'Cause we can take another trip outside if we need to."

"Hell no! It's cold as fuck out there, and I'm just starting to feel my fingers again. Besides I don't think I'd win any points with Raine if I made you any uglier."

"Did you see her face?" Hammer looked stunned. "Christ, I thought she was going to take a stick to us."

"I'm sure she would have if she didn't worry we'd use it on her ass next."

"That's a valid concern." He grinned slyly.

"You're right." Liam nodded. As silence prevailed, he glanced up the stairs, itching to hold Raine again, to finally see her whole. But they couldn't sweep this question under the rug. "I think we've sorted all our shit through. I've spewed everything—probably more than I should have—but I'm done."

"I think we both said our fair share. But it's nice to know that we've come out of it still friends. In some ways, I think we have her to thank."

"For making us see that we'd been idiots? I reckon."

Hammer gave a slow smile. "The only thing left to do is figure out how we're going to give her a night so fucking fabulous that she'll want another."

Liam grinned back. "And another. And another..."

C HAPTER
T WENTY

R aine put the last of the scented lotion on her body, then wrapped a clean towel around her as she fought back her nerves. Would they come tonight? Tomorrow? Ever? Would they still want her? Would they be able to share her even once? She didn't have any illusions; she was asking them for a lot. It wouldn't be easy for either of them to set their feelings aside to give her this fantasy.

Taking in a steadying breath, she pushed out of the bathroom to rummage through the suitcase Seth had brought up to her. She spotted Hammer shirtless and lounging on the bed, surrounded by easily a dozen candles. She stopped short, her heart stuttering with excitement. Then she scanned the room.

No Liam.

Her heart broke apart instantly. He'd tried for weeks to make her grow and blossom. He'd helped her so much here at the lodge. Had all the day's confessions been too much for him? He especially had wanted her all to himself. She put her hand to her neck, still missing the lovely weight of his collar there. The thought of never feeling the mark of his possession again shredded her.

"Hello, precious." Hammer's deep voice seduced her, a smoky murmur that stirred her memories of the pleasure they'd shared. Each and every day, that night haunted her. She'd never escaped the sharp pang of need to feel him again.

"Hi."

Tonight, she didn't know what else to say. All the confidence she'd built up in the bar with Beck, that had given her such strength when she'd delivered her proposition...it had evaporated. She should be happy that she was both a better submissive and a better human being. But if she'd finally pushed Liam away for good, how was she supposed to find peace with half of her heart missing?

The door kicked open a minute later, and her gaze zipped up. Beck and Seth carried in a big cheval mirror. An antique with a distressed black frame, its straight lines blended with the gentle curves of its legs into something truly stunning.

Raine clutched the towel over her breasts and watched the guys cart it in until they'd positioned it to face the bed, a few feet from the edge.

With a satisfied nod, Seth released it and straightened, then headed her way. He smiled as he cupped her arm. "Be happy."

God knew she wanted to be, but not without Liam. He'd become as essential to her as sunshine or food. As air. She pressed a fist to the aching hollow of her stomach.

Beck strolled over an instant later. "Try to keep it to a dull roar, huh?"

Before she could chastise him, he kissed her forehead, then clapped Seth on the back. Out the door they went, leaving her alone with Macen.

"Lose the towel, precious," he commanded.

Before they'd come to the lodge, Raine would have believed she could just stand naked in front of one of them and not realize how much she needed the other. But they'd opened her eyes. She had no way to unsee the truth.

How could she set him down gently? Just explain that she refused to give him half of herself, she supposed.

Raine clasped the towel tighter to her chest. "Macen—"

"Didn't Hammer give you an order?"

She turned to the familiar lilt. Hope surged. Liam strolled in, shirtless and carrying a small black bag. Like Hammer, the lean muscles of his shoulders and pectorals bulged and rippled with every move and sent her pulse skidding. He kicked the door behind him and sent her a wolfish smile. A quick glance back to Hammer revealed heat and expectation glowing in his eyes. The testosterone in the room swelled. Her breathing went shallow. Need settled right behind her clit.

They'd both come.

Raine dropped her towel. "Yes, Sir."

Automatically, she fell to her knees and sat back on her heels, head bowed, thighs parted. To her left, she heard the rustle of the bed covers and assumed Hammer pulled them free. To her right, Liam strolled closer until his bare feet filled her vision. He dropped the little black bag on the carpet beside him.

"Pretty. Rise, love." His voice was soft but whiplike in the hush. He held his hand out to her.

Placing her trembling fingers in his, she lunged to her feet and looked up at him, searching his dark eyes. They glittered with desire, too. With love, just like Hammer's.

For this moment at least, her world was complete.

Hammer approached on her right and lightly gripped her elbow. "Come to the mirror. Let us see you."

They guided her in front of the tall glass and positioned her to face it, totally bare. Her cheeks looked flushed already. Her nipples pebbled under their stares. Her pussy looked slick and pouting. God, they aroused her before they really even put a hand on her.

Raine glanced at them both. That worried female part of her wondered if they'd like what they saw on display. They'd both seen everything she offered them now, but did either of them feel differently knowing they wouldn't be taking her alone? It was probably a silly question. She had to believe they were here because they wanted to be, but nerves still wrenched her.

Hammer caressed his way up her arms. "You know, every time I see you, I want to fuck you."

It wasn't funny exactly, but she laughed.

"What's given you a giggle?" Liam demanded, looking very stern. "He's told you that he wants you."

She tried to wipe the smile off her face. "I was standing here feeling insecure, and he put that to rest with one sentence in his usual eloquent way. It struck me as funny." She sent a soft gaze to Hammer. "I'm not laughing at you, Sir."

"You'd better not be. Talk about a red ass..." he muttered.

"I second that." Liam smoothed a hand down her backside.

"Seems like you always want to spank me," she teased.

"I do," he admitted. "But like Hammer, I always want to fuck you, as well."

It wasn't the most romantic thing either of them had ever said to her, but it still made her feel beautiful and feminine. Wanted.

"I'm glad you both came, Sirs. I worried."

"Your honesty is gorgeous, precious." Hammer pressed a kiss to her shoulder. "There was no way we weren't going to come for you."

She shivered. "I'm still grateful you did. How can I serve you?"

More than likely, she should be bowing her head or something to show respect, but she really just wanted to look into their eyes and reveal to them both how earnest she felt. How much she loved them.

Judging from their sensual male smiles, they understood completely.

"You can start by putting your hands at your sides. Close your eyes. Spread your legs."

Liam's soft commands might as well have touched her where she needed it most. They ratcheted up her desire until it twisted her chest. But she did exactly as he'd bid, clasping her thighs lightly as she opened them and slid her eyes shut.

"Excellent," he whispered in her ear, then nipped at her lobe with his teeth. "We're going to take every inch of you in every way we can."

Raine swallowed hard. Her knees nearly went out from under her.

"When we're done, you'll damn well know you're ours," Hammer growled in her other ear.

"Your job, love, is to give everything to us. No holding back. No reservations. No thinking about anything but what you need. Is that clear?" Liam asked.

"Yes, Sir." Even her voice shook.

"Your safe word stands. What is it?"

Of course he knew, but he always verified with her. He always worried about her care.

"Paris, Sir."

"Thank you, precious." Hammer skimmed a hand down her right hip. "Are you wet?"

Excitement stole her breath. "Yes, Sir."

"Prove it. Show me," he barked.

She frowned, puzzling it out in her head. How? Finally, she lifted her hand from her thigh and dipped her fingers between her swollen folds, shocked to feel that she wasn't just wet but drenched. She gasped when she skimmed her clit, wishing that one of them would—

"That's enough." Hammer grabbed her wrist and lifted her hand from her pussy and led it toward him.

A moment later, she felt the wet heat of his mouth surround her digits. His tongue cradled them, swirling and licking as he moaned. The air left her lungs in a rush. It didn't make any sense, but the ache behind her clit became a throb.

"Do you like knowing he's tasting you?" Liam asked in a low, seductive murmur.

Raine wanted to turn to him and beg him to kiss her, lay her back and touch her, get deep inside her—something to alleviate the ache. Her nails dug into her thigh and she bit her lip to hold in her begging. A dizzy fever swam in her head.

When she didn't answer, Macen withdrew her fingers from his mouth. "I'll take that as a no. It's a shame, man. I wanted to taste that pretty cunt, but I guess she doesn't want that."

Was he crazy?

"I like it. I want it. Please…" No missing the pleading note in her voice, and she didn't care. Let them know she wanted them more than anything. It was nothing but the truth.

"Please…" A note of steel rang in Hammer's voice.

"Please, Sir."

"Better," he praised. But she still felt the loss of his body heat as he stepped away.

From her left, Liam's fingers skimmed the long line of her spine, then dipped down to skate over the cleft of her ass. A moment later, his touch disappeared, too.

Absolute silence and still blanketed the room. Anxiety gripped Raine's stomach. She wanted to ask what was wrong or open her eyes and see if they'd gone. *Trust*, she reminded herself. They wouldn't come this far to leave her. She wouldn't disobey because of her insecurities. They would give her the experience she craved if she let them.

After a calming breath, she centered herself and let the tension go.

"I'm very pleased, love," Liam said, sounding somewhere behind her, closer to the ground. She didn't have time to do more than frown in question before he raked his palms up her thighs. "Open your eyes and watch us."

Her lashes fluttered up, and Raine looked into the mirror. She sucked in a stunned breath.

Hammer crouched in front of her, his mouth so close to her pussy. The heat of his breath, the strong inhalation as he drew in her scent, the urgent thumbs he used to part her folds all made her gasp.

He settled his mouth over her clit and sucked deep at the same time Liam parted the cheeks of her ass and rimmed her rosette with slick, insistent fingers.

Raine mewled as desire rolled through her in a fresh wave, igniting nerve endings and silencing her fears. Nothing but the gaping, jagged ache of need remained, stealing her thoughts and overtaking her every cell, every vein, every heartbeat.

Maybe she shouldn't, but Raine reached out both to steady herself and to touch Hammer, rifling her fingers through his hair with a moan. He suckled her clit again, then laved it, toying with her, alternating the pressure and happily driving her out of her mind.

Behind her, Liam nipped at her cheek, his teeth gently digging, before he sank a finger inside her, shoving past the entrance, through the tight ring, right into the depths of her. Another followed, filling her with a snug tension that had her hitching in a breath. Then he kissed his way up her hip. His lips skated up her back as he stood, his body brushing hers and surrounding her with heat. Then he nipped across her shoulder blade, his mouth settling just below her ear.

"Are you liking this, love?" The sexy murmur all but dared her to say otherwise.

"Yes, Sir."

"What is it you want?" He thrust his fingers a bit deeper, parting them slowly and preparing her. "Tell us."

"I want you inside me," she gasped. "Both of you. Please, Sirs."

"I like the pretty way you beg."

Hammer chose that moment to nip at her clit, then soothe it with the tip of his tongue. An electric shock of tingles burst under her skin. She tightened her fingers in his hair. Blood surged and pleasure swelled. She'd fantasized about this for longer than she even wanted to admit to herself. But the reality made her imaginings pale. Every sensation was so crisp and loud. Her heartbeat drummed. Her legs felt like noodles. Raine wanted to serve and please them after they'd done so much for her, but they enslaved her with these sensations. She couldn't seem to do more than whimper.

"I guess that's enough, Hammer," Liam said. "She wants us to fuck her. Apparently, she doesn't want to come on your tongue."

"No," she contradicted. "Please, Sir!"

"Don't fuck you then, either?" He tsked at her. "Bloody demanding wench."

"Please may I come on your tongue, Hammer? Then will you both fuck me?" Saying the words sounded odd, a little embarrassing, but that barely pierced the haze of her need. And Raine had no illusions that they not only wanted her to say exactly what she desired, but they expected it.

She refused to disappoint them.

"Listen to that, mate. You don't have to guess what she wants now, do you?"

Hammer didn't respond verbally, just groaned as he set his mouth over the top of her cunt, anchoring his tongue in her opening and sucking. His groan vibrated through her entire body.

"I think that's his way of telling you to come," Liam whispered, his tone silky. "Do it now—and anytime tonight you have the urge. We want your pleasure, every last bit of it. Is that clear?"

"Yes, Sir," she managed to get out in one rushed breath before his fingers probed against sensitive nerves and Hammer's mouth startled her with another rush of ecstasy.

The sensations stacked, one on top of the other, until she was sweltering, dizzy, losing her balance and her mind. And she didn't care. The surge and rush of need slammed her. One more pull of Macen's lips, one more second...

"We want to hear you scream, love, loud and often," Liam demanded.

That wasn't going to be a problem.

Reality shifted, slipped, as the supernova of sensation exploded, bursting over her senses, taking her strength and balance with it. She wailed out, a high-pitched keening that bounced off the walls and filled her ears, echoing in the room around them. Her womb pulsed. Her fists clenched in Hammer's hair. With one hand Liam propped her up. With the other, his fingers filled her ass, wringing a staggering pleasure from her.

She ran out of air before the pulses stopped. With Hammer at the helm, the bliss seemed to last forever as they worked together to take every bit of her surrender and make it theirs.

Finally, panting, weak, stunned, she fell back into Liam's arms. Hammer stood and smiled down into her face, licking his lips like a very proud man.

A wave of love rolled through her as she looked into his hazel eyes. They'd darkened to something closer to emerald, and she knew from their one night together that meant he needed her, too.

"You're bad, Macen," she teased weakly.

Hammer shrugged and pulled her into his embrace. "I don't know. You made that sound like I was pretty damn good."

Her smile widened.

Liam disappeared into the bathroom to wash his hands, then returned to lift her in his arms. He laid her on the bed and covered her body with his own. As he swooped down to capture her mouth, she opened to him completely, rising up to crush their chests together, to take his tongue. For long moments, he'd played cool and collected, but she felt the urgency of his need now. He intended to put a stamp on her by making her crave him and scream for him, too.

Then he shimmied down her body, falling on her nipples that beaded and throbbed for his attention. He took one peak against his tongue and sucked hard, nipping and biting. A new wave of sensation formed almost immediately. She arched, trying to offer him more.

Hammer leaned over her. "Give him those pink nipples, Raine. Tell him you want them sucked."

"I do. I want them sucked, Sir," she managed to get out.

Above her, Liam growled.

Macen's eyes glittered. "You're going to get fucked, precious. It's been exactly thirty days since I've felt you grip my cock. Since then, I've craved the chance to be inside you once more. I'm going to stretch you and tunnel my way inside that sweltering ass again. And you're going to let me, aren't you?"

Oh, god. His every word set her ablaze. "Yes, Sir."

Liam pounced on her other nipple, making it every bit as tender and swollen as the first. He pinched the one he'd just worked, and every sensation jolted straight down to her clit. Her blood boiled as if she hadn't had an orgasm three minutes ago. As if she hadn't had one in the last five years.

"While I'm filling every bit of that ass," Hammer went on, "Liam is going to stuff your pretty cunt with every inch he's got. You're going to be a good girl and take all we give you. You're going to plead for us, isn't that right?"

"Yes, Sir."

"We'll hear every whimper and wail, won't we?"

"I promise, Sir," she vowed.

"And you're going to come for us."

It wasn't a question.

She smiled. "I'll be happy to."

Liam looked up at her, his dark eyes blazing. "Minx."

He gave her no time to even pretend to protest before he lavished more attention on her nipples. Biting, sucking, twisting, Liam was relentless, keeping at her until the little peaks crested hard, a little sore, but very well loved.

Until he'd used them so thoroughly, she felt herself crashing toward another climax.

As she panted and felt the flush creep up her body, Liam eased away and climbed off the mattress.

The moment he did, Hammer pulled her to her feet, facing the side of the bed. He hovered behind her. Liam positioned the mirror so that she could see herself...and they would be able to watch themselves penetrate her in whatever way they chose. She trembled.

When Liam had the mirror arranged, he bent to retrieve two items from his little black bag. One at a time, he threw them to Hammer. The first was something white and oblong. The second looked flat and square. Lube and a condom. She heard the fall of his zipper.

She turned to look at Hammer over her shoulder, searching for reassurance.

"You and I have done this part before, precious. I'll start first. We know double penetration will be new for you. We'll go easy. Just relax." He caressed her shoulder, his lips skating up her neck.

No way would he hurt her. She nodded. "I will."

Liam took up position on the bed in front of her, balancing on his knees, looming just slightly above her. "Look at me."

Raine couldn't have looked anywhere else if she tried.

"Good. Lean into me. We'll take care of you."

Behind her, she heard a delicate rip and knew exactly what Hammer was doing, what he had planned. Her insides danced with excitement, but she scanned Liam's expression. How did he feel? Was he prepared for this? She wasn't asking for more than a night; she couldn't force them to have a relationship, after all.

His dark stare reflected back her passion, the need and yearning that had her reaching for him and leaning in, just as he'd asked.

As she drew closer, he took her mouth, sweeping inside with a slow, sweet seduction that made her toes curl into the carpet.

Hammer chose that moment to slide his slickened fingers over her opening and add to the lubricant Liam had prepared her with earlier. Just his touch there thrilled her, but knowing he meant to sink deep into her and that Liam would steady her, kiss her, while Macen did...

A breathless wave swept over her as Hammer withdrew his fingers. He didn't wait an instant before he parted her cheeks and set the head of his cock against her opening. "You know what to do. Arch and push out. Take me, precious."

"Yes, Sir," she whispered, looking into Liam's eyes.

But he still looked steady, strong. She did everything Hammer asked as she stared up into Liam's gaze, hoping he could see the pleasure she experienced and how grateful she was to him for making this possible.

As Hammer popped past her tight ring, he eased his way in, a slow, molasses glide all the way inside her, so deep, she swore she could feel him in every corner of her body. Once he'd plunged in completely, she arched and tossed her head back, reveling in the raw ecstasy of the moment.

Hammer grabbed her hair in his fist and nearly withdrew. "Kiss him to show us both how much you're enjoying this."

"Yes, Sir," she eeked out, then reached up for Liam.

He met her halfway, his lips searching, parted, seizing her and making her feel so treasured.

Behind her, Hammer thrust his cock deep again. Liam's tongue filled her mouth. The sensation of being owned rushed through her bloodstream, unlike anything else she'd ever experienced. Between them, wrapped in their passion, she felt small, female, possessed...and shockingly submissive. Just like the night she'd taken them both into her mouth and pleased them, she wanted to give them everything she could, whatever would thrill them. She felt desperate to show them how much she yearned to give of herself.

Then Liam caressed his way down her waist, her hip, trailing his fingers into her aching pussy, adding fuel to the fire. As he found her clit and rubbed in gentle, insistent circles, Raine grabbed onto his shoulders and looked at him helplessly. Her pleasure was in their hands. His stare told her she had nothing to worry about.

Hammer thrust deep again, harder, rougher than before. She wanted it, craved it.

He tugged on her hair. "You're tightening on me, precious. Are you going to come?"

As incredible as it seemed, after the shattering orgasm they'd already given her, she would have thought it impossible. Instead, Raine knew it was inevitable. The pressure gathered. The blood collected. The need grew until she mewled into Liam's kiss, all but begging for just a bit more pressure and a lot more relief.

As if they had some silent communication, they suddenly ramped up as one. Hammer shoved his way in, one hard shuttling thrust after the other, electrifying every sensitive nerve gripping his cock, while Liam circled and pinched her clit. They controlled her. They knew precisely what she needed. They had the power to give...or take away.

After another seductive swirl of his tongue around hers, Liam pulled free and settled his lips against her ear. "I can feel your clit hard on my fingers. You want to come, don't you?"

"Yes, Sir!" She could barely find a breath.

"Liam..." Hammer growled, and Raine could hear his will to hold back.

"Suck it up, mate. We can't fail her." Liam rubbed the pad of his thumb directly over her sensitive little bud, and she saw stars. "Now, love."

Before he even got the words out, Raine twisted and screamed, arched and grabbed onto Liam for dear life as another cataclysm roared through her.

Hammer grunted, clutching her hip in a death grip, tugging on her hair as he fought for restraint. With a blistering stare, Liam watched her and groaned. The soundtrack merely added fuel to her fire. Everything inside her body beamed with ecstasy.

Slowly, the shattering stopped. She caught her breath. Hammer gentled his hold. Liam pulled away with a curse, tumbling to the floor and fumbling in that little black bag. Moments later, he ripped his jeans off and kicked them away, then sheathed himself. He clambered back onto the bed, teeth bared. He dipped under her and grabbed her hips, urging her onto the mattress to straddle him.

Raine climbed slowly, careful not to dislodge Hammer or disrupt his tight grip. Together, they positioned her over Liam's swollen, angry cock. She fell forward on her hands and knees. Hammer pushed her down with his next stroke, driving Liam straight inside her, one agonizing inch at a time until he filled her completely.

The dual invasion stretched her. She felt stuffed, impossibly penetrated. At the same time, it changed every perspective she'd held about pleasure. *This* was…beyond.

"Are you all right?" Just from his voice, the effort to ask that question clearly cost Liam.

"Fine, Sir." She stared down into his eyes. "Don't stop. Please." She didn't bother to disguise her pleading. She needed what only they could give her too badly.

"Look at us," Hammer commanded behind her, still sounding like he fought for control.

Raine turned her head to peer into the mirror Liam had positioned. She'd almost shied away from it earlier. Without Liam, the picture hadn't been complete. But now… The image seared itself into her head and blew her away—her between them, looking so much fairer, smaller. Them surrounding her, muscled, male, and determined. Possession stamped their faces. Determination tightened their bodies as they pushed their way into her, alternating strokes, setting up a rhythm that kept the tingles skittering under her skin, the need pooling in her pussy, and the lava flowing in her veins. Love poured out in every direction as they gripped her, filled her, gave their all to her.

This didn't feel like the one night she'd asked for. It felt like forever.

Another orgasm threatened to overtake her, and she looked at Liam, torn between panic and supplication.

As he ground up into her, sweat dripping from his temples with effort, he fused his stare with hers. "Don't you hold out on us."

Frantically, she shook her head, then cried out when the force and cadence of their thrusts notched up again. She wasn't going to last. Neither were they. And she wanted to weep. This couldn't end, not when she knew in her heart they could have so many more tomorrows together.

In seconds, the ecstasy would send her hurtling into the heavens. But she wanted to make one thing clear first.

"I love you both. Always."

Liam gripped her waist and forced her down onto his surging cock. "I love you, too. I'll never stop."

"Yes, precious!" Hammer bellowed. "I said it. I meant it. I love you. It's the fucking truth."

The insistence of their words, the pounding of their bodies, the way they all breathed and swayed together—it felt like total devotion, like nothing less than love.

Her entire body gathered, pooling and swirling. The power of this climax buzzed in her head. Raine glanced in the mirror one last time. They moved as one, the ebb and flow of breaths and limbs, of thrusts and gasps and heartbeats all converged.

Deep inside her, she felt them swell, heard their cries of passion as orgasm gripped them. They held her tighter and shouted her name, hearts pounding against her as they seemingly poured everything from their souls into her.

The explosion hurtled her, a cataclysm that broke and remade her, remolding her into not just a woman, but *their* woman. As they fell into a heap together on the bed and the men murmured and caressed her, Raine knew that, no matter what, she'd feel like theirs for the rest of her life.

Raine curled around Liam, her soft exhalations whispering on his neck. Her sighs and cries of ecstasy still played in his head. With them, she'd been giving, open, honest—revealing the dazzling submissive and woman he'd always imagined. Raine had drowned in the bliss of their tandem assault, bravely rising again and again for more, taking them both deeper into her body, her heart, with such splendor it had left him stunned and breathless.

The night had been beyond his wildest fantasies. No comparison with what he, Hammer, and Juliet had shared once long ago. That had been a sex act. This? Adoration and worship. Love should feel every bit this connected and necessary. The reality blew his mind, and he drew her closer, sliding a gaze over to Hammer softly snoring beside her, a coveting hand on her belly.

The room hung heavy with their combined pheromones until every lungful of air stirred the replay in his head again. Closing his eyes, he let it flicker through from beginning to end again, every moment, every sigh, scream and shudder of bliss indelibly carved forever in his memory. She'd loved every second of it, bursting into life and love in a way she'd never done with him alone.

Part of him grieved for what would never be again. Now that ecstasy wasn't ripping through him, so many of his insecurities came crashing back. Did Raine need Hammer because he alone wasn't enough for her? Would having Hammer back in the picture mean that she eventually wouldn't need him? Liam couldn't forget the way his friend had pounded into her soft body so roughly at times. Liam had nearly stopped him once or twice. But Raine's moans hadn't been of distress. Far from it. As much as he hated to, Liam wondered where that left him in her heart.

The buzz of his phone in the pocket of his jeans had him easing away from Raine. He searched the floor for his pants. Who the devil would be calling him now? Everyone who mattered to him was under this roof.

Seeing the light spilling from the pocket, he slid it free as he walked with it into the bathroom and closed the door quietly, answering quickly before the sound woke the other two.

"Hello?"

"Where are you Liam? The people at this Shadows club won't tell your wife where to find you."

Bloody hell.

"Ex-wife." She was in Los Angeles? At Shadows? "What do you want, Gwyneth?"

"You, of course. I need to see you. Now."

THE END

Liam's ex has returned—with a secret and a plan. Ready to see how her arrival threatens the fragile connection the trio has forged? Continue the epic, dark romance journey with Raine, Hammer, and Liam in The Brink now!

One Woman. Two adversaries. A dangerous web...

THE BRINK
The Unbroken Series: Raine Falling (Book 3)
by Shayla Black and Jenna Jacob
NOW AVAILABLE!
(available in eBook, print, and audio)

THE BRINK
The Unbroken Series: Raine Falling (Book 3)
by Shayla Black and Jenna Jacob
NOW AVAILABLE!
(available in eBook, print, and audio)

One Woman. Two adversaries. A dangerous web…

As rivals Liam O'Neill and Macen Hammerman work together to demolish the walls around Raine Kendall's wounded heart, Liam's ex-wife returns—with a shocking secret that threatens to destroy their new bonds. He leaves Raine in Hammer's care so he can expose his former flame's scheme…but the longer he's away, the more he worries Hammer will claim Raine for his own.

Though Hammer does his best to protect Raine from the threats to their budding happily-ever-after, when she discovers their subterfuge, it rekindles her insecurities. For her sake, the men resolve to bury the destructive past once and for all, but Liam's ex discovers his weakness and aligns herself with a monster who will do anything for a pound of Raine's flesh. With her life hanging in the balance, will Liam and Hammer banish their animosity in time to save the woman they both love?

EXCERPT

"Hammer. Wake up," a familiar voice whispered in his ear. "There's a problem."

Macen "Hammer" Hammerman jackknifed up, the fog of sleep dissipating. Liam O'Neill stood above him, over the bed.

Why the hell was his best friend waking him up in the middle of the night?

With a frown, Hammer rose on one elbow. "What?"

Liam's stare fell on Raine Kendall in the rumpled bed they'd all shared last night. Hammer glanced at the woman they both loved. Images of her moaning, melting, and writhing between them flashed through Hammer's brain like a sensual strobe. Thankfully, she was still asleep, her inky lashes fanning over her rosy cheeks.

But Liam's face tightened, the man's tense expression giving him pause. "Tell me."

"She's exhausted. Let's not wake her." He jerked his head at the open door. "Bathroom."

Hammer scowled. Had something happened after he'd crashed? Had Liam and Raine fought? No, he wouldn't have slept through that. Whether she was upset or in the throes of passion, she never held back.

What if Liam had reconsidered their arrangement and refused to share her anymore? That idea whacked Macen with fury. After years of denying himself her touch, he couldn't wait to have her again. If his Irish pal thought she still belonged exclusively to him simply because she'd once worn his collar, he'd lost his fucking mind. Hammer had rescued the scared runaway from an alley and taken care of her for six years. That damn well counted for something.

Besides, Raine needed them both. She'd only begun to lower those towering walls around her heart in the past two days, when they'd finally started working together. Sharing her might be a new arrangement, but he and Liam had been down this path before, though not with her...and not with success. Still, Raine made them better men— and partners. Hammer knew Liam had sensed the same perfection when they'd held her. Would he really want to mess with that?

Before Hammer could say a word, Liam grabbed his trousers, donned them, and stomped to the bathroom.

Hammer brushed his lips over Raine's forehead. "I won't let anything or anyone come between us, precious. I promise."

Feeling a twinge of pain in his jaw where Liam had punched him the night before, Hammer stood and worked it from side to side. Their fight had been inevitable. Jealousy and resentment had brewed for the past month, ever since Liam had taken an interest in Raine. Hopefully, the brawl had finally cleared the air between them.

Sighing, Hammer yanked his pants up and joined Liam, shutting the door behind them. In the light, Macen noticed his friend's nose was slightly swollen, but neither of them looked too worse for wear.

"I'm listening. What's the problem?"

Liam sighed. "Gwyneth just called me."

What did Liam's ex-wife want? The British beauty looked like every man's wet dream, but under the pretty exterior, she was his worst nightmare. "You keep in touch with that bitch?"

"Hell no." Liam reared back. "You know I changed my number after the divorce. I did it so she couldn't call me."

"How did she find you, then?"

"No bloody idea." But he didn't look thrilled.

"So…she called you. Why is that a problem?"

Liam hesitated. "She's at Shadows."

THANK YOU

Thank you for reading The Break! If you enjoyed it, please review and recommend it to your reader friends. That means the world to us!

If you'd like an easy way to keep up with the latest news, releases, and sales from Shayla and/or Jenna, subscribe to our newsletters for announcements about new and upcoming titles, series' previews, exclusive excerpts, teasers, random stuff about author life, and more!

Shayla's VIP Reader Newsletter or www.shaylablack.com

Jenna's Reader Newsletter or www.jennajacob.com

LET'S GET TO KNOW EACH OTHER!

Shayla Black is the *New York Times* and *USA Today* bestselling author of more than eighty contemporary, erotic, paranormal, and historical romances. Her books have sold millions of copies and been published in a dozen languages.

As an only child, Shayla occupied herself by daydreaming, much to the chagrin of her teachers. In college, she found her love for reading and started pursuing a publishing career. Though she graduated with a degree in Marketing/Advertising and embarked on a stint in corporate America, her heart was with her stories and characters, so she left her pantyhose and power suits behind.

Shayla currently lives in North Texas with her wonderfully supportive husband, her daughter, and two spoiled tabbies. In her "free" time, she enjoys reality TV, gaming, and listening to an eclectic blend of music.

TELL ME MORE ABOUT YOU.

Connect with me via the links below. You can also become one of my Facebook Book Beauties and enjoy live, interactive #WineWednesday video chats full of fun, book chatter, and more! See you soon!

Website: http://shaylablack.com
VIP Reader Newsletter: http://shayla.link/nwsltr
Facebook Author Page: http://shayla.link/FBPage
Facebook Book Beauties Chat Group: http://shayla.link/FBChat
Instagram: https://instagram.com/ShaylaBlack/
TikTok: www.tiktok.com/@shayla_black
Book+Main: http://shayla.link/books+main
Twitter: http://twitter.com/Shayla_Black

Amazon Author Page: http://shayla.link/AmazonFollow
BookBub: http://shayla.link/BookBub
Goodreads: http://shayla.link/goodreads
YouTube: http://shayla.link/youtube

OTHER BOOKS BY SHAYLA BLACK

CONTEMPORARY ROMANCE

WICKED & DEVOTED

Romantic Suspense

Wicked as Sin (One-Mile & Brea, part 1)

Wicked Ever After (One-Mile & Brea, part 2)

Wicked as Lies (Zyron & Tessa, part 1)

Wicked and True (Zyron & Tessa, part 2)

Coming Soon:

Wicked as Seduction (Trees & Laila, part 1) (March 15, 2022)

REED FAMILY RECKONING

Angsty, emotional contemporary romance

SIBLINGS

More Than Want You (Maxon & Keeley)

More Than Need You (Griff & Britta)

More Than Love You (Harlow & Noah)

BASTARDS

More Than Crave You (Evan & Nia)

More Than Tempt You (Bethany & Clint)

FRIENDS

More Than Dare You (Trace & Masey)

Coming Soon:

More Than Hate You (Fall 2021) (Sebastian & Sloan)

1001 DARK NIGHTS

More Than Pleasure You (Stephen & Skye)

More Than Protect You (Amanda & Tanner)

Coming Soon:

More Than Possess You (A Hope Series crossover) (Sept 28, 2021) (Echo & Hayes)

FORBIDDEN CONFESSIONS (SEXY SHORTS)

Sexy Bedtime Stories

FIRST TIME

Seducing the Innocent

Seducing the Bride

Seducing the Stranger

Seducing the Enemy

PROTECTORS

Seduced by the Bodyguard

Seduced by the Spy

Seduced by the Assassin

Seduced by the Mafia Boss

Coming Soon:

FILTHY RICH BOSSES

Tempted by the Billionaire (February 8, 2022)

THE WICKED LOVERS (COMPLETE SERIES)

Steamy Romantic Suspense

Wicked Ties

Decadent

Delicious

Surrender to Me

Belong to Me

Wicked to Love

Mine to Hold

Wicked All the Way

Ours to Love

Wicked All Night

Forever Wicked

Theirs to Cherish

His to Take

Pure Wicked

Wicked for You

Falling in Deeper

Dirty Wicked

A Very Wicked Christmas

Holding on Tighter

THE DEVOTED LOVERS (COMPLETE SERIES)

Steamy Romantic Suspense

Devoted to Pleasure

Devoted to Wicked

Devoted to Love

THE UNBROKEN SERIES

(co-authored with Jenna Jacob)

Raine Falling Saga (COMPLETE)

The Broken (Prequel)

The Betrayal

The Break

The Brink

The Bond

Heavenly Rising Collection

The Choice

The Chase

Coming Soon:

The Commitment (June 7, 2022)

THE PERFECT GENTLEMEN (Complete Series)

(co-authored with Lexi Blake)

Steamy Romantic Suspense

Scandal Never Sleeps

Seduction in Session

Big Easy Temptation

Smoke and Sin

At the Pleasure of the President

MASTERS OF MÉNAGE (Complete Series)

(co-authored with Lexi Blake)

Steamy Contemporary Romance

Their Virgin Captive

Their Virgin's Secret

Their Virgin Concubine

Their Virgin Princess

Their Virgin Hostage

Their Virgin Secretary

Their Virgin Mistress

STANDALONE TITLES

Naughty Little Secret

Watch Me

Dirty & Dangerous

Her Fantasy Men

A Perfect Match

THE HOPE SERIES (Complete Series)

Steamy Contemporary Romance

Misadventures of a Backup Bride

Misadventures with My Ex

Coming Soon:

More Than Possess You (A Reed Family Reckoning crossover) (September 28, 2021)

SEXY CAPERS (Complete Series)

Bound and Determined

Strip Search

Arresting Desire

HISTORICAL ROMANCE

STANDALONES

The Lady and the Dragon

One Wicked Night

STRICTLY SERIES (Complete Duet)

Victorian Historical Romance

Strictly Seduction

Strictly Forbidden

BROTHERS IN ARMS (Complete Trilogy)

Medieval Historical Romance

His Lady Bride

His Stolen Bride

His Rebel Bride

ABOUT JENNA JACOB

USA *Today* Bestselling author Jenna Jacob paints a canvas of passion, romance, and humor as her alpha men and the feisty women who love them unravel their souls, heal their scars, and find a happy-ever-after kind of love. Heart-tugging, captivating, and steamy, her words will leave you breathless and craving more.

A mom of four grown children, Jenna, her husband Sean and their furry babies reside in Kansas. Though she spent over thirty years in accounting, Jenna isn't your typical bean counter. She's brassy, sassy, and loves to laugh, but is humbly thrilled to be living her dream as a full-time author. When she's not slamming coffee while pounding out emotional stories, you can find her reading, listening to music, cooking, camping, or enjoying the open road on the back of a Harley.

CONTACT JENNA:

Website: www.jennajacob.com
E Mail: jenna@jennajacob.com
Facebook Page: https://www.facebook.com/authorjennajacob
Jenna's Jezebels Party Page: https://www.facebook.com/groups/jennajacobsjezebels
Instagram: https://www.instagram.com/jenna_jacob_author/
TikTok: https://vm.tiktok.com/ZMR8v5QWA/
BookBub: https://www.bookbub.com/authors/jenna-jacob
Amazon Author page: http://amzn.to/2Bmp0wP
Newsletter: http://bit.ly/JennaJacobNewsletter
Goodreads: http://bit.ly/2lZagNE

OTHER BOOKS BY JENNA JACOB

BAD BOYS OF ROCK (COMPLETE SERIES)

Rock Me (Prequel)

Rock Me Longer

Rock Me Harder

Rock Me Slower

Rock Me Faster

Rock Me Deeper

COWBOYS OF HAVEN

Coming Soon:

The Cowboy's Second Chance at Love (September 21, 2021)

The Cowboy's Thirty-Day Fling (October 5, 2021)

The Cowboy's Cougar (October 26, 2021)

The Cowboy's Surprise Vegas Baby (November 16, 2021)

THE DOMS OF GENESIS

Embracing My Submission

Masters of My Desire

Master of My Mind

Saving My Submission

Seduced By My Doms

Lured By My Master

Sin City Submission

Bound To My Surrender

Resisting My Submission

Craving His Command

Seeking My Destiny

PASSIONATE HEARTS

Small Town Second Chance

STANDALONE TITLES

Innocence Uncaged

UNBROKEN: RAINE FALLING

(Co-authored with Shayla Black)

The Broken

The Betrayal

The Break

The Brink

The Bond

UNBROKEN: HEAVENLY RISING

(Co-authored with Shayla Black)

The Choice

The Chase

Coming Soon:

The Commitment (June 7, 2022)